VILLA
HARMONY

VILLA
HARMONY

PHILIP WALSH

*"For none can thee secure
but one who never changes"*
HENRY VAUGHAN, 1622-1695

INTRODUCTION

I am not a writer. That is to say, I have never attempted to write anything of any substance before. What follows is an account of an extraordinary period in my life – a life which had previously been both predictable and ordinary – and the effect it had on others, not least my wife and children.

Perhaps I should make it clear at the outset that I love my wife and daughters very much, although it may not necessarily appear so from what follows. But you must know that for some time I was in the grip of an all-consuming obsession and truly believed that by yielding to it the course of my life would change for the better.

Looking back, I can see that I made mistakes, although none of them seemed serious at the time. In fact, quite the reverse – I could not swear that confronted with those same situations again I would behave any differently. For all that, my punishment seems out of proportion to my 'crime'.

I have recounted the story as it happened with the same emphasis on events as they appeared to warrant at the time. If I have left anything out it is for either or both of the following reasons: that I have found it difficult to recall some details of what actually transpired, or the task was too painful – or too shameful. Nevertheless, I have determined that it will all be set down by the end and I hope those who read this may judge me less harshly as a result.

I am not an evil man, nor have I ever intended harm to others. If I am guilty of any one thing, then it must be my failure to confront my true self.

Gerald Irving, May 1998

PART ONE

CHAPTER ONE

ANDALUCIA, SUMMER 1995

It was as if Harmony had never left the house before. At least, not recently and certainly not on her own. There was no mistaking the look on the faces of Henri and Oriole. They were terrified.

A family conference was convened, right there on the steps of Villa Harmony, by the "lake" complete with its fibreglass gondolas and plastic pink flamingos. The heat of the midday sun was becoming unbearable. I glanced uneasily at Blanche and could see that she, too, was wondering whether we might have haplessly (although with the best of intentions) stumbled into unknown territory with these people.

After what seemed an age but was more likely only a minute or two, Oriole broke from the huddle and approached us, Henri a pace or so behind her.

"Thank you. Harmony would be pleased to accept your kind invitation. She is looking forward to seeing the baby bulls. What time will you return her?"

"About six, I imagine," I replied reassuringly, "certainly no later than six-thirty. Really, you mustn't worry. She'll be quite safe with us."

"Yes, I know," said Oriole without a hint of any facial expression to match the conviction of her words, "it is good for her to go out."

By contrast, Harmony's face was a joy; I've seldom seen a child look so elated. She could hardly wait to climb into the back of our modest rental car and set about squeezing herself between Nikki and Paula. Oriole gestured towards the young woman on her right, Nina, whom we knew to be the children's nanny, a serious-looking, girl of imprecise Middle Eastern origin like Henri. She obediently made as if to follow Harmony into the back of the Opel.

"No, really," I protested, "this is quite unnecessary. Besides, there's no room, I'm sorry."

Again, troubled looks of fear and apprehension.

"Very well. Nina!" Henri's brief command was enough to cause the girl to retreat. He was resigned now. "We'll see you later then, around six. Enjoy the bulls."

Had he been able, I am sure Henri would have engulfed his daughter in a bear hug and smothered her with kisses – we had witnessed his suffocating affection for the nine-year-old several times during the day – but he could not get to her. By now Harmony was engaged in animated conversation with Nikki and Paula, oblivious to her parents' concern. Blanche was already in the front passenger seat. Forcing what I hoped was a calming smile, I took my place behind the wheel and opened the window.

"Don't worry," I said as I started the engine, "she'll be back!"

As we circumnavigated the fountain and made our way back down the palm-lined drive towards the huge remote-controlled gates, I glimpsed in the rear-view mirror the tableaux we were leaving behind – Henri, Oriole, Nina the nanny and little Max, on the steps, all waving goodbye to their beloved Harmony. The thought flitted through my mind that I had once seen something similar in a pre-war Hollywood movie.

It was only as the gates slowly opened and released us into the sun-baked outside world that I realised they hadn't believed a word I'd said.

Driving breezily along the Ronda road and up into the mountains with the three children chatting happily in the back, free from the oppressive atmosphere of Villa Harmony, how could we have foreseen that the events of that day would change our lives forever?

* * *

It had all started so innocently. When Lawrence, my editor, had shown me the stunning picture of Oriole he was proposing to use for the front cover of the magazine, it had occurred to me that an inside story featuring her at home with her family might be a rather glamorous (and inexpensive) addition to the issue. I guessed she was in her late thirties, but she looked much younger.

Lawrence had whetted my appetite in his clipped, assumed tone.

"She's rather fascinating," he enthused. "I first met her at the Bismarck's charity dinner. She got up, quite unexpectedly, and sang a duet with Julio in the middle of his cabaret. Superb voice, operatically trained by the sound of it. Julio wasn't too pleased although the rest of us loved it. Made quite an impression. She looked fantastic, too. Exotic make-up, designer kimono – the lot. Quite a work of art. They say she's a star in her own country, although I've not heard her confirm or deny it. Henri wants to promote her singing career. That's why he sent me the transparencies."

I looked at the pictures again through a magnifier on the light box. He was right, she did look stunning with her blue and green rainbow eye shadow lined with tiny jewels and sequins. It must have taken ages to create; this was serious showbiz.

"Is that what he is, then," I asked, "an agent or manager or something?"

"'Or something' is an apt description," Lawrence replied, dryly. "Truly, I don't really know what he does but he doesn't strike me as a showbiz type. He's wealthy, that's for sure – they live in magnificent style. But how they come to be living down here I couldn't tell you."

He moved away distractedly to shuffle some papers around his desk. I was a nuisance, I knew – the boss coming down with his family on vacation and disrupting his carefully orchestrated lifestyle, asking him to book restaurants, and make appointments. He was looking older, too, I thought, although his studiously quaffed red hair showed no trace of grey. Still, the once-tanned good looks were becoming blotchy, the veins around the nose harder to camouflage. Did I like him, I asked myself? It was hard to know.

We had started the magazine together, seven years before. I'd put up some start-up capital and provided some business expertise, he was the man on the spot with the contacts, the 'local knowledge', or so he'd told me. It had gone okay. I'd had ambitions at the start which later became clear were never going to happen. The trouble was that Lawrence would never kill himself through hard work and I simply wasn't there enough. My job at home didn't allow it and I couldn't afford to come out full time, even if Blanche and the kids had wanted to, which they didn't. So, we'd chugged along. He earned a living out of it, and I got a free meal here and there and the odd week of tax-free holiday. The good news was that the office suite we had purchased, right in the middle of the old town, doubled as a three-bedroomed apartment. We'd had a lot of fun there and the children loved it.

I picked up another picture, this time of a group of dinner guests smiling drunkenly at the camera. Lawrence was right in the middle, champagne held high in a mock toast (I've since learnt that real celebrities never have their picture taken with a glass in their hand) and I recognised the Bismarcks and the Foleys. Oriole was in the picture sitting next to an expensively dressed, swarthy man who looked about forty.

"Is that Henri?" I asked. Again, I wondered how old Oriole might be – she could be anything from fifteen to fifty with her delicate oriental features and flawless skin.

"That's him. Actually, the photograph doesn't do him justice. He's not so . . ." He was searching for the word,

". . . rough in real life. In fact, he's charming, well-educated and more refined than he looks. Lebanese, I would guess. Spent most of his working life in France. He told me his parents still live in Beirut. Extraordinary really. You know he's offered to buy them a home here, but they won't move. They say they prefer Beirut to Spain!"

This didn't surprise me as much as it obviously did Lawrence, but I let it pass. He'd committed twenty years to living and working on the Costa del Sol and would never return home, although he sometimes talked about retiring to Ireland. It was understandable that he professed an unwavering admiration for his adopted country.

Still, I was on holiday with Blanche and the kids – they'd enjoy seeing how the other half lived and it would make me feel better to do something useful. After spending the last three days lying on the beach, I was desperate for a change of any kind.

"Give them a ring. I'll take the family up tomorrow if that suits. I don't suppose they'll object to being featured in the magazine?"

Lawrence regarded me as if I had disturbed some crucial train of thought. "What? Oh sorry, no not at all! They seem to be pretty keen on putting themselves about. Odd that, they've been down here for three years but none of us had heard much about them until now."

None of *us* – he included himself amongst *them*, I thought. Of course, it wasn't so. He was only invited to everything because *they* wanted *their* photographs in the magazine. If it hadn't been for that, they would have dropped him as fast as they dropped their knickers.

* * *

So it was that the following day we found ourselves driving up towards the mountains looking for Villa Harmony. Blanche had protested mildly on the children's behalf saying that she had promised to take them up to see the baby bullfight in the afternoon. I explained that we could still do that after visiting Henri and Oriole. I had no intention of overstaying our welcome.

Lawrence had scribbled us a rough map and we found the house easily enough. They were expecting us. As we turned off the road to face the vast entrance gates with "Villa Harmony" in ornate wrought iron lettering above them, a man wearing what looked like a white waiter's outfit emerged from the gatekeeper's hut.

"Mr and Mrs Irving?" he enquired. I nodded and smiled. "You are most welcome. Mr and Mrs Nader will meet you at the house. Please, enjoy your visit to Villa Harmony."

"That's nice," said Blanche as the gates slowly opened. I could tell that the children were already impressed.

Soon the villa itself came into view. It was a large Spanish hacienda-style residence with a double exterior curved staircase sweeping up to what I presumed to be the principal rooms on the first floor. In front of the house was a three-tiered ornamental fountain and, beyond that, a small lake. The rest of the grounds were extensively landscaped with lawns and beds richly stocked with a variety of palms and brightly coloured sub-tropical shrubs and plants. The sound of sprinkling and cascading water was all around us. The total effect was startlingly impressive.

"Look," exclaimed Nikki excitedly, "aren't those flamingos!"

"And little boats!" added Paula. "I hope we can ride in them!"

"You'll have to wait until you're asked; *if* you're asked" Blanche replied in her school-marm voice. "Now, calm down, try not to look too overwhelmed, for heaven's sake. We don't want them to think we're complete strangers to their way of life!"

"Just be yourselves," I interjected sharply. Blanche's attitude on these occasions irritated me. But I left it at that.

As we came to a halt at the bottom of the steps another "waiter" wordlessly opened the car doors for us. That's when we had our first sight of Henri, bounding down the steps to greet us hand in hand with an exquisitely beautiful female child of nine or ten, dressed in a kind of kimono and, alongside her, a little boy, younger by a year or two and wearing European clothes like his father.

"Hello, hello," he bellowed, extending his hand, "let us introduce ourselves. I am Henri, this is my beautiful Harmony and this is Max."

"Good to meet you," I responded. "I'm Gerald, this is my wife Blanche, and our two daughters Nikki and Paula."

It was impossible not to be impressed by Henri. As Lawrence had said, his photograph failed to convey the charm or, indeed, the energy of the man. Of course, in the picture, he had been wearing evening dress, seldom flattering to a man of Henri's stature. Now, relaxed and informal, in a light, cream-coloured linen suit, he seemed totally at ease with himself, his family and his surroundings. His voice, too, despite a marked, middle eastern, accent and intonation, had a quiet depth and was noticeably easy on the ear.

As greetings were exchanged, I found myself looking around for Oriole. Henri was ahead of me.

"My wife will join us shortly," he sounded apologetic. "She has been resting. Her voice, you understand, and she so wants to be on top form for you. Please, follow me."

He led us up the curved staircase. I tried to sound casual and friendly, on equal terms: "I can assure you we weren't expecting her to sing for us," was my feeble effort.

This seemed to puzzle him and he paused for a moment. "Why should she not sing for you", he answered, "she is a singer?" And with that, we reached the top of the staircase and emerged onto a large terrace from which four sets of double doors led to the reception rooms.

"Would you prefer a glass of champagne here or inside?" Henri enquired politely.

"Inside, I think," Blanche replied, probably regretting that she had dressed in a blouse and slacks for the visit rather than something more lightweight, "it seems to be getting hotter by the minute and I'm afraid we're not used to it."

Henri raised his eyebrows slightly then smiled. "Of course, please, this way." He gestured towards the double doors and we preceded him and the children into a large, richly furnished salon. "Do make yourselves comfortable."

The cooling effect of the air-conditioning was immediate and comforting. I looked around at the impressive array of furniture, ornaments, paintings and objets-d'art. There was marble everywhere. It reminded me, a little disturbingly, of the Egyptian Room at Harrods. Towards one end was a suite of sofas and chairs flanking an encrusted gold and bevelled glass coffee table. Henri sat us down there. The children were already making friends and clearly wanted to explore.

"Nikki, Paula, do come and sit down, please," said Blanche,

worried they might break something.

"That's alright, let them see around." Henri placed a reassuring hand gently on her arm. "Harmony, show your new friends our home but be ready to join us again a little later for the photographs. And, darling, make sure you offer them some refreshments. Ask Abdul for anything they want, anything, do you understand?" But the enchanting Harmony only smiled fleetingly at her father before turning to Nikki and Paula.

"Come, I want to show you something downstairs," she chattered excitedly; and with that, they trotted off, out through the double doors, hotly pursued by little Max.

"You named the house after her?" queried Blanche.

"She is my jewel, my greatest prize," Henri answered. "There seemed little point in naming our home after anything else." I wondered what Oriole thought about that; Villa Oriole would have sounded pretty good, too.

Another white-suited flunky, whom I took to be Abdul, was placing a tray with eight sculptured frosted glass flutes in front of us and this was followed by a matching ice bucket containing two bottles of Dom Perignon. He took the first bottle and carefully wrapped it in a finely embroidered linen cloth. Henri nodded for him to open it.

"The children, they will get on well," Henri pronounced. "Harmony speaks fluent French, English, Spanish and some German. She will look after them."

I could tell that Blanche was rapidly getting out of her depth. "Four languages, good heavens! How can she have managed to learn them all at her age? At home, we'd never find a school that would agree to teach a young child so many languages."

"Fortunately, Harmony has never had to go to school," Henri answered tasting the champagne. "In each country where we have lived, she has had a tutor to help her master the local language, in addition to her other studies – except English, of course, which is her native tongue." He nodded to Abdul to fill our glasses. "It is the same for Max, although naturally, he is not so well advanced."

There was a lull in the conversation whilst Abdul completed

his task without spilling a drop of the precious liquid. The opened bottle was returned to join its companion in the Lalique ice bucket (for that is what I felt sure it must be).

"Your work has compelled you to travel a great deal, I suppose," I resumed. "What line of business are you in – if I may ask?"

Henri greeted my interest with a smile displaying rows of perfectly white teeth flecked with gold.

"I have been in many businesses, in particular heavy engineering, oil pipelines, as well as advanced electronics and medical technology. But for now, I am concentrating on Oriole and her career. You know she has a heaven-sent voice. You have heard her sing?"

"No, I'm sorry to say we haven't," Blanche answered. "We both love opera but seldom get the chance to go."

"Lawrence, my editor, was describing her voice with great enthusiasm," I added a little hurriedly, "he heard her sing at the Bismarck's."

For the first time, Henri's brow became slightly furrowed.

"Ah, yes, your Mr Miles. You cannot tell from that," he responded, "that was just a . . ." He trailed off and then brightened. "You know she has the greatest vocal range since Yma Sumac?"

"I had no idea, I'm sorry. I am afraid I have had very little opportunity to do any research. You see, we are really here on holiday, I—"

"No matter! No matter!" He paused to sip his champagne, then continued, animated, alive.

"Yma Sumac was a singer with an amazing four-octave range said to have been a descendant of Inca kings, an Incan princess, and one of the Golden Virgins. She was, in actuality, a housewife named Amy Camus. It mattered little because there has been no one like her before or since in the annals of popular music. She became a legend in the 1950s." I nodded. Words escaped me.

"Oriole is not world-famous yet, but she will be! Believe me, she will be." Quite suddenly he got up. I made as if to follow. "No, stay there, please, relax, listen and watch."

He moved around to the other side of the sofa and, unexpectedly, the doors of a large cocktail cabinet opposite us slid open to reveal a screen. I guessed that he must have had a control module hidden out of sight, behind us. As the screen sprang to life, the room filled with sound, not orchestral, but electronic, musique concrète.

The room was darkening, and I noticed that curtains were closing silently at the doors and windows around us. Slowly the picture came into focus. It was a huge crowd shot from high above, waving and swaying in time with the music which was now becoming more rhythmic and insistent.

We were watching an open-air rock concert. Wondering what this had to do with Oriole, I glanced at Blanche who seemed entranced by the images on the screen. The images were cross-cutting between blurred slow-motion close-ups of faces in the crowd and aerial shots of the whole amorphous mass. The compulsion of the pictures soon surrendered to the power of the music as it settled into a relentless riff, seemingly leading nowhere, yet preluding something. Suddenly, the crowd erupted as a single spotlight picked up a tiny figure, high up in front of them. At the same time, a piercingly high sustained note rose above the harshness of the accompaniment and three vast video screens filled with images of Oriole's surreal, painted face.

The effect was electrifying and as her ethereal voice swooped and soared above the fecundity of the rock backing, I knew I was hearing a classical aria of such sublime beauty that my senses were being torn apart by the assault of the two conflicting musical genres battling and yet, impossibly, complementing each another.

But there was something else, some other darker force contributing to the hypnotic power of this extraordinary performance which for the moment eluded me. When, finally, I realised what it was, I was profoundly disturbed by my own response. Again, I glimpsed at Blanche. Her eyes were fixed on the screen, pupils dilated, her tongue flicking her lips, her left hand inadvertently at her throat. So, she felt it, too, I thought – for Oriole's performance, pure and classic as it was, was unmistakably sexual. Although she hardly moved, and her appearance, though stunning, was not revealing in any way, there was no doubting the effect she was having on her audience. Briefly, the cameras roamed amongst the crowd and there again was clear evidence of the phenomenon. Sweating brows, frantic faces – the kind of adulation that might more usually be reserved for the overt antics of some overdressed, strutting group of male rock n' rollers instead of the solo performance of an opera singer. What I was witnessing was unlike anything I had experienced before.

Suddenly it was over: Oriole had gone, the music built to its own climax, and all that remained was the adulation of the crowd, screaming for relief in the only way they knew how. The screen went blank. The curtains opened. Enemy daylight flooded the room.

"More champagne?" It was Henri's voice, quieter than before, bringing us back to earth.

"Thank you, yes," I muttered; and then a little more firmly: "yes, please."

As he went around filling our glasses, I looked again at Blanche. Obviously disorientated by what she had seen and experienced, she was using these few moments to compose herself and regain a sense of normality. For that matter, so was I.

"Where was that filmed?" I asked Henri for want of anything else to say. "Seoul," he replied, replacing the bottle in the ice bucket and summoning Abdul to open the second, "the night before the Olympic games. Oriole is a heroine in her own country, you see."

"She has a wonderful voice," said Blanche returning to earth.

"She has, indeed. But there is more to it than that. The idea of combining operatic melodies with pop music is not so new but no one has done it quite like this before." He sat down, gently sipped his champagne and looked squarely at Blanche. "Did you find her performance arousing?" he asked.

Blanche blushed deeply, confused and embarrassed by the directness of the question.

"I'm sorry," Henri added, hurriedly, "that was not fair. It is just that many women find Oriole's singing very emotional and moving."

"Yes, yes it was," Blanche stammered, "I enjoyed it very much."

I looked at her and thought how girlish and vulnerable she was in these surroundings, she seemed hardly older than the children. Yet she was thirty-three, only two years younger than me. Blanche was a pretty woman, at her best lively and vivacious, if not a beauty. Other men found her attractive, I knew that. To be fair, I suppose I did, too. She still had the slim sensual figure, that had taken my breath away when we had first met, fifteen years before, in Paris, at the wedding of a mutual friend. The big brown eyes, silky fair hair, a little shorter nowadays, the soft freckled skin, accentuated by days on the beach and glowing with the sun – all were the same. The thing that had changed between us was not through any fault of hers – or mine. We had become friends rather than lovers, partners in the business of marriage and bringing up a family, resigned to our separate roles of carer and provider.

Now, confronted with Henri's exposure of her most intimate thoughts, I felt protective towards her, conscious of her lack of sophistication, and her need for moral support. I wanted to explain that people like Henri spoke matter-of-factly about such things, have few emotional secrets and expect a similar frankness from others; that she should be comfortable with his culture and that here, in this bizarre, cosmopolitan, post-Byzantine Aladdin's cave of a world, she should relax and try to be a bit less, well, bloody English!

As before, Henri was one step ahead of me.

"I ask because I am keen to know whether you think Oriole would succeed in England," he explained. "I have been in discussion with two video companies in London and also some major venues and concert promoters. But I do not want to move until I am sure the market is ready. Or do you think, perhaps, that Oriole's style of performance might not be to the taste of the UK audience, or the Americans for that matter?"

"It's impossible to say," I replied, feigning knowledge I didn't possess but not wanting to disappoint him. "When you see some of the artists who succeed at home, you'd think taste was immaterial."

"I'm sure Oriole would be a huge success," Blanche added keenly. "She's beautiful, talented and unique – I can't think of anyone else remotely like her. And, yes, she is very . . ." she hesitated, searching for an alternative word, "sexy. I don't quite know why – it's as if her performance was supercharged."

'Well done!' I thought admiringly, she had taken her courage in both hands and said what she had been thinking. Henri beamed.

"Thank you, Mrs Irving, Blanche. That is most encouraging." He got up. "Now, shall we attend to the business of the day? An interview and some photographs, was it not? One minute, I shall see if Oriole is ready. Excuse me."

"What do you think he means about her being ready?" Blanche asked me when he was out of earshot.

"I assume she is putting on her stage make-up and dressing up for the pictures," I responded to her querulous expression. "I'll get the camera out and check the film. Maybe I should've got a professional in for this!"

I opened the bright yellow carrying case and took out my old Pentax and some stock. "I need a dark corner," I added, looking around. "Maybe over there." I'd spotted a door which could have been a cupboard or storeroom, but when I opened it, I saw it led to a narrow, descending spiral staircase. It was darker below. "Shan't be a second," I said as I descended a few steps. Judging it dark enough I stopped, opened up the Pentax, removed the old film and slipped it into my pocket. There were a few exposures left but I meant to take plenty of Henri and Oriole and wanted them all on one roll, not confused with our holiday snaps. As I carried out the simple task of loading the new film, I became aware of voices as if in a room nearby, voices raised in anger, a man and a woman too faint to identify but who I guessed must have been Henri and Oriole. I was straining to hear what they were saying when I heard a door slam. The voices had gone. Guiltily, like a naughty child, I hurried back to Blanche, closing the stairwell door behind me. Within seconds, Henri reentered the room, preceded by Oriole.

"Hello," she said simply, extending her hand, "I am Oriole."

If there had been an argument, there was no visible sign of it.

Of course, it may have been someone else I had overheard. In any event, Oriole could not have been calmer, more self-possessed.

She looked just the same as in the photographs and on the video screen, except smaller. She was, without a doubt, a work of art and entirely compatible with the other pieces in the room. Even her fantastic make-up, contrasted against the pure white of her silk kimono, reflected the colours of the fine porcelains and ceramics dotted around the room. Her presence completed the picture – the room itself, the hues and textures of the fabrics and furnishings. Until now, the whole elaborate concoction had been like a jigsaw with a piece missing. Now she was there, the artist had taken rightful place, centre stage, the star in her own constellation.

I looked at Henri and saw from the proud expression on his face that this was his creation. He had done it all for her. If Oriole was his star, then Henri was her sun. They must love each other very much, I thought, very much indeed.

Oriole sat down and the rest of us followed. Abdul refilled our glasses, but Oriole waved him away.

"Now," she said precisely and with great courtesy, "please tell me all about yourselves."

Blanche laughed. "I don't think you'll find us very interesting! We live in a village in the South of England, Gerald owns a printing, sorry, publishing company, I'm a housewife, we have two daughters and we come here every year for two weeks for a holiday – and that's about it."

Again, the hint of a frown from Henri. "But, er, the magazine?"

"Oh, yes," I added, feeling that Blanche had sold us a bit short, "it's really only a part-time activity for me. I've had some publishing experience in England and when the chance came up to start a magazine here, I thought I'd give it a go. Lawrence Miles and I launched 'Costa Life' nearly seven years ago."

"And it has a been a great success, I believe? Everyone seems to want to have their picture in it. Look, I have it delivered here each month." He reached across to a nearby coffee table and picked up a copy of our latest issue. Almost certainly one of his staff had picked it up in a local restaurant and brought it to the villa.

"Yes, we've been very fortunate," I answered. "We happened to hit the boom in the property market which helped enormously. Needless to say things have been tougher recently." I wasn't being modest; the last two years had been miserable – we had been carrying hardly enough advertising to cover our costs. "Still, we've survived, others haven't. And things are bound to get better."

"Ah, the optimism of the entrepreneur!" Henri chuckled. "There is always light at the end of the tunnel! But you are too self-effacing. Your Mr Miles does a very good job. You should be proud of your achievements."

"Thank you," I said, genuinely grateful for the compliment. It was good to hear something nice about the magazine. Sometimes I wondered whether anyone read the damned thing at all and the advertisers were always complaining – usually when we asked them to pay their bills. Lawrence was right, this man was urbane and had charm.

'Now,' I thought, 'down to business, this is as good a time as any.' I went on: "I wonder, would you like to answer a few questions first and then I could take some pictures, perhaps some of the whole family both in the house and outside in the grounds?"

"Of course," Henri replied, "what do you need to know? Oriole will answer anything you care to ask."

I had surprised myself by remembering to bring a notepad and biro.

"Well, let's start at the beginning, Mrs Nader. Where do you come from, originally?" But before Oriole could answer Blanche interrupted.

"Will you excuse me if I go and look for the girls? I worry that they may be doing some damage somewhere."

"You need not be concerned," Henri said kindly, standing up, "but, please, come with me. We will locate them together. After all, this is an interview with Oriole not with me. Come." He extended his hand to Blanche and together they made for the double doors. "We'll join you again in ten minutes or so, with the children." And with that, Henri and Blanche left Oriole and me alone together. I relaxed slightly.

"Mrs Nader, may I . . .?"

"Please, call me Oriole," she interrupted, "we do not need to stand on ceremony." She settled back on the sofa and crossed her legs beneath the shiny, thin material. The kimono was slit almost to the waist. She wore no tights or stockings; she did not need them, the flawless, olive skin could not be improved upon.

"Thank you, Oriole. I was asking where you came from originally?"

"Originally, from Korea," came the reply. "But I left there as a child. I grew up and was educated in Paris. I did not return to Korea until last year, for the concert and the Games. My parents were exiled, you understand."

"And your singing," I asked scribbling away, "where did you train?"

"At the Paris Conservatoire. I was fortunate to be sent there when I was only a child. I showed early promise and eventually studied under Chalroix. They were wonderful years"

"Did you sing professionally in Paris?" I enquired.

"No, I met Henri when I was seventeen, we were married on my eighteenth birthday. After that, there was little time for singing."

I thought there may have been just the slightest hint of regret in her voice but hurried on. I couldn't avoid the question any longer and saw my opportunity. "How long have you been married?" I asked.

"Eleven years." So that made her twenty-nine.

"And, during that time you had your family?"

"Yes, Harmony is ten and Max is six. They are lovely children and also my friends," she said this with a fond smile. "But now it is time to use my voice again. It is a gift from God and cannot be wasted. That is why I am training intensively, and why we shall be arranging concerts all over the world during the next two years."

"Obviously with Henri's help. He is clearly committed to making sure your career gets off to a flying start?"

"He is a brilliant man, Mr Irving, and quite prepared to stay out of the limelight whilst helping me in every way. I could not do it without him."

"I can see that," I observed honestly. "I meant to ask him, does he have experience in the music or entertainment industry?"

"He does not need any – you do not know my husband. He is immensely experienced in businesses of all kinds. To him, this is just another one, another industry. We shall succeed, of that, there is not the slightest doubt."

I was beginning to believe her.

"Oriole, while we were waiting for you, Henri showed us the tape of your concert in Seoul. I was very impressed."

I thought I saw a shadow briefly fall across her perfectly composed features.

"Of course, that is only an extract from the entire programme," she went on, "although the whole event was filmed, that is the only segment which has so far been edited to Henri's complete satisfaction. That is the tape which we shall be using for promotional purposes and sending to booking agents everywhere. It is not for public consumption."

"What about recordings, do they feature in your scheme of things?"

"Yes, of course. Henri tells me we are on the brink of signing two recording contracts, one in France and another in the States."

"So, it is all going well, I'm pleased for you. Tell me, will you continue to live here or move elsewhere?"

"We already have homes in Paris, New York and England. We have scarcely spent more than a few months in one place since we were married. I cannot see that changing very much."

"Where is your home in England?"

Again, the shadow. "It's a house rather than a home. In the south, do you know the Ashdown Forest?"

"Of course," I responded, "we live not far from there ourselves."

Despite this innocent exchange, I could tell that beneath the calm exterior there was an unease and, had I been a real journalist, I would have pressed and probed until I had either found out what lay beneath or was prevented from probing any further. As it was,

I was more inclined to alleviate her discomfort, to be grateful for her hospitality. I changed the subject.

"Tell me, this idea of combining opera with pop, is this something you enjoy artistically or is it your way of bringing classical music more into popular culture?"

Her expression lightened at once. "Something I was fortunate to learn at an early stage of my life is that music is music. Of course, we want to make an immediate impact at this stage of my career but, at the same time, I have no problem creatively with combining the two different styles. Also, I do not believe that Verdi or Puccini would have had a problem either. I still treat their work with respect. We do not alter their melodies or their harmonies, the essential ingredients of their music are retained. Adding a contemporary beat and sound to the accompaniment is probably no more than they would have done themselves had they been around today. After all, they were writing popular music in their own lifetimes. They would not have wished their music to have been consigned to a backwater with the passage of time."

"But you would accept that you will inevitably upset the purists?"

"It is going our way, Gerald – may I call you Gerald?" She leant forward and the slightest waft of jasmine floated between us. I nodded. "You see examples of it everywhere. Yes, the die-hard classicists will protest when they hear what we are doing but they are becoming a smaller minority as we speak. Meanwhile, more and more people will have their horizons broadened and their eyes opened to the genius of the great masters presented in a way that they will find accessible. In time, who knows, they may re-discover the original versions in numbers greater than ever before." As she warmed to her theme, her accent had become a little thicker, her words faster and her eyes wider. Her lips were parted, her expression begging my comprehension and agreement.

"You make it sound like a crusade," I remarked.

"Not at all," she replied easily, "simply a commercial opportunity which is quite compatible with my love of all music."

That was enough, I thought, our readers (if there were any)

wouldn't take much more of this. Still, I had my feature. "May we look around this splendid house?" I asked, "I should like to say something about it in the magazine."

"It will be a pleasure, naturally. May I say I have enjoyed our conversation very much? You should do more interviewing, you have a flair for it."

A flair for letting interviewees off the hook, I thought to myself.

She led me towards the doors through which Blanche and Henri had gone. "Let us find the rest of our families. I imagine they will be in Harmony's room, she has so much to show your daughters."

The doors led to a wide descending internal staircase brightly lit by a two-storey window through which I glimpsed a view of the hillside beyond. Oriole went ahead of me. The jasmine was the real thing. From behind, I could see that her waist-length straight black hair had been loosely gathered at the nape of her neck with some freshly cut blooms. The effect was intoxicating in more ways than one. At the foot of the stairs, she led me along a cool marble-floored corridor towards a half-open door from which emerged the sound of children's laughter.

"I think we've found them," she smiled, and there, in an area rather larger than the entire ground floor of our house, were the four children, Blanche and Henri. Standing nearby, keeping a watchful eye on the children, was a young woman whom I presumed to be their nanny. Henri was quick to introduce her.

"This is Nina," he said, "her job is to look after the children, especially when we are away from home. Fortunately, she does it magnificently! We are lucky to have found her."

Nina responded with an appreciative smile. "Really, it is no problem," she replied, "they are wonderful children and I enjoy every minute of my time with them."

So, this is how the wealthy equip their kids' quarters, I thought. Harmony's room was a self-contained apartment with living and sleeping sections clearly defined, an en-suite bathroom beyond, and a fully fitted-out study. I estimated that the video installation alone must have cost £20,000. At one end of the room was a large-screen viewing suite complete with what looked like a dance floor and disco. Multi-panelled folding doors led onto a terrace and swimming pool.

In the centre of the room was the star attraction. Nikki and Paula were sitting in a miniature Corniche convertible, authentic in every detail, with Harmony demonstrating the controls. As Oriole and I watched, the car motored smoothly through the double doors and out onto the terrace.

"I bought it for her last year," Henri explained, "she has enjoyed it so much it was worth shipping over."

"From England?" I asked.

"No, it came from Macy's in New York. I saw it when I was over there on business before Christmas. I knew she'd love it. Well now, how did your interview go? I trust you have enough for your article?"

"Yes, thank you. You have a fascinating wife." It seemed an entirely appropriate thing to say, although Blanche looked up sharply.

"And so do you!" Henri replied happily, placing his hand gently on Blanche's forearm. She seemed relaxed in his company now. "We have been comparing notes on parenting."

"Well, shall we start right here with the photographs?" I suggested. "It's such a magnificent room. Let's get the children back in." I walked to the door and called out to Harmony. I was starting to enjoy myself. Here, in Harmony's magic wonderland, the atmosphere was infectious. Paula and Nikki were reversing the Rolls away from the edge of the pool with Nina helping Harmony and Max to pull it back. "I hope you've all passed the driving test?" I asked, to be met with giggles all around. "Come on, let's set up a picture of Harmony and Max in the Rolls just inside the window here."

A few minutes later, the pose had been agreed and I ran off six shots, the last two with Nikki and Paula in as well, bracketing the exposures as I had learned in evening class. "Excellent, now shall we go back upstairs?" I suggested. As we retraced our steps back to the salon above, I felt better than I had all day. The apprehension had gone and in its place was a sense of fun, of regaining some control.

Back in the salon, I looked around. The sun had moved to the west and was flooding through the double doors. "Now I shall need a picture of the whole Nader family, as well as one of Oriole on her own. Is there a particular spot in the room that might suit?"

"Here", said Henri, pointing to a large glass display case full of ornaments, "this would be a most suitable backdrop for a portrait of Oriole. The contents of the display are her most prized possessions salvaged from her family home." I looked with curiosity at the finely crafted items, gold encrusted with jewels, tiaras, brooches, clasps, armbands and other pieces whose functions I could not identify. The light was glinting in all directions and I was hopeful that the camera would capture this.

"Please, Oriole, would you mind standing over here? I won't come in too close, I want a full-length shot with as much of the room as I can get." She took her place, easily assuming the relaxed yet carefully contrived pose of a performer used to being photographed. I focused and released the shutter. Three exposures later I asked Henri to join her, which he did, formally, and with no physical contact. "Okay. Now, outside everyone, we'll do some more in the garden."

Once outside, the sun hit us like a torch. I instinctively moved into the shade afforded by the huge sweeping staircase. Blanche hovered at the top, preferring to stay within easy reach of the air-conditioned comfort of the interior. Oriole moved effortlessly to stand by the edge of the lake in front of the flamingos and the gondolas. Henri took his place at her side. They appeared exotic, I thought, glamorous and sophisticated as we imagine the rich should look.

"Why don't Harmony and Max get into one of the boats with us!" suggested Paula, "That would make a great picture." She was right, of course, and that's how we did it, a family group, adults and children. enjoying themselves in their own backyard. Finally, I ran off some exteriors of the house itself and gestured to Henri that I had finished. As the children set off in the gondolas for a ride on the miniature lake, Henri, Oriole and I climbed the staircase to conclude the proceedings.

"I have ordered some tea," Henri said, "although if you would like to stay for supper a little later you are most welcome to do so."

"The tea will be fine," I replied, "but I'm afraid we are committed this evening. We have promised to take the girls up to see the baby bullfight." Blanche was waiting for us in the salon. Oriole joined her on the sofa and Abdul appeared with the tea. Henri took my elbow and led me aside.

"It has been a real pleasure meeting you, Gerald. I wonder, does your present occupation keep you fully employed at home?"

"I'm afraid it does," I answered, wishing that it was not so. "The printing and publishing industry has been under siege lately – new technology, increasing paper costs, too much competition, the recession, you name it, we've had to cope with it. Why do you ask?"

"It is simply that I am rarely in the United Kingdom these days, although we have a house there. Often there is something that needs doing – perhaps the purchase and transportation of a picture or a piece of furniture, for example, things which are difficult to arrange from here. Also, with Oriole's career taking off, it would be good to have a contact to take care of certain matters when I am elsewhere. You work in the media, you understand these things." His flattery was skilful, never overstated. 'The print' is seldom considered part of the 'media' industry.

"Thanks for the compliment," I replied. "I'm flattered that you should ask, but I don't think I'd be much use to you. Of course, if we can help with more general things I'd be delighted. When you next visit England, we'd love to see you. I don't think I have a card, wait . . ." I took out my wallet and rummaged around. "Here, it's a bit scruffy, sorry, but all my details are there – or, you can always reach me through Lawrence Miles."

"Thank you. Here, please take mine." He produced an immaculate card from his top pocket and passed it to me. I don't know whether he intended to say more but at that moment the children came rushing in.

"Paula and Nikki have asked if I could go and see the baby bulls with them," she cried. "Please, I want to go!"

"Please, Mummy, can she come," pleaded Paula, "she's never seen them, it would be such fun!"

"Of course, she can," said Blanche spontaneously, "there's room in the car – just."

And that was when the family conference took place and I saw fear on the faces of Oriole and Henri for the first time.

* * *

The miniature bullring was proving to be not quite as simple to locate as I had remembered. We had only been there once before and that was a year ago. I felt sure I was on the right road and remembered clearly what the entrance looked like, but perhaps it had been optimistic to set off without a map. The children were oblivious to my difficulties, however, and were getting on famously in the back. Blanche, too, was absorbed in their conversation leaving me to navigate and drive. Had it not been for Harmony's presence it would have been interesting to compare notes about Henri and Oriole with Blanche. I wondered what her impressions had been, although, like me, she had clearly been much more at ease towards the end of our visit. But this conversation would have to wait until later.

We had already overheard that since she had been living at Villa Harmony, Harmony had only been out of the house once or twice, and then only with her parents. But she was a proud and intelligent child and would not admit anything unusual in that. We had, of course, seen for ourselves the elaborate security that protected them. Still, the children were far more interested in Harmony's globe-trotting way of life than they were troubled by her apparent imprisonment. Harmony, too, seemed happy and surprisingly unaffected by her precocious lifestyle. All in all, whatever secrets the Naders may have had, we were getting to like them.

Carried away by my thoughts of the extraordinary Oriole, I stopped the car. "I'm certain we are on the right road," I said to Blanche, "but we must have gone past it somehow, I don't recognise any of this."

"Turn around and go back then," she said, a trifle condescendingly, "this time I'll keep my eyes open as well." I executed a nifty three-pointer and soon we were re-tracing our steps. After a kilometre or so Blanche cried: "There it is! Look, there's the stone entrance wall and the gates."

"But there's no sign anymore, and the gates are shut. It is Saturday, isn't it?"

"Yes, of course it is. I don't understand."

"You did check there was a bullfight tonight, didn't you?" I asked, beginning to fear some mess-up.

"Well, it's always been on Saturday nights before," replied Blanche defensively. "But no, I didn't telephone if that's what you mean." I got out of the car and went up to the gates. They were chained and padlocked.

"I suppose it didn't occur to you that they might not be running the bullfights anymore? Honestly, for the sake of a phone call."

"Why couldn't you have checked, why does it always have to be me that's left to organise things for the children?"

"That's not fair," I replied. This had all the ingredients of a full-scale row. "It was your idea, you should have—"

"No arguing!" Paula shouted from the back. "It doesn't matter, we can go somewhere else. If you start an argument, it'll spoil the whole evening."

"Let's go into town for something to eat," said Nikki after an uneasy silence, "you'd like that, wouldn't you Harmony?"

"I would like to have seen the baby bulls," said Harmony quietly and we all felt as if we had let her down. "But I'd love a hamburger!"

"Right," I said, with a sigh of relief, "I think we know where we can buy you a brilliant half-pounder with everything in it, don't we girls?"

"'The Burger Factory," they chorused with Blanche in unison. "You'll love it, there," said Nikki, "they do the best burgers you've ever had!"

"I've never had a burger," said Harmony, "that's why I'd like to try one."

As I turned the car around and headed back to the coast, I wondered who had missed out most among these three children. Was it our two because, on the face of it, Harmony's life had had so much more packed into it than theirs? Or was it Harmony who had never enjoyed the simple pleasure of a hamburger? Blanche and I, whatever our other differences, had always believed we had done a pretty good job by the girls. But then they could die of mad cow disease by the time they were twenty. I put these impossible thoughts out of my mind.

We were all in a more cheerful mood as we neared the restaurant. I had to park a little way from the square and as we walked the short distance from the car Harmony broke into a trot. "Look, look!" she cried. Wondering what on earth it was she had seen, I ran after her and, following her gaze upwards, saw that the object of her attention was a brightly coloured plastic bag floating on the breeze, the sort that had come from a very expensive boutique. "I can't reach it!" she squealed. "You get it for me!" It was more like a command than a request, but, assisted by a lull in the wind, I reached up and caught it easily. "Thank you," she said, her face a picture of joy as she took the bag. I was becoming fond of this child who had everything, yet was fascinated by a simple plastic bag. For the remainder of the walk, Harmony played with the bag, running ahead of us and then back again, trying to make it fly again. We reached the door of The Burger Factory.

"I'm afraid you'll have to leave your aeroplane outside, now," said Blanche gently.

"It's only a bag." Harmony was looking around for a place to leave it safely. She found a hollow in the wall and carefully folded it up. "I'll put it here for when we come out again. I want to take it home."

The restaurant was busy, but we had no trouble finding a table for five by the window. Harmony grabbed the menu.

"Where are the burgers?" she asked. "Oh, here they are, yes." She was pointing to a picture and turned the menu to face me so that I could see it. "I would like that one."

"That's fine, you'll enjoy it, but it is rather large, you know." She looked again at the picture and pointed again with her finger.

"That one." The same picture; she was clear enough about what she wanted.

Paula and Nikki had their favourites and I thought I knew what Blanche would order. I gestured to the waiter who eventually came over to the table.

"Si, signor. You like drinks first?"

I was about to ask the girls what drinks they wanted but Harmony jumped in. "Say what you would like," she said.

Nikki and Paula both wanted Diet Coke, I asked for a San Miguel and Blanche a glass of white wine. Harmony took all this in and then relayed the information to the waiter in fluent Spanish. "Now, the food?" she asked. We went through the same procedure and again the order was placed by Harmony. The waiter had a query. "He wants to know how you want the burgers cooked," Harmony asked, clearly puzzled by the question.

"Tell him well-done", asked Blanche. Harmony translated this as best she could and after some confusion, the waiter went away. Harmony gave me a huge smile and touched the side of her nose with her finger. Sassy, I thought, clever girl.

"I have been taught to always speak in other people's language when I can," she explained. "It is courteous."

When the food arrived, complete with a huge bowl of chips in the middle of the table, Harmony's face was a picture and she set about consuming the enormous meal efficiently, if slowly. She watched Paula and Nikki carefully to see how they managed the big double-decker burgers and copied them. She was a fast learner and appeared to be enjoying every moment. When the remains had been taken away the three girls asked for some of those tall ice cream and fruit creations that adults seldom eat (but would thoroughly enjoy if they did). Again, it was Harmony who did the ordering.

As they demolished the sundaes and we sipped our coffees I glanced at my watch. It was past six-thirty.

"Well, young lady," I said to Harmony, "it's time to get you home. Your parents will be worrying."

Her face fell. "I would like to run along the beach," she stated, "I won't be long."

It was such a natural request, from a little girl who I guessed had never been allowed to run on a beach before. It seemed churlish to say 'no'. I was beginning to feel stupidly pleased that we were giving her the chance to enjoy some of life's simple pleasures – pleasures that for some reason we took for granted but had been denied her. Pleased and rather superior.

"Okay, but be quick, I promised to have you back at the villa by now." It was only a twenty-minute drive after all – surely Henri and Oriole would allow us some leeway? Harmony grasped Paula's and Nikki's hands and off they ran, across the road, towards the beach, leaving Blanche and me to gaze after them.

"A remarkable girl," I said.

"Isn't she, just," Blanche replied, "but what sort of upbringing produces a child like that?"

"Don't you like her, then?" I asked. It hadn't actually occurred to me that she might not.

"Yes, I like her," she said, "but I like ours better."

"Well, you would, wouldn't you?" I said. This felt like a good time and I put my arm around her shoulders. She seemed relaxed and inclined to be affectionate. Moments like this were becoming rarer between us – something we both knew but were reluctant to acknowledge. Now, with the sun low on the horizon and in the cool of the Mediterranean evening, it seemed as though things could be different, that we might still recapture and cling on to something calmer and more loving. Recently, she had frequently accused me of being unromantic. Only a few weeks ago, after a fruitless and angry analysis of the state of our marriage, she had told me she felt the need to have an affair –preferably with me, she added. In hindsight, I knew I had failed to react as she would have wished. Instead of taking her in my arms and promising to try harder to satisfy her needs, I'd felt hurt and emasculated, unable to cope even with the thought that she could have considered sex with another man, whatever problems we might have. To me, it was the same as being unfaithful. Another of the props supporting our fragile relationship had been washed away by the tides of time and familiarity.

"This is nice," she said.

"It's been a good week, good for us and for the girls. We should try . . ." I re-phrased it, ". . . I *wish* we could get away more often." I had said the wrong thing, treading on eggshells. That was her line, not mine and I steeled myself for the inevitable retort. But the sunset had softened her, too.

"Yes," she said looking at me, "so do I."

The three girls were running back towards us, faces gleaming, shoes dangling from their wrists, and their feet coated with sand. I offered my hand to Harmony, she took it, and the five of us walked back to the car, strewn across the width of the pavement, holding hands.

"My aeroplane!" Harmony said suddenly, stopping us all in our tracks. "I must keep it as a souvenir!" So, of course, we had to wait while she went back to retrieve her precious bag from its hiding place.

It was almost dark when we got back to the villa, the three girls asleep in the back. As we approached the illuminated portico, I could see the gatekeeper talking animatedly on his telephone. We did not have to wait as the big gates swung open. Driving towards the house, the unease returned. There were lights everywhere, not merely ornamental garden lights, it was as if the whole exterior of Villa Harmony had been floodlit.

Henri was already waiting by the fountain, Oriole scampering down the steps behind him – the looks on their faces fluctuating between anxiety and relief. As I stopped the car, Henri flung open the rear door and reached out for Harmony. Oriole's face appeared over his shoulder.

"They've been fast asleep for the last fifteen minutes," I explained, "we've had a good time."

"Where have you been?" Henri asked agitatedly. "We telephoned the bullring, you were not there and they told us there was no fight tonight. We were very concerned, we did not know—I'm sorry, please, come inside, please." He was dripping with perspiration, his white shirt darkly stained, the perfectly tended dark hair of earlier in disarray.

Harmony, Paula and Nikki stirred and opened their eyes. Harmony saw her father's worried face and smiled.

"I've had a wonderful time, Daddy." She spoke the words softly and with gratitude. Henri's eyes filled with tears and he took her in his arms.

"My darling, oh, my darling!" He was lost in some private and profoundly emotional state of mind and when he emerged his expression was joyful, trepidation replaced by joy and relief. He wiped away the tears and, without letting go of Harmony, put his arm around Oriole. Max and the nanny joined the group.

"You must come inside and tell us everything that happened," said Oriole.

"I have arranged a dinner in your honour," added Henri regaining his old enthusiasm. "I have invited other friends to meet you, please, do come inside!"

"We have already eaten, I'm afraid," said Blanche, "and so has Harmony, in fact, rather well!"

"No, no, you must join us, you must, come, I cannot take 'no' for an answer!" Henri strode up the steps one arm around Oriole, the other clutching Harmony tightly. Max and the nanny, Nina, brought up the rear. We appeared to have no alternative but to follow them. On the terrace, servants were already laying up a long cloth-covered table which looked as though it could seat thirty. The built-in barbecues were burning nearby. This was a banquet in preparation.

Blanche returned my questioning glance, 'the girls are dog-tired', she was telling me, 'and I want to go home now. Please.' For the first time, I gently touched Henri and turned him away from the others.

"Henri, this is rather embarrassing, I'm afraid, but I really don't think we can stay for dinner. We had a huge meal. When we discovered that the bullring was closed – I'm sorry, we should have checked before we set off, but we didn't – we took Harmony into town instead. Nothing special; as a matter of fact, we had hamburgers. Anyway, she thoroughly enjoyed the experience. I don't think any of us could do justice to more food and you can see my girls are very tired. I'm sorry, it was very generous of you." His face fell for a moment but brightened as Oriole joined us.

"I understand from Blanche that you can't stay," she said. "Gerald, I'm so sorry. I do hope we shall see you again, perhaps when we are in the UK."

"Of course," I answered, "it really has been a great pleasure spending time with you all. We'd love to stay in touch."

Henri took my hand and shook it warmly. "Thank you, for everything. It is so important for Harmony to mix with other children of her own age. It has been most kind of you. Do bring the girls up here any time to play."

"Say goodbye to Harmony, girls," I called to Paula and Nikki, "we're going now."

"One moment," said Henri, "there is something I would like you to have." He disappeared into the salon.

Blanche took a step forward. "It has been lovely meeting you," she said to Oriole, "and thank you for your hospitality." Oriole opened her arms. They hugged and I was aware for the first time that Blanche was at least six inches taller than Oriole. Meanwhile, the girls were saying their own farewells. Henri returned holding a box about the size of a small humidor, heavily encrusted with silver and ornamented with Eastern designs.

"A little something to remember us by," he said presenting it to Blanche.

"Really, we couldn't possibly accept such a generous gift! Why, it is us that should be . . ."

"You have given Harmony much happiness," replied Henri, "that is priceless to us. Please, with our love." Put like that he left us little choice and, again, as we strolled back to the car our unease gave way to feelings of affection and warmth.

For the last time, I circled the fountain and eased the car away down the drive, Blanche and the children with their heads protruding from the open windows, Henri's family returning their waves from the bottom of the sweeping, semi-circular steps, the entire picture bathed in the eerie light of the security lamps.

As we accelerated away from Villa Harmony, Blanche had the silver-encrusted casket on her lap. She turned it around in her hands to view it from all angles. "Why do you think he gave us this?" she said. "It is unusual and rather beautiful. I've never seen anything quite like it. Quite valuable, I would think."

"Presumably, for the reason he said – he was grateful", I answered. "Nothing that Henri might do could surprise me," I added, "the man's a one-off. You know they behaved as if they never expected to see Harmony again. What do you make of that?"

"Odd. They seemed torn between their concern for the child's safety and wanting her to have some freedom," Blanche said thoughtfully. "Oh, well, I suppose when you're living on a different planet you're bound to worry about safety and security. They say money doesn't buy happiness."

"I think there's more to it than that," I mused, "the question is what?" We carried on along the unlit mountain road nursing our thoughts.

"Mummy," said Paula from the back, breaking our reverie, "is there anything inside?"

"I hadn't thought to look, darling," said Blanche releasing the catch. She opened the lid.

Inside the box was a DVD. On the label was the single word *"Oriole"*.

* * *

That night, with the children asleep at the other end of the apartment, I made love to Blanche. It was tender to begin with, and then with the increasing urgency born of abstinence until we were both sated, exhausted and perspiring in the semi-tropical night. We said nothing – as if the intrusion of words or feelings would have endangered the moment. In the end, it was only sex born out of frustration, like two teenagers on heat.

I found myself wondering how she coped with the increasingly long periods between our lovemaking, whether she satisfied herself (I knew she had done at least once when, arriving home unexpectedly in the early hours, I had glimpsed her in the throes of her passion, one hand clawing at her breast the other moving frantically beneath the sheets. Although I had never mentioned it to her, the image had stayed with me) or, for that matter, whether she had taken a lover.

What I did know was, that during the final moments of our coupling, the face before me, contorted in orgasm, was not Blanche's but Oriole's.

CHAPTER TWO

The following Friday we had booked to go home. Barring last-minute problems, the flight was due to leave at ten o'clock in the evening. Nikki and Paula were missing their friends; I was worrying about the business. Blanche was the only one of us who, given half a chance, would have stayed on. Holidays suited her. Relieved of the day-to-day demands of family life – the ferrying of the girls to and from school plus Air Training Corps twice a week for Nikki, dancing classes for Paula, as well as the monotony when they were out of the house and the dramas when they were in – Blanche had become less edgy, more pliable. And with more time for me, it seemed.

Still, we had a few hours before we needed to set off from the apartment. Leaving the three of them on the beach, I went into the office to sew up some loose ends with Lawrence. I had bought him lunch at Simones the day before, a strangely formal affair when, as usual, we had both role-played for the other's benefit. He was keen to give me the impression that first and foremost in his mind were the finances and profitability of the business. I was trying to reassure him that the whole enterprise was more of a hobby to me, with no real commercial value other than the remote possibility that, one day, some vainglorious millionaire with nothing better to do might pay me a ludicrously inflated price for the title – with or without Lawrence Miles.

Today he was relaxed, confident in the knowledge that I would be leaving on Saturday and he would be rid of me for another three or four months, obliged only to keep me informed from time to time of the good news (whilst choosing to edit out the bad). Meanwhile, life would revert to how he liked it – invitations, some to be refused for effect, most accepted, diary complications, lunches and late nights. All of it fake; all of it fun.

He had hardly referred to our visit to Villa Harmony and I had left him with the rolls of undeveloped film and a quick draft of my article for him to polish.

"Sold another series last night," he pronounced in his clipped tone. He wanted me to leave on a high. "Something I've been working on all year finally paid off. Confirmed over dinner. Nice piece of business. 'SS *Aphrodite*'. No money problems, either, they've paid the full price for the first three insertions upfront, cash."

"Excellent, well done," I replied giving him a friendly pat on the arm. "'*Aphrodite*', what's that, a cruise ship?"

"Hospital ship, clinic. You must have seen her, gleaming white thing, moored out in the bay."

"Yes. I have. I thought she was a pleasure craft. A hospital, eh? Private clients only, I presume?"

"Very much so, yes. Laser eye surgery, you know, you've read about it, a permanent cure for short-sightedness, one of the first in the world, as a matter of fact. Idea of a chap called Chandrit Singh, brilliant man, a Sikh. Not the operation itself, that was invented by the Russians but, typically, they didn't know what to do with it. While they were waiting for the professional journals to publish their research papers so that the international medical establishment could pronounce its verdict, Singh had set up on board a ship and was cruising the Mediterranean. Queues of clients wherever he anchored. He's moved on a bit since – minor plastic surgery, facelifts, noses, boob jobs, that kind of thing, you know. Been here for the last year or so. Found a ready market here amongst the rich and would-be famous. Come from all over Europe and the States apparently."

"It is all bona fide, I suppose? I mean there's no need for us to worry about carrying the ad?"

"Good God, no. His ads have been appearing all over the world! That's how they do it, you see. The problem I've had until now is that he gets as much business as he can cope with from the coast without it. Still, I managed to persuade him that it's good PR to be in the local up-market mag and he's bought the idea at last." He looked at me sternly over his glasses. "Besides, I thought even doctors in England were allowed to advertise nowadays, aren't they?"

"Come to think of it, you're probably right," I recalled the advertisements for cosmetic surgery in some of Blanche's magazines. "Even so . . ."

"Really, I don't think we need to worry." He picked up a piece of artwork from a pile on the plan chest. "Look, all they want to do is advertise the eye operations and they're safe as houses."

I looked at the artwork. For some reason, 'SS *Aphrodite*' seemed familiar, maybe I'd read something about it in the UK. The advertisement was beautifully (and expensively) typeset, with a superb photograph of the ship and a smaller shot of a luxuriously appointed cabin. Tasteful, reassuring, I thought. It certainly wouldn't cause offence.

"Tell you what, why not go aboard, take a look around, I'll come too. Introduce you to Singh. You can take some more pictures if you like, write another article." I thought I detected a touch of sarcasm. "You'll like Singh and he'll be delighted to give you the Cook's tour. 'The *Aphrodite*' has a curious history. Used to belong to a man called Augustus Black. Singh bought it for a song from the receivers after Black disappeared, presumed dead. Take you an hour that's all. Interested?"

So that's where I'd seen the ship before. When Black had gone missing it had been all over the front pages.

"Oh, I don't know." I was in de-mob mode thinking about my real business at home.

"Listen, a bit of editorial to go with his first ad wouldn't be a bad idea. Take your camera, he'll be flattered. Good for future relations."

"Okay, sounds like another unique outing." The coast was full of them. "There's just one thing, who is the contracting party? Is it Singh, personally, or what?"

"No, it's a company," he picked up a thin file and opened it. "Here we are, Medici Medex Inc. Don't know much about them, I'm afraid. I didn't think it mattered – particularly when he paid in advance. His idea, not mine. Cheque's gone to the bank. We'll know on Monday whether it's cleared but I'm sure it'll be okay. Shall I give Singh a call? We could go this afternoon?"

"Sure, whatever you say. I'll take the camera, then?"

"Good idea, old man. Oh, and don't forget to take some film."

And that with only the slightest hint of sarcasm, I thought.

* * *

As always, Lawrence had organised everything well. He had briefly held a job as a butler, he had once told me, in between spells of eking out a precarious living as a writer. I could see why. One of his more endearing qualities was to regard people, their introductions, arrangements, appointments, and the day-to-day paraphernalia of managing one's existence, as important – or, at least, he gave that impression.

We were met at the quayside by a young woman wearing a pretty lightweight suit, who introduced herself in an easily recognised Californian accent as Julia Swartz, the *Aphrodite's* Cosmetic Consultant and assistant to Mr Singh. She was a 'perfect' West Coast specimen, in her late twenties I guessed, tall, tanned and blonde with an enviable bone structure, her face framed by a great halo of streaked, sun-bleached blonde hair. I wondered whether her job meant that she was obliged to tell others that she'd had cosmetic surgery when she hadn't.

Still, all she was required to do for now was get us to the ship in comfort and we were soon skimming across the rippled water of the harbour in the *Aphrodite's* launch heading for the only slightly less calm water of the bay. I had never been on board a luxury cruiser before and enjoyed a sense of anticipation as we tied up alongside. At close quarters, the *Aphrodite* seemed bigger and more substantial than from the shore. A few steps along a short gangplank and we were aboard.

"Please, come this way, Mr Irving," Julia drawled lazily, "Mr Singh is looking forward to meeting you. Of course, Mr Miles here is already a good friend of ours." She flashed a radiant smile and beckoned for us to follow her.

"Just a manner of speaking," Lawrence whispered to me as she led us along a corridor, "I've only met him once actually."

The route to Singh's office took us up a short staircase to another deck and through a luxuriously appointed panelled lounge, complete with a bar. A uniformed barman, drying glasses, smiled a brief greeting at us as we sauntered past. Beyond him, we could see a small area of open deck with a pool, sun loungers and shades.

"There used to be two other large public rooms on the ship," Julia explained, "but now they have been converted for use as an operating theatre and recovery room. However, we have preserved this area in its original state as a place for rest and relaxation." She stopped at a door and knocked. "Here we are, gentlemen, go straight in, Mr Singh is expecting you."

Singh was already on his feet to greet us. I admit to being taken by surprise. Far from the slight, self-effacing Asian doctor in a white coat I might have expected, Singh was tall and broadly built with finely chiselled European features. Only the dark red turban distinguished him as being from the sub-continent. When he spoke, his voice was mellifluous and his speech perfectly modulated. I guessed he must have spent some considerable time in England, possibly even been educated at Harrow or Eton.

"Charterhouse, Mr Irving!" He was smiling as he extended his hand. "Near Virginia Water in Surrey, do you know it?"

"Only by reputation, I'm afraid," I replied. He must have met with this same reaction many times before and was used to pre-empting the inevitable questions which might otherwise take too long to be asked.

"A fine school. I was there for eight years and then on to Cambridge where I took my degree. Afterwards, I was fortunate to get into Guys where I learnt everything I know about plastic surgery – well nearly. Nowadays, when I have the time, which is not often, I go back to Nuffield House to teach my successors the things I have discovered and pioneered since I left. The 'University of Life' it is rightly called, Mr Irving, would you not agree?"

He re-positioned two exquisitely gilded Louis XV chairs.

"But now you know all about me before I have even offered you a chair! Lawrence, it is good to see you again." He pumped at Lawrence's hand. "Please, both of you, sit down, can I get you anything to drink?" The large cocktail cabinet, also in the same style, was already open.

"Thank you," said Lawrence, settling himself, "a Scotch with water, if you have it."

"Of course. Mr Irving – or, may I call you Gerald – Lawrence has spoken of you so many times, in the most glowing terms I must add, that I feel I almost know you?"

"Yes, yes, of course. Thanks. Just a Perrier if you have one."

"Miss Swartz will do the honours." Julia sashayed over to the cabinet. Singh returned to his side of the desk and sat down in a swivel chair. "Well, Mr Irving, what do you think of my ship?"

"She's very impressive, from what I've seen so far," I replied. "I have never been on a luxury cruiser before. I'm finding the experience, er, enlightening."

"Good, good. In a minute I will show you the rest of her. Much is as it was when she was first built. She was commissioned in 1985 by a man called Augustus Black, the, er, 'entrepreneur', is how I think we might best describe him. He was fabulously rich, of course, but essentially a shy man. I have often thought that this ship was merely a manifestation of his alter ego – flamboyant, powerful, free and unfettered, a citizen of the world, belonging to no one nation yet able to lay anchor off any, conclude some business and depart into the night to tie up who knows where, or when?" Julia interrupted this reverie by handing him a glass of what appeared to be sparkling water. He sipped it appreciatively.

"When he went missing in such mysterious circumstances, I was fortunate to be one of the first to learn that his business empire was about to go bankrupt. I was looking for a ship to convert into a floating hospital with operating facilities and I knew that she would suit me perfectly. She was the right size and shape and already appointed to the high standards I required. You may have read that she had returned to Athens after Black's vanishing trick. I contacted the receivers in Geneva within minutes of their appointment being announced and made them an offer in cash. Possibly they should not have accepted quite so hastily, but they did. I changed her name to *Aphrodite* and took her to Dubrovnik where I began work on the conversion. Six months later we performed our first procedure on board. I'm happy to say it was a total success and we have not looked back since."

All of this he had related with a total lack of hubris. It was, indeed, an interesting tale. So far.

"Quite a success story," I replied, "but tell me, why should it be necessary for these procedures to be carried out in such circumstances, however pleasant, when, surely, the technology and expertise must exist in any number of conventional hospitals elsewhere?" I intended the question to be contentious, but he took it in his stride.

"In a perfect world, possibly, Gerald. But it is hardly so. You see, the expertise and technology to which you refer, whilst available in theory, are hindered in practice by two things: bureaucracy and the negativism of the medical establishment. And sometimes a third, even more regrettable factor, namely the entrenched self-interest of some power blocks within the commercial sector. Let me give you a simple example: the operation which I have pioneered, although I do not claim to have invented it, namely the application of laser surgery to cure short-sightedness. Its medical name is photorefractive keratectomy, abbreviated to PRK. This is a simple procedure, Gerald, with an extremely high success rate and, performed by a competent surgeon using the right equipment, virtually risk-free. The original operation was invented by a Russian nearly thirty years ago – to make tiny incisions on the surface of the eye in order to reshape the cornea and, thus, simply and permanently cure the condition that causes short-sightedness. But until relatively recently, there were no technical means to make such tiny incisions accurately – the only option was a surgical knife. When laser technology entered the field of medicine the problem was solved. Now we can actually remove a disc of tissue from the surface of the eye less than two-thousandths of an inch thick – less than half the thickness of a human hair! So, explain to me why millions of patients who wanted this simple operation had to wait ten years for it to become available to them. Let me tell you why. The policymakers didn't think it was important enough to invest in the equipment, the medical establishment had no surgeons qualified to do it and the optical industry – I'm talking about the people who prescribe and manufacture spectacles and contact lenses, Gerald, a multi-billion-pound industry worldwide – didn't want it! So, all I did was to satisfy a demand that was already out there."

"I can quite see how all that may be true, Mr Singh, but we have been brought up to have faith in the system and believe what we are told." I knew this sounded naïve, but I was committed now. "We still like to think that our family doctor knows all there is worth knowing and dispenses wise counsel as well as cures."

Singh chuckled. "Oh, that it were so! Yes, I know that you English cherish these myths, but you miss out as a result. Would I not be right in observing that you accord the same 'respect' to your solicitors and accountants? I lived and worked in England for many years, Gerald, I understand what it is like. But happily, others do not share your obsequiousness to the so-called 'professionals'. They know what they want, find out for themselves who can do it and then get on with it! It is called 'taking responsibility for your own welfare', Gerald, and it's catching on!"

"You know, Gerald, there is a lot in what he says," this was Lawrence putting his oar in. "Since I've been down here my attitude has changed. I don't trust anyone anymore. And when you can't trust anyone, you have no choice but to get better informed and rely on your own judgment. Maybe that's not such a bad thing."

"I'm not saying you should not trust anyone, Lawrence." Singh was so self-possessed it was beginning to annoy me. "I'd be most upset if my patients didn't trust me. What I am saying is that trust, like respect, has to be earned, certainly by example and preferably by results. In the end, surgery is a craft, not a science. There is no 'system' in the world that can make it foolproof. It comes down to the individual, in whom the trust is vested." His gaze flickered to his watch. "Still, enough of this, if you are ready, may I have the pleasure of showing you around?"

As we rose to follow, I felt as if I was being subjected to a gentle conspiracy.

We were to start at the top and work our way down. As we climbed the open spiral staircase, we glimpsed various aspects of the interior. The ship was very beautiful, no doubt about that. Clearly, when she was built, no expense had been spared. In fact, the personality of the original owner was still evident in the design, the furnishings and the decorations. Black had obviously never considered that his creation might one day be owned by someone else. It felt as if we were trespassing on private property and my camera stayed firmly in its bag.

"What kind of man was he?" I found myself asking as we emerged onto the open deck.

"I never actually met him," replied Singh. "Although I knew a couple of people who had. They spoke highly enough of him. Of course, he was driven, fiercely ambitious, a man with a destiny is how he would have perceived himself. He commissioned this ship at the height of his success. From the mid-eighties, his empire was in terminal decline – although that was not generally appreciated at the time. His personal life was in tatters, too. His wife was an alcoholic, something which he had kept from the press for nearly ten years, mainly by bribery and threats of litigation. His only son, Mark, had announced publicly that he would never take over the business and wanted nothing to do with his father's methods and practices. The two daughters had both left university, got married and gone to live in the States and his core businesses were badly hit by the recession. He had borrowed too much and the banks ganged up and eventually foreclosed. He wasn't the only one, but he was one of the biggest and most newsworthy. There was some suggestion of a scandal concerning the misuse of company money but nothing was ever proved. Still, the speculation didn't help. No, the greatest mystery of all was his disappearance."

"He quite literally disappeared, didn't he?" Lawrence chimed in. "One minute he was with a group of people in a bar, the next he wasn't. They assumed he'd gone to the bathroom or simply stepped out for a breath of fresh air. By the time the police were alerted, he'd been gone for nearly an hour. Not only was he never found, but there were no traces of him, either."

"I remember the reports at the time," I added. "Didn't the local court pass a verdict of death by misadventure?"

"That's right," said Singh, "disgraceful. If the case had been heard anywhere else other than in Monaco, there would have been a different verdict. After all, there was no evidence of death, in fact, there was no evidence of any kind. Quite extraordinary."

We were at the stern of the ship on a small area of open deck looking out to sea. Less impressive crafts were moored around us, rising and falling in the gentlest of swells. Beyond them, a speedboat towing a water skier left a trail of creamy foam in its wake. Behind, the pure white buildings of the port gleamed painfully bright in the early afternoon sun. A deeply-tanned, middle-aged woman wearing a flimsy negligée over a bright orange one-piece costume was sunbathing in a deck chair reading a copy of *Vogue* and sipping a long drink. She was wearing sunglasses and her legs were heavily bandaged – I had noticed her hastily covering them with a towel when we first emerged onto the deck. Two metal walking sticks were resting against the rail beside her.

"Hello, Mrs Thorpe," Singh greeted her cheerfully. "I'm sorry to disturb you. Just showing some friends around, we'll only be a moment. Is there anything I can get you?"

"No, thank you, Mr Singh," the woman replied testily. She was not English despite her name. "I chose this spot for some privacy – I was hoping to relax without being disturbed. Who are these people, more journalists, I suppose?"

"Well, not exactly," he replied then turned back to us. "Mrs Thorpe is staying on board for a few days, recuperating. Most of our patients go home the same day, of course, but Mrs Thorpe is the exception to the rule. Let us explore the rest of this deck and leave her in peace. Come, let me show you the bridge, I believe the captain is on board, you must meet him."

We left Mrs Thorpe to her thoughts and ascended another

short flight of steps.

"Some patients are rather sensitive after an operation," he explained. "Mrs Thorpe – which is not her real name, incidentally – has had some rather painful and unsightly varicose veins stripped from both legs and had some other blemishes removed. Not as easy as it sounds. Stripping out the offending veins is standard procedure but leaving the legs looking as good as new is a speciality of ours. Some of our patients don't want to return home until the after-effects of the operation have subsided. Mrs Thorpe has a new gentleman friend I am led to believe. People are not always honest with their partners, you know. Of course, we respect their wishes in these matters."

Singh opened a door and led us onto the bridge of the *Aphrodite*. "Well, gentlemen, as you see this is the nerve centre of my ship, and here is our master, Captain John Fairbanks."

The captain positively beamed at us. He was a short, dapper little man, about fifty years old, wearing a white officers' uniform complete with long white socks, white shoes and shorts. Fair-haired and bronzed he would have looked the part had he been six inches taller. When he spoke his rich baritone voice had an unmistakably Scottish burr.

"You've chosen a fine day to visit *Aphrodite*, gentlemen. Welcome to the bridge."

"If you had an hour or two to spare, the captain would no doubt take you through our navigation systems as well as show you the engine room," Singh interjected. "He is proud of his ship, as every captain should be, but tends to be overenthusiastic at times!"

"I make no apologies; maybe your friends are more interested in the technical aspects of this floating hospital than you give them credit for," said Fairbanks good-naturedly. "Still, I won't keep them, don't worry. Besides, I have to be ashore in ten minutes, I'm meeting the harbour master for tea." He enunciated the last word as though it would not normally crop up in his vocabulary.

"I leave the negotiations to the captain," explained Singh. "When we first arrived I did not envisage that we would stay for so long. The port authorities have realised that we are doing rather well and want their bite of our cherry. So far, we have got away with it fairly lightly, but the captain thinks we are in for a nasty surprise this time. We may even be obliged to move on."

"They're greedy people," said the captain, "determined to have their pound of flesh."

"Rather appropriate, you might think?" said Singh. It was a moment before we got the joke, but we all laughed. "Sorry, sorry! I don't think John quite appreciated what he was saying."

"How long have you been master of the *Aphrodite*?" I asked the Scotsman.

"Since she was launched," said the captain.

"So, you worked for Augustus Black?" I was stating the obvious.

"You could say I purchased him with the ship," Singh explained with a smile, "along with the rest of the crew."

"We were pleased to be able to carry on," said Fairbanks. "She's a fine ship and we wouldn't have wanted to leave her. Very little has changed and that suits us." He looked at his Rolex. "Now, if you'll excuse me, I mustn't be late for his nibs. Good day, gentlemen and have a pleasant tour." With that, he left us to roam his bridge at our leisure.

"A remarkable chap," said Singh after the captain had left. "He must have been to hell and back working for Black but he's a sea dog through and through. His loyalty is to the ship, not its owner, I'm well aware of that. Fine captain, though. I think he's frustrated at the moment – we've been at anchor here for nearly four months. Not a lot for him to do. He'd like nothing better than if we had to look for another mooring further along the coast. Maybe Nice or Monaco." He paused in thought for a moment. "Very well, shall we continue? I know you would like to take some photographs – feel free, but not of my patients, please. Follow me."

We made our way back through the lounge and down to the deck below where we had embarked.

"Now let me show you my part of the ship," said Singh. "The medical facilities of which we are so proud. I must tell you, Mr Irving, they are infinitely better than most you will find on land, with the possible exception of one or two clinics in California and Switzerland." He opened a door. "Preparation room," he explained. "This is where patients have their pre-meds prior to being taken into the theatre." He led us on through a pair of flexible double doors.

"How wide a range of treatments do you offer?" I asked. "I was under the impression that the eye surgery was your principal activity."

"It was to start with, and still is to a large extent," Singh answered, "but from the beginning, there has been a demand for other treatments which we were well qualified to provide. You know, many cosmetic surgery procedures could be carried out by a first-year student, Mr Irving, the removal of small blemishes, skin flaps, moles, that kind of thing, but people still want them done by experts – quite understandably, of course. Then, once they discover how pleasant and discreet it can all be," he waved his arm around him in a gesture of endorsement, "they come back for more. Often, once a patient has experienced successful cosmetic surgery, they want to do it again. I'm sorry to say some people find it almost addictive."

The operating theatre was smaller than I had expected, running the entire width of the ship, and packed with gleaming and spotlessly clean equipment.

"We could undertake a multiple bypass heart operation here if we needed to, although, we have not been called upon to do so – yet!"

"Would you?" Lawrence asked naively.

"It would have to be a real emergency and a most unusual set of circumstances," laughed Singh, "and we don't have a heart surgeon on the team. When I said it would be possible, I was referring to the facilities, not the personnel!"

"Forgive me asking, but if you are only performing minor procedures, in medical terms anyway, why did you install equipment and facilities beyond your requirements?"

"A good question, Mr Irving, and one that deserves a full explanation, but first let us move on lest time gets the better of us. This way."

We returned to the passage and walked towards the stern of the ship passing several unmarked doors. The thick carpet yielded under our feet and the walls were hung with individually lit prints of Shakespearian subjects. Singh stopped outside a door with a brass plate bearing the name *Oberon.*

"All our suites are named after characters from the Bard's plays," he explained. "It is a personal thing, I have always loved Shakespeare, even before I went to England." He opened the door to reveal the kind of accommodation you might expect to find in a luxury hotel. The light from a large window flooded the room.

"Each patient has his or her own bathroom en suite and, as you see, television and video. Although they may only spend a few hours in here recovering, maybe a night or two in certain cases, they are afforded every comfort. There are ten suites like this which are all we need at any one time. At present five are occupied. Also, at the end of this corridor, I have my own private quarters, so I am always on hand."

"You were going to answer my question about the facilities and equipment?" I reminded him.

"Yes, indeed. Let us return to my office, we can go via the library which I would like you to see, and perhaps you might like another glass of champagne before you depart."

We spent a few minutes looking around the library with its bleached oak panelling and maritime objets d'arts, but nothing more of note transpired until we were seated once again in the ornate chairs in Singh's room. The spectacular Julia reappeared on cue.

"So, have you enjoyed your visit, gentlemen?" she enquired politely.

"Very much," I replied, "I think we've seen everything and I think I have some good pictures."

"Well, not everything, by any means," said Singh, "but enough to give you an overall impression, I hope."

Julia was pouring fresh drinks into clean glasses.

Singh sat down and placed his hands under his chin, fingertips together in a symbolic gesture of reflection. "Mr Irving, when I first relaunched *Aphrodite* I had twin objectives. Firstly, to provide a worthwhile and commercially successful treatment centre to satisfy a market which I believed I had correctly identified. Secondly, to give myself a base where I could carry on my research into new techniques – research which, for a variety of reasons, I had found it difficult to conduct within the confines of the conventional medical environment. *Aphrodite* is not only a hospital ship, she is also a centre for research into new plastic surgery procedures. Therefore, she is overequipped as you correctly observed."

"And may I ask where this research is leading?"

"That is harder to answer, Mr Irving. Medical research does not always sound so acceptable to those outside the profession. One must be careful about how much one reveals and time such revelations carefully. When I am ready, everyone will know."

He must have seen my brow furrow. He laughed.

"Don't worry! I can assure you there is nothing sinister going on! I am only concerned with cosmetic and plastic surgery after all – I am not Frankenstein, am I, Julia?"

Ms Swartz took up his note of humour. "Not that I know of, certainly," she said. "I think I'd have been aware of any new life forms aboard if there were any."

This broke the slight tension and we all relaxed, chuckling.

"Gerald, doesn't your youngest daughter suffer from short-sightedness?" asked Lawrence.

"Paula? Yes, she does, why?"

"Why don't you consider asking Mr Singh if he can help?"

"How old is she?" asked Singh.

"Just ten," I replied.

"That's rather young, as a matter of fact, although, contrary to what the so-called 'experts' will tell you, we have had some outstanding successes with children. In some ways, it is the best time to perform the operation."

"I'll talk to my wife about it, thank you."

"Let me give you some literature," offered Julia, getting up.

"Very well, thank you. Now, we should think about getting back." I rose to follow her.

"Julia, make sure the launch is ready. It has been a great pleasure meeting you, Mr Irving. I hope we shall see you again. And, of course, if there is any further information you need concerning your daughter, call me at any time, or, better still, come back and bring her with you so that I can meet her personally."

"Thank you." I extended my hand which he shook warmly. "It has been most interesting. Oh yes, there was one other thing I meant to ask you, it's been niggling in the back of my mind. What was this ship called when Augustus Black had her? It wasn't *Aphrodite,* was it?"

"No, Mr Irving, *Aphrodite* was my idea, appropriate don't you think? Augustus Black originally christened her *Oriole.*"

* * *

It was still early afternoon when we got back to the apartment. Lawrence had enthused profusely about Singh and his set-up but had said very little when I quizzed him about the name of the ship.

"Coincidence, old man. If you'd met the Naders twelve months ago instead of yesterday you wouldn't even have made the connection. You've just met a beautiful woman called Oriole – who, incidentally, obviously made quite an impression on you – and Augustus Black called his ship *Oriole* eight years ago; now, I ask you, what are the chances of the two things being connected, really?"

Put like that I suppose I might have been reading too much into a coincidence, but I didn't think so. Maybe he was right, meeting Oriole had affected me more than I cared to admit.

"It's such an unusual name," I replied. "How many people do you know called Oriole?"

We'd left it at that, besides which Lawrence seemed far more interested in talking about the possibility of Paula having the eye operation. I began to wonder if he had negotiated some commission for himself.

* * *

It was after four by the time Blanche and the girls had returned from the beach. Blanche wanted to get on with the packing so I decided to leave any discussion about Singh and the *Aphrodite* until later. We were bound to have plenty of time hanging around at the airport or on the plane.

"Have you telephoned to reconfirm the flights?" she asked me, in a flurry of bedclothes and beach towels.

"Just about to," I lied, making my way to the telephone in the living room. As usual, it was engaged. I'd try again later.

As I put the tickets back in my inside pocket, I felt the shape of a business card and took it out; it was the one Henri had given me as we were leaving Villa Harmony. I knew then that I wanted to call Oriole, to say 'goodbye', to ask her about the ship and Augustus Black, too – and yes – to make sure she was alright. It was absurd and I knew it; Blanche would think it was a ridiculous thing to do. And she'd be right. But Blanche was at the other end of the apartment, preoccupied with clearing up and packing.

I quietly pushed the lounge door shut and dialled the number. It was ringing but no one answered. This was silly; what would I say if Henri picked up the phone? He didn't, the female voice that replied in Spanish was not one that I recognised.

"Hello, is Mrs Nader there?" I asked, my voice more hushed than she might have expected.

"Mr and Mrs Nader are not in residence, right now," said the woman in poor English. "Would you leave a message?"

What to do, what to say?

"No," I replied. "Well, yes, alright, would you tell Mrs Nader that I telephoned? My name is Gerald Irving– you may recall I was at the villa with my family yesterday?" No reaction to this. "She may care to call me sometime tomorrow. I shall be in my English office most of the day."

I gave her my office number and there was a pause as she wrote it down. "Thank you, Mr Irving. I will give her your message as soon as she returns. Good day, sir." The voice was gone and I found myself listening to a dialling tone. I replaced the phone knowing that Oriole would never return the call.

I tried the airport number again. This time there was a recorded message; our flight had been delayed until half past eleven. That meant nearly two hours to kill and an arrival back home in the early hours of the morning. I told Blanche.

"That's dreadful! Why do they do this to us?" Blanche's plans had been disrupted and she was cross.

"Possibly because you always insist on buying the cheapest possible tickets," I replied, not quite managing to keep the irritation out of my voice. "If we travelled on scheduled flights we wouldn't have these problems."

"Do you know how much we save by going through the bucket shops?" she asked angrily. "We couldn't afford to go scheduled, for heaven's sake, not four of us!"

"Stop arguing!" Nikki interrupted. She had overheard the raised voices. Paula was behind her at the door.

"I'm sorry," I said trying to take the heat out of what I could see was going to boil up into another domestic crisis. "I was just trying to point out that if you go for cheap tickets, which I don't say is wrong, then there's no point in complaining if you get the odd delay like this. At least it's not being cancelled completely."

"We hate it when you argue," said Nikki.

"Mind your own business, Nikki," Blanche said sharply. "Well, I don't think it's right and I don't see why they have to do it." But she seemed somewhat mollified and I decided to press home the advantage.

"Listen, if the children don't mind, why don't we use the spare time to go out to dinner, just the two of us, we'll go to Mamma's in the port?"

"Yes, good idea," Paula answered. "A romantic dinner, just the two of you. We won't mind, we'll have fun here. Go on, Mummy, say 'yes'." It was touching how much the children wanted us to get on.

"Alright then, but are you sure you'll be okay?" she added anxiously. The two girls nodded happily. "Very well, we won't be long and don't answer the door to anyone! Oh, and I want you to get some sleep while we're out, you'll get precious little on the plane."

Then panic. "What am I going to wear? I've packed everything!"

"Wear that little black sleeveless dress, Mummy, show off your tan!" Nikki was burrowing in the suitcase. She emerged triumphant. "Here it is! And these to match, look!" She had picked out a pair of the highest heels Blanche owned. Her antics were so endearing that we all felt better.

"Ten minutes, then?" I suggested.

"Fine," said Blanche, happily, "ten minutes it is."

I'd booked an early table while she was getting ready and we got a taxi easily. By half past seven, we were sitting at our table reading the menu. Blanche looked spectacular and I was beginning to enjoy myself. There was one other couple at a nearby table, otherwise the little restaurant was empty so early in the evening. Mamma came from the kitchen and welcomed us like long-lost family members. Soon, we were enjoying her delicious baby lamb accompanied by a bottle of excellent Rioja.

"This is really nice," said Blanche, smiling at me over her wine, her slim fingers on either side of the big balloon glass. She seemed very sexy in the half-light, both our moods softened by the alcohol and the novelty of eating on our own without the children.

"Do you think they'll be alright?" she asked.

"Having a great time, I shouldn't wonder," I replied. "It's as much fun for them to be without us as vice versa. But for once, let's try not to worry about them, shall we?" I knew this was easier for me than for her, but it seemed she was prepared to try.

"How was your day? What was the ship like, you never got around to telling me?"

"Rather interesting," I replied. "Lawrence has sold them a series of ads. I was a bit worried that it might not be up to scratch, but everything seems fine and above board – excuse the pun."

She laughed and her eyes sparkled.

"They do these eye operations, don't they?" She ate delicately, taking the smallest pieces of the succulent meat but relishing every mouthful.

"Yes, laser surgery, that seems to be their main line of business. Lawrence mentioned that Paula was short-sighted and they gave me a brochure about it. It's back at the apartment."

"Surely you wouldn't think about Paula having eye surgery – and, if you *were*, not here, and not on a ship?" She was surprised rather than indignant.

"No, I'm not thinking about it seriously, really. It's just that I was impressed with the set-up, and with Singh, too – the guy who runs it. He's a smooth operator. Sorry, another unintentional pun!" Blanche laughed again. "He said the operation is virtually risk-free and can be very successful with children. What do you think? Is this something we could do for Paula?"

"She doesn't like glasses, that's for certain," Blanche said thoughtfully, "but I'd need to know a lot more about it before we even mentioned the idea to her. I'd like to check the whole thing out at home, too."

She had finished eating and seemed to be warming to the notion slightly. "Besides, surely, we couldn't afford to have it done privately, could we?"

"I'm not sure it's available any other way. And, actually, yes, we could afford it, down here anyway. There's a few thousand on deposit, don't forget, which we've never touched; what better use for it? Still, there's nothing we can do now, we're flying home in three hours."

"Yes, of course."

As we ploughed on through the main course, our enjoyment of the food overtook conversation. Time passed quickly and, long before we were ready, Mamma was standing beside us with the sweet trolley. Blanche rolled her eyes.

"Just some fresh fruit, Mamma, please. The lamb was so delicious and filling I couldn't do justice to anything else." I nodded my agreement.

"But you will have a brandy with me, I hope, on the house?" This was a ritual and not to be declined.

"Thank you," I replied formally, "we'd appreciate that very much. Your choice, as usual?"

"Leave it to me." She went off happily, gesturing to her man behind the bar. Some others had come in and were sitting at the bar drinking quietly, two men and a woman, barely visible from where we were sitting in the dim light.

Blanche let her hand rest on mine. A troubled look crossed her face.

"Gerry, I don't want to spoil the evening, but now seems as good a time as any. I'm terribly worried about us."

This was not what I wanted. Not because I was afraid to talk about our problems, but because whenever we tried, it never seemed to solve anything. In fact, I was beginning to wonder whether we weren't better off keeping our feelings about each other to ourselves.

"Go on," I replied flatly.

"You know as well as I do that things haven't been right between us lately, well, for some time. We seem to constantly upset each other, you're so sensitive and I admit I get angry sometimes over things that must seem unimportant to you, but I want you to know, despite all that, I still love you and always will. The rest of it I can put down to pressures, in my case the children and a pretty boring and unfulfilling life, I suppose, and with you, the worries of running the business." She paused, looked down at the table and then seemed to summon her strength. "I need you to understand that I can wait for things to get better – if you can, too. If that's all it is. It is for me. If there's anything else, anything on your side that I don't know about, I would prefer if you told me."

"No," I said, relieved that I was able to be honest. "There's nothing else. I wish things could be better between us, Blanche. I don't understand the way we are and I don't know what to do to help. All I can see are your faults, but my brain tells me that whatever's gone wrong must be down to me as well. It must be the same for you. Yes, I can wait and hope. Try not to worry, I love you, too."

I clasped her hand tightly as if hanging on for dear life. I wanted this to last; I wanted *us* to last; there were too many good reasons to even think that we might not. A tear ran down her cheek and spilled onto the linen cloth.

"Then I won't worry?" It was a question more than a statement.

"No, don't worry."

We stared into each other's eyes for a long time not daring to add anything to what had already been said. It was a rare moment of intimacy tinged with hope.

I had not seen the woman approach our table but suddenly she was beside us. She was dressed in a figure-hugging yellow dress, sun-streaked hair tumbling about her bare, golden shoulders, her eyes heavily mascaraed, and decidedly tipsy. Her two men friends watched cautiously from the bar.

"Mr Irving, Gerald, how nice. Twice in one day, what a coincidence!"

"Ms Swartz, er, Julia." I rose slightly out of my chair, barely recognising her in a different context. "May I introduce my wife, Blanche? Darling, this is Julia Swartz, she works for Mr Singh on the *Aphrodite*. We met earlier today."

"Hello," said Blanche pleasantly, "nice to meet you. We were just talking about the *Aphrodite*. Will you join us?" Just then Mamma arrived with the brandies.

"I'd love to," said Julia, taking a seat between us, "the company this evening has been decidedly lacking." She cast a scornful glance at the two men at the bar who were now preparing to leave and waved a hand in the general direction of our newly arrived drinks. "Oh, and Mamma, I'll have one of those, too."

The two men had paid their bill and were making for the door. Both Spanish, I guessed, young and handsome, but whether they were Julia's friends or had just met her was impossible to fathom. They said nothing and left the restaurant without fuss. Mamma looked at me questioningly then, on my nodded approval, went back to the bar for another brandy.

Julia was striking, there was no questioning that, even when worse for a drink. Her skin glowed, the swell of her firm breasts beneath the thin cotton of her micro dress, her aggressively female scent, the whole effect was pure Hollywood. She was vibrant, alive, young – and bored.

"So, Mr Irving, did you enjoy your tour of Mr Singh's floating bazaar?"

"Bazaar, Julia, that's a little unkind, isn't it?"

"Yeah, I 'spose. How much did you see?"

"Enough to give me a good idea of what the *Aphrodite* has to offer," I replied.

"Eye operations and cosmetic surgery, yeah?" Her West Coast accent seemed more pronounced than ever.

"Yes."

Mamma returned and placed the brandy in front of her. She took a large mouthful and coughed in an unladylike manner, or as close as someone so gorgeous could get.

"Did you see both theatres or just the one at the stern?" she asked.

"I don't know where it was precisely but it was near the stateroom called *Oberon*, I think."

"Not being used, right?"

"Right." I was beginning to wonder where all this was leading. But she changed tack.

"You know, Gerald, people think I have a glamorous job." She took another slug of brandy. "God, if they knew!"

"I can imagine worse things than spending your days on a floating luxury hotel dealing with people who, I imagine, are generally grateful to you for what you have done."

She looked as though she couldn't believe what I had said.

"Grateful? Grateful? You don't know the rich, Gerald, that's for sure." She seemed genuinely sad and remained silent for a moment. I was beginning to feel sorry for her. I glanced at Blanche who I could see was beginning to resent this intrusion into our precious time together.

"No, you're right, I don't know much about the rich. But I can see that you're unhappy. Which is a pity, you're young, you're beautiful, and you should be enjoying life."

"I've been working on that ship for nearly a year. Sure, he pays me well, I've got the beachside apartment, the clothing allowance, and the car. But I didn't know, I didn't . . ." She tailed off, lost in her thoughts and the effect of the alcohol. She went on, "The joke is I couldn't get out now if I wanted to." The laugh was self-deprecating.

The drink was taking its toll and she was finding it difficult to frame her thoughts. Even Blanche was feeling sorry for her.

"Of course you can get out," she said gently, taking Julia's hand, "it's only a job. I don't know what your problem is but if you're not happy, leave!"

Julia looked at her, a bitter look in her eyes.

"You don't get it, why should you?"

"What is it, then? Your job seems straightforward enough. Is it his research that bothers you?" I asked.

"Research? Growing ears on the backs of rats? Don't make me laugh!" But she did. Noisily. Mamma was observing anxiously from the shadows of the bar. "Listen, I'll tell you something. I'm not a trained nurse, you know that? He has nurses, medically qualified, yes? Me, I'm a salesgirl." She looked at us for confirmation. We nodded and she went on. "Right, a salesgirl. Then you tell me why I'm counselling transplant patients?"

For a second the significance of what she had said didn't sink in.

"Transplants? What kind of transplants?" What was Singh transplanting, I wondered, ears, hands, faces, genitalia?

"What? Oh, yeah, well, you know, I'm not qualified, that's all." She seemed to realise through the haze that this line of conversation had gone far enough. "I shouldn't have gone there. Sorry, I'm not making much sense, am I? Just a teeny bit too much to drink, sorry."

She hauled herself up and stood shakily, leaning on the back of Blanche's chair.

"Listen, you guys, I gotta go." She looked quizzically at her watch but the haze was too thick. "Late. Too late. Early start and everything. I'll see you around. Yeah, definitely. Forget it, right? Just forget it." She seemed to be trying to pull herself together and got to her feet unsteadily. "Hey, Mamma," she called, "do I owe you?"

Mamma approached anxiously from behind the sanctuary of the bar. "Nothing, it's okay. Now you be careful, Ms Swartz, be very careful, you understand?"

"Sure, Mamma, thanks." She put a hand on Blanche's shoulder. "Mrs Irving, you look lovely, it's been a pleasure meeting you. I sure hope we get to see each other again."

With that, she tottered confidently to the door and was gone. I had to hand it to her, she got drunk in style. It was nine-thirty. Mamma came over with some coffee.

"I've seen her enjoy herself before," she said, "but never like that. Poor girl, so lovely, so sad."

"Yes," I agreed, "will she be alright, do you know where she lives?" I was wondering if we should have seen her safely home.

"She'll be fine, she's got a nice apartment over Jackie's shop only fifty metres from here. She'll go straight there, and straight to sleep. She's not stupid."

"No," I said, "I'm sure she's not. Well, we must be off, too. My bill, por favor, Mamma." She scuttled back to the bar.

"Sorry about that," I turned to Blanche, "totally unexpected and rather intrusive, I'm afraid. I hope it hasn't spoilt the evening for you," I took her hand. "I thought it was going rather well."

"It was," said Blanche. "And, no, it hasn't spoilt it at all. But we should get back. I hope those children have had some sleep; we'll need to leave for the airport by ten o'clock."

Ten minutes later we were back at the apartment and, surprisingly, the girls were in bed and fast asleep.

"Don't wake them for another minute or so," said Blanche, "let me get changed first." She turned to me and said: "Thank you, that was lovely, despite the inebriated Miss Swartz!" I took her in my arms and kissed her, tentatively at first and then with more confidence until we were kissing like teenagers – the memories flooded back. I put my hand on her breast and felt the nipple hardening at my touch. She wanted to make love and so did I. She pushed me away very gently.

"Darling, we have to leave, we'll miss the plane!"

She was right, of course, and I eased away from her savouring the sensation of wanting her again and being wanted. We both knew that we had reached some sort of turning point that night.

"I'll get changed," she whispered. I knew she was wearing next to nothing under the dress. "In the circumstances do you think you should wait in the other room?" Her eyes were twinkling in the half-light.

"Yes," I said, "I think I probably should."

CHAPTER THREE

We were at Gatwick by three o'clock in the morning, at home and in bed by half past four. The day was a write-off and I didn't expect to see Blanche or the girls until later that afternoon.

I slept restlessly for an hour or so and then got up, slipped on my watch and dressing gown, and made my way silently to the kitchen. On the way, I passed the front door and collected the Sunday papers.

By the time I had made a cup of tea and fed the cats, another fifteen minutes had elapsed. I looked at my watch. It was half past seven.

I remember the hour exactly because the front page of *The Sunday Express* carried a headline and picture of such significance that the moment became frozen in time.

"Millionaire's Daughter Kidnapped –
Million Dollar Ransom Demand"

Beneath the large type was a picture of the Nader family together with a smaller head and shoulders of Harmony. The report went on to say that she had been taken early on Friday afternoon from the garden of Villa Harmony. Apparently, the kidnappers, as yet unidentified, had managed to penetrate Henri's elaborate security and whisked her away without anyone seeing. I knew how difficult that must have been.

The only communication the local police had received had been a single telephone call demanding a ransom of $1 million – payment instructions to follow.

Rather surprisingly, I thought, Henri had immediately issued a statement saying that he could not raise $1 million in cash quickly enough but pleading for the return of his daughter in exchange for granting the kidnappers amnesty. No one, apparently, had any idea who the kidnappers were. No political faction had claimed responsibility, nor had the single phone call given any indication of where Harmony was being kept.

It dawned on me that, like it or not, I was involved in this whole business – for the simple reason I not only knew that Henri was aware of the danger to his daughter, but he was expecting just such an event to occur. It was only common sense that if he believed a kidnapping to be imminent, then he almost certainly had a good idea of who might have taken her. It also occurred to me that at the time I had made that ill-advised telephone call to Oriole, Harmony had already disappeared. The household must have been in turmoil. No wonder Henri and Oriole weren't taking calls.

The inside pages carried a further in-depth piece, this time focusing on Henri and, to a lesser extent, Oriole. The writer had researched his background well. It appeared that Henri had made his way to London in the late fifties having arrived penniless from Beirut. He had quickly landed a job as head of security for a wealthy Soho nightclub owner, some of whose seamier activities had been exposed in the wake of the Profumo affair. The racketeer had gone to prison and his key staff deported. Henri was one of them, although the police had never been able to make any specific charges against him stick.

The article went on to chart his subsequent success in France where he had set up a small business designing and manufacturing security devices – miniature cameras, sound and surveillance systems, lie detectors, night vision equipment, and so on. A "techno-freak", Henri had rapidly acquired an international reputation for his ingenious inventions and by the early nineties was supplying governments with anti-espionage equipment and dealing in small arms and military equipment. In fact, Henri was head of one of a handful of leading European companies that had government contracts to develop anti-radar detection technology for the new generation of "stealth" surveillance aircraft. He was rapidly making a fortune which, in turn, he invested in several other businesses, transcontinental pipelines being just one of them.

By now, Henri Nader was living the lifestyle of an extremely wealthy man, used to entertaining presidents and politicians, film stars, and even royalty. More recently he had set out to identify new opportunities for his genius to flourish and had expanded his activities into the field of miniaturised medical equipment. The article stated that his products were sought after all over the world.

It went on to briefly mention that, in 1988, Henri had married Oriole, an exiled Korean princess, in Paris. It had been the wedding of the season. Oriole was a trained opera singer and her recently recorded CD of popular classical arias was about to be launched in the UK. In 1989, in his wife's honour, Henri had part-funded and pioneered the building of a brand-new hospital in Seoul, the capital of Korea, which had been greeted with great public acclaim and bore her name – *"The Oriole Nader Hospital and Foundation for Medical Research"*.

I had learnt more about Henri in two minutes than I had found out from him face-to-face over several hours. A complex and remarkable man. I made a mental note of the name of the journalist who had written the article, someone called Vincent Lythgoe. It might come in useful.

I decided to go into the office rather than disturb the others. Although it was Sunday, some of the production staff would be in and they would be impressed to see me. Besides, it would be a good opportunity to catch up with what had been going on in my absence without the pressures of a Monday morning to cope with as well.

Blanche and the girls needed their sleep and would see the headlines when they woke up. I scribbled a note to that effect and left it on the hall table where Blanche would see it. I had slept in the spare room and my clothes and toilet bag were still there. I washed, shaved and got dressed, tiptoeing around. Letting myself out quietly, and walking the few paces to the garage, I couldn't help but compare the dank English January morning with what we had so recently left behind. They say you can get fed up with the sun, well, I thought, you can sure as hell get fed up with this.

As I eased the Jaguar along the deserted Sussex roads to the factory, I knew that the last two weeks in Spain had made a difference in some way. I didn't yet know why or how, but I sensed that a profound change of some kind lay just ahead.

There are times when even the most ordinary amongst us will reflect and take stock, usually when some ambition has been realised or a dream shattered. With success – or failure – comes a keener insight into one's limitations. As if your strengths have taken you as far as they will and what remains to be done is beyond the resources you have left.

I had never expected nor wanted very much. My upbringing was typically middle class; my father worked in insurance, mother was a teacher. Everything had gone according to plan until I left school and was about to go to university. My parents were killed in a car crash the day after my eighteenth birthday. From then on my comfortable, unthinking young life went into free fall. Too old to want to live with relatives, and too young to be self-sufficient, I was trapped alarmingly in the no-man's land of young adulthood. There was some equity in the house, the money from my parents' life policies and the settlement on the car. Fortunately, there were few liabilities: five thousand pounds of mortgage to pay off and a few monthly payments and direct debits to meet. Like Mr Micawber, I was on the right side, but only just. I had to get a job and start supporting myself.

I'd sold the house, paid off the mortgage, cancelled university and, instead, enrolled at college working behind a bar in the evenings to get by. As an only child, I had spent most of my life on my own, enjoyed my own company and so seldom felt lonely. I cannot recall ever feeling sorry for myself. With the small amount of cash remaining from the sale of the house, plus my casual earnings, I had made ends meet, living in a small rented flat near the Elephant and Castle until I got a permanent job with a firm of printers in Streatham. With my minor public school education, my easy manner and early maturity (so I was told) – plus a willingness to work all hours of the day and night – I had got on quickly and had shown an aptitude for assisting the company's clients with copywriting and design problems as well as delivering my work on time.

When I was twenty-five, I had been invited by an old school friend, Simon, to attend his wedding to a French girl in Paris, all expenses paid by his father. It was there I met Blanche, a school friend of the bride. I had fallen in love with her instantly. She was the first and only one and we were married within the year. Blanche was already pregnant with Nikki. Having a child accelerated my ambition and within two years I had been made General Manager with a seat on the small board.

The following year we were pregnant again and I set about forming my own business, writing and designing publicity material and placing print on commission. By the time I was thirty-three, I had a printing business of my own and was publishing a local free sheet. We were able to move into our first proper home – a three-bedroomed detached house in the village of Mayfield in Sussex. The mortgage was large but manageable, and things were going well.

Ironically, it was about this time that our relationship began to deteriorate. Blanche seemed to be preoccupied with everything except our marriage, our sex life had virtually ground to a halt, and communication between us was at an all-time low. I felt unloved and so, evidently, did she. All our affection, care and attention were channelled into the kids. In a naive attempt to stop the rot I had booked a week's holiday in Spain without the children but, far from cementing the marriage, it had resulted in things being said which had only made matters worse. I began to worry that I was not the man to give my increasingly independently-minded wife what she needed.

It was also on that trip, by chance, that I had been introduced to Lawrence Miles. He was scratching a living writing odd articles about Spain for English papers but wanted to start a local society magazine. He was charming and appeared to be very much the man about town. We went into partnership and within the year launched the impudently titled *Costa Life*.

All this went through my mind as I drove to work that Sunday morning. Why? Because I had met and learnt something about Henri Nader? Possibly. Compared to his, my life seemed of no consequence whatsoever, my modest achievements paling into insignificance. Who was it had once said that life was a banquet with most people complaining they were starving? Henri was eating his fill and replenishing the table tenfold with his philanthropy, a man who had started, incredibly, with nothing at all. Where had I gone wrong? Was there more left in life for me? Or was it just that Henri had played with higher stakes and gambled against a different set of odds? One moment building a great new hospital in some far-off place, the next suffering the agony of his little daughter's abduction. How would I feel if something similar happened to Nikki or Paula? It was impossible to imagine and, anyway, why should anyone want to kidnap them?

This, then, was my frame of mind as I let myself into the works. I could hear the presses grinding away beyond the empty reception area and knew that only a few key staff would be in catching up on orders ready for the finishers to collect on Monday morning. I climbed the stairs to the offices on the first floor above the machine room.

Pru, my secretary, had left my desk neat and tidy expecting me to be in bright and early on Monday. On top of my mail, opened or left sealed according to her instinct as to what might be business, personal or private, she had left a note hoping that I had enjoyed my 'holiday' (she refused to accept that my trips to Spain had anything to do with business) and listing the appointments she had made for me and telephone messages that needed to be returned. The list was complete until six o'clock on Friday night when she had left for the weekend. The red light was flashing on the answerphone in the outer office so any calls recorded on the machine would have been made either late on Friday or earlier this morning. My heart missed a beat as I imagined whose voice I might hear on the playback.

I pressed the switch and waited for the buzz and clicks of the rewind mechanism to finish. The voice was hushed and anxious. I could hardly believe it.

"Gerald, it is Oriole. Listen, Harmony has been taken, we are worried sick. Henri is spending all his time with the police. Do you know anything about this? No, of course you don't, I'm sorry, how could you? It's just that you telephoned, not long after we discovered she had gone. You'll understand why I couldn't answer. Please, call back."

Maybe I was deluding myself, but it sounded to me as if it was important to her, very important, that she spoke to me. I reached into my inside breast pocket for Henri's business card and placed it carefully on the desk in front of me. I stared at it for a moment. Did she really want me to ring her or was she just returning my call out of courtesy? How could I possibly help? Should I make the call at all? What maelstrom of events would I be unleashing if I did?

I suppose, in the final analysis, she was the damsel in distress and I couldn't resist seeing myself as the knight in shining armour. It was juvenile and I was surprised to discover there was still enough of the romantic in me to believe it might be real. I picked up the phone and dialled her number.

This time there was no mistaking her voice. Of course, she answered in Spanish first, then French and, finally, in English, a polished and well-rehearsed routine.

"Oriole? It's me, Gerald. I'm returning your call."

"Gerald?" The voice was distant, distracted. "Yes, thank you for calling. Do you have any idea where Harmony is? We're worried sick." The directness of the question threw me.

"No, no, I can't imagine. I mean, why should anyone want to take her?" There was the briefest hesitation at her end. I went on.

"Oriole, forgive me for saying this, but it seemed as if you knew she was in some danger. You were so anxious when we took her out and were late returning. Do you not suspect who might have done this and why?"

"Gerald, it's complicated, I'm going out of my mind here. I need to talk to someone, someone I can trust. Could we meet, do you think?" My heart missed another beat.

"I'm pleased that you should think I can help, Oriole, but I'm back in the UK now. Surely Henri is doing everything that can be done?"

"If only it was as simple as that." I could hear the despair in her voice. "I can't talk over the telephone. I would like to see you. I won't ask you again, it wouldn't be fair. If you don't want to get involved I will understand." She was waiting for my answer and I didn't know what to say.

"I don't think I can get back to Spain immediately," I needed time to unscramble my thoughts.

"You don't need to," she replied, "I will come to you."

"But, surely, with Harmony missing, you should stay where you are—"

"Harmony is not in Spain, Gerald, of that I am certain. It makes no difference where I am. Will you meet me tomorrow, at Heathrow? There is an Iberia flight that arrives at 11.50?" She must have already checked the flight, possibly even booked a seat.

"Yes, of course, if that's what you want, I'll be there. You will stay with us, of course?"

"No, it would be best if I stayed in London. Please don't tell anyone I am coming, Gerald, not even Blanche. Is that okay?"

Somehow she was managing to make all this sound perfectly reasonable, day-to-day stuff.

"If you say so. How long will you be here, do you think?"

"That depends."

"On what?"

"On you. I'll see you tomorrow. Thank you, Gerald."

Before I had a chance to ask her any one of the dozen or so questions forming in my mind she had gone and for the second time in forty-eight hours I found myself listening to a dialling tone.

I would tell Blanche, of course. There was no reason not to.

I got up from my desk and wandered down to the machine room. The monotonous rumble of the two big Heidelbergs grew louder as I weaved my way through the narrow avenues between piles of printed and unprinted sheets. Derek, the senior minder, only looked up when I was by his shoulder.

"Hello, Mr Irving, we weren't expecting to see you today."

The greeting was amiable enough, I thought. I picked up a printed sheet from a nearby pile.

"Looking good," I said.

"Yes. We had a bit of trouble with the fit early on. Had to have the magenta plate re-made. It's fine now, though. Client was in on Friday night and gave us the go-ahead. It'll all be ready for the cutters tomorrow."

I was pleased the job was going well. A new client, a major FMCG company, with their head offices nearby, had given us the job as a try-out. It was a short run, suited to our machinery, but delivery time and price were of the essence. Larger firms tended to be inflexible in these situations thus creating an opportunity for smaller outfits to compete and make a decent margin. I had brought in this piece of new business and I wanted it to go well; there was more to come if we got this right.

"Well done," I said, "and thanks for the overtime. It's appreciated."

Derek's face spread into a grin. "Let's hope there's more where this came from," he said.

I couldn't help thinking how much more cooperative staff were now that work was in short supply. Five years before when the order book was overflowing, you couldn't get them to do overtime for love nor money. How times change. Now, with the same amount of admittedly less profitable work, I had half the number of workers putting in twice the hours for one and a half times the pay. The operation was three times as efficient. So much for unions.

For the sake of appearances, I walked around to the second machine and exchanged a word or two with the other minders before making my way back to my office.

I wondered if they had noticed my preoccupation with other things. I doubted it.

I left a note for Pru explaining that I wouldn't be in the following day but would call her during the morning. I knew she would wonder where I was since I invariably told her my movements. Another innocent victim of my little white lies.

I knew then that I wouldn't tell Blanche, either.

When I arrived back at the house, Blanche was up, still in her dressing gown, reading the paper. She looked up at me wide-eyed as I came into the kitchen. She was about to speak but I got there first.

"I've already seen it," I said. "They knew this was coming, didn't they?"

"Yes, but what can we do to help? We must ring them or something straightaway. Poor little Harmony! Poor Oriole and Henri!" She was already up and on the way to the phone. "Do we have the number? Didn't Henri give you a card?"

"Just a minute, hold on!" I held her shoulders in what I intended to look like a calming gesture. "Listen, what good will it do? They are probably inundated with calls from friends and acquaintances. We're hardly close to them, are we, we've only met them once. In fact, do we really want to get involved at all? Why has Harmony been taken? For all we know, Henri could be tied up with the Mafia or God knows what. We're just ordinary folk, Blanche, do we want to get mixed up in all this? Really, do we?"

At the same time as I saw that my words were having the desired effect on her, I knew that my chance to share the truth with her had gone. There had only been one opportunity to tell her that I had already spoken to Oriole and that we were meeting the next day, and that had been the second I'd walked through that door. The die was cast. In that moment the course of my life changed.

"I suppose you're right," she sighed and sat down again on the kitchen stool. "I just feel so sorry. I rather liked them, I suppose, and it's terrible to imagine anything like this happening to a child – to think how we might feel if it happened to us." She shuddered and pulled the gown tight around her. "I'd better go and get dressed. There's some tea in the pot." She paused at the door. "Oh, how are things at the office, I presume that's where you've been?"

"Fine, everything's fine. The Baker order is on schedule, that's the main thing."

"Good, I'm glad." But the enquiry had been cosmetic. "Poor Oriole." She went off back to the bedroom. I poured myself a cup of lukewarm tea and looked again at the paper. In the morning, before I set off for the airport, I'd call in at the office for a minute or two and ring that journalist, what was his name, Vincent Lythgoe. At least if there was any up-to-the-minute news of Harmony I'd have it for Oriole as soon as she stepped off the plane.

The rest of that momentous Sunday passed without incident. The children didn't get up until after lunch and we were all lethargic with no real objective other than getting ready for Monday. Paula and Nikki reluctantly did an hour's schoolwork and collected their things together, Blanche conjured up spaghetti for supper and I spent some time at my desk under the stairs catching up with the household bills that had come in while we'd been away.

The girls were horrified over the kidnapping and, like their mother, instinctively wanted to do something to help. Blanche had used my arguments from earlier, but they were harder to convince.

Later, we turned the television on and caught a short piece about Harmony on the news, but there had obviously been no further developments during the day. They showed the same picture of the family that had appeared in the newspaper and simply referred to Henri as a multi-millionaire entrepreneur and businessman.

We watched a family film on Sky until about ten and then we all felt ready for bed. As I kissed the girls goodnight, Nikki asked me: "Daddy, if Henri knew that Harmony was going to be kidnapped, why did he let her go out with us?"

I pondered the question before answering. "I suppose he must have trusted us, darling," I said. "Maybe we look honest?"

"What does an honest person look like?" was Nikki's inevitable response.

"Like you and Paula and Mummy," I replied.

"And you, Daddy," she yawned, her eyes closed, nearly asleep.

I kissed her again on the forehead and, as I carefully closed her door and walked back to my room, I studied my reflection in the landing mirror curious to see whether my appearance had changed.

I slept uneasily that night, distanced from Blanche who seemed untroubled. Restless and fretful, my mind was filled with confused, cartoon images of Henri laughing uncontrollably, hands on his belly like a fairground clown, and huge fibreglass flamingos. Chandrit Singh was bearing down on me with what seemed like tools of torture and, swooping and soaring above it all, a giant Bird of Paradise, exotically plumed, hanging motionless and then plunging down and swallowing me whole. As the monstrous beak engulfed me, and I spiralled down and down into the uncharted labyrinth within, I heard a woman's voice saying over and over again: "Gerald, give yourself, give yourself up, to me . . . to me . . . to me . . ."

There's nothing very subtle about dreams.

CHAPTER FOUR

We slip into deception. It is rarely a conscious thing, planned and pre-meditated; more often an accident, an oversight, an error of judgment. Unfortunately, the deceived don't see it that way and, more often than not, find it impossible to forgive. To them, your lie is deliberate and malevolent, destructive, causing wounds that won't or shouldn't be allowed to heal, a betrayal, a punishable offence against their person.

My lie to Blanche was no more than an omission, or so it seemed, at the time. But how soon the omission compounds into conspiracy, how quickly the error – itself just a facet of frailty, –leads us to abuse another's trust and loyalty. Should that be someone you care for, love even, then you are on a one-way road to wretchedness.

Setting off from home that grey Monday morning, knowing that within an hour or two I would be meeting Oriole – who wanted to see me so badly that she had flown over spontaneously – such thoughts were far from my mind. Rather, I felt a great sense of anticipation. Excitement at the prospect of seeing her certainly – for I was beginning to face the fact I was falling in love with her – but also that I was embarking upon a roller coaster of an adventure. Like an actor on the eve of his opening night, I was in a state of heightened emotion; the adrenalin was back in training, the pheromones rehearsing their routine in readiness for the bravura performance that lay ahead.

Pru noticed the change in me immediately.

"Good gracious, Mr Irving, the break has done you good!" She was pleased to have me back. I knew she felt disorientated when I wasn't there; she was the old-fashioned kind of secretary who worked for me and not for the company. In my absence, no one on the staff related to her at a personal level. They only spoke to her when they wanted to know whether I had left any instructions that concerned them or if they needed her to second-guess my reaction to something they intended to do. They thought of her as mine and knew that anything they confided in her would immediately be passed on to me and that she would keep no secrets, and harbour no confidences. That is how Pru had set out her stall and there was a price she had paid for her loyalty to me.

Of course, with clients, it was a different story. They loved her, appreciated her cheerful honesty and knew that whatever she told them was as good as coming from me first-hand. Where production staff could appear evasive and devious, Pru was a breath of fresh air. In short, she was a great asset and I treated her accordingly.

"Yes, we had a good time," I said pecking at her upturned cheek, a formal gesture of affection we had performed a hundred times. She had worked for me for eight years and in all that time we had never shared an off-duty moment, never visited each others' homes and only met our other halves accidentally, if Blanche had come into the office or Mr Pru (whatever his name was) had collected her from work.

She followed me into my office.

"I see you were in yesterday," she said chirpily. She had the mannerisms of a young girl. I knew she was disappointed; my Sunday visit had deprived her of the chance to bring me up-to-date with everything in her own way, something she would have been turning over in her mind for several days. As it was, she couldn't tell me what I already knew. Wrong-footed, she had to revise her routine without giving me any hint of her discomfort.

"You'll have seen that the Baker job is on schedule?"
She was fishing so I fed her some line. "Good, that's what I wanted to hear. I saw they were working on it yesterday but I didn't know the overall state of the job."

"I know that Mr Etherington spoke to Bakers on Friday, but I thought I'd better check and ring Janet Struthers myself last thing. I told her that you'd be back today and that delivery would be on time."

"Well done, I imagine she was pleased?"

"Yes, and she sends her regards. Wonders if you would meet her for lunch next week?"

"Miracles do happen, then! I never thought I'd get a lunch invitation from the redoubtable Mrs Struthers."

"She's not as bad as you think," said Pru, confidentially. She was enjoying this, I thought, united with me against the common foe, in this case, the client. She sat down opposite me crossing her legs, notes on her lap. She had nice legs, I had noticed many times, but the rest of her was sexless, unawakened, unaware. She was probably forty – I suppose I had her birth date on file somewhere but then she kept the files – and, had she been dealt a better hand, might have got further in life. But she was bright and intelligent, hard-working, and she played the cards she'd been dealt pretty well. I believe she was happy in her own way. Blanche had once told me that Pru was in love with me, that all long-suffering secretaries had to be in love with their bosses, but the idea had made no impression on me. I was prepared to admit that I had a relationship with Pru, maybe there was mutual regard, even admiration, but nothing approaching love.

"The kettle's just boiled, would you like some tea?" she asked.

"No, no thank you, I shall be going out again in a moment. In fact, I wonder whether you'd mind if we left the catching up til tomorrow, I don't think I shall be in much, if at all, during the rest of today."

This surprised her, my immediate departure again was not what she had been expecting. She looked at me with questioning eyes. Where was I going? What could be so important as to take me out of the office again so soon when there was so much to do? She wasn't going to ask but she expected me to tell her just the same.

"I have to make a couple of phone calls first, that's really the main reason I came in," I went on, "so if you'll excuse me, I'll do that now."

She looked at me disbelievingly, but I held her gaze. Then she got up and left without a word, closing the door firmly behind her. Damn, I thought, annoyed with myself for upsetting another innocent party.

I reached for my copy of BRAD and looked up the number of the *Express*. A few seconds later I was waiting to be put through to Lythgoe.

"Lythgoe." The voice was gruff, disinterested.

"My name is Irving, Gerald Irving." My mind raced ahead trying to find an easy way into what was still a jumbled web of incidents and unrelated suppositions. "I was reading your piece about the kidnap of the Nader girl," I started.

"Who are you, Mr Irving, anyone I should know?"

"No, not at all," I replied, non-plussed by the question, "I was just interested in your story. Well, that's not quite true, actually, I was with the Naders last week."

"Were you, indeed?" A distinct change of tone at the other end. "And where would that have been, may I ask?"

"At their home, in Spain, the Villa, near San Pedro, where the little girl was kidnapped. We took her out for a meal as a matter of fact."

"I see. Can I just take a few details down Mr, er, Irving? What did you say your first name was?"

"Gerald. Look, I haven't got a story or anything you'd be interested in, I just wondered whether you had anything further on the girl, you know, that hasn't made the news yet?"

"Have you got a contact number, Mr Irving, somewhere I can get hold of you?"

"Yes, of course, it's—" I was about to give him my number at home but thought better of it. "I'll give you my office number." I did and he took it down.

"Friends with the Naders are you, Gerald?"

"No, not exactly. Look, have you heard any more or not?" The man was beginning to annoy me.

"No, not at the moment. Do you want me to call you if anything comes in?"

"Yes, please, but no messages, please. I shall be out most of the day, perhaps I could call you, later?"

"Certainly. Gerald, you say you took Harmony Nader out a day or so before she was kidnapped, did I hear you correctly?"

"Yes."

"So, other than the kid's family, you could be'the last person to have seen her alive – apart from the kidnappers, that is?" His question took me aback.

"I suppose so, but that presumes she's . . . that they won't find her?"

"Got to be a possibility in cases like this, wouldn't you say? Not a very good prognosis, is it? Disappearing without a trace, nobody claiming any connection with the incident, a ransom note that doesn't make sense and a father who says he can't pay anyway; clueless local police force. What do you think, Gerald? You obviously know the people involved better than me. How does it stack up from where you're sitting?"

"I don't know. What do you mean a ransom note that doesn't make sense?"

"Think about it, Gerald, one million dollars? That's less than three-quarters of a million pounds. Henri Nader could pay that out of petty cash! If this whole thing is about ransom money why not go for broke, five million, ten million – it wouldn't make any difference to Nader. He's devoted to the child, we know that he'd pay anything. But instead, he says he can't afford to pay at all. Made a mistake there, Gerald. Then, by the time the second editions are out, he retracts and says he can but he'll need time to raise the cash. Smells a bit, wouldn't you say? Fishy, eh?"

I was shaken not only by what he'd said but by the dispassionate way he'd said it.

"I don't know, I hadn't really thought about it," I replied foolishly.

"Well, I suppose everything will take on a different slant if the young woman recovers."

"What young woman?"

"Oh, yes, sorry – that's the bit that didn't make the paper. Apparently, the girl's nanny was hurt. Shot – badly wounded, but not dead, not quite. They're waiting for her to regain consciousness.

See, if she does, she'll be able to identify the kidnappers. Anyway, that's what the police are hoping. Gerald, are you still there?"

"Perhaps I shouldn't have troubled you, I'm sorry." This time he didn't say anything. The silence lay heavily on the line. "It's just, well, I'm seeing . . ." I stopped myself from saying any more.

"Yes, Gerald, seeing who?"

"No, it doesn't matter. Well, goodbye Mr Lythgoe, and thank you. Maybe I'll call you again, later in the day." He detected the nervousness in my voice.

"Call me Vinny, Gerald, everyone does. We're not the police, you know, you can talk to us. We're not going to arrest you." I thought I heard him chuckle. "How about we get together for a chat, what do you think?"

"No, I don't think so. Thanks for the suggestion. Goodbye."

"Oh, Gerald, just one thing before you go. You know Mrs Nader, of course, er," he paused as if he was consulting some notes, "Oriole, isn't it?"

"Yes."

"You might like to know she's disappeared, too – for the moment at any rate. No one knows where she's gone. The Spanish police made an announcement about an hour ago. Now they are looking for her as well as the girl. That's the only bit of news I've got for you. Speak to you later, then. Thanks for calling." There was a click as he put down the phone.

I put the receiver down not knowing what to make of it all. Assuming that Oriole was on her way to see me, why hadn't she told anyone? Why didn't she want Henri to know? No wonder she had asked me not to tell a soul, even Blanche! Lythgoe had said she'd 'disappeared', what did it mean? What was I getting myself into?

I looked at my watch. If I was to meet the aircraft, then, allowing for the vicissitudes of the M25, still in the throes of constant 'improvement', I should have to leave within the next few minutes. I called Pru on the intercom. She came in, the slightly hurt expression still securely in place.

"Pru, I'm sorry, there are one or two things going on at the moment I really can't tell you about, personal things, I'm sure you understand."

The troubled look left her face instantly.

"Oh, I'm so sorry, Mr Irving. Of course, if there's anything I can do, you'll let me know, won't you?"

"Thanks, yes, there is something. I'm not sure where I shall be during the next few days, my movements are likely to be erratic and I may not always be able to call to let you know."

"I see." She didn't, but some ideas were forming in her mind.

"I don't want to worry Mrs Irving too much. Of course, she knows what all this is about," I lied, "but, even so, I am anxious not to involve her unnecessarily. You do understand, don't you?"

"I think so," she frowned. "May I just ask, I mean I know it's none of my business, but . . . "

"Go ahead," I encouraged her.

"It isn't your health, is it, I mean, you are," she struggled for a word, "alright, aren't you?" She'd finally blurted out the question and had inadvertently given me my alibi. In fact, I had been suffering the occasional bout of nausea which she had certainly noticed. Despite everything I was touched by her concern.

"I just need some time, Pru, and then everything will be back to normal again, I promise."

"Yes, of course. Please, don't worry about anything. I'll hold the fort here and if Mrs Irving calls I won't say anything to alarm her."

"Thanks," I said and meant it. "I'll speak to you very soon. Now, I have to go."

By the time I'd put on my coat, she was back at her desk typing happily away, secure in the knowledge that I had confided in her, needed her, and that she was not excluded from any part of my life to which she should properly have access. How grateful I was to be later that I had bothered to stage-manage that little scenario.

* * *

By the time I got on to the M25 I was concerned that I might be late for Oriole's flight. How often I had done this – tried to calculate things so finely that I spent half the journey worrying about whether I'd miss the plane? The state of the motorway didn't help; long stretches were being repaired and the heavy traffic was reduced to one lane for miles reducing traffic to a standstill.

Still, once I had cleared the junction with the A3, the variable speed limits were up to sixty again and I made Heathrow with some minutes to spare. Parking the Jaguar in the short-stay multi-storey, I made my way to Terminal Two arrivals. The electronic information board told me that Oriole's flight had arrived and that passengers were in the customs hall. I leaned against the restraining rail, picking a place where she could not fail to spot me, and waited for her to emerge through the big glass sliding doors.

It occurred to me now that my anxiety had little to do with the car journey and everything to do with seeing Oriole again. It was hard to believe that this was actually happening.

"Have you got a light, by any chance?" The voice belonged to a short, youthful man who had appeared beside me. He had a camera slung around his neck and a photographer's bag over his shoulder.

"Sorry, I don't smoke," I replied as amiably as I could. Passengers had started to appear in dribs and drabs and I didn't want to be distracted from the task of recognising Oriole.

"Oh, good for you," he replied looking around to see if anyone else nearby was likely to be carrying smoking equipment. Obviously not. He put his cigarette carefully back in the packet. "Well, I don't suppose it'll do me any harm to go without. Are you meeting someone in the team?"

"What team?" I asked disinterestedly. The trickle of passengers was becoming a steady stream, but he seemed determined to get into a conversation.

"The PGA boys," he went on oblivious to my cold shoulder. "You're not a golfer, then? Valderrama, the Volvo Masters, they've all been down there, you know the big names, Nick, Colin, Ian, all of them – and they're coming back on this flight." As if to prove the accuracy of his words a group of tanned, fit-looking young men, wearing identical blazers and flannels, accompanied by pretty, predominantly blonde, women similarly attired, appeared through the doors pushing trolleys with large golf bags dominating their baggage.

"Scuse me," said the young man, dodging underneath the rail, "got to get some pictures of the conquering hero!"

As more golfers appeared, some of whom I vaguely recognised, intermingled with returning holidaymakers and the occasional businessman, I was dimly aware that other cameramen were flashing away. As yet there was no sign of Oriole.

"Hello, Gerald." For the second time, I was being addressed from out of frame. It was a woman's voice and my heart leapt. I looked around and there she was, not as I remembered her in the lush surroundings of Villa Harmony, of course, but unremarkably dressed in a thick navy blue sweater and jeans, her hair scragged up into a baseball cap and her face disguised with a pair of large-framed sunglasses. She was standing there, clutching the handle of a luggage trolley bearing a single medium-sized suitcase, looking up at me, waiting for my response.

"I'm sorry, I can't believe how I missed you, I was here, waiting for you to appear, I don't know how—"

She put a finger to my lips, a gesture I later learnt was a habit of hers. "You didn't miss me," she said. "I was already here. I came in about an hour ago on an earlier flight." She saw my furrowed brow. "Don't worry, I'll explain everything. Do you have a car?"

"Yes," I stammered, "yes, it's in the short-stay car park." I grabbed the trolley from her. "Let me take that, here, this way." As we left the concourse the golfers were still flocking out and the cameras flashing.

We walked briskly up the ramp to the car, me pushing the trolley, and Oriole hanging on to my arm. Soon we were driving out of the airport and heading towards the M4. She cast the odd glance over her shoulder but otherwise seemed calm enough.

"Where are we going?" I asked as we reached the junction with the motorway.

"London," she replied. "I've made a reservation at the Lanesborough." Obediently I turned right onto the M4 and headed for the West End.

"So, why the earlier flight?" I ventured.

"Just to make it a little harder for anyone who might be trying to catch up with me," she replied.

"Do you mean Henri?" I asked bravely,

"Of course. When he discovers I have gone he will be out of his mind. First Harmony, then me. It is only a matter of time before he goes to the police."

"He already has," I commented.

"How do you know that?" she seemed genuinely surprised but there was a note of suspicion in her voice.

"I called one of the newspapers just before I left in case there was any further news of Harmony. They told me that you had disappeared as well. Henri must have called the police soon after you caught the flight."

"If he believes that I have been abducted as well, that might help us," she replied thoughtfully looking back through the rear window. "I chose not to leave a note or message of any kind. I had hoped that he would not discover I had gone until later."

I wondered how far I should press her. We still had a twenty-minute drive ahead of us and I decided to stifle my curiosity for a little longer to see if she came up with anything else of her own volition.

"It won't take them long to discover which flight I was on so they will know that I am here in England. Hopefully, no one saw us leave the airport so it will be harder for them from now on." She seemed perfectly calm and in control of the situation.

We drove on in silence for some time, both lost in our thoughts. Eventually, the motorway ran out leading us onto the dual carriageway west of Chiswick.

We stopped at some traffic lights and for the first time since we had been in the car together, I studied her. The hat and the sunglasses had gone and there, gently bathed in the orange glow of the streetlights, was that incredible face with its flawless olive skin and deep-set almond eyes, the face which had been etched in my mind since I had first met her. I wanted to take her in my arms, then and there, to tell her that she would be safe with me and that I would cherish and protect her, whatever agony she was suffering. As if reading my mind, she rested her hand lightly on mine. The effect was electrifying.

"Thank you," she whispered.

The impatient sounding of a horn from behind jolted me back to the here and now. The lights had changed; I engaged the gears clumsily and we leapt forward.

Oriole looked over her shoulder again.

"I think we are being followed," she said.

I looked in the rearview mirror.

"Two cars behind," she said, "the red one. It's been there since we left the airport."

So had a lot of other cars travelling into town from Heathrow, I thought.

"It's probably just a coincidence," I said. "We'll know for sure when we get into town. I wouldn't worry just yet."

We were making good time now. The worst of the traffic had dispersed, and I could see the Chiswick flyover looming ahead of us through the mist and drizzle. In a minute or so we would be at Hammersmith. I had already decided to take the less likely route past Olympia and down Kensington High Street. It would be interesting to see if the red car did the same.

"Sorry about our English weather," I said trying to keep the tenseness out of my voice, "it's not what you're used to, I'm afraid."

She laughed lightly, musically, I thought, and then retreated back into her reflective mood. It was a while before she spoke.

"Gerald, I know I have a lot of explaining to do and that none of this makes much sense to you. But, please, be patient for a little longer. I promise I'll tell you everything very soon – everything I know that is."

Again, we drove on in silence. I looked at the clock on the dashboard. The time was two-fifteen.

"Oriole," I broached the point as delicately as I could, "I need to know what you are expecting of me. Am I simply giving you a lift to your hotel or is there something else?" Put like that the question sounded childish. I tried again. "I mean, if you need me to spend some time with you, that's fine – I'll do anything to help you get Harmony back, I think you know that – it's just that I need to make arrangements, I have a business to run and there's Blanche and the children."

My premature attempt to straighten things out between us was faltering hopelessly.

"I have checked into the hotel as Mrs Irving," she said.

I couldn't believe what I had heard. "But, Oriole, that's absurd—" but she went on quickly, stifling my protest.

"Gerald, you must understand that I was desperate. I had to get away and I needed help. I couldn't go to anyone I knew, that way Henri would have found out where I was in no time at all. The few true friends we have are his, not mine. When you telephoned it seemed like fate. I don't know why but I knew I could trust you." Her grip tightened on my left hand, resting on the gear shift. "Gerald, I had so little time to make any arrangements. When the hotel asked me my name, I said the first thing that came into my mind."

The possibilities of what she was saying flooded my mind. Was this simply a subterfuge to disguise her identity or was she intending to go on masquerading as my wife?

As we rounded the Hammersmith one-way system I signalled left towards Kensington and checked the red car in the mirror. He did the same, but I could still not bring myself to believe that we were actually being followed.

"Is it behind us?" she asked, for the first time with a note of anxiety in her voice.

"Yes, but it still doesn't necessarily mean we're being followed," I replied. "Incidentally, why did you choose the Lanesborough?"

"I don't know London, Gerald. I have spent very little time in England, and have never been to London. I had only heard of the

Savoy and the Ritz and I thought they would be too obvious. We were at a dinner a few weeks ago and someone mentioned that the Lanesborough was very good so I made the booking."

"Was Henri at the dinner, too? Did he overhear that conversation?"

"He may have done," she said hesitatingly, "it didn't occur to me."

"I think you may be safer somewhere rather less pretentious. London is full of perfectly acceptable low-profile hotels. What do you think?"

"You may be right. Do you have anywhere in mind?"

"No, but give me a minute and I'll come up with something." I felt a flush of self-congratulation – at last, I was doing something positive to help her. The rearview mirror was telling its own story. There was the red car (it looked like an old Sierra) still two places behind us in the slow-moving traffic as we approached Kensington High Street.

For the first time, Oriole was showing some interest in the surroundings.

"Is this your famous West End?" she asked.

"Not quite," I replied, "in fact, I was thinking of avoiding the West End entirely. Unless you want to do some sightseeing, of course – it might give us a chance to lose our friend?"

She turned her head to look behind us. I sensed the atmosphere had lightened a little.

"Why not?" she said. "The longer we go on driving, the more likely we are to lose them and if we don't know where we are going, then they won't know either, will they?"

There was a touch of humour in her voice and I marvelled at how ordinary this extraordinary woman could be.

"Very well," I said, "Hyde Park Corner, here we come!"

She laughed, freely and unreservedly for the first time. "I have read about it, isn't that where the Duke of Wellington lives?"

"Yes, his house was once called Number One, England, but now it's something else, I think. And we'll pass the Lanesborough. Do we need to cancel your booking? Did you give them a contact number or can you think of any other way they could trace you?"

"No, I made up a name and address. I can't remember what I said but they seemed to accept it."

"Good, then we have nothing to worry about apart from this chap behind us, that's if he is following us deliberately. Well, we'll soon know."

I took a sharp left into the park just past the Albert Hall and immediately right towards Park Lane. I looked behind to see the red Sierra carrying out the same manoeuvre. I was beginning to think that Oriole's fears were justified.

"I think you're right," I said. "I'll tell you what I'm going to do. There's an underground car park at The Four Seasons. The attendants know me, I'm often there with clients. We'll drive in, you can stay in the car and I'll walk round the block to see if they've stopped near the hotel, then we'll know for sure."

"Okay," she said, "but be careful."

Getting to the Four Seasons from where we were involved a number of twists and turns which I had negotiated many times before. If the Sierra was tailing us the driver would assume that we were making for the Hilton, The Four Seasons or the Intercontinental, all clustered together at the end of Park Lane. Seeing us disappear into the car park I hoped they would conclude we had arrived at our destination. After that, it was a question of whether they stayed around or went off to report to someone else.

The red car followed our every move, even into Hamilton Place where the entrance to the car park was situated. I turned into the narrow archway, stopped for a brief second and watched in the mirror as the Sierra carried on down the road. The driver was on his own. Continuing down the ramp I stopped at the attendants' kiosk.

Nassim, one of the regulars, came over and opened the door.

"I need a favour, Nassim," I said addressing him with a smile.

"Of course, Mr Irving, how long will you be with us today?"

"About five minutes, I should think. Could you just make sure Madam is alright, she'll be staying in the car, I have to call in at reception to collect a package?"

"Certainly, please, just leave the keys in the ignition as usual."

"Thanks," I said and then to Oriole, "I won't be long." She gave my hand a squeeze, I got out and Nassim shut the driver's door behind me.

I walked around the perimeter of the hotel and quickly spotted the red Sierra parked on an opposite corner near the entrance to the Hilton. It was empty. I wondered where the driver was – looking for us inside the hotel, in a phone box, or pursuing me as I was pursuing him? Casting my eyes around the immediate vicinity I could see no one who appeared remotely interested in me. When I was close enough to the Sierra, I made a mental note of its index number. There was a sticker on the windscreen which looked familiar although I couldn't make out what it said. Not wishing to arouse any suspicion I turned on my heel and went back to the car park and Oriole. I had only been away for a minute or two but already I was concerned about her safety.

I need not have worried. Nassim had been true to his word. The car and Oriole were exactly as I had left them. I pressed a five-pound note into Nassim's hand, thanked him and wondered whether he had noticed there was no package. Getting into the car, I flashed a quick smile at Oriole and started the engine.

"If we move quickly, I think we might lose him," was all that I said.

Emerging from the car park, I turned right, away from the Sierra, down a short stretch of a lightly used one-way street and out into Green Park. Strictly illegal, of course, but a justifiable risk under the circumstances. If our pursuer saw us at all, it would be difficult for him to give chase without attracting considerable attention to himself.

Once we were in the mainstream I made a wide detour via Berkeley Square and Grosvenor Place heading back towards Notting Hill where I thought there was a good chance of finding some nondescript but comfortable, reasonably priced accommodation. There was no sign of the Sierra.

I had spent the night once at an ordinary but pleasant enough hotel called the Concorde in Maida Vale and it was there that I was heading, hoping it was not full; I didn't fancy trailing around the area looking for a room.

By the time we got there the drizzle had turned to steady rain and, having to leave the car some distance away in a side street, there was no alternative but to get rather wet. Oriole clung onto my arm as we half-walked, half-ran to the hotel's modest front entrance.

"Blast, I've forgotten the suitcase!" I didn't want to get wetter going back to the car.

"We'll get it later," she replied, "they may not even have a room for us." As we entered through the revolving door the 'us' was ringing in my ears.

The receptionist was a middle-aged, gaunt-looking woman with peroxide blonde hair, "Good afternoon," I smiled, "I wonder whether you might have a room available?"

"Certainly, sir," she said politely consulting her computer terminal, "for how many nights will that be?"

"Two," Oriole answered quickly. I thought from now on she might prefer to make the running.

"Non-smoking, I presume?"

"Yes, please," Oriole replied.

"Good, that'll be room 404 on the fourth floor. That's a double room with an en-suite bath and shower, television and mini-bar. The rate is £80 per night. Will that suit you?" This woman must have worked somewhere better than this at some earlier stage of her career, I thought appreciatively. She reminded me of Pru apart from the peroxide.

"That will be excellent," said Oriole.

"Would you kindly fill in the registration form?" She passed it to me and laid a pen on top. I picked it up and, with only the slightest hesitation, began to fill it in. In the first box, beside 'Guests Name(s)', I wrote 'Mr and Mrs G. Irving'. Instead of a private address, I put care of my office. This seemed to satisfy Peroxide as she cast a perfunctory eye over the completed form.

"How will you be settling the account?" was her next question. I reached for my wallet, but Oriole was ahead of me.

"Cash, if that's acceptable," she said.

"Yes, of course, madam," came the unflinching reply, "but, in that case, we do require payment in advance."

"Certainly," I said, "darling?"

Oriole reached into her bag and produced a most exquisite purse. From it, she took four carefully folded fifty-pound notes and handed them to me. I passed them straight over to Peroxide.

"Do you have any luggage?" she asked, sorting out the change.

"Only one suitcase," I replied, "unfortunately I left it in the car – it's around the corner."

"I would like to say that someone will fetch it for you whilst you go on up to your room," Peroxide replied, "but we don't carry front desk staff anymore." She looked sadly out of the window behind her. "You're going to get wet again, I'm afraid." She returned two twenty-pound notes.

I turned to Oriole. "You go on up," I suggested, "I'll only be a minute. Oh, and order some tea!"

"Fourth floor, room 404, you'll find tea-making facilities in the room; there's no room service, sorry." Peroxide handed Oriole the key. "The lift is in the corner over there. Enjoy your stay."

As I trotted back to the car, the importance of Oriole's visit, the mystery of why she was here at all, the danger she might be in, Harmony's disappearance, why I had become involved – all this I had neatly consigned to the back of my mind. All I could think about was that I would soon be alone with Oriole in a hotel room and that no one knew where we were. I found the idea intoxicating.

I retrieved the suitcase from the boot of the car and paddled my way back to the hotel.

"Everything okay?" enquired Peroxide as I passed her in the foyer, my clothes darkly stained by the rain.

"Yes, thank you, just a little damp round the gills." From the expression on her face, I wasn't so sure she believed Oriole was my wife. I remembered a previous time, before we were married, when Blanche and I had checked into a west country hotel for an illicit weekend, convinced that the proprietor knew the truth and would throw us out at any moment, most likely bursting into the room whilst we in the middle of wildly abandoned sex. Of course, it hadn't happened then, and it wasn't going to happen now.

The lift was waiting and I pressed the button for the fourth floor. It occurred to me that we hadn't seen another soul apart from Peroxide since we'd been in the hotel.

Room 404 was only a few paces from the lift. I stopped outside the door and knocked gently. Oriole's voice was hushed, "Who is it?"

"It's me, Gerald."

She clicked back the locks and opened the door. I slipped in. What I saw before me was the last thing I had expected.

Set free, her hair cascaded in luscious waves almost to her waist. The sweater and jeans had gone, too, replaced by a loose-fitting red kimono. Only her reddened eyes and tear-stained cheeks detracted from her beauty. I didn't know what to say, ashamed that I had forgotten the weight of her grief, ashamed of my selfishness.

As we stood facing each other I knew that I was about to take another stride in the marathon of commitment to another living soul.

Without a word she fell into my arms, weeping uncontrollably; her private torture, her grief pouring out in a great waterfall of emotional release. Boyishly, I kept my hands at my sides and then, tentatively, put my arms around her and tenderly stroked her silky hair. She made no attempt to break away. Gradually, the weeping turned to sobbing and we cried together.

I carried her gently to the bed and laid her down beside me, rocking her until the spasms subsided and she was calm again. I don't know for how long we slept but I woke first and lay gazing at her. Eventually, she took a long, deep breath, opened her eyes, turned and lay on her back looking up at the ceiling. Her hand found mine.

"Thank you," she said, "now I shall make your tea."

She got up, filled the kettle from the bathroom, plugged it in and waited for it to boil. She put the teabags in the pot and only then turned towards me. She leant back against the fitted side unit, hands behind her, and tossed her hair away from her face.

"I am so terribly afraid for Harmony," she said simply. "I am so frightened that I shall never see her again." Her eyes filled with tears but this time I made no attempt to comfort her.

"You will," I said. "Whatever they might say, whoever they may be, they have to keep Harmony alive. Dead she's worth nothing to them. No, when they get their money – and that's what this is all about isn't it – you'll have Harmony back in no time."

She frowned. "I'm afraid it may have nothing to do with money, Gerald, that may be just pretence."

"You make it sound as if you know who has taken her," I said.

The kettle was boiling. She switched it off and transferred some water into the pot. Her actions were precise and mechanical.

"Until last year we had no fears about the children's safety and then, suddenly, one day when we were at our home in Paris, Henri became desperately concerned and warned me that they might be in danger. When I asked why he said it was because we were wealthy and well-known, therefore, our children were likely to become targets for ransom attempts. That was when he installed elaborate security systems in our homes. It was frightening. He was always nervous after that and, naturally, I became apprehensive, too."

"So, you think there may be more to it than simply being rich and famous?"

She poured the tea carefully into the cups which she had arranged neatly on the tray. She made the mundane task seem like a ritual.

"Milk?"

"Yes, please."

"Sugar?"

"No, thank you." She stirred the tea slowly round and round in the cup and then passed it to me. I sipped it appreciatively and smiled at her. She smiled back as if she had performed a duty well. Tidying the tray, she picked up her own cup and sat beside me on the bed.

"Something else happened at that time in Paris," she went on. "Henri had some visitors."

"Was that unusual?" I asked.

"No, except that when they left he was scared; I had never seen him frightened before. I didn't meet them, but I saw them. I could tell they were not clients or the kind of people he would normally see. I tried to find out – I was worried for him – but he insisted that there was nothing for me to concern myself about." She got up and walked to the window, staring through the net curtains at the dismal scene outside. "Our lives changed from that moment on. We seldom stayed in one place for very long and wherever we went he surrounded us with staff and, what do you call them, minders? Harmony had to go everywhere accompanied by a trained nanny, except the only thing she was trained in was self-defence." I thought of the middle-eastern girl we had met briefly at Villa Harmony now lying comatose in some Spanish hospital.

"So, you think these people who came to see him in Paris were enemies of some kind who had threatened Harmony's safety in order to – to what, to get Henri to do something he didn't want to do?"

"I don't know. But I am sure there must be an important reason why Henri has not been honest with me. That is why I do not believe that Harmony has been taken for ransom money and why I cannot trust him to get her back."

I let her words sink in and sipped at my tea. I looked at my watch. It was five minutes to six.

"Why don't we watch the news," I suggested, "in case there's something about Harmony?" I switched the television on, the volume turned down, waiting for six o'clock.

"Henri is devoted to her, that's obvious," I said eventually. "It's hard to believe that he won't do everything within his power to ensure her safety."

"That is precisely my concern, Gerald. Getting her back may not be within his power at all." I was beginning to understand why she had left home.

"You told me on the telephone that you didn't think Harmony was still in Spain. What made you say that?"

"If she were, I believe the police would have some idea who might have taken her and where she might be," Oriole replied. "The kidnappers would have had to give an address for the ransom to be delivered. To my knowledge, there has been no such clue, certainly until the time I left. Besides, I believe that I would know if she were near to me."

I thought for a moment – as a mother, she was being led by instinct.

"You say you saw these people in Paris, what were they like?"

"I only glimpsed them briefly, Henri let them in and out. They weren't there very long. One of them was short, fair-skinned, and fair-haired, but his accent was not French, he could have been American or even English. The other two were dark-skinned, probably African. There was some shouting, but I could not hear very much of what was said. It was obvious they wanted something from Henri and he was refusing to let them have it. Henri was in a rage at the end. It sounded as if they were threatening him."

"I don't know much about Henri's lifestyle, is he often abroad, does he go off alone on business trips?"

She had finished her tea and put the cup back on the tray: I handed her mine. She came back and lay full-length on the bed, innocently, hands behind her head, the thin fabric stretched taught across the swell of her breasts, her nipples alert, the olive skin of her face and arms glowing in the half-light. I felt myself harden with the lust I had been suppressing all day.

"Yes, he travels a lot but seldom alone, he nearly always has members of his staff with him. Most of his work nowadays is the manufacture of medical equipment. His companies design and manufacture a whole range of miniaturised surgical tools, without which many modern-day operations would not be possible. I think it is acknowledged throughout the medical world that Henri has pioneered the means by which micro-surgery exists."

"You must be very proud of him," I said, "he is a remarkable man."

"He is a brilliant but complex man. Despite outward appearances, he is deeply troubled, and secretive, too. You asked me about his travelling. Soon after the visit to Paris, he set off on a trip alone. He told me it was business but he would not tell me where he was going or why. But I found out – it doesn't matter how. He had gone to Africa, he was there for three weeks. When he returned he seemed even more worried than when he left."

"Whereabouts in Africa?" I asked.

"I don't know. The flight was booked into Johannesburg."

I was only half listening to her. The news had started on the television. I picked up the remote and increased the sound slightly.

"Do you know if he had ever had any connection with South Africa before? Was he involved politically at all? Had he made any enemies there?" I still had half an eye on the TV but there was nothing, just routine news items, journalists' words we don't hear, and pictures we have become immune to.

"There was a time, yes, when Harmony was ill, he used to call someone there."

"I didn't know Harmony had been ill, when was this?"

"When she was five. She had kidney failure, the doctors said that she was going to die. Henri saved her life."

"Henri? How?"

"She needed at least one, preferably both kidneys replaced, but there were no donors available. The hospital in Paris was trying very hard but time was running out. In the end, Henri managed to find a surgeon who could carry out the operation and who had located a suitable kidney. We flew Harmony to South Africa, and the operation was a total success. Harmony still only has one kidney but, as you saw, she is fit and well."

Again, her eyes filled with tears. I switched the set off and offered her my arms. She fell into them, sobbing quietly.

"She's been through so much for a little girl, Gerald, I can't bear to think that she's suffering now!"

I thought for a moment and then asked her, "What was the name of the surgeon?"

She looked at me wide-eyed

"Why should that matter?"

"Was it Chandrit Singh?"

Her surprise was obvious. "No, but I remember the name. He was connected with it all in some way. How did you know?"

"It was a guess. I've met him. He's in the port, Oriole, and he lives and works no more than five kilometres from your home! Surely, that's not a coincidence, is it?"

She dried her eyes, got up and walked over to the dressing table. Unzipping a small toiletries bag she took out a long-handled hairbrush and began brushing the luxuriant, waist-length hair.

"It was as a reward for helping save Harmony's life that Henri set Chandrit up in business," she replied eventually, "he felt it was the least he could do."

"So, *The Aphrodite* belongs to Henri?"

"To one of his companies, yes. As a matter of fact, Henri hates Singh being so close to us. Originally, he was supposed to have been sailing all around the Mediterranean, not stuck in one place. It is not a line of business with which Henri particularly wants to be associated."

"Is that why *The Aphrodite* used to be called *Oriole*?"
She was shocked by the question; I was trespassing on uncomfortable territory. She carried on brushing, more vigorously, carefully avoiding my gaze.

"There's nothing to be gained from talking about this, Gerald," was all she had to say in reply. Her sudden reticence was irritating.

"What do you mean, nothing to be gained? I'm trying to make sense of all this so that I can help you, Oriole – don't start being selective about what I should and shouldn't know!" I got up and strode to the window. "What is it, don't you trust me? Haven't we gone a little too far for that?"

I had raised my voice and regretted it. She didn't deserve that, not now. I sat down on the bed again.

"Yes, I trust you, would I be here otherwise?" She was looking at me anxiously, then knelt in front of me, holding my hands.

"I'm sorry, I shouldn't have spoken like that." I smiled, glad the uneasy moment had passed.

"Gerald, there is so much you don't know and I hope you will never need to know. I'm sorry." She let go of my hands and stood up. "Just now you asked me to trust you and I said I would. Will you trust me to tell you these things if, and when, the time is right?"

Her upturned face was a picture: this woman was used to getting her way not because she manipulated or capitalised on her beauty but, I thought, quite simply, because she naturally evoked compliance in others. Her charm was a function of her beauty, certainly, but it was just as much to do with her honesty. Somehow, I could not imagine her telling lies.

"Of course, I will," I said, knowing there was no alternative. "You call the shots, okay?" I looked at my watch again. It was getting late. "But right now, I need to know what you have in mind. Remember, I have a real wife and family who expect me home in the evenings and a secretary who will be surprised if I don't turn up in the morning."

"I understand." I thought I detected a note of sadness in her voice, but I wasn't sure. She went on: "I was hoping you might be able to help me for more than one day." Her voice was trembling. "But I understand I have no right to your time. Of course, you must go home."

"Oriole," I said a little more firmly, "I must know what you plan to do next. I think you are safe here, but sitting around in a London hotel room isn't going to find Harmony, is it? For God's sake, why doesn't Henri just pay the ransom money?"

"Because he believes that once they have the money they will kill Harmony. As long as he can keep them talking she will be safe."

"But as far as we know they're not talking, are they?" I knew that once we started the process of analysis it could go on for a long time. "Would you like me to stay a bit longer to help you really think this through?"

Her face lit up like a child's. I had seen the same expression on her daughter's face.

"I must make a couple of calls, then." I lifted the receiver by the bed and dialled the office.

"Thank you. Shall I make some more tea?" I nodded just as Pru came on the line. I was glad she was working late.

"Pru, it's Mr Irving, listen, I shan't be back to the office tonight, can you do something for me?" Pru's voice at the other end was concerned, curious.

"Of course. There are some messages, would you like them?"

"In a minute, firstly, make a note to call Mrs Irving, and tell her I'm unexpectedly out of town with a client. I may be late. If we end up drinking, I'll probably book in somewhere for the night rather than drive home. Tell her I'll ring later. I tried just now but she was engaged." The lie came easily and landed softly. "Is that clear?"

"Yes, I'll do that immediately. As a matter of fact, Mrs Irving called earlier, so she knows you are out."

"What did you tell her?"

"Simply that you were out on business."

"Good. Now, the messages, please." I had a notepad and pen at the ready.

"Actually, there's nothing urgent that can't wait or that I haven't dealt with. Oh, yes, there was one call, from a rather odd-sounding gentleman, I don't think I've spoken to him before, I'm sure I would have remembered, he just said his name was Vinny. He left two numbers; he said not to hesitate to ring him at home."

I scribbled them down recognising the first one as the number I had called earlier.

"Good, thanks, Pru. See you in the morning, then. Any problems I'll call again." I replaced the receiver and immediately picked it up again, dialling the first of Vinny's two numbers. I guessed he would still be in the office – a lifetime of waiting for the pubs to open after work would have made sure of that. The operator put me through. As before his voice was curt, abrupt.

"Lythgoe. Who is this?"

"Gerald, Gerald Irving," I answered. Why did this man make me nervous?

"Ah yes, the elusive Mr Irving. I've been trying to get hold of you. Where are you?"

"That doesn't matter, Lythgoe," I tried to sound as menacing as I could. "Why are you hounding me?" I was aware that Oriole was hanging onto every word I was saying.

"Au contraire, Gerald, au contraire. If you remember, it was you who asked me to call you if I found out any more news about the kid. Well, I've got something – still interested?"

"Yes, look, I'm sorry, it's been a difficult day."

"Has, hasn't it? By the way, how's Mrs Nader I take it she's still with you?"

The question hit me like a blow in the solar plexus. "W h a t do you mean?" I spluttered, I was no good at this. "She's not with me and I don't know what you are talking about!"

"Saw you with her at the airport, Gerald, we had a team down there covering the return of the Volvo boys. It was just a hunch on my part, happened to come off. After all, you very nearly told me this morning, didn't you – wasn't hard to put two and two together? Anyway, young Peter made the connection and I've got the pictures in front of me as a matter of fact. Don't do the lovely Mrs N justice, really. Still, it's her alright – and she had been on the road, as they say."

"Was it you who followed us in the red car?"

"Not me, young Pete again. Once the golfers were out of the way he had to come back to town anyway. Good practice for him. Still, you gave him the slip – clever you. What did you do, wait till he was round the other side of the hotel then dodge down the one-way street? Got to be careful pulling tricks like that, Gerry, you might get done."

The man was contemptible. I drew a deep breath.

"You said you had some news for me?" I said levelly.

"Oh, yeah. Nothing on the girl I'm afraid. Her bloody stupid father is still saying he won't pay the ransom. No, the news is about the nanny. She took a turn for the worse this afternoon, they don't reckon she'll make it. So, it might only be kidnapping today, Gerry, but it could be murder tomorrow."

"I see." I tried to take in the significance of what I was hearing. "Listen, these photographs, allegedly of me with . . ." I didn't want to frighten Oriole. "You're not proposing to publish them, are you?"

"Depends on you, Gerald." His voice was cheery. Could it really be that this was all in a day's work for some people?

"Why? How do you mean?"

"Well, it's a story, of sorts, isn't it? *'Kid abducted, mother goes missing, turns up at Heathrow with a mystery man who no one's ever heard of.'* Course, sounds a bit bald put like that, but dressed up with some nice shots of you, the wife and kids, er, Blanche, isn't it? A bit of background – you know how I work. You're not a bad-looking bloke, Gerald, tallish, fair-haired, blue-eyed, nice dresser by the look of it, I think our female readers might see you as quite a hunk. It'll make page one, Gerald, not the big story perhaps, but it's got legs. Syndicate well, too, come to think of it. 'Mystery man', yes, I like that."

I was in a daze, my head spinning, but he was relentless.

"Sorry, Gerry, it's my imagination, it's what I'm paid for. You see, it's what one might call a speculative piece. Not as good as hard facts, of course, but then I'm old school, aren't I? Nowadays, most of our readers treat the paper like it's a fuckin' magazine, anyway. They're not too fussed about facts, frankly."

"You said it was up to me," I mumbled, "what did you mean by that?"

"Ah, well, that's a different way forward entirely. Thing is, will you choose to take it, I wonder?"

"What?"

"Cooperate with us, Gerry, and I'll cooperate with you. Unless I'm very much mistaken you and the lovely Mrs Nader are about to set off on a grand expedition to find – and hopefully bring home – little Harmony, am I right?"

"I, I don't know, I really don't know." It was true, I didn't.

"Well, I can't see what else she's got in mind, Gerry, maybe you should ask her? What would you do in her position, eh? She's lost her daughter, her husband's behaving like a prick and she doesn't trust him to play the game with a straight bat. What do you expect her to do, sit patiently on her pretty butt waiting for a miracle? It's not in the nature of the beast, is it? Now I don't know how you've got tied up in all this – maybe she fancies you or something – like I said you're not a bad catch. Anyway, she's chosen you as her hero, Gerry, her fuckin' knight on a shining white fuckin' charger – come on, it's what women do! Believe me, you're in this up to your neck, old son, until the kid's found, safe and well. Or not. Either way, I want the story, Gerry, every day, every step of the way. Thus, you keep your anonymity, and your wife and kids stay out of the frame. Fair enough? What do you say?"

"You give me no choice." Game, set and match in straight sets.

"Good boy. Now, where are you?"

"I, I can't tell you that," I mumbled.

"Can't tell me! What's wrong with you? You deaf or something?" He was shouting at me.

"Listen, listen," I said hurriedly, "I'll do everything else, the daily calls, keeping you updated, everything, but I can't tell you where we are. It's not safe, please, Lythgoe, leave it at that."

The seconds ticked by. I heard him sigh hugely at the other end. How could this man who I had never met force himself into my life?

"Alright. I'm a soft bastard, aren't I? But you better deliver, Irving. If so much as a day goes by without me hearing from you, we're down to Mayfield, do I make myself clear? Oh, and Gerry, no talking to the other hacks, they'll be on to you, sooner or later. This is a strictly exclusive arrangement? I'm trusting you, got it?"

"Okay, okay," I was drained. Drained by the conversation, drained by images of Blanche and the girls spread all over the front pages of a national paper, drained by the knowledge that I had so overwhelmingly fucked up. What a fool, what a stupid, stupid fool.

"I'll speak to you tomorrow, then."

"Great, Gerry, great. I'll be here. Bye for now."

I looked at Oriole. She could only have pieced together a fragment of the conversation from the few sentences she had heard but the despair written all over my face told her everything else she needed to know.

"Oh Gerald, I'm so sorry! I am so sorry!" It was her turn to comfort me. I tried to pull myself together.

"It's my cross to bear, Oriole, not yours. I got myself into this with my eyes wide open, it's not your fault. Still, if it's any consolation we now know who it was following us from the airport, and it wasn't Henri."

"Who, then?"

"Press, believe it or not. Acting on guesswork, would you believe? Bloody hell, what a piece of work! I'm out of my depth, that's for sure. The bastard!"

She was more in control than I was, now.

"I know something about handling the press, Gerald. The first rule is to give them something rather than nothing, that way you keep the upper hand. Did you tell him you'd stay in touch, keep him informed?"

"Yes, I suppose that's exactly what I did. But I didn't tell him where we are, he knows you are with me, but not where."

"Good. You did the right thing."

"So, what are we going to do?" She was going through her tea ritual again.

"I think we should have something to eat, then get some rest. Tomorrow, we – I – must set off in search of Harmony. If the men who threatened Henri in Paris are responsible, then perhaps Africa is the place to begin."

"But, Oriole, it would be like looking for a needle in a haystack! Where on earth do you start? What do you have to go on?"

"I have a mother's instinct, Gerald, it may not seem much to you but to me, it is like a beacon, a guiding light."

"It's a big country, Oriole, where will you start?"

"I will start at the largest hospital I can find. They will know of Henri and his activities. I shall tell them that our daughter has been abducted and see if anyone knows anything about it. I have descriptions of the men who came to visit Henri in Paris, maybe someone will recognise them."

"Oriole, it really isn't very much to go on." I felt heartless saying so, but it was true.

"What else can I do?" she cried. "I must start somewhere! Even if I never see Harmony again, I could never forgive myself for not trying! Gerald, please, support me, I am so frightened, I need to know you are on my side."

Her face was within inches of mine, pleading, hoping. I put my right hand behind her head and, grasping her neck, pulled her towards me, closing the gap between us. I kissed her roughly, uncompromisingly, my lips hard against hers, my tongue forcing her mouth open. Momentarily, my newfound confidence faltered as she failed to respond to this crude imposition, but then, magically, she opened her mouth, her tongue exploring mine, her hands on my neck and shoulders, nails digging into my flesh, her body pressed hard against me. The sensation was so intoxicating that I felt sure I was losing my senses, and yet she was making the pace now, directing my movements, her need urgent and pressing. Now we were lying together, she on her back, me half straddling her, as I tugged at her clothes, pulling them away. Her gown had fallen open, and for the first time I saw her fully naked, the big almond eyes half closed and heavy-lidded, her breath coming in short bursts. I kissed the already erect nipples, my right hand reaching down to part her legs. Her hands were scrabbling at my waistband now, and I eased my position to help her undress me. She was already moist and swollen, ready for me to enter her, but before I could, she sat up and rolled on top of me. As she rode me with a fierceness and passion that took my breath away, I knew she was already on the brink of orgasm. I looked up, supporting her breasts with my hands, and saw the anxiety on her face; for, in the full heat of her passion, she was unmistakably asking my consent for her to come. "Yes, yes, don't hold back!" I whispered and immediately she convulsed in orgasm, head thrown back, her hands clasping mine against her breasts, first one, then a second and a third shuddering climax, until, like an angel, she fell forwards onto my chest, showering my lips, face and shoulders with a flotilla of tiny kisses, until, in the aftermath of her relief she began to calm down, her breathing subsiding into long, deep regular sighs.

Such was the urgency and speed of her lovemaking, the all-consuming necessity for her orgasm, that, fleetingly, I was not sure whether I had climaxed myself. Now, feeling my hardness still inside her, I began a rocking movement of my own, a compelling pressure building in my groin to come as she had, without inhibition, without restraint. Immediately, I felt her stir again, and, pushing herself back up to a sitting position, she again started riding me, this time in slower, more measured thrusts, teasing and massaging. But if she had meant to stay in control for longer this time, the intention was short-lived as the stimulation of her own movements overtook her. Now she was panting, eyes half closed, head thrown back, mouth open, flicking at her lips with a moistening tongue, until, bucking again on top of me, I saw that same pleading look on her face, begging my consent to her release. This time I responded with my body and raising myself easily beneath her, arched my back and matched her urgent movements with thrusts of my own. She was already coming, this time in one long, continuous spasm, as I exploded inside her. Hands behind her neck, holding her hair away from her face, she continued to shudder and jolt long after I had finished, before finally collapsing on me, another shower of butterfly kisses, signalling her descent back to the here and now. I had never experienced anything like it and lay there marvelling at the miracle of what had just happened.

The whole experience had been so vividly erotic that simply recalling what we had just done was enough to revive me and, gently moving her onto her back, taking care to remain coupled, I raised myself above her and, slowly at first, started to fuck her in long, deliberate strokes, looking at her directly as I did so. Her eyes were closed, relishing the fresh sensations of our new juxtaposition. "Open your eyes," I said gently, "look at me." Her eyelids fluttered back and she returned my gaze. Instantly her body began to respond and a low agonised moaning emanated from the back of her throat. Her eyes closed again. "Open them." I said sharply, "look at me!" She opened them, and her hand went to her mouth, stifling the sounds of her mounting excitement. I noticed a fleck of blood by her mouth and saw that she was biting the soft fleshy part of her hand. She was hurting herself, trying to delay her climax to coincide with mine. I kissed her hand and gently removed it from her teeth, then transferred the kiss to the softness of her open mouth. She could prolong her battle no more and, as she moved her pelvis rapidly against mine, gasping for breath against the insistence of the kiss, she was lost and climaxed again, breasts trembling, legs locked together behind my back, nails digging into my shoulders. I felt the pressure inside me reach its peak and, this time, to make sure she knew, delivered some powerful final thrusts as I climaxed again inside her. A smile fluttered across her face; my orgasm had resolved the turmoil within her, so anxious had she been to satisfy me as I had satisfied her.

We lay together for some while, recovering from the intensity of our lovemaking which, from beginning to end, had probably lasted no more than a few minutes, but had seemed like a journey into another space and time. Wondrously, as I looked at her lying in my arms, glowing and fulfilled. I felt how I imagined a mature man might feel having deflowered a virgin, without pain or fear, initiating her into a world of new and everlasting sensual pleasure from which she had been precluded only moments before. If life can change people, then surely people can change life.

"I love you," I said, the words coming easily and unselfconsciously. "I have loved you, wanted you, from the moment I set eyes on you."

She put a finger to my lips. I didn't know how to conduct this conversation, but I desperately wanted to cement the significance of what we had shared.

"Oriole, you seemed to want me so very much, I must know whether—" But the finger was at my lips again.

If I had been a smoker, now would have been a good time to light up. Instead, I hugged her tightly and kissed her forehead. As the heat of passion subsided the room began to feel chilly. The quilted bedcover was on the floor. I got up, retrieved it, and laid it carefully over her before climbing under it myself, beside her. She snuggled up to me, intimately, her warm wetness pressed against my thigh.

Time had no meaning that afternoon, I could easily have lain with her all night. Not a thought of regret entered my head; I did not contemplate Blanche or the girls, or the business, the past or the future. I was in a time warp, consumed by my obsession with Oriole, whom I found so exciting that it seemed beyond belief that she could exist at all. I was living purely for the moment. That she did exist and wanted me as her lover was, to put it mildly, immensely flattering to my self-esteem. This was a sophisticated woman who needed a man and, for the time being, at any rate, had chosen me. Yet my feelings for her, whilst predominantly sexual, were interlaced with tenderness and love.

"Oriole, darling," I tried again, "I can't believe this is happening, please, tell me what you're thinking?"

She stirred at my words and snuggled closer.

"I was thinking how wonderful it is to make love," she answered simply tilting her head to look up at me. Her eyes were wide, and a smile flickered around the corners of her mouth.

"In general, or in particular?" I replied.

The smile broadened. "Isn't it always 'in particular'," she said, "is there any other way?"

I knew she was teasing me and didn't mind. "Well, you know, in general, I would say it's different for everyone."

She laughed happily, sweetly, innocently.

"Making love is very special to me, Gerald, it is not something I give or take lightly. But, just now, with you, it felt natural, inevitable. All I wanted was to make you happy." She tailed off as if puzzling to find an explanation.

"You make it sound as if you don't make love very often," I said. It was a crude thing to say, intrusive and insensitive. It broke her mood. She pulled away.

"I'm sorry," I added hastily, pulling her back towards me, "that was crass, it doesn't matter and anyway it's none of my business." But the spell was broken and I didn't try to stop her as she got out of bed and slipped the kimono over her.

"Would you like another cup of tea?" she said coolly looking at my reflection in the mirror. I propped myself up on one elbow not sure whether to stay where I was or get up too.

"Yes, thank you, that would be wonderful."

Again, she performed her ritual, silently, until she brought me my cup. Again, she waited for my verdict. I took a sip.

"Delicious," I said with a reassuring smile. She poured herself a cup and took it over to the window. She parted the curtains. It was dark.

"You are right, Gerald, I don't make love very often." She turned towards me and for the first time, I saw her look angry. "Now, are you satisfied?" I remained silent, drinking my tea.

"I just assumed that . . . you and Henri seemed so devoted to each other, I suppose it never occurred to me that—"

"That we might have any problems?" I was seeing another side of her now, her voice sharp and accusing, as if being my lover permitted her to speak to me differently than before.

"I'm sorry, I didn't mean to pry," I said.

"Of course, we are devoted," she continued. She paused for a second. "Henri is impotent," she said finally, "he always has been." The statement was so brutal I didn't know what to say. She went on: "It has caused great strain over the years." She still wasn't looking at me and clearly didn't mean to until she had finished.

"But Harmony and Max, surely?"

"Max is adopted, Harmony is ours."

I was at a complete loss. "But, I don't see—"

"We had Harmony by artificial insemination. She is Henri's daughter, he is her father. That is why he is so," she was searching for the right word, "so infatuated with her." I wasn't sure whether I detected a hint of jealousy in her voice.

"I see." I got up and put my arms around her. She seemed to relax a little at my touch. "Oriole, my darling, it must have been impossible during those years, to tolerate a marriage without love."

"Not without love, Gerald, without sex. It is not the same thing." She was right, of course.

"Even so, surely, you must have," I was struggling to find the right words. "Were you never tempted to?"

She spun round to face me.

"To take a lover, that's what you want to know, isn't it?" She looked away again, the almond eyes beginning to brim with tears. "Yes, I had a lover, once, only once, Gerald, until tonight. That is why you are now in danger, why you must be terribly careful!" "Why? Why should I be in danger?" I asked.

"If Henri were to find out he would forgive me, but not you," she replied, looking at me again, fondly, but with fear in her tearful eyes.

"He would convince himself that you had seduced me against my will. You see, despite everything he is madly possessive and believes he can keep our marriage together – God knows he makes up for it in a thousand other ways. But he is used to having what he wants and can be insanely jealous."

"He won't find out, how could he," I said, "not unless circumstances change, or we choose for him to know?" I felt no concern, no anxiety, the courage of the fool. Instead, like a smitten teenager, it was more pressing for me to know the details of her love life. "Oriole, you say you had a lover once before?"

She resumed her position at the window.

"Yes," she paused and took a deep breath, "five years ago. To begin with, I believed I could conceal the affair from Henri. Later, after he found out, I even thought he might understand. I was wrong. In the end, it made no difference."

"Why, what happened?"

"He – my lover – just disappeared and that was the end of it," she answered.

"I'm sorry, that must have hurt you very much."

"I had thought we might have had a future. It would have been difficult, but it seemed like a . . ."

"Who was this man, what happened to him?"

"Nobody knows," she answered wistfully, turning to face me. "Surely by now, you must have guessed who he was?"

I shook my head in disbelief at the answer I knew was coming. "His name was Augustus Black."

* * *

I left soon afterwards. She was determined to fly to South Africa the following day and I had made her promise to call me at the office before she left. She had wanted me to go with her, but I'd explained I could not just drop everything and leave the country on the spur of the moment, for who knows how long? Pride had prevented her from asking me twice, although, in hindsight, I don't think it would have taken much to change my mind. In the end, we had kissed fondly, without passion, and I slipped out of the hotel just before midnight. There was no sign of Peroxide; her place had been taken by a desultory and bored night porter. As I unlocked the car, I glanced up to room 404 in time to see the light switched off.

Once clear of central London, there was little traffic about, and I was soon driving through the suburbs heading for home. Even so, I had more than an hour's drive ahead of me. I don't know why but I found myself really looking forward to seeing Blanche and the girls.

My mind was racing with the events of the day, trying to fit together just some of the pieces in a complex jigsaw. If Henri thought that his daughter had been abducted by his enemies from Paris, then it might explain why he had not been taken in by the ransom demand; he would think that was a smokescreen. On the other hand, supposing he was wrong? It must have occurred to him that Harmony's abduction could be a straightforward demand for money and have nothing at all to do with his Paris visitors. What might he do then?

Oriole clearly believed the two things were connected and was convinced that, for whatever reason, Henri could not be trusted to get Harmony back alive. Why I wondered? She had not really explained. At precisely the time she and Henri should have been united by a mutual concern for Harmony's safety, she had chosen to go it alone. What's more, she had gone out of her way to track me down, someone she hardly knew.

Then there was our lovemaking. Of course, if their marriage lacked any physical dimension, then her desire for sex outside was quite understandable. But then I had read of treatments available for such conditions – surely Henri with his wealth and experience of medical matters would have succeeded in overcoming his problems at least partially?

Then there was the mysterious connection with Singh and his floating hospital, not to mention the link with Augustus Black who had mysteriously disappeared soon after Henri had discovered he was having an affair with Oriole. Without saying so, did she think that Henri had 'got rid' of Black?

In the reassuring environment of the car, away from the intimacy of the hotel room and Oriole, I felt myself regaining some reason. There were too many unanswered questions, too many coincidences, and too many loose ends. Lythgoe's unveiled threats meant I was involved whether I liked it or not. I could no longer maintain my anonymity, even if I wanted to withdraw from the whole messy business. I was in it up to my neck and I needed some answers, fast. But where was I to get them?

My thoughts soon returned to Oriole. Was I in love with her or was I merely infatuated? How was I to tell the difference? My experience with the opposite sex was too limited to know. I thought back to when I first met Blanche. There had been a powerful sexual attraction there, too, but it had been nothing like this. Besides, she had never wanted me in the same way as Oriole clearly did. Even allowing for my heightened emotional state, finely tuned as it was by recent events, my nerves raw and exposed, still I knew that my feelings for Oriole were in my heart as well as my body. Just thinking about her, knowing that I might not see her for days, or weeks, left me with a sense of emptiness.

What should I do? What *could* I do?

Soon I would have to face Blanche. With luck she would have been preoccupied with her own routine during the last twenty-four hours and might not have noticed anything out of order – after all, I had been home in the early hours of the morning many times before. How much, if anything, should I tell her? I suppose if I had not made love to Oriole . . . no, the deceit had set in long before that. I had no choice but to extend it, to brazen it out. Above all, I had to keep my head. I knew I was guilty of some serious errors of judgment, but if I used my brain and stayed in control, things might still turn out for the best. For the moment, I desperately needed to know that Blanche, Nikki and Paula were still there for me. They were my port in a storm, my secure haven when, suddenly, my life had been turned upside down.

Please, loved ones, be there for me, trust me and give me the strength to see this through.

CHAPTER FIVE

There were no lights on as I eased the car into the drive. I looked at my watch; it was twenty-to-two. I parked, shutting the car door as noiselessly as I could and tiptoed to the porch trying not to crunch on the gravel. Once inside all seemed quiet and undisturbed. I made my way silently to the spare room, looking in at Nikki and Paula through their half-open door on the way. Their sleeping forms were just visible in the suffused moonlight through the drawn curtains.

I threw off my clothes and, without stopping to wash or clean my teeth, gently closed the bedroom door and got into bed. I lay staring at the ceiling for a moment or two then switched off the bedside lamp and turned onto my side ready to attempt sleep. I did not expect it to come easily.

At first, I did not hear the door. As I opened my eyes I saw her shape silhouetted in the shadows. I whispered, "Blanche, I'm sorry, I tried not to wake you."

She flicked at the switch and the sudden light took me unawares. She was standing there staring down at me, her tear-stained face and dishevelled hair giving her a wild, unkempt appearance. I had never seen her like this before. She said nothing.

"Blanche, darling, what's wrong, come here, lie down, you don't look well." I held out my arms proffering an embrace. She stood there for a second, then turned and left, closing the door behind her.

I lay there, shocked, wondering whether to go after her or leave it until the morning. Any disturbance now would be certain to wake the girls and they had to be up early for school. Clearly, something was terribly wrong; I racked my brain to think what it might be. She couldn't possibly know about Oriole; how could she? Nor would the vile Vinny have contacted her – he had not given me time enough to 'file' a report yet. Surely, he would keep his word? No, the only possibility was that she suspected something – bad enough, of course, but not the same as knowing. I could deal with her suspicions in the morning. I switched off the light again and turned back on my side.

A few days ago Blanche's state of mind would have been of paramount importance to me. Now it had to take its place on my list amongst other, equally pressing priorities. I was disturbed to note it was no longer at the top.

I slept fitfully, or so it seemed, the hurricane of events that had assailed me playing on my mind, not least the forthcoming, inevitable confrontation with my wife.

Still, it seemed as if I was woken almost immediately by the sound of the children getting up and clumping around between bedroom and bathroom, their early morning complaints and demands interspersed with Blanche's routine rancour. I got out of bed and threw on a dressing gown sensing that it was particularly important this morning to say goodbye to the girls as they left for school.

I caught them up in the kitchen wolfing down their cereal.

"Hurry Paula," Nikki was saying, "she'll be here any second!"

"I've got to clean my teeth!" wailed Paula. A horn sounded in the driveway.

"Come along," chivvied Blanche, "you mustn't keep her waiting two days running."

That was when they saw me standing in the doorway. They froze at the sight of me. Blanche broke the tableaux.

"Hurry up!" she said. "Paula, you've got ten seconds to clean your teeth."

Paula dashed past me on her way to the downstairs cloakroom.

"Bye, Mummy," said Nikki, kissing Blanche on the cheek, "don't forget to pick me up at five." She forced a half-smile as she passed me.

"Bye, darling!" I shouted from the kitchen door.

Paula emerged from the loo smelling of mint, wiping her mouth on her sleeve. She grabbed her school bag.

"Bye!" she said, generally, to anyone it might concern. And they'd gone.

"What's wrong with them?" I asked Blanche as she went back into the kitchen to clear up. I hadn't had the chance to look at her and now she had her back towards me. She didn't answer straightaway seeming to gather herself together.

"The police were here last night," she said eventually. Her voice was strained, impersonal.

"Good God, I'm sorry," I said, "I should have been here. What did they want?"

"They wanted to talk to you about the disappearance of Harmony Nader, Gerald." At last, she turned to face me. She still looked strained but more composed than a few hours before, "I tried calling you everywhere; I had no idea where you were."

I knew I had to be careful, not knowing where she had checked, or who she had rung.

"Pru knew where I was, I asked her to call you to let you know."

"Don't lie to me, Gerald!" she screamed. "Don't lie!" and then, more quietly, "don't lie." She sunk onto one of the kitchen stools, her head slung low, her shoulders sagging. "It's over, Gerald, I can't go on like this."

I rushed to her, and put my arms around her, but she backed away from me like a startled cat.

"Don't touch me!" There was fear and loathing in her eyes. I moved away. She looked down at her hands, fingers intertwined and went on, her voice trembling but full of quiet resolve. "I think you should leave, Gerald, as soon as possible."

"I don't know what you mean, Blanche, what has brought this on, what am I supposed to have done?"

"Gerald, I really don't want to speak to you anymore. You are hurting me and the children. If you love us, you won't want to hurt us and the easiest way for the hurting to stop is for you to go somewhere else as soon as possible. Get some treatment, if you can." She stood up and walked to the door. "I am going to shower and get dressed. I would be grateful if you had gone by the time I have finished." She turned and left the room. Without thinking, I chased after her.

"Blanche, what are you talking about? We must speak. I can't just leave. We can't just end everything like this! Besides, I don't want to leave, for God's sake!" I needed to find out what she knew and how much of this was supposition.

She was huddled over her dressing table, clutching the dressing gown tightly around her. When she spoke her voice was quiet, barely controlled.

"Gerald, I know things have been strained between us for a long time, but I have always trusted you. I have always been optimistic that, in time, we – you – would sort things out, that whatever was wrong now, there was hope for the future. I didn't realise, I had no idea." Her words died away, and she stood up, squaring her shoulders, and turned to face me. "How could you do this to me, to us, to the girls? What have we done to deserve it?"

"Blanche, darling," I was at a loss, there was so much she might know, but what and how? "I really don't know what you are talking about." A desperate sadness enveloped me. All my instincts were screaming that this was the end, that one of the few good, reliable things left in my life was about to close down.

"Don't lie!" she was screaming now, on the edge of hysteria. "I know you were in London last night, at a hotel with . . . " and then more quietly, "a woman."

"Blanche, it's not true. Yes, I did spend the night in town, but not with any woman, I promise you!" I didn't know what I should say but I knew that admitting the truth would leave me no chance of redeeming the situation later on. I had to play for time.

"The police said they were investigating the kidnap of the Nader child and that you were involved." Her voice hardened; she wiped her eyes. "God, it was humiliating. Do you know, that was the worst part, the humiliation? 'Can you tell us the whereabouts of your husband during the last twenty-four hours, Mrs Irving?' 'Of course,' I said, 'he's been at the office or with clients.' What a joke. They must have felt sorry for me, I can see that now. Sorry for me! Then they asked if I was quite sure. That's when I started to make the phone calls. Pru told me you were up at Bakers. When I rang them they said they weren't expecting you. So, I rang Pru back but I could tell from the sound of her voice that she was bluffing on your behalf, in the end, I rang off. What was the point? They just sat there watching me, listening to me making those calls knowing all along that I hadn't the faintest idea where you were. Then they showed me a photograph of Oriole and Henri and asked if I recognised them. I said I did. They wanted to know how well you knew them. I explained that we had only met them once, in Spain. Then they asked me if I could think of any reason why you might have spent several hours with Oriole in an obscure London hotel. To start with I didn't believe them. Then they showed me a photograph. It was of the two of you together, you and Oriole, in your car! I was shattered, Gerald, but mostly I was ashamed. When it dawned on them that I couldn't help anymore they apologised for any inconvenience and left. Inconvenience! My God, if only they knew!"

She was sobbing profusely now, lost and betrayed, desolate and alone. It was my fault. I had caused her to suffer all this pain. What on earth had happened to me? I knew I wasn't a monster but, clearly, I had behaved like one. I had to tell her the truth. To try to take her with me in the vain hope that she still loved me enough to understand; to forgive, help me get through the rest of this nightmare, in time, maybe, even forget. There was no turning back. I had to face up to the truth now or I would be lost. It was my last chance. I put my hand gingerly on her shoulder, she stiffened but this time did not shrink away.

"Blanche, I have been very foolish, I'm sorry. I'm afraid the truth will hurt you even more than you've been hurt already but I know that I must find it within myself to tell you everything, that if there's any way forward for us, you have to know—"

She turned to me eyes blazing. "I don't want to know!" She was shouting now. "What gives you the right to unburden yourself on me, Gerald? How can you be so, so arrogant? What makes you think that I want to 'go forward' with you?" Her words were laden with irony. "It wasn't as if we had much anyway, was it? If you hadn't taken a lover, it wouldn't have been long before I had. Don't you think that I haven't thought about it often enough? I've had offers, men still find me attractive, you know, but then I don't suppose you'd think that possible, would you?"

"Blanche, I know it sounds ridiculous but none of this has anything to do with you, if you'd just let me—"

"Do you know something? It's not the fact that you've been seeing another woman. Oriole is beautiful, certainly, although why she should bother with you God only knows, but I suppose given time I could understand that – it's the deceit, the dishonesty, the total disregard for my feelings, the children. I thought I knew you better, but that was a long time ago. Whatever your faults, I didn't know you could be such a, such a . . . bastard! Get out, Gerald, just do me a favour and get out! I can't even stand the sight of you anymore. You're sick!" Now she was composed and dismissive, with a steely determination in her manner. She turned and looked me straight in the eye, half demanding half imploring. "Just go away, please, now."

I stood there for a moment, then turned and left the room. Within minutes I had thrown a few things into a suitcase and was back in the Jaguar heading for Maida Vale.

* * *

It didn't take the blonde receptionist very long to tell me what I needed to know. 'Mrs Irving' had checked out an hour ago. The porter had helped put her luggage into a taxi; no she had no idea where she had gone. There was no note. Sorry, Mr Irving – this with a hardly perceptible rise of an eyebrow.

I went despondently back to the car, the breeze blowing my raincoat about my legs. It was getting cold, the leaves swirled around my ankles. I had let her down and she had left. She had come to London to enlist my help, for some reason I had been the only person she could turn to in her lonely quest to search for the daughter she had loved and lost.

In that moment, I knew where she had gone and where I

had to go to find her. To stop her, if possible. God knows where Harmony was, but she wasn't in Africa, I don't know how I knew that, but I did. I couldn't bring myself to believe that any part of the answer lay there. With luck I could catch Oriole at Heathrow; it was possible that she had left herself plenty of time to catch the flight and I could get to her in time to talk to her, and save her a wasted trip.

Soon I was speeding back along the motorway, grossly exceeding the speed limit but not caring, simply wanting to get there before she boarded her flight. I assumed from the night before that there was a good chance she would be heading for Johannesburg. There were only three airlines on that route to my knowledge: SAA, British Airways and Virgin. Only SAA had a morning flight – the other two were much later in the day.

As I headed through the tunnel into the airport the boards directed me to Terminal Three. Parking the car in the short-stay park, I half walked, half ran into the building.

There was a pretty young African girl at the SAA enquiries desk dealing with a middle-aged man asking routine questions about luggage allowances and who pedantically checked and repeated every answer she gave him. My patience at breaking point, I interrupted rudely.

"Excuse me," I asked, "how can I check whether someone I know is on your nine o'clock flight?"

The girl looked at me coldly.

"I am sorry, sir, would you kindly wait until I have finished dealing with this gentleman?"

"Look, forgive me, this is important, and the flight is due to leave in ten minutes. Please, can you tell me if a particular person is on board?"

The man turned and looked me full in the face. He was a burly fellow, casually dressed in a tracksuit and trainers.

"What's the matter, you deaf or something?" The accent was strongly Afrikaans. "She told you to wait, nicely. Now, wait."

Realising that I wasn't going to get anywhere, and with time of the essence, I turned on my heel and ran over to the ticket sales desk opposite. This time there was no one in front of me.

"Can you check if a Mrs –" I hesitated not knowing what name Oriole would have checked in under. The woman behind the counter glanced at me curiously, "if a Mrs Irving is on your nine o'clock flight to Johannesburg, please?"

"I'm sorry, sir, we are not allowed to give that information."

"But I'm her husband!" I blurted indignantly. "Please, it's very important."

"Well, the flight has closed for boarding, I suppose it's alright, just a moment, please." She tapped a simple command into her terminal and soon had the passenger list in front of her. "Mrs Irving? No sir, there is no one of that name onboard." My gamble had failed. Hastily, I re-grouped, aware of how clumsy this must all have seemed.

"A Mrs Nader, then, she could be travelling under her maiden name?" I knew I was pushing my luck.

"I'm sorry, sir, this is most irregular."

"Please, please, help me. Mrs Nader, is she on that list?"

The woman glanced sideways in both directions. Another check-in girl was heading her way. She looked at the list again and nodded, an almost imperceptible inclination of the head, hastily tapping at her keyboard to clear the screen. I heaved a sigh of relief. Of course, in her rush to leave Spain, Oriole would have had no choice but to travel under her true identity.

"Thank you. The flight is closed, you say? Is it impossible to get on?" The woman looked at a large clock on the wall.

"I'm sorry, sir, by now the aircraft will be taxiing for take-off."

"Blast. When is your next flight?"

"Not until nine o'clock tonight, I'm afraid."

"Is there nothing before that?" I was aware that a note of desperation was creeping into my voice.

"Virgin have a flight at four o'clock, you could try them, but everything is pretty full today."

"Thanks, you've been most kind," I said.

Seeing the Virgin ticket desk further down the concourse I found myself breaking into a run. The blonde girl in a white uniform was on the telephone. When she saw me she turned her head away as if I was going to eavesdrop on her private conversation. It seemed an age before she put the phone down and turned to me disinterestedly.

"Do you have any seats left on your Jo'burg flight?" I asked. She tapped into her computer.

"One in first-class, that's all. Would you like to take it?"

"How much will that be?" I thought how strange it was that cost should even begin to enter into the equation at a time like this. But so used was I to bargaining for the best prices when it came to untangling the complex web of airline seat pricing that I couldn't help myself. Tap, tap, tap . . . wait . . . tap, tap . . . wait.

"Three-thousand-and-twenty-pounds return," came the eventual reply.

"Have you nothing cheaper?" I asked incredulously.

"Sorry, nothing. That's the only seat left on the flight. So, do you want it?"

Another anguished decision. "Very well," I said getting out my wallet and credit cards.

"It is fully transferable," said the girl, as if in consolation, "will that be on Visa?"

"Visa, yes," I replied producing the plastic. The transaction didn't take long.

"Thank you, Mr Irving." She pushed an assortment of bits of paper towards me. It didn't seem much for three thousand pounds. "You don't need to check in until three o'clock." She glanced at her wristwatch. "That's six hours from now. Will you be staying in the airport or returning later?"

Another decision. Six hours at Heathrow with nothing to do seemed an interminable prospect. On the other hand, what else was there? Both office and home seemed far away and home wasn't an option anyway.

"I'm not sure," I replied. "Anyway, I'll be back at three."

'Do you have any luggage?" she asked. "Can I arrange for it to be stored until you come back?"

"Yes, just this suitcase, thanks." I passed it around the side of her desk. She scribbled a receipt and handed it to me.

"We'll see you later, then." A big smile and her attention had moved on to the next person in line. I turned and walked towards the telephone kiosks. Something felt slightly at odds, but I couldn't say what; maybe it was just that I'd just spent ten times more on an airline ticket than I'd ever done before. I looked back at the Virgin girl expecting to see her in conversation with the young man who had been behind me. There was no sign of him. That hadn't taken long, I thought.

I was jerked back to the here and now by the sound of my mobile ringing in my pocket.

"Hello, this is Ger—" but something stopped me from giving my name.

"Where you off to now, Gerald?" It was the unmistakable Lythgoe. My heart sank.

"Oh, fine. Are you having me followed again?" I tried to sound as firm and in control as I could.

"Not especially, no. Why do you say 'again'? Hasn't the penny dropped? You're being followed all the time, Gerald – and not just by me, either."

"What? Who else is—" but he wasn't interested in this line of talk.

"Now listen, we've got an arrangement. You didn't call in yesterday and I told you what would happen. How did you get on with the police?"

"That was you?" I couldn't believe what I was hearing. "You tipped them off because I hadn't phoned you!"

"This isn't a game, Gerry. There are people here playing for high stakes, very high. And they don't always tell the truth, either. Now, I'm not saying whether I tipped off the rozzers or not. You'll have to work that out for yourself. What I am saying is that you better start taking our little arrangement seriously. 'Cos, if you don't, there's worse to come. Far worse."

I said nothing.

"So, I'll ask you again. Where are you off to now, Gerald? Jo'burg?"

"If you know, why are you asking me?"

"Do I take it that's a 'yes'?"

"Yes."

"So, that's where the scrumptious Mrs Nader is heading, obviously. Or, at least, that's what you think."

"I know, Lythgoe. I know. I checked the manifest. She flew out on the nine o'clock SAA flight."

"What, like she flew in on the eleven o'clock flight from Malaga?" He was right. She'd changed her flight time. How had she pulled that off? I hadn't bothered to find out.

"She's clever, this one, Gerry. Light years ahead of you, matey. So, you're following her, are you? Why's that, I wonder? Gotta hand it to you, you're up for investing in a bit of high-class tail. Hope they didn't sting you for first class. Don't be surprised when you see plenty of empty seats in tourist." The sneer in his voice was palpable.

"Lythgoe, Vinny," I was getting to the end of my tether. His voice softened.

"Listen, you're booked on the four o'clock. What are you doing until then?"

"I don't know, just hanging around here getting depressed."

"Maybe it's time we met up. Listen, I'll be there in an hour. There's a disabled ramp leading from departures to arrivals. Meet me there."

"Okay, how will I know you?"

"You'll know me." The line went dead.

I put the phone back in my pocket. Almost immediately it rang again. I answered. It was Pru.

"Thank heavens you've answered, Mr Irving." Her voice was hushed, anxious. "The police are here. They want to talk to you."

I tried to conceal the panic welling up inside me. "What about, Pru? What do they want to talk to me about?"

"They won't say, I'm afraid." I could tell that she was struggling to stay in control; trying not to give the police any more reason to be suspicious.

"Pru, will you explain to them that I—" A male voice

interrupted me.

"Mr Irving, this is DC Stevens, Met police. We called to see you at your home last night and had the pleasure of meeting your wife. It's important we talk. Don't worry, you're not in any trouble," (if only he knew) "it's information we want. Can we meet up, ASAP?"

I took a deep breath. "It's rather difficult. I'm at Heathrow, just about to catch a plane."

"Ah, and when are you back?"

"Tomorrow, I'll be back tomorrow evening," I lied. "Listen, give me your number and I'll call you when I land, okay?" I held my breath.

"Alright. I suppose that's the best we can do, then. Tomorrow evening?"

"Fine, give your number to Pru, she'll text it to my mobile. Oh, and could you pass me back to her, please?" I heard the receiver change hands. "Pru, I'm just off to Rotterdam, the UCI job. Back tomorrow night. I've said I'll ring them, then." No response. "You alright?"

"Yes, of course, Mr Irving. Everything here is fine. Give Mr Bruinse my regards. Goodbye and good luck, see you on Wednesday."

Marvelling – not for the first time – at Pru's presence of mind, I switched the mobile off again. Instinctively, she had corroborated my story.

I felt sick and hungry at the same time and looked around to see what was on offer. There was a Garfunkel's across the walkway. Could I face breakfast? Yes, suddenly it seemed like a good idea. Vinny wouldn't arrive for another forty minutes. A WHSmith kiosk caught my eye. I went in, quickly scanned the front pages, and bought a copy of the *Daily Express,* wondering if there would be any more about Oriole and Harmony.

At the restaurant, a monosyllabic dark-skinned girl showed me to a table. She took my order and I settled down to scan the paper. Nothing on the front page but there it was on page three with Harmony's sweet face staring back at me. Much the same story as the day before, rewritten with a different slant, but no new material other than an update on the state of the injured nanny who was still unconscious. It carried Vinny's by-line and I could see why he was so keen to get more to go on. His editor must be pressuring him for a bigger story for the late edition.

Not for the first time my mind started to retrace events, trying to make sense out of the jumble of facts and assumptions, some of which were already becoming vague and disassociated. Every aspect of my life was involved, of that I was sure, and it only remained to be seen whether I emerged from this mess better or worse off than before.

I found myself falling back on the metaphor of a play. Oriole, Harmony and Henri were clearly centre stage, whilst the others, Blanche, the children, and even Pru, although they featured in the cast, somehow appeared to be on the sidelines, extras making the odd entrance and exit, rather than principal players, driving the twists and turns of the plot. Why should this be, I asked myself. I knew perfectly well that my family was the most important thing to me and that I should be putting them ahead of all other considerations, and yet . . .

My musing was interrupted by the waitress who busied herself wiping the table, then carelessly laying out knives, forks, a napkin, little tubs of jam and marmalade. "Food will be here shortly," she said. "Do you want your coffee now, or later?"

"Now, thank you," I replied, jolted back into the reality of the moment. She sashayed off. Something irritated me about the way she had laid out the bits and pieces and I found myself rearranging them, putting the little tubs in neatly arranged rows, squaring and lining things up. It was a habit; Blanche often referred to it. She said I was obsessed with straight lines. It was true. Too many years in design and print.

I looked at my watch, surprised that Oriole had already been gone nearly an hour. She'd be flying over northern France by now. I conjured up a mental picture of her, looking much as she'd appeared when I collected her the day before, simply dressed, with no make-up, hair scragged back, so different to the exotic creature

I had made love to in the hotel. The intensity of my feelings came flooding back and I felt myself hardening at the recollection.

She was back, the waitress, this time with my order. I shifted uncomfortably on the bench seat as she placed the plate of food clumsily in front of me. "Full English, no beans," she announced as if getting this right was a minor triumph. "Will there be anything else?"

"Just the coffee," I replied.

"Oh yeah, on its way." She was gone.

I picked up my knife and fork, took one look at the greasy plateful and knew I was going to be sick. Grabbing a handful of paper napkins, I got up and made for the toilet as quickly as I could trying not to make an exhibition of myself. A few customers looked up laconically as I passed their tables.

I found a cubicle, locked it behind me and knelt over the bowl just as I started to retch up the bile which was all I had inside me. Eventually, the spasms subsided. I gave myself a minute to get my breath back, pulled the chain, and walked to the basins where I splashed my face with cold water.

Feeling better, I returned to my table. The Full English was still there.

"Everything okay?" Her voice came from behind me as I sat down.

"Yes, thank you. Actually, I'm not feeling very well, sorry. Would you mind?"

She looked at me quizzically. For a girl with no O-Levels, she was doing okay.

"Shame to waste it," she looked sadly at the congealing mass. "Probably jet lag, you wouldn't be the first." She picked up the plate and nodded towards the coffee pot, cup and saucer. "I brought your coffee, won't do you no harm, that. Do you still want it?"

"Oh, yes, thank you," I stammered.

She gave me another look. "Settle your stomach, you'll feel better in a moment." Gone again.

This was happening too often, I thought. I'd been experiencing these sudden bouts of vomiting for some while, usually for no apparent reason. Only Blanche had noticed. I'd been to the doctor who had found nothing wrong. She thought it might be stress-related which would certainly explain the current attack.

I sat there drinking the hot bitter liquid.

CHAPTER SIX

By the time I found the disabled ramp, Lythgoe was already there. I hadn't imagined him in a wheelchair. He seemed less frightening. I'd been expecting a thickset man, pugnacious, intimidating physically. Instead, he was thin and bespectacled, with lanky hair, looking more like a university don than a journalist. But the voice was unmistakable.

"So, we meet at last, Gerry." He looked almost pleased to see me. "Let's treat ourselves to some breakfast, shall we? Pete!" An anonymous-looking young man who had been reading a paper and leaning against a nearby wall walked over. He looked familiar despite his obvious ability to blend into his surroundings.

"Pete's with me," Vinny explained. "Don't worry, I'm perfectly able to propel myself in this contraption, look." With a flick of a switch, the chair spun on the spot and quickly moved level with me. I noticed that it was quite a sophisticated piece of machinery. "Pete's been working with me on this since the start. He was as keen to meet you as me."

The younger man proffered his hand. I took it, more out of courtesy than enthusiasm. "Pleased to make your acquaintance, Mr Irving," he said, genuinely enough.

Vinny was motoring, well ahead of us by now. "There used to be a Garfunkels a floor up," he shouted over his shoulder, "used to serve a great fry-up. Nearest to a greasy spoon you'll find this side of the Chiswick flyover."

My stomach turned over at the thought. "Just been there," I said, then lied, "and, yeah, the fry-up was pretty good."

Vinny stopped in his tracks. "I thought I said I'd meet you for breakfast, didn't I? What, you couldn't wait or something?" He winked at Pete. "Still, I suppose you need to replace all that energy you've been using up, eh?"

"Sorry, I don't remember you mentioning breakfast. I was filling in time."

He was on the move again. "You won't mind sitting with us while we have ours, will you? We're on expenses. I'm starving. Been at it since seven this morning. Shame to waste the opportunity."

"I'd rather not."

"Come on, Gerry boy, have a coffee or something, you don't have to eat anything."

If my friendly waitress was surprised to see me back, she didn't show it. Within minutes we were seated at the same table and she was taking orders from Vinny and Pete. Sickeningly, they both ordered fry-ups. When she'd done her business, Vinny got straight down to his.

"So, where have we got to, Gerry? Let's run it through, eh? Right up to date. One way or another, don't ask me why, you've got yourself involved up to your neck with some dangerous people, people you don't know, but who don't think twice about abducting a child. Now, the law of unintended consequences, Gerry, let's think about that. You've got two little girls of your own, right? Have you considered the possibility of one of them disappearing? Your focus shouldn't be on where Harmony Nader is, rather you should be concentrating on keeping your own family out of danger. How do you think you might go about that? Or, hasn't that even occurred to you? Let's conjecture for a moment. Just suppose that Henri Nader is somehow involved in all this, even in the disappearance of his own daughter. How do you think he might feel about you sticking your nose into his business, let alone his wife? Eager to play the knight in shining armour, right, but unwilling to face the dragon, eh? You need all the help you can get, son, more than you know."

Everything he said rang true, and those realisations baffled me. How had it never occurred to me that I was putting my family in danger by getting involved? I had only been dreaming like an idealistic fool, moved by the hope of a blossoming romance with Oriole.

His words compelled me to be cooperative. "No, that's not possible. The man is devoted to his family. I have been to their villa, as I told you. I spent time with the girl. The child is protected beyond all measure. Believe me, she had never experienced the simple delight of a hamburger; she wasn't allowed to step out of their property. Poor thing didn't even have kids around her age to provide company. My daughters became friends with her, so we took her out for a meal and got back a bit late. Henri was flying off the handle. It appeared to me that they anticipated her disappearance."

Without missing a beat, Pete started taking notes. "Now, you're talking," Vinny said. "So, it seems Henri's involvement in her disappearance is out of the question?"

"Can't discard the possibility yet." As I said that, shaking my head, a memory that I had put at the back of my mind started emerging. "On my first meeting with the family, I heard the couple shouting. Seemed like Oriole was being forced to do something. He definitely sounded threatening. I don't know the subject of their disagreement, though."

"That doesn't mean much. Every couple fights. Seems to me like you're stalling. Give me something substantial if you want to be taken seriously. What did you find out from the lovely Mrs Nader?"

The question made me stop in my tracks. Oriole had trusted me with that information in her moment of weakness. I was certain I was the first to witness her in that state of turmoil and the only soul to bear her secrets. Her tear-stained face, her fragile frame rocking in my arms, and her vulnerable voice flashed through my mind. I recalled her advice to filter the information I offer these prying ears.

"Why don't you go ahead and ask me questions? I'll answer everything best to my recollection," I offered.

He was too quick to miss that moment of hesitation. "Very well. It's unlikely of you to forget any of the blissful moments you spent holed up with her now, am I right?" I had to agree with him. He continued, "They have two children. Don't they? Why isn't the other one as guarded as this Harmony?"

"Max, the other one, is adopted as far as I've been told. Harmony is their biological child."

"Why's the other one adopted? Is the couple not intimate anymore?"

"They are intimate," I replied bitterly. "I don't know. They are certainly rich enough to afford adoption."

"I see. Something tells me there's more to this child than meets the eye; I imagine, something you must have heard people saying about you as well?"

"Hardly. The girl is far more interesting than I could ever be," I addressed his remark, trying to feign ignorance about her and acknowledging his comment on me with sincerity.

If I could help it, I didn't want to give him Harmony's medical history. There was something very fishy about the floating hospital and the man who disappeared into thin air. If Vinny found out about Oriole's affair with Augustus Black and his disappearance, it would certainly push the narrative of Henri as a possessive and dangerous man, but I couldn't risk giving him this advantage over me.

The waitress returned with their breakfast, bringing with her the retching feeling in my stomach. Excusing myself for the toilet, I tried to compose myself and think straight. In fact, now that Blanche had found out about the affair, I was off the hook. There was this problem of Henri learning about it, but Vinny didn't know what Henri was capable of. Whatever he had guessed was all speculation – a shot in the dark.

I had revealed nothing about the men Henri met with in Paris either. I could use that to my advantage, I thought with a guilty conscience. I knew I was betraying Oriole, but the ball had already dropped. This was the only way I could survive in this game. After calming myself down, I returned to my acquaintances.

"You took your time, Gerry boy. I was about to send someone in to check up on you. I must say I'm concerned. Will you really be able to survive your expeditions?"

Everything Vinny said foretold a hidden agenda. He made a

simple question sound like an accusation as if he knew more about me than I was letting on.

"I'm sorry to keep you waiting. I haven't been feeling too well the last couple of days. Some bug I've picked up. Sorry."

"Oh, don't worry about us. Don't mind if we carry on with our repast if you're feeling better?"

"Much better."

"We won't take your time up much longer. Right, so do you know where Mrs Nader is headed?"

"Johannesburg. It all started when a few African men came over to meet Henri in Paris. According to Oriole, these men looked really shady. She said she could tell at first glance they weren't his normal clients. By the sound of it, he was demanding something from them. She said she heard him shouting and threatening the men. A few days later, he received a letter. She said he went pale and started throwing things around. The letter was sent anonymously but the very next day he booked a flight and left Paris without telling Oriole where he was going.

"She subsequently discovered that he'd gone to Jo'burg. He was away for three months, and when he returned, he beefed up the security around Harmony and Oriole. He wouldn't let Oriole meet with anyone without meeting them first. Really possessive and constraining."

I had barely altered the truth. Just exaggerated some bits to my advantage. Vinny didn't fail to detect and press on those bits.

"Didn't you say they were intimate? If he is the villain you're making him out to be, Oriole is still an independent woman, very much capable of handling herself. So, what's binding her to him?"

"I don't know. His wealth? A promise of stardom?" I gave myself the satisfaction of a smirk.

"I hate to admit it, Gerry boy, but you make a good point. But then there's the fact that she ran off and shacked up with you when they were supposed to be fighting off these struggles together." His sneer didn't put me off this time. "Alright then, here's what I'm going to print. 'Harmony Nader – Abducted or Escaped?' will be the headline tomorrow.

"I will detail every bit of your exaggerated story in an even further exaggerated narrative. Mrs Nader's lovely pictures at the airport will be on the front page. It will paint the perfect picture of a corrupt billionaire turning out to be an abusive man; the daughter runs off, opening up an opportunity for the mother to seek help from a mystery man. The public will eat it up, possibly benefiting the lovely Oriole in advancing her career in the future. You'll be off the hook, and Henri will take the fall for now. See, I said I'd help you."

"What's the catch?"

"The catch? No catch. You'll obviously track down the exotic one in Africa and update me when you've found her."

I flinched at the words 'track down', thus dissipating the fleeting amiability we'd established a moment ago. Watching the two of them guzzling their disgusting meals, I saw my own dishonesty reflected as Vinny laid out his plans. I knew I had come too far to assume the higher moral ground now. I recalled Nikki's innocent voice asking, "What does an honest person look like?"

Had I left my honesty behind in pursuit of love? No, it was more than that. Too afraid to let my unconscious spill into my consciousness, I'd put those thoughts away. I reminded myself of the obvious differences between us. Vinny could never be my ally. To him, this was just his usual work, even when there were lives at stake.

"I'm disappointed to sense your loyalty lies elsewhere, Gerald, but I am hoping you're a smart man. She needs to be in your sight at all times; bug her if necessary. You need to know her every move and keep me posted. Folks like her are not easy to tackle – make a single slip-up and she'll know."

I was losing patience with every word he uttered. "I will make no such filthy commitments to you. I am sure she will rely on me, and I'll keep you informed to the best of my abilities."

"Easy now. Remember, you have three days. I'm sure you understand by now the price of breaking your word. I won't go so easy on you next time."

I knew he was not bluffing, but I needed to know his next

move. Sadly, the public believes what the press tells them and Vinny held the reins. Reminding myself of his influence, I realised yet again that I needed him on my side, even if temporarily.

"It's interesting how you think you can keep pulling my strings. Just as you said, I have already lost my family; I have no home to go to and barely enough money to even pull me through this journey. My life is already on the brink of complete ruin. The woman I have risked it all for is miles away, God knows only where in South Africa. I'm afraid soon enough you'll have used up all your cards against me; that is if you haven't already."

There it was, that creepy all-knowing stare accompanied by an even creepier, provocative smile. "Oh, no, Gerry, don't you worry about us. We can take care of ourselves, can't we, Pete? You're a fast learner Gerald but not fast enough to outwit me. What's more interesting is how this entire sequence of events has turned out in your favour, giving you the only thing you currently desire, isn't it?

"With Henri and little Harmony out of the way, you can run off with your pretty little princess into the sunset. Except you being the last person to see the girl before her abduction doesn't really help you, does it? Do you think the police might have already put two and two together? Maybe that's why they're so eager to have a little chat with you. What do you think, eh?"

Suddenly, it felt as if every pair of eyes in the restaurant were focused on me and that everyone was listening to our conversation. This was nothing but a baseless insinuation, yet his words were having such a profound impact that I could barely think straight. I wanted to know his next move, but he wasn't leaving any hints for me to figure it out.

This time I made no attempt to hide my frustration. "Where is your evidence for these bloody accusations?"

Vinny scraped up the last congealed smears of egg yolk from his plate, carefully placed his knife and fork together and wiped his mouth with his napkin.

"I'm not accusing you of anything, Gerry, just speculating. You'll have to forgive my imagination running wild from time to time. I told you, it's part of the job. But you don't have anything to worry about since you're one of the 'good guys,' aren't you?" He drew out his last words with a chuckle. "Well, it's certainly been a pleasure to make your acquaintance. I'll see you around I hope."

And with that, he pulled back his motorised chair, gestured at Pete to follow him, and left me staring at the remnants of his coffee.

***

I still had hours to kill. My stomach growled. My appetite is becoming ridiculous, I thought. Especially when nothing stayed down. The waitress eyed me up, wondering if I had nothing better to do than sit there occupying her tables all day long. Finally, I ordered a smoothie. I thought of this morning, of Blanche's heartbroken look and her desperate words. She'd always taken care of me when I got nauseous and made sure I had something to eat.

Of course, she was right. I had been misplacing the blame on our failing marriage. In truth, I had failed her and my children. There was a sense of protectiveness I felt towards Blanche that came out even when I was the one causing her pain. Tender and vulnerable as she looked, Oriole knew what was best for her and would always put herself first. Unlike Blanche, who had stayed by my side despite being the victim of my neglect.

It hadn't even occurred to me that I might never see them again. Leaving England without kissing them goodbye hadn't seemed that significant until I realised that I might get killed and die without hearing Nikki's and Paula's laughter ever again. As I sat there in that dismal place, the thought almost brought me to tears.

Suddenly, I had the urge to drive home and try to end things on the right note with Blanche. I knew she deserved better and that after all that had happened, she wasn't going to take me back. The least I could do was let her know how much I still cared and that I was not going to discard her.

Glancing at my watch, I rashly decided I could make it home and back in time to still catch the flight. My mind was made up and I drove back to Mayfield with as little regard for the speed limit on the seventy-mile journey as I'd had earlier. I managed it in an hour and twenty minutes.

In my frenetic state of mind, it hadn't occurred to me that no one would be there to welcome (or shun) me. There was no car in the drive and, with another glance at my watch, I realised Blanche must have gone to pick up the girls from school. They would be back soon.

The spare key was hidden under a potted plant, so I let myself in. It was odd, but I could already feel the house becoming alien to me. I recalled only too well the single-handed efforts Blanche had put into decorating it. Now I felt like a visitor in someone else's house, as I took it all in – a cramped but homely space with walls painted pale blue and teal and white furniture to provide a contrast and liven it up.

I needed a pee and as I went upstairs I tripped over Paula's dancing shoes. Nikki liked their shared bedroom neat and tidy, her space clean, but Paula couldn't help turning it into a dump. They had been complaining and asking for separate bedrooms for a while. As I had always kept the spare bedroom for myself, I wondered if they would now get their way with me gone.

Gently, I folded Paula's clothes and cleaned up the mess as much as I could without misplacing her stuff. These two are a handful, I thought to myself, smiling. Picking up one of Nikki's neatly arranged glitter pens, I scribbled down a message in purple ink: '*I am always here for you and will always love you*'.

Finally, I went to our bedroom. It seemed ages ago that I had last slept in this bed. I averted my eyes and opened up the closet to grab a few photographs of my family from the photo album. Having taken what I wanted, my eyes fell on the silver-encrusted casket. The memory of Oriole's sensual voice overwhelmed me, and without hesitation, I grabbed the casket.

I was headed for the stairs when I heard Nikki's voice from downstairs. "It wasn't my fault, Mummy. Mr Kennedy must have lost his kitten again."

"It still doesn't give you leave to—" Blanche caught sight of me and stopped in mid-sentence, lost for words. It might have been wishful thinking, but I thought her first fleeting expression could have been hope rather than anger, but her face quickly hardened. "I thought I told you to leave."

Holding up the photograph, I rushed to explain myself. "I just came to pick up some stuff." Her expression softened, looking at our joyful faces in the picture; sadness replacing anger. Tentatively, I continued, "I'm not here to ask you to take me back. Can we just talk? Just for a moment?"

"Nikki and Paula, go to your . . ." Her voice trailed off as she noticed what I was holding. The girls followed their mother's gaze and mirrored her expression.

"Oh my God, Gerald! How could you possibly be so cruel?" She looked visibly weakened and the girls took her hands in support.

I tried to reach out, racking my mind for any excuse that could help me out of this situation. My family were shying away from me, eyeing me with contempt. Everything about this was wrong.

I felt like there wasn't enough air in my lungs and something had triggered a flight-or-fight response. I felt my body shuddering, my self-possession hanging precariously by a thread. It was me against them – my own daughters shielding my wife from me. Their looks of hatred stirred me to defend myself, to claw my way out, to shake them until they acknowledged their love for me.

A rational part of me looked on as I unleashed my desperation on Blanche. "You had no right to turn my daughters against me! Nikki, Paula! Whatever she told you is a lie! She's lying to make me look bad! Please, believe me!" It was Nikki who calmly took me on.

"Daddy, please go. Mummy is scared, and Paula is crying. I really think you should leave."

It was her soft voice and composure that brought me to my senses as she looked up at me with pleading, fiercely determined eyes. This was a different Nikki. So brave, and so mature for her

143

young age. It shook me to the core and without another word I left, slamming the front door behind me.

My drive back to Heathrow passed in a blur, my thoughts and feelings in tatters. I arrived eighty minutes earlier than my flight and went straight through security. After locating my boarding gate, I waited in the lounge for boarding to start.

I took the opportunity to check my phone. There was a call from Pru, who recited my messages – a reminder to call back the policeman, a client I needed to get back to, and Mrs Irving had rung.

She continued mechanically before I realised there was no message from her. I jotted down everything she had said, with only a hitch at the mention of my wife.

". . . I repeat. This is the final boarding call for Mr Gerald Irving. Thank you." It was a voice over the tannoy.

"Isn't that you?"

"Sorry?"

"The boarding announcement. Isn't that your call?" A lanky guy standing nearby pointed to the boarding pass I was clutching, bringing me back to reality. Looking around, I was the only passenger left in the lounge.

"Oh. Yeah, right. Excuse me."

I boarded the plane sheepishly, internally cursing myself for my lack of concentration, my recklessness, my – well, everything really – before finally I sank into my seat and closed my eyes.

The ability to dissociate myself from my inner turmoil had always been my strength. Stepping out of my being, I had learnt to become a bystander in the maelstrom of my life, watching those relentless waves crash around me.

This time, whilst I knew I was in the middle of a maelstrom and that those same vicious tides had again turned against me. Detached, I watched as they dragged me far into the depths of the heaving ocean, too fatigued to stand my ground. All concern for my family and Oriole floated away, my consciousness cloaked in darkness.

CHAPTER SEVEN

"Oh God, Jack. I'm not going to tell him. You have to do it yourself. He was so excited."

"I'm sorry. Look, I had it all planned out as well. The car really did need repairing. I've been on a shoestring budget for months to manage this trip for the lad!"

I heard Mum and Dad fighting – no, conspiring to let me down – through the door. Deep down, I knew it wasn't going to happen. Every summer, I got excited at the prospect of this adventure, and every year something got in the way. The only safari I'd ever experience would be through the National Geographic Channel.

I decided to act nonchalantly. My parents may not have learned how to let me down easily, but I had learned that it was always in my interest to let them off the hook. I'd rehearsed my latest white lie in my head: "Daniel and Kevin are going to Centre Park. I want to spend my summer with my friends. Can we go on a family trip next year instead, please?"

Putting on my best façade, I got out of bed to fake this excuse for my parents. But the moment I stepped out of my room, everything changed, and I was falling off a plane, trying to fight gravity.

I woke up with a start, secure in my seat. It took me a moment or two to get my bearings, the events of the day flashing through my mind. Dreaming about my parents was unusual for me. After all these years, I could barely conjure up their faces.

To claim that my family had struggled with poverty would be a stretch, but those disappointments in my own childhood had made me determined that my girls would never have to worry about family finances or miss out on the happy memories they deserved.

I don't consider myself to be particularly optimistic, but

I enjoy the pleasures that fate occasionally allows me without feeling guilty. Unlike Blanche. In fact, it was probably one of the reasons for our falling out.

Surprisingly, my first-class flight from London to Johannesburg was such an experience. After an undisturbed six-hour slumber, I woke up with a fresh perspective and a healthy appetite.

I asked for a meal and was served garlic and ginger prawns, Thai green curry, sticky rice, and bok choy, apparently, a speciality of the chef, or so the rather pretty young flight attendant informed me. I prefer to stay sober when I'm flying, but it was hard not to indulge as she repeatedly topped up my glass with an excellent 1986 Pinot Noir.

The plane landed around three o'clock in the morning. As I disembarked ahead of the other passengers, I couldn't have been more pleased to have bought a first-class seat. Still, I felt a certain sense of anticipation thinking that Oriole might be on the other side of the terminal awaiting my arrival as I had awaited hers.

My nerves were on edge from the flight – probably not helped by the alcohol – as I tried my best to get my act together, reminding myself that rushing to enquire after Oriole wouldn't magically send me to her. Unsteadily I stumbled past the throngs of people, hardly mustering the patience to get through the queues at security and immigration.

Collecting my luggage, I hurried to the SAA enquiry desk. The entire ordeal had taken less than thirty minutes, but it felt like more.

I frowned as a woman pushed past me, seemingly oblivious to the loud cries of her distressed infant as she yelled into her phone.

The bustle of the airport mixed with the effects of the wine was giving me a throbbing ache in my forehead and my earlier good spirits were quickly dissipating. To my relief, a middle-aged woman sat idly at the desk, searching for someone – anyone – to help relieve her monotony. I was ready to oblige.

"Excuse me, ma'am, can you tell me the arrival time for flight BA57?"

"Just a moment, sir." She looked up at me nervously, then

continued tapping at her keyboard. Glancing at the screen momentarily, she said, "BA57, right? It arrived at 8:05 p.m."

"Right. Thanks – er, thank you so much."

I was heading for the exit when it dawned on me that I had neither a place to go nor any directions as to how to get there. With the comfort and security of my flight fading, the gravity of my present situation seemed only too real.

In my hurry to rush after Oriole, I hadn't thought about how to navigate this strange city. Plus, I was finding it hard to think straight.

I returned to the lovely lady at the counter. "Sorry to bother you again," I slurred. "Can you please tell me where I might find a currency exchange kiosk?"

If she was bothered by my irksome questioning, she was trying hard not to let it show. "To your left, just after the sign to Arrivals, Terminal A." I thought I saw her glance in the direction of a nearby security guard.

She'd spoken too quickly for me, or maybe it was her accent. "I'm sorry, could you repeat that?"

She looked at me and sighed, realising I was drunk and repeated the directions again slowly, as if to a child.

"Thanks a lot," I said apologetically and wandered across the concourse to the exchange. I presented my credit card and asked for £200 in Rands. Having enough money in my wallet to get me through a week put me slightly more at ease and I made my way outside. The heat and humidity of the late evening hit me in the face.

There were no taxis waiting so I used the nearby taxi phone to call one. While I waited, heavily perspiring, I decided the immediate task was to check in to a nearby hotel. Once there, I figured I could sober up and plan my next move, shuddering as I recalled Vinny's warnings to expose me.

The taxi arrived within five minutes and seeing the driver's pained efforts to lift my overstuffed case, I heaved it into the boot of his vehicle myself. He was a dark-skinned, tallish, yet fragile-looking man. If his physical strength hadn't given away his age, the greying of his hair certainly did.

The man smiled at me in appreciation, his friendliness comforting me in this unknown land. "Evening, sir, my name is Sib." He looked me up and down. "Where would you like me to take you?"

I felt myself relaxing, away from the crowds of reuniting families, rude businessmen and meddlesome ladies with infants.

"Any cheap hotel nearby. I don't have a reservation and I don't know my way around this place."

He looked at me sympathetically. "Rhodesfield has all sorts of accommodations, just a few minutes drive from the airport. Usually, I drop my passengers there; from guest houses to upscale hotels, it has lodgings for everyone. Been there with my wife to get away from the kids and all for a weekend."

I struggled to maintain consciousness as I climbed into the back seat. He courteously closed the door behind me before taking his place upfront. "You away on a business trip?" he rambled on as we drove off.

"No. Chased out of my homeland by the police, I'm afraid," I muttered, laughing. He glanced at me sideways, visibly disturbed by my risible 'joke'. I couldn't stop chuckling. Even that sardonic answer held some truth. My uncontrollable laughter led to aggressive coughing, which gave way to unloading the contents of my stomach on the back seat of the taxi before I could stop myself.

We had barely left the airport perimeter behind when he braked sharply to a halt. "Oy, man! What the hell? You are drunk. I must ask you to get out."

My ears, along with my vision, were deceiving me. I was beginning to panic. What was I thinking? Talking nonsense to a stranger in the middle of the night with nowhere to go. I needed all the help I could get.

"I am so sorry!" I blurted out, "I'll pay for the mess. I told you I have no way to get around. Please, just drop me at a hotel," I pleaded, abandoning my last shred of dignity.

He was unyielding, "No, man. Out, I said."

"You have to be kidding! We're in the middle of the road! I

don't know a soul in this entire city, right? So, start driving now!"

Had I given in to my conscience, I'd have been too ashamed to yell at the man, but my survival instincts overshadowed my civility.

"Get the fuck out of my taxi!" he said.

I stuck two stiff fingers between his shoulders. "Start. Driving. Now!"

***

I woke up drenched in sweat in a single bed I didn't recognise, stinking of vomit, dressed in the same clothes I'd been wearing the day before. Groggily, I lifted my arm, trying to adjust my eyes to read the hands of my watch. It showed half past seven. As I sat up and looked around, nothing about my surroundings made any sense.

The air conditioning was doing little to counter the suffocating heat, whilst a mosquito repellent spray was doubling up as an air freshener. There were two separate beds in the room, placed against opposite sides of the room. The walls were covered in floral wallpaper. Between the two beds stood a small wooden table, and to the right of the bed I was occupying was a window dressed with tribal-patterned curtains. Opposite was an ageing TV. The room was neat and tidy and the bedlinen clean enough, but the decorations badly needed an upgrade.

I racked my brain trying to trace any recollections that might explain why and how I came to be here. From the traces of sick on my clothes, I could just remember throwing up in the taxi and could only assume that I'd passed out and the driver had been kind enough to bring me here. As that thought struck me, I jumped out of my bed to check my belongings. Nothing was missing except for some money equivalent to the amount of the taxi fare. I felt intense gratitude for the driver. The man must have been a saint after the mess I'd made of his car – not to mention that I had left myself completely vulnerable to theft.

Realising how much time I had already wasted, I rummaged

through my things for a change of clothing. I hadn't given myself much choice, but managed to find a clean pair of jeans and a shirt. I'd have to find a cleaner's shop later for my soiled clothes.

I dug my cell phone out of my jacket pocket. The battery was dead. Searching through my luggage to find the charger, I tried not to think of any dreadful mishap that may have befallen Oriole.

Almost immediately, I was startled by the 'ding' of my phone – five missed calls from Vinny, one from Pru, and two from an unknown number. I called Vinny back, ignoring the other messages, listening to the dialling tone, waiting to hear that course, mischievous voice.

"Rise and shine, Gerry!" There it was, I hadn't had long to wait.

"Hello," I replied curtly.

"I see you're not a morning person then. I presume from your grumpiness, that you haven't located Mrs Nader yet?"

"Of course, I haven't. I've only just got here. Why did you call me?"

"Really, what's been occurring for the last twelve hours, then?"

I ignored the question rather than admit I didn't actually know. "Why are you calling me, I've got nothing to tell you."

"Because I have some good news." He sounded smug. "While you've been frigging around doing God knows what, I – well Pete actually – anyway, we've located your precious Mrs Nader."

"What? Where? Why are you wasting my time then?"

"I'll send you the location. Same tactic. My guy started tailing her when she landed in the city. She's a smart one, tried to lose us, but we're smarter." His sense of victory was palpable. He continued more seriously. "Be quick, you'll have to leave right away to catch her. I'll text you the location."

My phone dinged again, as I received the location: Ecomotel O.R. Tambo Intl. 44 Voortrekker Rd, Kempton Park Cbd, Kempton Park, 1619. I didn't bother to say goodbye to my tormenter.

Within fifteen minutes, I was in the back of another taxi, hurrying the driver to my destination. My heart was pounding with excitement. When I woke up, she'd been a fantasy image. Now, I couldn't believe I'd actually be seeing her within a few minutes. I pictured her reaction when she realised I'd chosen her above all else.

The journey took less than thirty minutes. Looking at the hotel, I couldn't help but smile as I saw how drastically Oriole had stepped down from her five-star status. Suddenly conscious of how I looked, I stopped by a shop window to fix my dishevelled hair before proceeding to the reception.

"Good morning. Could you kindly tell me if Mrs Irving is staying in one of your rooms?"

A freckled teenage-looking girl was sitting at the desk paying no heed to her surroundings, engrossed in some puzzle in her lap. "We can't – oh!" she paused, solving something in the labyrinth of letters before continuing, "Sorry, we don't disclose our guests' information. It's a breach of privacy." I was beginning to get used to this, but the 'my wife' trick had worked successfully so far.

"Look, this might seem unreasonable, but my wife and I got separated at the airport. I have her belongings. I really need you to understand that she's alone and helpless."

"Can you show me your ID? I need to confirm that you're her husband."

Accepting my passport as proof, she started scanning through a file. I held my breath hoping that Oriole had chosen to check in using my name.

"Yes. Mrs Irving checked in last night around half past ten," she raised her hand to shush me as I opened my mouth, "and she checked out again twenty minutes ago."

"Are, are you sure?"

"Yes. Sorry to disappoint you."

"Thank you. She must have gone out looking for me. You've been a great help." I couldn't keep my voice from cracking. Where was that urbane facade when I needed it?

I bolted out of the building and visited every hotel in the neighbourhood, my lies spilling out mechanically at every reception desk. *She couldn't have gone far,* I kept telling myself. I ran and walked around for hours, calling at banks, grocery stores, restaurants, a hospital – even at the shopping mall, all to no avail. I had found her only to lose her again.

Dejected, I wandered back to my motel. It was only then that I remembered the plastic carrier bag containing the filthy clothes that I had been carrying around for nearly two hours. I spotted a 363 launderette and sat there for twenty minutes while my trousers, underwear, shirt and jacket spun around in front of me. It was hypnotic.

I started running through everything that had happened since I'd arrived in Jo'burg. If only I hadn't drunk so much on the flight, I wouldn't have passed out. If only I had woken up earlier, I would have caught Oriole before she'd checked out. If only I had asked her where she was heading. My life had become a series of 'if only's'.

I combed through everything Oriole had said, trying to find a clue, any clue that might lead me to her. But there weren't any.

My phone rang. I knew who it would be even before Vinny's name came up on the screen. This time I ignored its incessant ringing. This time he would have to wait for me.

With my anger and frustration fading, I realised how starved and thirsty I was. I'd had nothing since I'd been on the flight nearly twenty-four hours ago, let alone since I'd emptied my stomach in the back of the taxi. Collecting my still-damp washing, I wandered back in the general direction of my motel. It was a pleasant enough stroll and it occurred to me that parts of this city were really quite attractive.

As I approached my motel, I had a chance to observe it for the first time. It was called The Cottage and although it had clearly seen better days, it remained picturesque with pavements lined with brick and palm trees shading the sidewalks. Exotic flowers – red, orange and violet – hung from the boxes outside the windows. There was a small pool, too, surrounded by rocks, giving it the appearance of a hot spring.

I chose the restaurant attached to the motel and ate and drank with little awareness of what I was putting in my mouth.

I wondered whether this time the food would stay down. Before retiring to bed, I even went for a brief swim and fell asleep with newfound hope for the following day.

The next morning, I woke up early feeling refreshed. The last vestiges of alcohol had worked their way through my system and for the first time in forty-eight hours, I felt I had my wits about me.

After breakfast, I braced myself to tell Vinny the bad news. He picked up on the first ring.

"I hope you have something titillating to compensate for missing last night's update. See, I'm not a monster so I pardoned you this time. After all, you have better things to occupy yourself with than talking to a poor crippled man." He spoke without a greeting or a break in his quippy speech.

"No, I do not."

"Oh, Gerry, are you finally warming up to me?"

I didn't even have the energy to disagree with his ridiculous remark. "I mean, I didn't find her."

My news was followed by prolonged silence, interrupted by me awkwardly clearing my throat.

Finally, Vinny spoke in a curt voice. "Gerald, I knew you had trouble keeping your word, now I assume lying is another one of your endearing qualities?"

"I'm not lying. She'd been at the EcoMotel, but she checked out before I got there."

"And you couldn't bother letting me know?" He sounded angry. "My guy boarded his flight back last night after our conversation. Now you're on your own." This was the first time I'd heard him lose his composure.

"Don't worry, I'll find her if it's the last thing I do," I tried to reassure him (and myself).

"You have till tomorrow midnight. Call me when you've done it." The phone clicked as he left me to do his job for him.

The rest of the day was much the same as the one before, except that I didn't hear from Vinny. I went around the city, asking about Oriole. Even without Vinny's countdown ticking away in my head, I would have still felt lonely without her. I had never experienced such solitude before. I missed her terribly.

Around dusk, I was enquiring after her at a shopping mall when I remembered her DVD in its silver-encrusted box still packed away in my suitcase. I asked a guy I was passing if there were any electronic shops nearby.

"Yeah, sure. Just around the corner, you'll find a store called CJ Electronics."

"Thanks a lot."

I found the place quickly enough where an eager young man found me a portable DVD player that met my requirements. I went over to the girl behind the counter to pay. "Hey, how much does this cost?" I asked her.

"That'll be 650 Rands," she answered. I handed over the cash and left the mall with more enthusiasm than I had felt in the last two days combined.

Back in my room, I found the DVD, inserted it into the player and connected the player to the TV. A countdown was followed by smoke and neon lights. My anticipation grew with the pounding electronic music. A crowd roared as Oriole's silhouette appeared, her white dress diffused with the smoke.

It was breathtaking how within moments of her appearance, the roaring voices of the crowd were replaced by total silence filled only by her singing. Then, when she'd finished, the uproar returned.

The scene changed, and she was signing autographs for overzealous fans. I was surprised by her humility. Truth be told, I'd always thought there was an arrogance about her. But now I could see that was wrong; it's easy to mistake shyness for haughtiness. The scene changed again, and she was talking excitedly yet agitatedly with Henri backstage.

"Do you think they liked me?"

"Of course, darling! They love you." She didn't look convinced. "What's wrong?" Henri asked.

"Well, my performance is meant to move people to express feelings they normally suppress. I want to do that for people, to make them experience raw primal emotions that they're ashamed to feel and I, I'm not sure I have the assets." She said this shyly but with a slight smile, enough to make the viewer wonder if she was being entirely serious.

Henri roared in laughter and I was just as surprised. I could never imagine that Oriole was troubled with insecurity, especially when it came to her looks. With a pang, I compared her level of intimacy with Henri with ours.

"Oh honey, you have no idea the effect you have on people!" he said in a low voice, almost growling. "However, if you're really concerned about that, I can talk to Chandrit."

I paused the video. As well as her performance it included some behind-the-scenes footage of the tour. This must have been the original unedited version, presumably only for the eyes and ears of close friends and acquaintances.

Here I had the best and only clue since I had landed in Jo'burg. Searching for Singh's number in my contacts, I called him. The line was busy. Two minutes later, I called again, and this time it went through.

"Hello? To whom am I speaking?"

"Gerald. I don't know if you remember me. Lawrence introduced us."

"Oh, Mr Irving! How could I forget?"

"Listen. This is urgent. Did you ever serve in a hospital in Johannesburg? Or do you know anyone who has?"

"Yes, actually. My friend from college, Diopka Sharma, serves at Wits University Donald Gordon Medical Centre. Does this have anything to do with that business at our last meeting?"

"What do you—" Knowing I didn't have time to deviate from my purpose, I interrupted him. "Never mind that. Can you give me your friend's contact number? I need to get in touch with him as soon as possible?" I quickly jotted down the number Chandrit recited and headed out to WDGMC.

* * *

I arrived at around eight o'clock that evening. Walking through glass-lined lobbies, I searched for a counter to ask after the doctor.

A sign at the entrance led me to reception, where I had to wait another few minutes to be attended to by a smartly uniformed male nurse. "I need to see Dr Diopka Sharma. Is he here?" I asked.

"Do you have an appointment, sir?"

"No, but a friend of his sent me here. The matter is really urgent."

"Sir, you'll have to wait for the end of his shift. I'll see what I can do for you."

"Okay! Thank you. Please tell him that Mr Irving, a friend of Dr Chandrit Singh, is here to see him."

Nodding his head, the young man jotted down the two names. In one corner of the hall, a TV played at a low volume. A seat, sandwiched between a shivering man and a sleeping child, stood empty. I sat down to wait.

Time passed with much fidgeting and pacing when, just as I was about to seek an update, the receptionist appeared and directed me to Mr Sharma's office.

A man clad in green scrubs with brown skin and enviable lashes was waiting for me. I held out my hand to shake his. I judged there was little time to dwell on preliminaries.

"I am pleased to meet you, Mr Sharma. Thank you for your time, I'm sure it is precious, so I'll be brief. I recently met with Chandrit on a visit to his ship and he told me you've been friends since college. I apologise for my unexpected arrival but I'm here on urgent business."

"Hello, Mr Irving. I'm afraid I haven't heard about you but Chandrit, yes, a good friend with great talent – although with some . . . peculiar tastes, I must say. Still, no matter. What brings you here?"

Without beating around the bush, I stated my concerns. "Well, I know this is a shot in the dark, but I'm looking for a missing person. Do you know Oriole Nader?"

His look of surprise and a hint of nervousness in his voice were answer enough. "May I ask how you know her?" he responded cautiously.

"I met her quite recently, but we have become close. I went to the Nader's villa for an interview, accompanied by my family. My daughters struck up a friendship with their daughter, Harmony. I presume you remember her as you performed her transplant?"

The fact that I had rightly guessed such an intimate connection encouraged the surgeon to trust me. "Yes, poor child. It's a shame she's still suffering, God knows where she might be. Her mother came to see me a week ago. She wasn't in good shape herself, frankly, understandably so, I suppose, given the distressing circumstances. She's staying nearby. She asked me to call if I heard anything about the child."

I was stunned and relieved at the same time. "Is she safe, please tell me she hasn't come to any harm?" There was no answer. "Well then, can you at least give me the address where I can find her? I need to reach her, urgently."

Unnerved by my obvious anxiety he grew a tad hesitant. "I'll need to speak to her before I go around handing out her location to strangers."

"Believe me, Mr Sharma I'm no stranger. Look, it's really important that I reach her soon. Talk to Chandrit, he'll vouch for me."

"You say you met him a few days ago?"

I remembered the photographs I had been carrying around in my wallet ever since Blanche turned me out of my home. I placed them in front of him. "You see? I know the family quite intimately."

The surgeon nodded and smiled at Harmony's sweet face. "She's a charming child, isn't she? Well, I'm going by my instincts here. You seem like a good man, and God knows her mother needs a friend now more than ever." He scribbled an address on the back of a card and passed it to me.

"Thank you," I said sincerely as, with a firm handshake, we parted company. I left. I was experiencing a rare sense of desperation, praying to a God I didn't believe in to give me the chance to hold Oriole in my arms again.

The scribbled address was for a hotel in Midrand which turned out to be halfway between Jo'burg and Pretoria, a good forty-five-minute drive. It was nearly midnight when the taxi got me there. I entered the deserted reception area and had to ring several times before a middle-aged man appeared, smoking a cigarette. I had never been more grateful for a total lack of security as he gave me Mrs Nader's room number with no questions asked.

With a pounding heart, I knocked on the door twice and heard a slight shuffle of footsteps. At my third knock, the door opened an inch and I glimpsed her standing on the other side holding a heavy lamp above her head, ready to smash my head open.

As soon as she saw me, her fright quickly turned to relief and, dropping the lamp on the floor with a thud, she fell into my arms. We held on to each other for what seemed like an age, standing in the doorway, neither daring to let the other go.

Oriole finally murmured, "Do you want to come inside?" As she moved back into the room, I thought she looked feverish and weak.

"Yes, please," I said, following her and closing the door behind me. "I left London on the next flight after yours and got here maybe three days ago, I don't remember. I've been looking for you all this time and I was so scared, scared that something might have happened to you . . ." My voice cracked. Putting her finger on my lips, she shushed me.

"You're here now. I was scared too. You have no idea how happy I am to see you."

She sprawled across the mattress; her hair splayed on the sheets. I followed and sat beside her legs, putting my hand on her knee.

"Where have you been? I missed you at the EcoMotel by twenty minutes."

"You've been missing me by twenty minutes quite often, then, huh?" She looked up at me with a smile, but the sadness in her eyes was evident.

"I'm so sorry."

She clasped her fingers in mine and paused for a minute before she started speaking. "Henri's men have been following me, so I had to change my location. Someone else was tailing me as well. I stayed there for one night. The next day, I met with Harmony's surgeon, and he connected me with a few people Henri had been involved with."

"I know," I interrupted, "I went to see Sharma myself and he told me where you were staying. That's how I found you."

"That was clever of you, Gerald." Then after a short pause, she went on. "Anyway, I sent out a message to the people he'd put me in touch with saying that I have what they want – as if Henri had sent me as his trusted messenger. But, I'm not sure they bought it."

I felt myself stiffen. How could she use herself as bait for these people? "Oriole, you can't be serious! I can't believe you've agreed to meet them on your own. These people could be dangerous, surely you know that? How will you be helping Harmony by putting yourself at risk?" Then, as an afterthought. "Besides which, you are putting them at a huge advantage over Henri, don't you see?"

Tears started to spill down her cheeks. There was no fight left in her. She was a mother, desperate and isolated, who would do anything to see her daughter safe and sound. At that moment I saw how much I loved and needed to protect her.

Gently wiping away her tears, I climbed into bed next to her and made a vow to this new woman in my life. "We will get through this together."

I hoped she believed me because I had no idea what we were going to do next.

CHAPTER EIGHT

Beads of sweat glistened on Oriole's brow. Her eyelids fluttered like butterfly wings. A few jet-black strands of silky hair were stuck to her face with perspiration and the rest cascaded over the white linen, like spilled ink soaking into the material. One delicate arm rested above her head whilst the other cradled the pillow I had slept on.

She was wearing a grey t-shirt and jeans. I marvelled at the sight of her – never had I seen her look so ordinary, so innocent and, yes, so childish and vulnerable, with her features relaxed and soothed as she slept.

Along with a gold chain, taut across her throat, I spotted several tiny moles decorating her neck. Imperfections? Not on her, I thought. The pendant on the chain, a golden oval engraved with a treble clef, lay on the pillow beside her ear. I gently picked it up and held it in my fingers. The surface was patterned with ruby red lines along with the treble clef. I moved it so that it nestled above her breasts, brushing her neck along the way.

Finally, she stirred. "God! It's hot."

"Yet, you slept well enough," I teased her affectionately.

She noticed the crack of bright light at the edge of the undrawn curtains. "What time is it?" There was a slight, early morning rasp in her voice.

I chuckled. "Darling, it's past noon. You've been sleeping so long that I've been back to my hotel and fetched my luggage."

Raising her head slightly, she noticed my half-unpacked suitcase placed untidily in the corner of the room. "Oh, so that's why you're all . . ." she searched for the right words in her half-conscious state, "dressed for this hot hell," she mumbled, piecing her thoughts together.

Noticing she felt better than last night, I attempted to further lighten her mood. "Would you rather I not be?"

Ignoring my flirting, she grumbled, "I would rather you arranged an ice bath."

Instead, I poured her a glass of water. "Drink. You'll feel better." Drinking in quick gulps, she smiled up at me sweetly.

"Better?" I asked.

"Yes, thank you. For everything."

I returned her smile, trying to think of what to say next. I was only too aware that however intimate our previous encounters may have been, we knew very little about each other.

"I noticed your pendant. It's beautiful."

She fondled it gently. "Thanks. Henri got me this as a present for my first official performance."

I considered pursuing this, but I wasn't interested in hearing about her life with Henri on tour, or anywhere else for that matter so responded with a curt, "Oh, right."

Unable to come up with anything to fill the silence, I resigned myself to watching her again. Her face was bathed in the sunlight streaming through the window, and I noticed a wedding ring glint on her hand as she bundled up her hair and secured it in a bun at the nape of her neck. She gathered a fresh silk kimono from the drawer of the bedside table and flashed me another smile before going into the bathroom.

The sound of the bath taps filled the awkward silence and I wondered whether things had somehow changed between us. I found myself thinking about our last encounter. In hindsight, she hadn't seemed overly enthusiastic about our tryst in London until after we'd made love.

Contrary to the bond I shared with my wife, Oriole and I had absolutely nothing in common. Blanche and I had hit it off right from the start when I first met her at her friend's wedding in Paris. Like silly teenagers, we had taken shots at stupid bets until, in a pleasant alcohol-fuelled stupor, we had escaped from the wedding to get laid.

But these thoughts did little to diminish my arousal as Oriole stepped back into the room with her kimono loosened and water droplets escaping from her hair onto her cleavage.

She cleared her throat and mentioned the elephant in the room. "I'm meeting with the 'mafia' guys for lunch in two hours. I don't think I'll be able to stomach anything during the meeting so I'm heading out there for a light lunch now. Do you want to join me?"

"What else would I have to do? Of course, I'll join you. As a matter of fact, I haven't had anything myself since yesterday."

Our drive passed in silence with only the odd remark about the weather and our glorious surroundings. The restaurant itself was in a beautiful setting very much at odds with the seriousness of Oriole's business. Once inside, the exquisite décor, complemented by a stunning view created a romantic ambience.

An elegant brunette woman greeted us at the entrance and led us to a table on the outdoor terrace overlooking the gardens. She probably thought we were a couple out on a date. But if Oriole had thought the same, she gave no sign. In fact, she showed little interest in the drink I had ordered for her, the menu or, when it eventually arrived, the food on her plate.

Unable to contain my curiosity, I broke the mood with one of the many questions that had been plaguing me. "How do you know the people involved are members of some mafia group?"

"Just an assumption," she replied. I suspected this wasn't the whole truth, but I didn't press the point. This wasn't the first time she'd been less than open and I doubted it would be the last.

Adopting another approach, I asked, "Do you have a good relationship with Mr Sharma?"

She smiled. "Yes, yes. He's the kindest man and most expert at what he does. If not for him, my . . ." Swallowing the lump that formed in her throat, she concluded her sentence, determination replacing apprehension, "Harmony wouldn't be alive today."

"He spoke of you fondly, too. Have you known him long?"

"Yes, we go way back. To start with he was friends with Henri, but he and I grew closer when Harmony got sick. He's a compassionate man and it was he that found us the kidney. He was very supportive throughout the entire ordeal."

It was some consolation that she'd been able to rely on

somebody here and hadn't been left entirely alone. However, there was another thing I found strange. "You didn't mention him before, back in London."

"No, I didn't. He moved back to India after he got married. I had no idea he'd been divorced and returned here. Henri hasn't stayed in contact with many of our acquaintances since that meeting in Paris."

I nodded, suspecting this was the truth, when another pressing question occurred to me. "How did *he* connect you with the mafia members – a respectable guy like Sharma?"

Finally, irritated by what must have felt like an interrogation, she cut me off. "I think your definition of 'a respectable guy' might differ from ours. People from all over the world attended Henri's parties." I sensed a touch of pride in her voice. "Everyone wanted a piece of him, and many different types formed connections with him." She was warming to her theme. "Of course, these parties were held under very tight security. No shady incidents ever occurred, but they obviously couldn't screen out all the bad guys."

Embarrassingly, I found myself reddening at this stark reminder of the gulf in our social status. I kept my mouth shut for the rest of the meal, wondering if this was what our future would be like. If, indeed, there was any future for us at all.

Eventually, she ordered a glass of wine to calm her nerves and asked the waitress to clear our table as we were expecting guests.

It felt like an eternity had passed when she clutched my arm under the table. She was looking through the window as a broad, dark-skinned bearded man in an expensive navy-blue suit stepped out of a black Mercedes S600. He was accompanied by two slightly taller men and gestured to one of them to stay outside whilst the other stayed with him.

He was welcomed into the restaurant by the brunette. Leaning towards her, he whispered something in her ear that alarmed her, and she hurried off in the direction of the kitchen. The man scanned the room, quickly spotting Oriole. He walked towards us briskly and extended his hand towards her greeting her in a deep, cultured voice and a respectful manner which neither of us had expected. "Hello, Mrs Nader. My name is Richard Jones, a friend of your husband. I'm glad to finally meet you."

With a confidence I knew she lacked, Oriole extended her hand and replied in a steady voice, "Hello, Mr Jones. I am glad to make your acquaintance, too. This is Mr Irving."

He extended his hand towards me and chuckled, "Mr. Irving! I knew I recognised you from somewhere. You're all over the British press!"

Oriole looked confused and with a grimace I explained for her benefit. "The press caught us at Heathrow Airport. Remember?"

"These bugs ain't got no soul, am I right?" Jones said, shaking his head.

"Yes," Oriole agreed. "Our privacy gets compromised with no regard to us nor our families." Without waiting for a response, she continued, "Please, be seated Mr Jones, we have much to talk about."

"For sure." He settled his bulky frame beside her and picked up the menu. "Do I take it you've already eaten?"

"We have," I explained.

"Well, you'll forgive me if I order," he said summoning a waiter. He took a long look at Oriole and then said: "I took Henri for a chauvinistic pig, but here you sit, Mrs Nader, right opposite me, very much the independent woman." He chuckled at his own jest before asking, "Has he finally learnt to put some trust in you?"

If Jones had planned to unsettle Oriole, it hadn't worked. She returned his provocation with a firm response. "Rather, I'd say that I have learnt to take matters into my own hands. So, let's get straight to the point, shall we? Where is my daughter?"

This appeared to catch the guy completely off guard. A look of surprise and confusion flitted across his face before giving way to amusement. "Mrs Nader, your daughter! Why the hell would I know where she is? Is that why you're here? Man, this is going to be a waste of time. I should've taken my girl out instead."

A waiter came to the table and he ordered a steak and a large beer.

I could see Oriole had had enough and had we not been

interrupted by the waiter, I'm sure she'd have slapped him in the face. Under the table, I slid my fingers into hers hoping to calm her down, glancing nervously at the man standing guard only a few feet away.

Oriole had obviously decided to take a different tack. "How can that be possible? I can't have come all this way for nothing. You're the one who came to see Henri in Paris, I recognise your face. Ever since, he has been on edge about Harmony's safety. If you have her, we will give you whatever you want in exchange. But please, please, just give our daughter back!"

The desperation in her voice looked as though it might have done the trick and Jones appeared to soften. With his food ordered and seeming to forget about time-wasting, he sat back, relaxed, ready to converse.

"Mrs Nader, I can only imagine how much you must be hurting with your daughter missing after everything you went through to bring her back to life. We may have been involved in the girl's surgery back in the day, but believe me when I tell you we have had no hand in her disappearance."

He leant forward and took a large gulp of beer before continuing. "Let me explain. In exchange for us providing the means to save your daughter's life, your husband agreed to extend our business with Singh. He had the staff, the equipment, and the perfect cover. Your man wasn't blackmailed into the deal. No, Ma'am. It was all his idea."

A terrible dread was creeping over me and with every passing moment I was regretting my involvement in this wretched business. My instincts were telling me that I was about to bear witness to something dreadful. Even worse, Oriole's nervousness hinted that she might not have been entirely unaware of what he was saying.

Suppressing a rising sense of nausea, I turned to her and asked, "Oriole, do you know what he is talking about?"

Ignoring me, she went on pressing Jones. "If you have nothing to do with her kidnapping, why did you agree to meet me? In what way is Henri involved with you?"

"You are likely correct about him notching up personal security around your family since he started working with us," Jones replied. "I can only imagine he was concerned for your safety because of his involvement in what some might consider our 'questionable' activities – although that's a matter of opinion. Anyway, he has been a valuable part of our activities since our meeting in Paris." He took a deep breath. "Honestly, ma'am, consider me baffled with how little you seem to know about all this – but your man is the real boss here."

Oriole was clearly shocked by this revelation. "You talk about a business, Mr Jones, what business is that, may I ask?"

"Well, we are charity to be accurate. On the one hand, a charity involving homeless or orphaned kids here in Africa – kids who need to be taken care of one way or another – on the other, helping save lives all over the world. There are hundreds of unwanted, abandoned youngsters here, some with parents some without, who have no future, thousands if you go further afield. These kids are matched by others, mostly on the other side of the world, desperate for help at almost any price. Henri was the father of one of those. He found us and we were able to do for him what no one else could, namely, provide a suitable kidney for your daughter together with a highly skilled surgeon to execute the transplant. We saved your daughter's life, Mrs Nader, and he felt indebted to us. He decided to help our charity in its work."

He took another gulp of beer as his steak arrived. He looked at it appreciatively, taking his time to tuck his napkin into his collar. "Well, using his contacts, he extended our business to the rich, the very rich. We were never in a position to deal with them ourselves. They were out of our league – your husband opened up a valuable new market for us."

No amount of forewarning could have prepared me for this. The truth hit me like a ton of bricks. The mafia (if that's who they were) were involved in the illegal trading of human organs and Henri hadn't been able to find a donor when Harmony needed a kidney. Her life had been sustained in exchange for another.

Every piece of the puzzle was falling into place – the mysterious remarks of the inebriated Julia Swartz, Singh's evasiveness when I'd asked him about procedures carried out on the ship and, most obvious of all, Henri's involvement in the project. I looked to Oriole for her reaction to this bone-chilling revelation.

Beneath what appeared to be genuine horror, I thought I detected an expression of thinly-veiled guilt, as if all this hadn't come as a complete surprise. But within a moment, that expression had gone, disbelief returned, and she was quizzing Jones again. "You still haven't told me what you are demanding from Henri or what he wants from you? Otherwise, why on earth would you agree to meet me?"

Jones spoke sporadically between mouthfuls.

"Henri has been getting cold feet for months about his involvement with us, what with your rising popularity pushing you both into the limelight – or so he said. Still, our business with him is not nine to five, he could try to quit, but we wouldn't want that, not while we need his cash, his laundering skills and, most of all, his clients. You see we've trebled our business since Henri's been onboard, sending us wealthy customers from all corners – tycoons, politicians, celebrities, public figures, even royalty. Of course, he's been making a small fortune out of us, too, but right now he is not concerned about that. He wants out. So, can you see how we can't let that happen? Still, we never thought about kidnapping your daughter to get our way with him. Perhaps we should have."

He was slaughtering his steak and talking with his mouth full, there was blood all over his plate – in fact, I was feeling nauseous just watching him, never mind what I was hearing.

"Though I had my doubts about meeting you," he went on, "I assumed you'd come here on Henri's behalf to renew our 'gentleman's agreement', because that's all that's bound us to your husband – apart from getting him a kidney for your daughter, of course. You said you have what we want, but since you don't, I'm starting to see your value. Let's assume Henri has kidnapped his own kid to make you more famous – which is most likely what's happened – I wonder what he'd pay to get you back?"

Without thinking twice, I lashed out. "You lay a finger on her, and I'll . . ." This time, it was Oriole's turn to calm me with a firm hand on my shoulder. I had my glass raised, ready to smash it into the man's head, when she gestured towards the guy standing behind Jones, who had his hand inside his jacket pocket.

"What do you mean get rid of his own daughter?" Her voice was threateningly low.

"What I said. Henri has stopped talking to us. We've not heard from him for months. He wrote explaining that you were getting interviewed a lot and the publicity would raise questions. Said he couldn't risk the exposure, so he wanted nothing to do with us no more. He's been getting rid of every piece of evidence that might link him to us. You tell me, Mrs Henri Nader, what's the biggest piece of evidence that links him to us?"

Oriole was lost for words.

"That's right. Your daughter."

She sat there, shivering despite the scorching heat. She was shaking her head in denial, refusing to believe the possibility that her husband would abduct, possibly risk the life of his own child.

Having demolished his T-bone and found her weakest link, Jones abandoned all pretence at humanity. "Since you came all the way here, Mrs Nader, would you be so kind as to deliver a message back to your husband? Tell him that Richard Jones has refused to accept his letter of resignation. We will be looking forward to his response."

Pushing his knife and fork aside and wiping his sweaty face with a napkin, he walked out of the restaurant leaving his bodyguard to settle the bill.

I didn't want to confront Oriole in such a situation, but I had to find out. "Oriole, how much did you know about all that?"

I was ashamed for even thinking she knew anything; on the face of it she was just as much a victim as her daughter, but I had to alleviate my own conscience. "Did you know where Harmony got her kidney from?"

Covering her face, she just shook her head. I saw her anguish and my resolve gave way. I took her into my arms. There was only one good thing that had come out of this meeting, it had affirmed Oriole's reliance on me.

On our way back, she clung to my arm, barely able to stand on her own feet. When we arrived at the motel, we were stopped by the middle-aged lady who was supposed to be responsible for servicing our room,

"Mr Irving! That's you, right?"

"Yes. What is it?"

"A man came looking for you," the lady said, taking a long drag at her cigarette.

"Oh, that's unusual," I said, feigning surprise. "Did he give a name?"

"Yes, yes. It slipped my mind. I wrote it down somewhere . . ." the woman sifted through some grease-stained newspapers on her desk before finding the name scrawled over the headline of a magazine. "Jake Winston," she announced.

The name meant nothing to me, however, it caused Oriole to gasp, then shudder. I turned to her but not for the first time she addressed the messenger, not me. "Thank you. Excuse us for now."

* * *

Once we were back in the privacy of our temporary home, Oriole began to gather her senses. "Gerald, I don't know how, but Henri has located us. I knew I was being followed but thought I had got away from him. With you by my side, he must be growing even more impatient than before. Jake used to serve for the U.S. government before he was hired by Henri as our head of security and bodyguard. He's a skilled hitman. I believe he's the one who . . ." she hesitated, "took care of Augustus."

Augustus, her previous lover? So, that is how he met his fate. Such an obvious threat to my own life drained the blood from my face. If that had been the reason for Augustus Black's disappearance, then the same thing could happen to me.

Seeing my distress, Oriole stepped forward and gently held my face in her hands. Her touch was so tender that I couldn't help but close my eyes, savouring the feeling of her soft palm against my skin. Her thumb moved over my lips, brushing slightly, hesitant to give in to me again.

Her struggle took my breath away. My eyes flew open, and I saw gratitude reflected in hers. Grabbing my shoulders, she propped herself up, and I leaned in to meet her lips halfway.

As she moved tentatively against me I felt I was descending into a trance. Her touch betrayed fear, loneliness and pain. We were both only too aware of the fragility of our relationship, scared of rushing things for fear of losing what we had.

Her hands fondled my hair as mine slipped under her kimono. Circling one arm round her shoulders and placing the other under her hips, I lifted her up and placed her on the mattress, following her without missing a beat.

As she struggled to unbutton my shirt, I noticed her hands shaking in contrast to her steady movements during our lovemaking in London. I eased her into the motions as I took off my clothes and gently removed hers.

If a looming threat on my life was supposed to quell the intoxication I felt for this woman, it hadn't worked. My eyes feasted over her body with the same fascination and desperation as the first time. Enthralled, I watched her breasts heaving as she lay panting with her eyes shut.

With a pang of concern, I saw how much weight she had lost and with this physical symptom of her misery, my passion erupted. I started leaving a trail of butterfly kisses from her neck down to her chest, caressing the soft flesh of her thighs with one hand. Hugging my shoulder, she pulled me close and raised her hips, pleading with her eyes for the missing contact her body craved.

I entered her, and she matched my rhythm with slow, deliberate motions, lacking the urgency in her movements she had displayed before. As the momentum built, with every stroke, the unspoken words, burdens, and differences between us dissolved. Without any promises or explanations, the doubts in our minds evaporated.

We lay in a cosy embrace, spent. Peering into her eyes, I saw pure, unfiltered love for me and no longer felt the need to ask questions that would leave painful memories in their wake. Brushing her cheek slightly, I whispered softly in her ears, "Let's go back together."

My statement was met with a frown. "Go back? What do you mean?"

The moment was gone, this mysterious, perplexing woman was beyond my understanding. I exclaimed, "Now that it appears Henri faked Harmony's disappearance, we can seek help from the police. They will not only give us protection, but they'll investigate everything that Henri has been involved in."

She moved away from me, standing up.

"You don't know Henri." Her voice revealed the years of disillusion and defeat. I felt a flash of anger at the man who had not only abused this incredible woman but profited from the deaths of his innocent victims.

"Darling, you don't need to worry about him. They have methods of cracking the toughest nut. Trust me, Henri will reveal where he's been keeping Harmony. For years he has hidden behind his great wealth and never been challenged. But it's going to be different from now on because I'll be there to help you and Harmony escape his clutches."

With determination in her eyes akin to religious faith, she said deliberately, "Henri does not have Harmony, and I'm not going to leave here until I get her back."

"Are you kidding me? You heard what Jones said. Do you seriously still trust him?" This was harsher than I intended but her resolve didn't falter.

"No. Far from it, Gerald. But I don't expect you to understand. I fell in love with Henri when I was just seventeen! We have moved mountains together. You can't imagine the struggles we have gone through to bring Harmony into this world and sustain her life. Yes, you could be right, he might be a vile man. He'd kill you or hundreds of innocent children if he felt it necessary, but he would never, ever harm Harmony or me. Don't you see, everything he does, he does for us!"

"Can you hear yourself? 'He *might* be a vile man'? You're

excusing his crimes like I excuse Blanche's whining." I was getting angry now. "God, this sounds like a fucking case of Stockholm Syndrome!"

"What are you talking about? I'm not excusing anyone! All of this is just speculation and I'm refusing to take a stranger's word over my husband's!"

"Then, why are you in bed with a stranger instead of your husband, Oriole?" The words were spat out venomously.

I regretted getting into this argument so soon after our passion had waned. Did her conviction come from her trust in Henri or her refusal to believe that her daughter might even be dead? Would Henri go that far?

I yielded. "I get it. You don't believe that Henri has anything to do with Harmony's disappearance. Okay, I'll buy that. But I still think it's a terrible idea to stay here. If not London or Spain, let's move somewhere else, where no one knows we are there, at least temporarily."

"This is not over. If you want to go, I won't stop you, but I can't leave here yet."

Her intransigence was out of character. So far, she had rarely contradicted plain common sense. I knew she must be hiding something from me, but there was no point in forcing the issue. Gathering the facts as I believed them to be, I tried again to persuade her she was wrong.

"Listen Oriole, Henri knows where we are, and that bastard Jones will use you to get his way with Henri. It's only a matter of time before we get caught. Neither of us knows how to combat these people, and we have no way to protect ourselves from them." I continued in a gentler voice, coercing her like a child. "What will become of Harmony if you get kidnapped as well?" An idea was taking shape in my mind. "I say let's stay off the radar and see what further clues we can come up with."

Heaving a sigh, she muttered in a wearied voice, "You don't understand. You won't get it."

"Try me."

For a while, she remained silent, pondering over the right words to convey her feelings. "Alright. Have you ever felt stuck in one place in time? Like, the clock has stopped and you've been frozen in one specific moment of your life? Your whole existence gravitates towards that one single moment, and you just feel like – if you could fix that, you'd stop the entire domino effect from happening. I believe everything started here with Harmony's surgery, and our life became a shambles ever since. My heart tells me that in this place, I'll find the answer."

Everything she'd said made perfect sense. And yet I could not recall a single moment in my own life when I'd felt the same. Pulling her closer and resting my chin on the top of her head, I committed, "I'll stay by you whatever you decide. But we'll move to a different hotel tomorrow. We can change our appearance and pretend to be a newly married couple on vacation. That way we can keep on the move."

She let out the breath she had been holding in. This was another fascinating thing I was finding out about her – she had learnt to conceal her emotions with a façade so poised you didn't see anything fragile underneath. I planted a kiss on the top of her head and she looked up at me with a heart-warming smile. "Thank you, Gerald. I mean it."

"I know you do." I tried to lighten things up a bit. "I'm assuming you hadn't had sex with Henri for so long that you're not ready to get rid of me just yet."

My teasing tone seemed to have worked and with a little giggle, she pulled herself out of my arms. Propping her head up on her elbow, she placed a finger on my lips and said, "Gerald, you should know, you really suck at pillow talk."

CHAPTER NINE

The following morning, Oriole overslept again. I had woken up early and found myself restless and in need of some fresh air.

Besides, there was something worrying me or, to be precise, someone. Mr Sharma, the surgeon. The man who had saved Harmony's life. Had he simply accepted the kidney supplied by Jones or was he involved in more than just the surgery?

I decided to pay him another visit hoping he would see me without an appointment and leave me time to get back to the hotel before Oriole came to. I dressed quietly and slipped out, closing the door as silently as possible.

It was still early when I arrived at the hospital although it was already buzzing with activity. I announced myself much as before and, again, was soon ushered into Sharma's office. He rose to greet me with a warm smile.

"Mr Irving, how is it going? I hope you were able to track down Mrs Irving?"

"Yes, thanks to you, I did. She was very pleased to see me and, if you saw her now, I think you would notice a great improvement in both appearance and state of mind."

"That's very good news, well done. But what about little Harmony, is there any news of her?"

"That's what I wanted to talk to you about, if I may."

"Please," he looked at his watch. "I have my first operation scheduled in half an hour, but please carry on."

"Oriole and I had lunch with a man called Jones, Richard Jones, do you know him?"

The surgeon shuffled in his chair and turned to look out of the window. "I know of him, that's all I can say. He works for the charity, Hope for Black. He's quite high up there, I believe, but that's really all I can tell you. I'm sorry."

"That's alright. Can you tell me about Hope for Black?"

"Yes. It was started by a rather remarkable man called Augustus Black. He was wealthy and a rare philanthropist in this part of the world. I met him some years ago and liked him very much. He was deeply concerned about African children, especially in the townships, living in extreme poverty and after many failed attempts to persuade the local and national authorities to do something about it, decided he would have to take matters into his own hands. That's how Hope for Black came into being."

"That all sounds fine," I said. "I know something about Augustus Black and what you've said all fits. But what did Hope for Black actually do?"

"That's public knowledge, Gerald. He started by taking these young children – abandoned babies or children who had lost their parents – and putting them in hostels he'd either built from scratch or converted from empty properties. Once they had been nursed back to a reasonable state of health, he would organise adoptions and find homes for them."

"That sounds like wonderful work," I said, "what happened next?"

"He built up a multi-million-pound charity and called it Hope for Black, which I always thought was a rather clever name. Most of his financial support came from wealthy overseas donors – in fact, our Mr Nader may well have been one of them, I often wondered. Anyway, as his charity grew and the medical workload increased, Augustus got in touch with me and asked if I would help run the medical side of his operation. I accepted and did so happily on a voluntary basis for some years."

"But not anymore, I presume?"

"No, not anymore, Mr Irving," he replied with a hint of sadness. "Tragically, Augustus disappeared as you may know, which was never satisfactorily explained. You will probably understand that the subsequent investigations may not have been, shall we say, as thorough as they might have been, but this is South Africa, Mr Irving, and for many reasons that is not uncommon. Without him at the helm, things changed."

I began to anticipate what might be coming next and wondered how far he would be prepared to go.

"In what way did they change?" I asked.

He poured himself a glass of water, took a sip and glanced at his watch.

"It is complicated and difficult to explain," he went on. "Imagine the situation. By this time Hope for Black was handling hundreds of children, mostly parentless, with no prospect of any future. The few who were taken in or adopted were the lucky ones. With the shelters and hostels becoming overcrowded, the others were living in hopelessly overcrowded conditions and, as this became more generally known the donations from overseas began to dry up. Children began to die, Mr Irving, tragically, because the resources to sustain them were no longer there.

"I am sure, had Augustus still been in charge, he might have been able to turn things around. But he wasn't. I don't know how it happened, but someone saw that if these children were going to die anyway then it might be possible for their organs to be used to help others live. In fact, the government at the time were encouraging people to sign paperwork allowing for their organs to be donated after their death, so the suggestion wasn't seen as unreasonable. And that's what started it."

"Started what, exactly?" I asked.

"I think you can guess. Hope for Black was a large organisation with contacts all over the world. Once it became known that the charity was in the business of providing human organs, particularly from children, the floodgates opened. Before long, organ donating became their main activity and, it has to be said, source of income."

I sat there not knowing what to say. Sharma had explained everything, calmly and rationally. I could quite understand how all of that could have come about.

"And then? Where do Richard Jones and his colleagues come in?"

"Once you put money and the need for human organs together, you are inviting the possibility of illegal activity. The people you mention, Gerald, are the kind who sniff out these opportunities. And that is what Jones and his kind managed to do. How they infiltrated Hope for Black, I don't know – blackmail, bribery, threats, your guess is as good as mine – all are likely, especially in this part of the world, but they succeeded. And now they are running Hope for Black."

"That's terrible," I replied, "and, presumably, when supply no longer meets demand, a poor child's life in Africa becomes expendable?"

"Possibly, probably. When I save a child's life by transplanting an organ, I don't ask where that organ has come from. If that makes me party to a crime, so be it, but my job is to save the life of the child lying in front of me – and I guarantee you that the vast majority of my colleagues would feel the same."

"But surely we are talking about organ trafficking. It must be someone's responsibility – the Government's – to stop them? It's illegal, after all, unethical and immoral, so who is enforcing the law, for God's sake?"

"I wouldn't go too far down the moral and philosophical route if I were you, Gerald, it tends to be a bit of a minefield. Of course, you are right. For example, I don't know where Harmony Nader's kidney came from, what I do know is how desperate her parents were to save her life. If that kidney was trafficked, who are we to say they were wrong or to blame them?

"Let me tell you something you may not know. Even the World Health Organisation estimates that ten thousand kidneys are traded on the black market worldwide annually. That's more than ten percent of all organ transplants that involve trafficked organs. Regardless of where or how they are obtained, they can be transplanted to recipients in the most reputable of hospitals in major cities throughout the world. This is a lucrative global trade worth billions of dollars a year, Gerald, and the truth is, many governments turn a blind eye."

He glanced at his watch again. "Look I'm running out of time." He opened a drawer in his desk and took out a sheet of paper and a pencil.

"If you think it will help find Harmony, you might pay a visit to the headquarters of Hope for Black. Here's their address. It's a big place and I'm just doing a rough sketch of the layout as I remember it." He passed me his drawing. "Here, it might help you get in and out. I don't know what you'll find out, if anything, but good luck. I'm sorry, I must leave you now. Good luck."

He got up and left me sitting there, immovable for several minutes, contemplating and stunned by what I had heard.

CHAPTER TEN

"Is it short enough? It doesn't look even, does it?"

"No," I replied briefly, sparing Oriole a cursory glance before returning to study Sharma's roughly drawn map.

She had been sitting at the dressing table when I got back, wielding a pair of scissors, seemingly unconcerned by my absence.

"Do you think you'd be able to recognise me like this if you spotted me across the street?"

"You could be clad in rags with your head shaved, and I'd still be able to recognise you from miles away," I replied.

"Ha, ha. Seriously, Gerald. I have never cut my hair before, and I've no idea what I'm doing. A little help would be appreciated."

Putting away the drawing, I turned my full attention to Oriole. She sat there, her bottom lip trapped between her teeth, with an intense look of concentration. I got up from the bed to help her.

Her ethnicity and beauty would always make her stand out from the crowd. Now, I studied her face with some anxiety, realising that her youthful features made her a far more convincing student than me.

"Trim a bit more from the left side of your face," I told her. To me, she was still unmistakably Oriole. "Maybe you should go for an even more boyish look. Or have a total makeover like me. It's worked okay, hasn't it?" I asked nervously.

I looked over her shoulder at my own reflection. Besides the pale blue eyes, the fake-tanned guy staring back at me was a complete stranger. A dyed black fringe fell across my forehead and my features looked more angular.

"Don't worry about me," she said, "when you get into showbiz, you learn to do wonders with a bit of slap and some hairspray. Tomorrow, I'll be as unrecognisable as you, Mr Julian."

I stood up, sharply. "Why are you calling me Julian? Who's that?"

"Sometimes when you're asleep you ask me to call you Julian. Did you know you talk in your sleep?" Her amusement grew with my embarrassment. She continued, faking my voice and accent, "My name is Julian. Stick to your side of the bed, woman, and don't call me that awful name." She smiled up at me. "So, you tell me, who is this menacing guy called Julian – an imaginary friend?"

I was lost for a sensible answer. "The only Julian I know is a character in a TV series and I don't look anything like him. Not even with this makeover." Why I would call myself 'Julian' I had no idea.

* * *

Almost three weeks had passed since the meeting with Jones. We'd moved into the inner-city Yeoville district immediately and since then, we'd been changing our location every few days, avoiding staying longer than twenty-four hours in any one place. Last night, we'd decided to move to the Bella Casa Guesthouse in Devonshire Avenue first thing in the morning.

Blending in had worked well for a while, but during the move, we'd had a second near encounter with the guy Oriole had nominated as my potential assassin, Jake Winston.

As I stepped out of the cab, Oriole held me back by discreetly gesturing towards a bunch of pedestrians across the road. A red van passed revealing a big white guy in his mid-thirties among them. He had a jutting chin, piercing eyes and was dressed in khaki pants and a wrinkled white cotton shirt. We slipped back inside the cab and asked the driver to carry on round the block until he'd gone.

So far, our search for Harmony had led us nowhere, so, following my meeting with Sharma, we'd decided to try to get into the headquarters of Hope For Black on the off chance of getting more leads. As I'd left the hospital clutching Sharma's map, I'd also managed to solicit two fake IDs for fifty rands each from a couple of medical students. They'd been delighted!

The complex turned out to be in the residential suburb of

Rosebank, near the bustling Mall. Our plan was to infiltrate the building under the guise of interns and gather whatever information came our way. The idea had been Oriole's – an absurd plan full of loopholes, but when I pointed that out, she simply said, "Can you come up with a better alternative?" I couldn't.

Neither of us acknowledged the danger of our mission or its probable failure. Oriole disguised her anxiety with playful remarks. I did the same by obsessively going over her plan in my imagination. Anyway, that was our frame of mind when we retired for the night.

My sleep remained fitful, with disturbing images crossing the barriers of my subconscious. Paula was spinning in her ballerina shoes when she sprained her ankle and stumbled onto the ground. As I rushed to her aid, the girl lying on the ground turned into Harmony. When I called out for help, the scene changed, and suddenly I was running for my life. A haunting operatic melody overwhelmed me as I sprinted away from whatever it was that was chasing me. As the chilling sound grew louder and closer, consuming my entire being, I woke up, out of breath and dripping with sweat.

We relaxed over a breakfast of shakshuka and mimosas, before hailing a cab and heading out to our destination. The only weapon we had managed to get hold of was an aggressive-looking karambit knife, which I'd tucked into the waistband of my jeans. No matter how hard I tried to put away the thought of it, I could feel its metal handle digging into my waist.

Seeing my discomfort, Oriole rubbed her thumb gently over my knuckles and that tiny gesture had a deeply calming effect. How she was managing to keep her composure was a mystery.

It was a short journey and we were soon standing before the entrance to the building, looking at it in awe. The frontage was well-maintained, adorned by an exquisite water fountain and jacaranda trees. Green metal boards emblazoned with quotes by Nelson Mandela outlining our responsibility towards children lined the pavement to the entrance.

Looking at this building, I wondered aloud, "What are the

chances of anything criminal happening in a place like this?"

Oriole laughed bitterly and responded, "If my husband is a criminal mastermind, and if it's true he's been involved in trafficking human organs and the murder of innocent children, well then, I think I've been let down rather worse than Mr Mandela!"

She pushed through the revolving glass door ahead of me. We were on our way to the lady sitting behind the reception desk when we were intercepted by a lanky security guard who jumped to his feet and snatched Oriole's bag out of her hands. As he passed a detector wand over her bag, its alarm was set off by the spiral-bound notebooks she had stuffed inside.

"What's this you're carrying around, girl?" The guard asked rudely, emptying the contents onto a small table.

"Why, was I supposed to bring along my transcripts? Oh no! I think I forgot." Oriole chattered loudly in a panic-stricken voice.

I had no idea what she was talking about but seized the moment to make myself as inconspicuous as possible, slip behind the guard and work my way through the lobby to a narrow stairway leading to the floor above. My lungs were bursting as I started to climb the stairs, trying to keep my footsteps steady and to look casual. I'd almost made it to the floor above when I heard the lady at the front desk calling me out, "Mister! Hey, you! Come back here."

Every person in the foyer turned in my direction, but my eyes searched for Oriole's, pleading with her to 'go back, get away'. But she stayed resolutely rooted to the spot.

Back at the front desk, far from being admonished, I was greeted with a warm smile. The lady addressed me politely. "Good morning, welcome to Hope for Black. Please state your business?"

I replied in a similar vein. "We are students at the University of Johannesburg. We were requested to come in for an interview today."

"Right. May I see your ID, please?"

I produced the fake ID from my breast pocket. The lady scanned it, extracting Tim Sheldon's information from the card. Returning my ID, she cleared her throat to attract Oriole's attention who was looking towards the spot on the staircase I had recently occupied. Standing there was a slightly chubby, bespectacled young man.

He looked to be in his early twenties and was clearly focused on Oriole. Caught staring, he looked away disconcerted.

Oriole turned her attention back to where it was required and after going through the same drill as before, the receptionist picked up her phone and dialled a number handing us some forms to fill in at the same time.

Five minutes later, she led us to an elevator and pressed the button for the fifth floor. "Go to the first room to your left on the fifth floor, Mr Harris will be there to interview you shortly."

The privacy of the elevator gave us both the chance to catch our breath.

"Now what?" Oriole asked.

"Let's just play by the rules, it's worked so far, right? We'll meet the man and see where it takes us."

"I don't have a good feeling about this."

"Well, what other choice do we have?"

We made our way to the first room on the left as instructed and found the door open. Inside was an empty desk and a couple of chairs.

Before we could sit down, we were joined by another burly guy in a black suit. He paid us no heed and continued talking on his mobile, speaking nervously. His facial expressions ranged from threatening to the look of a man facing defeat.

We hung onto every word spilling fretfully from his mouth. "But you said you'd transferred the money . . . Obviously! Yes . . . that doesn't matter anymore . . . He went to Paris . . . No, no, there's no need to get him involved." Momentarily, he glanced in our direction as if surprised that we were there.

Scowling, he stepped out of the room, closing the door behind him and hollered, "I am not here to babysit! Just take care of the girl yourself!"

Oriole drew in a sharp breath. The man could be referring to anyone, any girl, but it was impossible not to make the connection.

The door crashed open again. "Now, who the hell are you two?" the man demanded.

"Int-interns," Oriole stuttered, caught off guard. "We're PR majors at the University of Johannesburg, and we were called in for an interview."

"By whom?"

Losing her composure, she went silent for a moment. I interjected. "The name has slipped our minds, I'm sorry. We only spoke to him on the phone. Reception sent us to this office. Perhaps you could enquire with your HR team?"

"We're not recruiting, you'll have to leave." He dismissed us curtly.

"Please, can we at least take a tour? It's been our dream to work here, for this charity. We've been really excited about today."

"No, don't waste my time any more than you already have."

In a final desperate attempt, I blurted out, "Jones! I remember! It was a Mr Jones who asked us to come here."

The man stopped in his tracks. Clearly, the name had an intimidating effect and he immediately pulled his phone out of his pocket again.

Throwing caution to the wind, I tried to excuse myself. "Listen, don't worry, you don't need to bother him, he's a busy man. We'll just be on our way."

But there was no way out now. By mentioning the one name we knew in the organisation, I had jumped out of the frying pan into the fire. Oriole's eyes questioned me silently, *'Should we make a run for it?'*

But our torment was short-lived due to the appearance of the bespectacled guy we had seen staring at Oriole from the stairs. He went straight to her, his hand extended.

"You're here! I'm so sorry, I'd been told you were running late. Not the best first impression, is it?"

Oriole sprang to her feet. "We've been here for over twenty minutes!" She appeared to know the boy although I had no idea how or why.

He turned to the guy called Harris and said, "Really? That's very rude, Harris. I'll take it from here." There was a clear tension between the two of them.

"You stay out of this," Harris warned.

But the young man was not to be bullied. "They were called in for an interview today. Val O'Brien will vouch for them."

"Who? Your work mommy?" Harris laughed at his own joke. "Since when have you been involved in recruitment? Why don't you just stay hidden behind your computer?"

But the younger man was not to be intimidated. "They're coming with me," he insisted.

"Isaac – look, don't be difficult. You'll get us both into trouble. They say they're interns and were called here by Mr Jones. Tell me, why would the boss concern himself with these people? Eh, why?"

"I don't know, but I would take great pleasure in telling him you've disclosed sensitive information in front of outsiders."

The two men stared each other down. Harris was the first to back down. "Fine, okay. But you're on your own – and don't come running to me if it goes tits up."

Isaac nodded and gestured for us to go with him, slamming Harris' door behind us, leaving him to fret on his own.

He led us outside, through the grounds to the south wing of the building. We had no choice but to put our trust in this strange boy. Whenever I tried to say anything, he talked over me in a loud voice, asking about our ambitions as potential employees.

Oriole seemed equally bewildered but played along, remarking on the "great work" Hope for Black was doing until we reached the elevator. The moment the elevator door closed behind us, Isaac grinned at Oriole and said, "Can I have your autograph, please?"

Oriole looked more clueless than ever. But before Isaac could explain, the elevator door opened, revealing a man whose appearance wiped the grin off his youthful face. He joined us in the lift. The moment we reached the ground floor, Isaac scurried past him and led us through carpeted hallways to a tiny cubicle where he arranged three chairs.

He spoke hurriedly. "I think you must know the danger you are in. This is all I can do for you, right now. There's an exit through the parking lot. Get out of here, as soon as you can."

Oriole interrupted him. "We didn't succeed in getting in here to immediately leave again. I'm trying to find the whereabouts of my daughter. She's been kidnapped. Thank you for your help but we won't involve you any further." But her curiosity got the better of her. "Who are you, anyway? Why are you at odds with everyone? How do you know me?"

He chuckled nervously at her maternal tone of voice. "I'm your biggest fan! My uncle took me to your concert in Yokohama. That was the best day of my life. I remember you were wearing a red kimono with sakura flowers printed over the hem of your sleeves – and you extended your concert in honour of a little boy who had been murdered in the city."

Oriole flushed at the memory. "I remember that concert very well. I met someone important that day. You seem a sweet boy, what on earth are you doing in a place like this?"

Isaac's excitement at meeting his heroine was replaced by a weary sadness. "My uncle was the founder of this organisation. When he was finally declared dead and they discovered I had legally inherited everything he left, they wouldn't let me go. I don't know why. I've been expecting them to get rid of me ever since."

"Augustus was your uncle?" Oriole exclaimed.

"You knew him?"

"I'm sorry. Yes, I did. I was very fond of him." She smiled wistfully. "And my husband was probably . . . oh, never mind, that's all in the past. I'm so sorry. When I get home, I promise I'll arrange some way for you to get out of here. He has to listen to me."

"Henri Nader? Do you really believe your husband has any influence here? You're underestimating the scope of this operation. It spans across the globe."

"Mr Jones said—"

"You can't believe a word that backstabber says. Do you

know that my uncle's wonderful charitable vision is now at the centre of an international organ trafficking cartel?" Our blank expressions said it all. "You don't seem surprised. Anyway, there's nothing you or I can do about it." He was staring at his feet, wringing his hands, then looked up with a smile. "But I wish you luck in finding your daughter. How do you plan to go about it?"

I shared a worried glance with Oriole. Isaac picked it up immediately and shook his head. He had turned out to be more than the naïve young man we had first taken him for.

"Listen, maybe I can help you. There's a guy here who's involved in transportation. Usually, he knows the ins and outs of everything that goes on. He's a bit tough to crack, but if you can get it out of him, he'll fill you in on anything. The security camera in the kitchen doesn't work, so you can take care of him there."

Isaac looked directly at me. "I don't know you, but I'm assuming you are on Mrs Nader's side?" He didn't wait for a reply. "Come with me," he added, "and I'll show you the way to the kitchen. Oriole, you should wait here since you look pretty recognisable. Put on a show of being a student and occupy yourself with printing these documents."

I liked the idea, but Oriole put her foot down, pouting at this insult to her makeover skills. "No way, we're in this together."

Ignoring her protest for the moment, I addressed Isaac. "Right. I already have a rough idea of the layout of the building. Just point out the guy, and I'll take care of it."

Leaving Oriole behind to deal with the grunt work, he led me to the floor above. Passing between rows of occupied desks, we stopped at an empty one. Isaac asked no one in particular, "Hey, where's Roach?"

"Restroom."

"Okay, thanks."

Returning along the corridor, Isaac led me to the door on the left. "There you are! Roach, why are you hiding in here?"

Roach looked nothing like his unfortunate surname. Apart from a few freckles on his cheeks, the guy was of medium build with smooth, chiselled good looks.

"Nothing, I'm not hiding," he responded. "What's up with you, freak?"

"Amanda said you wanted some help with your IT."

"She was playing you. Now, get out of my way." Roach got up, pushed past Isaac and left without sparing me a glance.

"I can't help you," said Isaac apologetically. "I'm not too strong in the combative department. You'll have to get him to talk yourself."

I replied gratefully. "That's fine, don't worry, you're truly our saviour. I guess it's time for us to split, then?"

"Yeah, good luck!" He handed me a card. "I hope we meet under different circumstances one day."

I took it, wishing him a good future and found my way to the kitchen. For some reason, perhaps the time of day, it was deserted, except for Oriole who appeared unexpectedly from behind a refrigerator.

"Hey, you were taking so long. I got worried!" she said, her brow furrowed. There was no way she was going to leave me alone.

"Okay. We'll make it out of here in no time," I promised, bending down and pressing my mouth on her lips.

Returning the kiss, she whispered, "I think you were right about Henri all along. We'll find my girl, and we'll run far, far away."

"I love you." I waited in vain, but she didn't say it back. She never did. Instead, she turned to a jar of spices behind me. "Hey, we can use this!"

A few minutes later, I saw Roach approaching. I gestured to Oriole, and we quickly concealed ourselves behind a free-standing cabinet. Roach made his way towards us and stood virtually beside me, taking a cup. As he looked down to pour some water, I slammed the cabinet against his head with resounding force. Before he could recover, Oriole blew a handful of spices over his face.

"Ah! What the hell!" he screamed.

Yanking the knife out from my waistband, I placed it against his throat and hissed, "Don't make a sound."

The guy had tears running down his cheeks from the spices. I think the loss of his vision contributed more to his terror than my blade against his throat.

"What do you want?" he asked.

"What do you know about the disappearance of Harmony Nader?"

"Nader's daughter? I don't know crap about her."

"What do you know about him?"

"Only what's good for me. I know not to mess with him."

"Apparently, you don't." I pressed the blade against his flesh, drawing out a few drops of blood.

"All I know is he's incredibly useful. Makes my job much easier." Then, unexpectedly, he kicked my shins, slipping out of my grip. I lost my footing, but Oriole immediately grabbed his arm, giving me the advantage I needed to pin him to the ground.

"I see how you've earned your reputation, tough guy. Darling, heat up that butter knife, will you? We need to melt some eyeballs." Oriole didn't need telling twice. I didn't know where my sudden courage had come from, but it had the desired effect on Roach.

"Okay, okay! What do you want to know?"

"Everything, we'll decide which bits we need."

"Alright. When we started out we had a network primarily throughout Africa and the Middle East. The products were shipped through buses, business jets and, you know, common vehicles. Mostly to third-world countries or any place with minimal security. The whole business was messy and bumpy. Lots of our guys got caught or hunted down.

"Nader owns this ship at the Port of Málaga in Spain. Used to belong to Augustus Black, but Nader had his eyes on it. We agreed to get rid of the man and split the prize. Ever since, it's been at the hub of our operation, and the risks involved have been minimal.

"The kids stay aboard in the hold until there's an operation. Don't worry, they're taken care of, we need them healthy."

Incredulously, Oriole asked, "He got rid of Augustus for the ship?" She had heard far too much to still be shocked over her husband's actions. "You're saying every child you people abduct stays aboard until they're needed? No secret mansion. No shabby hotels. Just this enormous wandering piece of metal, carrying innocent children along with random civilians and passengers?"

"You heard me."

"I don't believe it."

"Woman, I'm not stupid enough to lie to you in my current position. I've told you everything I know. Let me go, now."

The chat with Roach filled in most of the blanks. We had got what we came for. Leaving him to clean himself up, we crossed the floor in quick strides. Since it was approaching lunch hour the place was getting crowded.

"Hey! Please, hold the elevator for us!" Oriole called out to a man who had just entered the lift. He looked up from his phone at the sound of her voice. Everything happened in a flash. The moment he saw us, we recognised him as the man who had stood guard at our meeting with Jones. Mercifully, the elevator door closed as he was about to lunge in our direction.

Grabbing Oriole's hand, I bolted down the stairs, abandoning any attempt at discretion. Pushing people aside, I dragged her behind me without pausing for a breath. The moment we were outside, Oriole pulled me back at the sound of the elevator's ding. Ducking our heads, we managed to conceal ourselves in a small closet containing a generator.

"Guard the stairs and every elevator in the building! Don't let them go," the man shouted.

Just a few steps away, I could see the guard's silhouette against the bright light of the day streaming in through our only way out. Our escape was so close, but he stood guarding the exit without budging. For what seemed an interminable time we stayed rooted to the spot.

Seized by fright, I shouted "Isaac - help!" as loud as I could. A minute later, I heard Isaac's voice echoing through the parking lot. "They've been found! They're in the kitchen!"

The guard left his post and ran towards Isaac. Taking advantage of his momentary absence, we left the closet and headed for the light. But we'd made our move a second too early and, shoving Isaac out of his way, the guard turned back and rushed after us. Oriole dashed into the road, stepping in front of a car with her arms flailing wildly. The vehicle came to a sudden halt.

"Stop! Stop, or I'll shoot!" the man called, revolver in his hand.

Urgently, she pulled the car door open. Her adrenaline was rushing, and she didn't look back. Not when the gun was pointed at her head, and not when the shot was fired. Without thinking twice, I jumped in front of her.

However, to her surprise, the name I called out in horror was Harmony.

* * *

Oriole was leaning over me. I could just make out her face through my bleary eyes. Her features were contorted as she tried to suppress her sobs. I tried to reassure her that I was okay but choked on the words. She was thanking me and thanking the man who'd been kind enough to give us a lift and was now driving at breakneck speed away from Hope for Black.

"He's bleeding! Oh my God! Why can't he breathe? No, no, no. Gerald, stay with me!"

I wasn't feeling any pain but the blood soaking through my sleeve gave my injury away. I was struggling to breathe and with every gasp, I knew I was losing touch with reality.

The driver was a level-headed man. He spoke over Oriole's frantic cries, "Calm down, lady. He's not dying, he was only shot in the arm." He glanced at me in the rearview mirror and added. "Put some pressure on the wound."

"Why can't he breathe?" Oriole sounded frantic.

"He's having a panic attack, and you're not helping," the man said. "Take deep, calming breaths. Both of you. Try to anchor yourself in the present."

Surprisingly, his reassuring voice started to calm us both down. I tried focusing on the fragrance of Oriole's perfume. She started speaking to me in a hushed voice. "We'll make it out of here. Stay with me."

By the time we drove through the iron gates of the hospital, I was barely conscious. The driver stopped. "I have a family. I'll drop you off here, but I won't get involved any further. Hope you are both okay."

Oriole's reply echoed in my ears. "Don't worry about it. You saved our lives today. May God bless you."

* * *

I woke up in bed with Blanche. My surroundings were so vivid that the scene felt more like a memory than a dream. One look at her face made me realise that she was pretending to be asleep. Tears were leaking down her temples into her hair. Irritated, I walked out of the bedroom without making a sound.

It was uncharacteristic of me. Not even the version of me in my dreams would have been heartless enough to resist offering her comfort when she looked so heartbroken. Sitting in the living room, I noticed that it was newly furnished. Blanche also looked much younger. Her vibrant beauty, before the years of neglect, was still intact. Something was agitating my nerves so much that I pulled out a bottle of beer in the middle of the night. I coughed violently as I gulped it down.

Blanche had followed me out of the bedroom, a look of concern plastered on her face. "Gerry, please. I don't want to fight anymore."

She was wearing nothing but a white silk camisole that fell to the middle of her thighs. The porch light shining through the window silhouetted her body. The night was chilly and she stood shivering with her arms and legs bare. The emotion I felt at the sight of her vulnerability felt wrong and foreign.

She eyed me cautiously as I slowly lowered the empty bottle onto the side table. As my footsteps drew closer to her, I felt the predator in me unleash. I brushed my finger under the strap of her camisole down to her collarbone. "You're so beautiful." But though I voiced the words, my tone was full of contempt.

The guilt was eating me alive. Shutting my eyes, I willed my way out of the nightmare, only to enter another one. Blanche was standing by my side at a seashore. We looked on at the sight of our girls and Harmony chasing after a plastic bag. They ran around gleefully, leaving tiny footprints over the sand. Eventually, Blanche left me alone to look after them.

At a distance, I saw the girls huddled around something. I went over to see what they were looking at. The sight before me left me cold. There was nothing suspicious about the glass bottle that had washed up on the shore.

I had seen countless model ships in glass bottles before. Harmony held the bottle delicately in her hand, trying to remove the cork from its mouth. Nikki asked, "Daddy, how did the ship get into the bottle?"

Ignoring her question, I told Harmony to leave the bottle where she found it. The girl refused and the moment the cork came off, my vision was obscured by a cloud of smoke. I looked through the smoke, calling out the girls' names, but they were nowhere to be found.

When the smoke cleared, it revealed a crowd of people, Oriole, Blanche, Henri and my parents amongst them. Everyone was sneering at me, cursing me. The more I tried to defend myself, the louder their voices grew.

I was desperate to escape from my nightmare and woke with a start, drenched in sweat. My eyes took a while to adjust to my surroundings. I was lying in a hospital bed with an IV tube attached to my hand. The humble room looked more like a small clinic than a hospital.

I tried to lift myself up, but it brought on a wave of dizziness. My head was throbbing with excruciating pain. I laid back again in silence and, eventually, I heard Oriole's voice faintly as she approached the room.

"Diopka, what's wrong with him? Are you sure it was a minor

gunshot? Why isn't he waking up?"

"I'm positive, of course. He's in a state of delirium, a bad fever. It's just the after-effects of shock. He'll come out of it when he wakes up."

"I'm actually very concerned about his emotional state as well. Something strange happened when he got shot. I was their target, and he jumped in front of me. He saved my life, but when he took the bullet, he called out Harmony's name instead of mine."

"Well, he's putting his life on the line to find her. In a state of panic, it wouldn't be unusual if he called you by your daughter's name."

"Right." But Oriole didn't sound convinced.

Finding me awake, her concerns disappeared, replaced by overwhelming relief. I tried to return her affection, but the anguish of the nightmares still fresh in my mind restricted my efforts. I tried to concentrate on what she was saying.

"How are you feeling?" she asked

"Okay," I replied weakly.

She took my hand in hers. "You saved my life. I don't understand why you'd go so far for an awful person like me. I don't have the words to express my gratitude for everything you've done for me."

"I can't help it," I said truthfully.

"As soon as you get better, we'll go back to Spain. We'll tell the police everything we've discovered here. I should've listened to you in the first place. I just couldn't believe my daughter could be so nearby, yet so far out of reach."

"Most abduction cases that make the news happen right under your nose. It's not uncommon." It was the best I could do.

"You're right. I should've listened to you." I could see the guilt weighing on her.

"Hey, I made a vow to stay by your side. This is my choice."

We had been staying at Mr Sharma's private clinic. Apparently, I had been out for two days straight. Oriole kept fussing over me, trying to get me to eat. She had become much more attentive.

During our stay, I was frequently visited by Isaac as well. It transpired that he had been there to witness the entire thing play out. On his first visit, his eyes and lips were swollen, and his body was covered in bruises. It was a wonder he could walk around, though he brushed it aside nonchalantly.

"You should see the guard who shot you. When Jones found out it all happened in broad daylight and there was a witness, he went off the rails. That guy's been well and truly punished."

The young man seemed to find joy in his visits. He had struck up a real friendship with Oriole. Both badly needed someone to talk to and Isaac was ecstatic to have found Oriole who remembered his uncle so fondly. On one occasion Isaac said to me, "My parents died young in a car accident. Since I was an only child, I've been pretty much on my own all my life. My uncle was the only one who used to look after me."

This got my attention. "Really? I went through the same thing, but I didn't grow so close to my relatives," I confessed.

Oriole turned toward me sharply. It occurred to me how little she knew about me. "You never told me that," she said, almost accusingly.

"You never asked," I replied simply.

"You truly are a mystery man." She shook her head.

"Get a room, you two," Isaac interjected.

* * *

When the fever subsided and I was able to move around, we changed to a new motel again. My mental state was starting to recover along with my wound. Things were starting to look better. Oriole was more spirited and paid more attention to everything I said.

However, the night before our flight back to Spain, she went to bed in a miserable mood. After several attempts to get her to confide in me, I gave up. After all, we had remained holed up in an inconspicuous motel. Her mood was understandable.

I was woken in the middle of the night by the sound of her sobs. She was curled up on her side of the bed as if she was trying to disappear into herself. Alarmed, I took her in my arms. "Hey, hey, darling, what's wrong?"

She tried to free herself from my arms, visibly disturbed by my endearment. "If you knew me, Gerald, really knew me, you'd never be able to love me."

"Darling, what are you saying? Of course, I know you, and I love you. Even if you can't return my feelings now, I'm ready to wait."

She sobbed harder. "I'm sorry. I'm so sorry."

"Shh. It's okay."

"No, Gerald. It's not. I did something awful."

I looked at her with questioning eyes but didn't want to hear more. She contradicted all my claims of love with a single sentence. "I agreed that Henri should arrange for Harmony to get her kidney from the black market when we couldn't find a donor."

I couldn't believe what I was hearing. "What?"

"I'm so sorry! Please, God, forgive me!"

"Oriole . . . a child may have been murdered to save your daughter?"

"Don't say it like that. Please, try to understand. My daughter was dying!"

"That excuse," My outrage was becoming all-consuming, "it's not enough! Not—"

"Please, I beg you, try to understand. I had to! No. What am I saying? It has haunted me ever since. Believe me, losing my daughter, almost losing you, has made me realise . . . I've changed. I would never . . ." I tried to get away from her, but she clung to my arm.

I needed to be on my own. To think. Her very presence, every word she uttered, repulsed me. I could no longer stand to spare her even a glance. In my mind, she had taken the form of a monster. "Let me go!" I demanded.

And she did.

* * *

My arm was throbbing with intense pain when I woke up. I noticed beams of sunlight pouring through the window. Oriole was nowhere to be seen. Shards of a broken vase were scattered across the floor. The sheets were torn to shreds. The whole room was a mess. My knuckles were bloodied.

The possibility of being the cause of this disaster sent chills down my spine. With tears in my eyes, I recalled the memories of the night before. Was it possible I could stop loving Oriole? She may have been a spoiled rich woman before, but the woman I fell in love with was kind and strong. In time, possibly, I'd learn to accept her and her past.

I looked for her in the shower, but she wasn't there. I started to panic. What if she had been harmed? I ran around the motel, calling out her name. The man at the front desk told me she had checked out. He eyed me warily and told me to leave the woman alone or he'd ring the police.

I paid the bill, left the motel and staggered around the neighbourhood with little sense of direction. After turning a few corners, relief flooded over me as I spotted her at a pharmacy. "Oriole!"

She turned to face me, and the blood drained from my face. Her left eye was swollen. A patch of hair from the top of her head had been yanked out and a purple bruise was forming over her lips. "What happened?" I asked stupidly, reaching out for her, but she recoiled from my touch.

"Stay away from me!" She was trembling in fear.

A man in his forties appeared to stand by her side. "Is this man bothering you?" he asked.

"Yes," was all she said.

"Stay away from her," he told me in a menacing voice.

"Look, you don't understand. I know her. I can explain."

"Security! Show this guy out of your store! He's dangerous!"

I was pushed out of the store by a guard, and the man gently led Oriole away.

For the rest of the day, I looked for her in every hotel we had stayed at, the memories of our time together replaying in my head. I was burning up with a fever, and my wound was starting to bleed again. I hadn't eaten a thing or had a drop of water. I had absolutely no recollection of what had occurred the night before.

Agonising thoughts tormented me as I sat on a bench in a park. Why was all this happening to me? How had things turned out this way? I made no attempt to hold back the tears, letting out pent-up emotions.

The sound of a ringtone stunned me back to earth and it took me a moment to realise it was my mobile. I cleared my throat, but my voice was weak.

"Hello?"

"Irving, right?"

"Yes?"

"We have Mrs Nader. This is between Henri and me. Stay out of this if you value the lives of yourself and your family." The call ended before I had a chance to respond. He'd hung up but I recognised the voice only too well. It was Jones.

With no tears left to shed, I felt calmer. I'd heard what he'd said but felt nothing, whilst only a few days ago, I'd taken a bullet for her.

I dialled a number on my phone. A reassuring voice answered after a single ring.

"Mr Irving! Hello! Where are you? Are you okay? Have you seen the news? Is it all true?" She paused abruptly to compose herself. "I'm so sorry. I wasn't expecting you to call."

"Pru, I need you to book me a flight. I'm coming home."

"Oh, that's good news," she replied excitedly, "when, tomorrow?"

I surprised myself by stalling, quite why I wasn't sure. "No, I still have one or two loose ends to tie up. Another week should do it. Book me a flight for next Friday."

What I was going to achieve in another week, I had no idea.

CHAPTER ELEVEN

In hindsight, implausible as it might sound, I suppose I didn't want to go back with less than I'd left with, and that included Oriole. Although I'd risked everything for her during those last desolate days in Jo'burg, I must have known deep down that I would never see her again. But my mind refused to accept it.

After her disappearance, I'd tried to reach out to Isaac but he, too, seemed to have vanished. I feared for what may have happened to him. With nowhere to go and nothing to do, I'd sought distraction and had been wandering in parks and open spaces in the mornings. In different circumstances, there would have been much to see and enjoy but I had little interest in sightseeing. By the evening, I was invariably to be found in bars seeking solace if not good company – with periods of oblivion in between.

In truth, I was procrastinating. Whether it was because I couldn't contact Isaac or was still hoping that miraculously Oriole might still re-appear, I don't know. In hindsight, all that time was wasted.

Then, two days before my flight, my stroll in the glorious Melville Koppies was interrupted by the call I had been waiting for.

"Hello, is that you, Isaac?"

"Hey, Gerald! Thank God, you picked up. Why do you keep hanging up on me, man, I've been calling you for days?"

"What are you talking about? When did I hang up on you? I've been trying to reach *you* for days! More importantly, Isaac, have you heard anything about Oriole?"

"Must have been the alcohol talking, I called you back several times. Yeah, I heard about her. Is it true, have they really kidnapped her?"

"I think so, I'm not sure. Can we meet up? I need to talk to you in person."

"Oh my God, I hope she's safe!" Isaac took a moment to digest what I'd said. "Sure, we can meet. It's getting tricky at work. Until things settle a bit, I'm staying here. Can you come over now? I'll text you my address."

The prospect of seeing him cheered me up. "Yes, yes, that sounds good. See you soon." A moment later, the phone pinged with his address.

Isaac lived in a studio apartment a fifteen-minute cab ride away. The elegant red brick block with its shuttered windows sat amongst pleasant surroundings. Not a bad place to live, I thought.

I climbed the wrought-iron staircase to the second floor and there was Isaac, standing in his doorway, paying a delivery man for a pack of beers. Obviously pleased to see me, he welcomed me in with open arms and we hugged before he stood aside, pointing to a well-worn sofa. The room was sparse but comfortably furnished. He cracked open a can of beer.

"Alcohol this early in the day?" I said to him with a smile, as I sat down.

"Not much else to do at the moment – anyway you're a fine one to talk!" He handed me one, too.

"My circumstances called for it, what's your excuse?" An incredulous expression was all I got. I looked around fishing for another line of conversation. "This is a nice space."

"I hate it here. Not the flat particularly, it's okay, but the whole situation. I feel trapped."

"Yeah, I can imagine. Actually, that's why I'm here. I've had an idea, been thinking about it for a few days." Of course, I hadn't, the idea had just come into my head, but I continued, "I've fixed my flight back. Why don't you come with me?"

Isaac raised his eyebrows as if I was mad.

"What in heaven's name are you talking about? What would I do in England?"

"I'm flying back the day after tomorrow. I mean it, come with me. We could rent a small place together then, once you're settled, you could find a place of your own – if you want to." Isaac was still at a loss for words, and I wasn't giving up. "Seriously Isaac, are you really going to spend the rest of your life here, in the clutches of these criminals?"

Realising I was serious, his initial shock was replaced by anger. "So, you are going to abandon Oriole? I thought we were going to talk about how we might rescue her."

I winced at his words. "Isaac, I can't offer her anything anymore, least of all safety. I can, however, offer you a new life. I know how widespread these people's influence is, but you'll be ten times safer in England than you are here."

"It's impossible. They'll never let me go – anyway, I repeat, what happens to Oriole?"

"Look, one way or another, Henri will look out for her. I know for a fact that whatever his sins, he is as devoted to her as he is to Harmony. I've seen it. His whole life centres around those two. He won't let them come to any harm. But, after everything that's happened, right now I have to think about my own family. I've got a wife and two daughters who through no fault of their own are in danger, too." I thought that summed up my position convincingly enough. "I should never have come here in the first place."

"Don't say that, man! Since the day you arrived, people have started sniffing around Hope for Black. It might only be the media, but it's a start. The police won't be far behind."

I knew his words were intended to give me some comfort, but they had the opposite effect. "Don't you see, that makes things even worse? Flush them out and who knows what they might do, what lengths they might be driven to?" I wasn't sure where to go from here. "Believe me, I know how seriously I've hurt the ones I love and the danger I've put them in and I have to make them my priority. But I do know I can help you. Please, give me the chance to get something worthwhile out of the mess I've created."

Isaac looked up, surprised at this display of vulnerability. I went on: "It's the perfect time for you to escape. With everything that's going on, you'll be the least of their worries." The ideas were coming thick and fast now. "You could even start working at my business. When I get back, God knows I'll need all the help I can get."

Isaac stepped away and leaned against the kitchen counter. Lost in thought, he stared at his can of beer.

"When do you leave?" he finally asked.

"The day after tomorrow. The flight goes at seven o'clock Friday evening. Make up your mind and I'll take care of everything."

He looked up grinning. "Perfect! I've always wanted to sneak out in the dead of night! There's one condition, though."

"What's that?

"If we're going to lodge together, you'll have to promise me you'll lay off the booze."

"No, problem," I replied, "No problem at all."

* * *

The return flight went without incident and arriving at Heathrow early the following morning, we picked up the Jag from the multistorey car park and drove straight to the address Pru had given me. As loyal as ever, she'd managed to rent a nearly new two-bedroom apartment not far from the factory and left the keys with a neighbour. After an hour to unpack and settle in, we decided to go to the office.

I felt apprehensive as we approached the gates to the industrial estate. It was barely light at seven in the morning and my building was completely desolate, perfectly mirroring the state of my life, I thought. My mood was lifted by Isaac's excited chatter.

"Impressive, Gerald. Did you really build this up from scratch? On your own?"

"It's nothing."

"Oh, don't be modest. It's great!"

"Believe me, there's still a long way to go."

"Okay – and how may I assist you – boss?"

I had to smile. "By giving me some peace and quiet, that's what! Give me a chance to catch up and soon you won't have time to scratch your head."

We made our way up to my first-floor office where, obligingly,

Isaac decided to go off and look around leaving me to start sorting through the plethora of business emails in my inbox.

Most of the staff wouldn't be in for another hour and by the look of it, Pru had carried on dutifully in my absence. I suppose I should have expected no less from her, but I still marvelled at how she'd managed to balance the books, keep the creditors at bay, chase up payments, deal with difficult customers like Janet Struthers – even, it appeared, picked up a couple of new clients in my absence.

As I worked through dozens of emails and messages, summarily discarding those that needed no immediate attention, my head began to throb with an oncoming migraine. Logging out of my system, I stood up to fetch a cup of tea when I heard Pru's chirpy voice harassing Isaac in the hallway. Before I could get out from behind my desk, she was dashing over.

"Mr Irving!" She exclaimed, looking me up and down with motherly concern. She didn't say a word about the remnants of my disguise – in fact, if anything, it merely caused her to be more attentive.

I greeted her with a customary kiss on her cheek and a teasing remark. "I see you've been doing absolutely fine on your own."

"Hardly! We missed two consecutive deadlines on the Baker project." Momentarily, her voice was full of shame but, before I could praise her further, she continued enthusiastically. "Still, enough about me. Fill me in on your journey! Is it all true?"

"Is what all true?"

"Have you been living under a rock? Did Oriole Nader really elope with you?"

"Elope? That's a stretch." Pru continued to look at me expectantly and I gave in. "Her daughter went missing. Heavens Pru, why would she elope with me?"

Sensing my change in mood, she proceeded more cautiously. "Is that why you went to help the Naders, to help look for their daughter? But how did you become involved with them in the first place?"

"They're family friends."

She considered this for a moment. "But from what I read, the girl still hasn't been found, has she? And you've come back." Then, more anxiously: "Mr Irving, are you in trouble? That police officer has been here enquiring after you several times." I felt guilty that this woman had so much faith in me.

"Yes, I'm back, and as far as I know I'm not in any trouble, at least, I hope not." Before she could go on, I interjected, "Trust me, Pru, you don't want to know too much about any of this. Everything that's happened is confidential and it would be putting us both at risk if I told you all the details."

She nodded understandingly before she remembered something else that was weighing on her mind. "What am I supposed to do with this . . ." she hesitated, ". . . kid you've brought back?"

Isaac, who had been silently standing in the doorway, cleared his throat. "Hi! I'm Isaac," he said waving to her across the room.

Pru looked him up and down, unimpressed. I broke the ice. "Isaac, meet my PA, Pru, she has been my most valuable asset for a long time, nearly eight years. Pru, this is Isaac, a new member of our team. He's an IT wizard. Please show him around."

Isaac stepped forward with the keenness of youth, his hand extended towards her. "Nice to meet you, Mrs Pru. Gerald's told me a lot about you, and I look forward to working with you."

Mollified by his youthful charm, Pru led him to the door. "That'll be my pleasure, Isaac, do follow me. IT expert, eh? Then we'd best start in the design department." So, with a possible new ally who seemed to share her regard for me, Pru had relaxed. With one last curious glance at my changed appearance, she led him out of my room, quietly closing the door, leaving a heavy silence in her wake.

I tried to focus my attention on a brief for a job that had been attached to one of the emails, but my mind wouldn't take it in. Nearly two months' absence from work had muddled what little attention span I had left.

I turned away from my desktop to the blinking red light on the old answering machine. I should probably have attended to voice messages first, but fear of whose voices I might hear had been holding me back. My stomach lurched thinking about how Blanche and the girls would react towards me knowing what they must have read and seen in the papers and on television. Bracing myself, I pressed the playback button and waited. Hoping to hear their familiar voices, I barely paid heed to McGraw, the policeman who had left me a warning, or Vinny, who had left me a sarcastic but cheery greeting. When Paula's quiet voice finally came up, it almost brought me to tears. She sounded as if she was calling in secret, her voice hushed and guarded.

"Hello, Daddy! I tried to reach you on my phone but Mummy barred me from making overseas calls. Do you know what happened last night? I saw you on TV, but Nikki changed the channel. She said you don't want to see me anymore." Her voice was cut off after the sound of a beep, but my girl wasn't done talking. "Daddy, it's me again. Nikki has become really mean, and Mummy always sides with her. I miss you so much. Please come home. I'm going to sleep now. Bye-bye."

The rest of the day passed in a blur, my spirit exalted by her call. She wanted to see me! It was a start and opened the door for me to ring Blanche. Given how apprehensive I had been, I felt I'd had a useful day – the call from Paula having been the cherry on the cake. Now, as it neared its end, I went to check on Isaac in the studio.

When I entered, Isaac was in an animated conversation with his new friends which was quickly cut short by my appearance. I realised I looked different, but the staff stared at me like I had grown a second head. It wasn't difficult to guess what they were thinking.

"Is that really Mr Irving? I always took him for a family man!"

"Look at him!"

"That girl's abduction is a farce."

"I'm not so sure. Did you see the news? That woman is drop-dead gorgeous. Even the best of us can go astray sometimes."

It was to be expected, and I wasn't going to get upset by their idle gossip. In any event, Isaac seemed to be doing pretty well. With his natural charm and boisterousness, I could see that everyone had taken a shine to him. And that was what mattered now. He waved goodbye to his new colleagues, and we left to make the short trip back to the flat.

Isaac turned out to be equally good company as a roommate as he was an employee. Living with him, I could see how he'd turned that cramped space in his Jo'burg apartment into a comfortable home. If I had a complaint, it was his inability to keep his nose out of my business – for someone who had spent most of his life without a friend, he was seriously inquisitive.

* * *

Generally, I felt life had more or less returned to normal, or as close to normal as I could hope for. The policeman, McGraw, had caught up with me and I'd given him an edited version of my adventures, much as I had done with Vinny. He was suspicious and probed more thoroughly than Vinny but, without any hard evidence, he seemed prepared to me let me off the hook, at least for now. My days continued peacefully, until one night, this short period of relative calm was brought to an end.

As my phone rang, I rushed to answer it, hoping it might be Paula, maybe even Nikki or Blanche. But it was Vinny who had come back to hound me.

"You have some nerve calling me. I'll give you that," I told him.

"What are you saying, Gerry? Shouldn't you be a little more grateful? I saved your life?"

"What do you mean, who saved my life?"

"Oh, didn't Davis send you my regards, then? I guess he must have been more concerned about you bleeding out all over his back seat."

"That was you? I should've guessed." It was hard to express gratitude, given his obnoxious manner. "Anyway, what do you want?"

"Well, to fill in the blanks, of course! Now I certainly know that the girl's abduction has something to do with this organisation, but not much else. One of my men spotted a truck full of children leaving their building, but the incompetent arse lost them in traffic."

"Send someone else, then. Why would I work for you now after everything that's happened? You were the one who was so eager to get rid of me. Neither of us has any more to gain – or lose."

"You had one job, Gerald. I ask you, where is the fragrant Mrs Nader? One minute you had her in the palm of your hand, the next you've lost her again! Brilliant."

I had no idea where this fruitless conversation was going.

"Oh, and who's the boy you've replaced her with? Isn't he a bit young for you?"

"Sorry to disappoint you, Vinny, but I can't help you anymore. You'll have to get to the root of it on your own."

"Gerry, don't be like that. You owe me one."

"No, I don't, Vinny, they've threatened my family! I can't get involved any further, I daren't, even if I wanted to – which I don't."

Now, I had Isaac's attention. He rushed to my side, wildly gesturing for me to put the call on speaker. Frowning, I turned away and continued: "Believe me, I want to expose them as much as you do, but try to understand my situation, please!"

"I do understand, only too well," Vinny replied, "but let me give you a word of advice. You'll stay involved whether you like it or not. I've met men like you before, men who like playing with fire. Let's see how long you can stay under the radar. Mark my words, I'd give it days, not even weeks."

For once, I had an answer for him, bolstered by the confidence that only comes from nearly losing your life. "Then take this as a warning from me, Vinny, from the man who has played with fire.

You be careful too, this is much bigger than you can imagine."

He laughed disturbingly, and his voice sounded excited. "Listen to me, Gerry boy, it was me who warned you about that in the first place – and it ain't over yet." He hung up, and I put my phone down uncertainly.

Isaac looked at me expectantly, so I filled him in. At the mention of Oriole, he appeared uneasy as if he suspected something had happened for me to give up on her. But he said nothing. Instead, he decided to press on another issue.

"Why don't you try to meet with your family?"

"I will. When things settle down."

"You're stalling. Why?"

I was tired and inclined to tell him. "Because I'm scared I'll hurt them!"

"You told me you'd lost your family, so you probably never had a father figure in your life. I did. Believe me, they'd rather have you in their life than not. Everyone makes mistakes."

"Mistakes? Yes. But your uncle's mistakes weren't broadcast all over the press and TV for the world to see."

"It doesn't matter what your daughters see on the news. And you're wrong – you wouldn't believe the shit the tabloids printed about my uncle. All your kids will remember is that you abandoned them because you were too scared to face up to your mistakes."

For the first time in a long time, someone had said something to me that was worth hearing.

Thank you, Isaac.

* * *

The following morning, I was too absorbed to focus on anything. Pru looked almost offended when I asked her to reschedule a meeting with Mr Strasser, a new client.

After a hurried lunch at my desk to allow plenty of time for the drive to Mayfield, I covered my head with an old baseball cap. The last thing I needed was my daughters failing to recognise me.

Excited and apprehensive in equal measure, I arrived at the

school just as the bell rang for the end of the last lesson. Boys and girls of all ages spilled out into the playground. I scanned the throng of red and white uniforms for my daughters.

I had little trouble spotting Paula's neon green bag and rushed to meet her. She recognised me, even with my black fringes, fading tan, and hollow cheeks. She ran into my arms.

"Daddy! I knew you'd come! I told Mummy so!"

I cared little about the two teachers watching who looked surprised to see such a heartfelt reunion between a father and daughter at the end of a school day. "How are you, darling? How's Mummy? Where's your sister?"

"Nikki always takes too long to pack her bag, and Mummy is okay, but she cries at night. Nikki is always picking fights with me, but I'm good and very happy because I won the pop quiz today!" She excitedly pointed at the gold star pinned to her blazer. I was proud and overwhelmingly pleased to see her. I hugged her again. "Well done, darling," I said, "well done!"

Behind her, I saw Nikki, standing with her mouth agape, tears threatening to spill out of her eyes. I stood up to hug her, but she angrily ran off back into the hallway. Paula noticed her and ran after her. "Nikki, it's Daddy, it is! He looks different, but it's him!"

Before I could go after them, I spotted an unmistakable presence amongst a group of parents in the waiting area. Jake Winston was making his way toward me in a few long strides, thwarting my attempt to escape him. "A word, please, Mr Irving."

"I – please, not in front of my girls, I beg you."

Nodding slowly, he stood aside to let me pass and followed me to my car. "You're safe for now."

"I didn't kidnap Oriole. She spent every moment with me willingly."

"So I've told Mr Nader. He wishes to know why she hasn't returned with you."

For a moment I was amused by how far Henri was out of the loop. But the amusement was quickly replaced by concern as I said to myself: "That's strange. How come they still haven't reached out to Henri?"

"What are you mumbling?"

"Oriole was kidnapped by an organisation called Hope for Black. I'm sure you're familiar with them?"

His eyes widened in shock. "Do they have Harmony as well? My God! Is she even alive?"

This took me by surprise. If, as I had assumed, Henri was responsible for his daughter's abduction, how could his man Jake be ignorant of that? What's more, he didn't seem to want to kill me. "They don't seem to have her, and I'm assuming you haven't found anything either?"

"Nothing. Mr Nader is losing his mind. Wait, how do I know you're not lying? It's unlikely for Jones to go so far, given Mr Nader's influence over him."

Rolling up my sleeve, I showed him the gunshot wound. "The influence he *had*. This bullet was meant for Oriole, not for me. *(Why was I so sure about that, I wondered?)* Henri has been systematically extricating himself from Hope for Black and they don't like it."

His darkened expression was enough to tell me how truly dedicated he was to the Naders. When I stopped him with a hand on the forearm, I didn't expect my voice to shake as I pleaded for the second time to this ruthless man. "Please, save her."

Could it be that Jake and I might actually be on the same side? In that short exchange, he had as good as said that he and Henri were just as much in the dark as I was.

I looked back at the school. The girls had gone, presumably collected by Blanche and driven away during my altercation with Jake. If they had witnessed that, then this wasn't the time to press ahead with my plan for an early family reconciliation.

In fact, something else was troubling me. What was Jake even doing in Mayfield? Why was he there? And then I remembered. When we'd first met Henri and Oriole, hadn't they told me they had a home in Sussex, not far from where we lived?

The thought filled me with dread.

* * *

When I got back to the flat, I found that Isaac had left me a note saying he wouldn't be back for the night. I was glad he was finally living his life but, as the evening wore on, the loneliness dragged me back into an only too familiar void. I assumed he'd made some new friends of his own age and had become less interested in finding out more about me, the business or what was happening in my life. Disappointing, but understandable. He was young.

However, the next day he was at the office as usual and, passing me in the corridor, suggested we might meet up for dinner together that evening. I readily agreed and offered to get a Chinese takeaway which we could have together at the flat. I thought no more of it, Pru had the day off which gave me the chance to concentrate on paperwork without any interruption. I spent all day at my desk, pretty much insulated from the rest of the staff.

When he arrived at the flat, he was unusually quiet and wary. After a few mouthfuls of the Chinese, he cleared his throat nervously and asked: "Have you seen the news this morning? You've made the headlines again."

I was surprised but, not overly concerned. I suppose I had gotten used to it. "No, I haven't followed the news since we got back. What are they saying now?"

He pulled a folded page from his inside pocket and offered it to me.

"No, I don't want to read it. Just tell me what it says." Most likely, not the reaction he was expecting.

"Interesting." He unfolded the paper. *"Gerald Irving – knight in shining armour or wolf in sheep's clothing?"* Isaac let out an uncomfortable laugh.

My lack of interest didn't elude him. "Exaggeration sells," I said, shrugging.

Isaac went on monotonously, *"According to sources, Gerald Irving, a publisher from Sussex, was introduced to the Naders when they visited their holiday home, Villa Harmony, on the Costa del Sol. Irving is accused of returning their generosity by beating up Mrs Oriole Nader, wife of multi-millionaire and philanthropist, Henri Nader, and the mother of their abducted child, Harmony, who went missing three months ago. Psychologists have commented on his motives and possible state of mind. Some think he may be driven simply by greed and money, whilst others suggest he may be suffering from delusions of envy leading him to punish the wealthy."*

He looked up, his eyes demanding, begging me, to dispel the rumours. I struggled to say, "Isaac, there's so much you don't—"

He coldly went on, "Oh, there's more! *"Harmony Nader's lavish peacock hair clip was found in the glove compartment of Gerald—"*

"Enough, Isaac!" I dug my fork against my palm to keep my composure. Isaac stopped talking as my body trembled violently and a trickle of blood seeped from my hand.

Suddenly there was a loud banging on the door. I was almost thankful for this intrusion into what had become a tense situation but, the moment I opened the door, the bulky figure of Jake burst in. He looked furious.

Before I could make sense of the situation, Jake's fist came flying in my face. I took the blow on the side of my head and it hurt.

"You lied!" he shouted.

My heart leapt as I saw Isaac approaching out of the corner of my eye. If my attacker hadn't been so consumed with anger, he would've spotted the shake of my head directed at my friend. Stay out of this, I was signalling.

I tried to stall to give Isaac a chance to hide. "No, I did not! They've got Oriole, and I've no idea where Harmony is!"

Jake was having none of it. "If I hadn't been told to bring you in alive, I would take you out myself, now. We found Harmony's hair clip in your car in Spain!"

"What were you doing searching my car, for God's sake? Anyway, one of my daughters could have had the same clip."

"Yeah, after what you'd told me I decided to give you the benefit of the doubt. But I'd seen Harmony wearing it and when I showed it to Mr Nader, he said it was no ordinary clip. He'd had it specially made for her in Paris and it was unique!"

"So, you tracked down my car, broke into it, took the hair clip and that made you think I'd kidnapped Harmony? That's absurd. Did Henri not tell you she'd been out in the car with us? That must be when she left it there and obviously, none of us noticed."

"It makes no difference, either way. If you laid hands on Mrs Nader, you're already a dead man. Count your days, Irving."

"Listen to me. I could never hurt her, I love her! It wasn't me – it couldn't have been! I saw her, yes, but I don't know how she got hurt!" Even though I was terrified, a sense of injustice was sustaining my resistance. What Jake was saying was just plain wrong.

Jake wasn't listening anymore and as he squared up to throw another punch, Isaac decided to do something. Silently sneaking up behind him, he smashed a bottle of wine against the side of Jake's head, knocking him flat.

"Thanks," I said.

"I'm not talking to you until you explain yourself," Isaac replied.

But Jake was up again and threw a third punch. This time I wasn't so lucky, and it caught me square on the chin. His fingers curled against my throat, and he dragged me up against the front door. Isaac tried to come to my rescue, but Jake swatted him off like a fly.

"I suppose you enjoyed playing the big macho man, eh, lording it over an innocent, powerless woman?"

My reply remained choked in my throat as Jake constricted it harder. I was fighting to breathe and on the edge of consciousness when, I saw Isaac's frantic hands fumbling at Jake's pocket.

The last I saw of him before the darkness enfolded me was him shaking violently yet determinedly, holding my attacker at gunpoint and saying, "Let him go."

* * *

When I came to, neither Jake nor Isaac were to be seen. Surprisingly, I woke up on the couch in the flat and would've taken it all for a dream had it not been for the soreness of my throat, the stinging in my jaws, and the blood and shards of glass on the floor. It was nearly nine o'clock. When I couldn't find Isaac, I panicked.

Digging my phone out from where it was buried under the armrest of the couch, I called Isaac's number, there was no reply. I wasn't ready to lose yet another person I cared for. Desperate situations require desperate measures, and I rang the man I least wanted to speak to.

"Hello, Vinny, is this a good time? I can't believe I'm asking, but I need your help," I croaked out painfully.

"Hello, Gerald. You sound terrific! I knew you'd come crawling back. Where are you?"

"At my new apartment. It's near—"

"I know where that is, Gerald. Are you crazy? The police will be out looking for you. In fact, after today's news I'm surprised you're not behind bars now. Wait at Nando's, just down the road from you. I'll pick you up in fifteen."

Just in case, I packed my phone, charger, a change of clothes, a knife, and the cassette of Oriole's performances in a backpack. Heaven knows why I wanted it with me, but I did. I made an attempt to tidy up the flat and locked up behind me.

I'd only been standing outside the pizza shop for a couple of minutes when, true to Vinny's word, Pete sidled up and asked me to follow him to a Hyundai Tucson parked a few yards away on the other side of the road.

Vinny was sitting in the passenger seat and greeted me with a lopsided smile. I could see his wheelchair stowed behind him in the back.

"Ready for another trek are we, Gerry?" He was almost friendly as he noticed my backpack. "Where are we off to this time, then?"

"I have no idea. Never mind about me, Vinny, I need your help to find someone else."

"Heard you the first time. So, tit for tat, are you willing to open up now?"

"Under certain conditions. Please, Vinny, a young man's

life may be at stake." I'd promised Isaac safety and if anything happened to him I knew it would be my fault.

"Fine. I'll send my men to look for him. What's his name?"

"Isaac. I don't recall his surname, but his uncle was Augustus Black. Is that enough to go on?" He nodded. "Thank you. I'm in your debt."

"Yes, you are and you'll pay up one day, I'll make sure of that! Now, get in." As I climbed into the back, he was already on the phone.

I didn't ask how he'd found it but it was near midnight when we arrived at a nondescript block of flats in a decidedly scruffy area. I have no idea where. If this was Isaac's new home, it was even humbler than the one we had shared together.

Pete was despatched to ring the doorbell. A few minutes later he was back. There was no answer. With nothing to do but wait, Vinny got down to business right away.

"Good opportunity to spill the beans, Gerry. Pete will take notes."

I looked at Pete with his notebook ready in hand. "No," I demanded, "not in front of him."

"Pete stays."

"I told you I'd tell you everything under certain conditions. This is one of them. Pete leaves, and I'll make sure not to leave anything out. Isn't that enough for you?"

Vinny reluctantly gestured to him, and Pete got out of the car. Left alone with me, he frowned. "So, should I get some candles? A medieval dagger? Draw blood to seal the deal?"

"We don't have time for your nonsense," I replied impatiently. "Considering everything that has been said about me in the press, you're supposed to be my enemy. You're the last man I'd trust right now, but I don't have much choice."

Vinny raised both of his hands in the air defensively. "How offensive! 'Malicious envy against the rich'? That wasn't me, I'm better than that! Do you seriously think I'm the only reporter in town?" Then, as an afterthought, "By the way, is it true?"

Throwing him an incredulous look, I said: "Well, you're

about to find out – if you promise to keep quiet until Oriole and Harmony are safely back with Henri."

"What's that, another condition? That's very unfair. Basically, you're telling me to give my competitors a head start until the entire thing blows over? I'm not doing charity work here. Let's leave that to your friends in Joburg."

"Vinny, you're on the right track with the charity thing," I told him. Suddenly, he was all ears. "But if you're not careful, they'll take you and your men out before you know what's hit you. Your competitors have no clue about the connection the Naders have with this organisation, but you do. What I'm going to tell you will blow away the competition."

I went on to tell him every detail since my first meeting with the Nader family. My voice got smaller as I recalled how Oriole got hurt. I expected the man to laugh in my face, but to my surprise, he nodded sympathetically.

"Holy shit! You mean you actually had no part in the girl's abduction?"

"What the hell, Vinny? After everything I've told you, does that still surprise you?"

"You can't blame me. My instincts are always right. Still, for what it's worth, you've convinced me. Okay, I'll stay schtum for now. You might be right about putting people's lives at stake."

Things were going in the right direction for once. "My expectations are low, Vinny, I just hope you've got enough now to stop you backstabbing me again."

I'd hit a nerve, but his anger was short-lived. His eyes narrowed. "I never backstabbed you, you self-pitying idiot! I gave you several chances but you failed to keep your word. That's how it works in my world, Gerry, simples."

We remained silent for a moment, and then he spoke again. "But there's one thing I don't understand. If you are actually innocent – and I'm not saying I believe you a hundred per cent – so, why are you hiding? Why not simply give yourself up, then you and your family will be under police protection? They might even help you find your friend, too. If they can beat me to the chase, that is."

"Because. I don't know." I had no answer or, if I did, it would be too difficult and take far too long to explain.

Pete knocked on the window. "I don't think he's coming back, Guv, there's no sign of life."

"Okay," Vinny said, "we'll drop you back at your place, at least you now know where you might find your little boyfriend. I'd come back another day if I were you."

* * *

Why had I listened to him, the son of a bitch?

So much for finding Isaac, so much for not putting me behind bars and protecting my friend and family. What had I actually expected from the police? A stern telling-off for beating up a woman? A full-scale investigation by Interpol to rescue poor children under threat of losing their lives at the hands of an illegal international organ-trafficking organisation? That they'd take my word over that of a billionaire entrepreneur and benefactor?

"I hope all your introspection hasn't come to nothing," McGraw remarked, seating himself opposite me. "Let's start again. Where is the girl?"

"I said I don't know. Go and ask Henri Nader. But you wouldn't do that, right? Did he buy your silence or threaten you? That's his style, you know."

My head was throbbing. I'd thrown up what little I had eaten more than twenty-four hours ago and my entire body was burning with pain. Nearly a day had passed since I'd given myself up. My written statement had been followed-up by a "friendly" line of questioning by McGraw, but when my answers didn't match his pre-conceived conclusions, I'd been detained further and, frankly, now I was being bullied.

"Leave the questioning to me, Gerald. Does this object look familiar?" He produced a plastic bag from his pocket containing the hair clip. It took me a single look at the exquisite piece of jewellery to realise how Jake had recognised it at a glance. The metal was carved into the shape of a peacock, with emeralds and sapphires studded into its feathers.

"Not exactly, but it's not surprising it was found in my car, and I've already told you how it got there."

He let out a sigh and tried a different tack. "Do you confess to beating up Mrs Oriole Nader?"

"Not that I can recall ever hurting her, but I can see that the evidence suggests that I might have."

"She has given us her statement that you did."

"Has she been returned? Is she safe?" My voice cracked, and I couldn't argue with the accusation.

"Yes, but she is not in good shape. In fact, she has come forward specifically to report the physical abuse she suffered at your hands." When I didn't deny the charges, he continued in the same vein. "You've already taken one step towards redemption. If you can confess to one crime, why not the other? Or are you working with someone else?"

"No, I'm not." Seeing the change in his countenance, I pleaded my case again. "Officer, if Oriole has returned, she'll confirm everything I've told you. I'm not lying and while we are sitting here wasting time, my friend's life might be at risk."

"So you are working with someone?"

With growing horror, I realised my mistake. "What? No, no, no, no! He's just a boy!"

He went through his notes and asked, "Isaac Black, right? He's been working for you at Irving Press. Correct?"

"No, I mean yes, but you're barking up the wrong tree."

"Answer the question, please, Mr Irving."

"I've already told you everything. It's all in my statement. Have you bothered to read it?"

Before he could react, a knock came through the metal door. Sending me a look of warning, he left the interrogation room, leaving me to seethe alone. I knew talking back at him wasn't helping but my patience had run out and my growing hunger was taking a toll on me.

After nearly twenty minutes, a rather elegant, tall middle-aged woman entered the room. After pleasantly introducing herself as

Doctor Muriel, she went about her business setting up a recording machine and sorting through some papers. I got the impression she was putting on an act to make me feel comfortable, giving me time to observe rather than be observed.

"How are you doing, Mr Irving?"

"Fantastic! I've been in here for seven hours. What about you, doctor?"

"I'm doing pretty good as well. Thank you for asking." She offered me a smile. "There's no reason to be suspicious. This is a safe space. You can trust me."

Unlike McGraw, her kind, honeyed words were matched by her expression, but I kept my defences up. "So said Officer McGraw before subjecting me to hours of interrogation."

"His role and duties differ considerably from mine."

"I see," I said dubiously. "So, what exactly is your role, doctor? Have you been sent to find out whether I'm a pathological liar, or is this just another way to get a confession out of me?"

"Neither. You may not believe it, but I'm here to help you. To ensure you're mentally fit and well. You've been through a lot, Gerald, more than most people go through in a lifetime. So, I ask you again, how are you doing?"

When my eyes met hers, I wanted to accept her help with all my heart, but a voice inside my head held me back.

Instead, I replied, "I'm fine."

PART TWO

PROLOGUE TO PART TWO

Vinnie Lythgoe

Let me be honest. When I first encountered Gerald Irving, I didn't like him. I thought he was a loser and a liar.

Plus, I thought he was stupid. Not 'thick' stupid, more 'weak stupid'. Not properly grown up. 'Silly' would be a better word. Yes, that's exactly right, I thought he was silly. Silly to be getting involved in something far bigger than he understood. Silly for falling head over heels with a woman a million times out of his league and a lot brighter and manipulative than he realised, who only wanted him because she needed someone, anyone, some fool to help her in her 'hour of need'. Yes, and the quote marks are intentional - at the time, I was far from convinced that she wasn't totally in control of their relationship. But, mostly 'silly' for thinking that he could take on the likes of Henri Nader, one of the wealthiest and most powerful men in Europe who, with a click of his fingers, could mobilise a small army if he had to.

Judging by what he has written, Gerald felt much the same about me – for different reasons, of course. I don't think he had any reason to think I was stupid, but I have no doubt he was scared of me. Hated me. But as I got to know him, the less sure I became. He puzzled me. On the face of it, he was a prick, but perhaps there was more to him than met the eye.

Later, when I spoke to his wife, Blanche, I saw him as an ordinary bloke who had got in over his head. By the way, I liked her very much. She was open and honest, there was no side to her. Pretty, too. With lovely kids. A nice family. It didn't seem possible she would have chosen an idiot for a husband.

People usually make a simple error when they talk to me. They think I am only talking to them when nothing could be further from the truth. I know 'the press' aren't rated highly by the public – hacks, purveyors of sensationalized, personalized, and homogenized trivia – call us names and say what you will. Shoot the messenger, if it makes you feel better about the sick world we live in. But that's only half the story. The other half - what we mainly do - is seek out the truth.

That's what got to me about Gerald Irving. In the course of our conversations and odd meetings, to my great surprise, I started to believe what he was saying. I even began to like him. You'll have gathered by now that I'm a cynic. Years of doing this job has given me that right. People of all types, particularly the great and the good, are invariably disappointing, so it's rare to come across an exception. Gerald Irving was one. A perfectly nice, ordinary bloke, hopelessly overtaken by events. Which doesn't make him a bad person.

So, let's come back to seeking out the truth, which like all proper journalists I'd been trained to do from an early age – even to the extent, you might think of going to extremes. Above all we were taught to seek corroboration. Like a good policeman, to check and double check, to make sure that A's story tallies with B's - that his or her 'truth' doesn't distort the picture. Do this often enough and eventually you will get to the facts – not versions of the facts, the facts themselves.

That's what I decided to do with Gerald's story. As his predicament got more complicated and his version of events more contradictory, I began the process of contacting the other principle players - which wasn't easy with them strewn all over the world. Some were happy to talk, others not, or not so readily. One or two were totally incapacitated, the nanny, for example. Others, like Julia Swartz, seemed to have disappeared off the face of the earth until she finally emerged, happy as Larry, when everything was as good as over. Others, Mrs Nader, for example, were impossible to get anything out of until afterwards and even then, I believe, only to justify her part in the whole sorry saga. Singh, too, was desperate to give me his account in order (as he put it) to protect his reputation within the medical profession. Believe me, a session with that man was as exhausting as anything I've ever done. When the nanny, Nina, came to - and with no little persuasion I might add - she told me a lot over two sessions. She was quite a character, tough but attractive and vulnerable. I had no luck with the South Africans who were under arrest. I kept it all in my office safe, in anticipation that one day there might be an article there.

So, a year or so later when Gerald, surprisingly, told me that he too had written everything down, I asked to see it. It was in a pretty chaotic state, as you'd expect from a man who had never written anything before. But it had something, so I got to editing it and included the material I had extracted from the others.

The tape recorder is a wonderful invention. Once people get going, they are inclined to go on for ever. Some are frightened to begin with, others almost over keen to put 'their side of the story'. But, once they are in the swing of it, it's amazing what they'll reveal. All in confidence, of course. Well, sue me.

So, this is what I did. I transcribed the tapes, embellished them with some dramatic license (otherwise known as imagination) and put them into some kind of chronological order, filling in what I thought might be the missing bits.

My greatest achievement was to get telephone interviews with the Naders. Funnily enough, Mrs Nader's version of events was almost a mirror version of Gerald's. Henri's, on the other hand, shed a completely new light on the events following Gerald's arrest. Of them all, his testimony was the most incriminating – which as the eminently entitled man he believed himself to be, didn't seem to worry him in the slightest.

So, shall we press on?

Vinnie Lythgoe

CHAPTER TWELVE

Henri Nader

I am fortunate to live in a magnificent house in a glorious location where the sun shines most of the year. But I can hardly recall the last time I was able to sit in the sun on my terrace, enjoy a cocktail and reflect.

However, right now, with both my wife and daughter missing, that is exactly what I am doing, reflecting on the past and hoping to figure out how I have come to be in the desperate state I am today.

My few true friends have told me that I'm an eternal optimist and that is not always for my own good. They will say that I anticipate the best outcomes, however unlikely, and that I showcase events, and for that matter myself, in the best possible light at all times. I don't deny any of that.

Of course, I'm not that clichéd billionaire with a tragic backstory that you see in films, read about or rarely if ever come across in real life. I know that the hand on my moral compass sits steadily between genuine concern for my fellow man and my own selfishness. I admit all that, too. Ask any wealthy, successful tycoon and they'll tell you the same thing – that there is a perfectly achievable middle course. Well, may be after a couple of cocktails, they'll say that.

These facets of my character first revealed themselves to me when I fell out with my parents and my father kicked me out of the family home when I was seventeen. Back then, I had no intention of departing from the straight and narrow, but that didn't stop me from ruining my only close friend a few years later.

I was a penniless kid when I'd arrived in Soho and Cavalotti had taken me in. He'd put food on my plate, given me a roof and a job. But when I saw the chance to expose him and take over the club, I didn't hesitate. Ruthless, possibly, but that was my first step towards fortune and fame. Of course, Cavalotti fought back. Threatened with survival, people usually do. I could have lost, but I didn't and, as any gambler will confirm, when you don't lose, you keep playing. And that's what I did.

So, instead of what could have been a tragic backstory, I've been blessed with all of life's privileges – great wealth, fame, an enviable lifestyle, handsome looks (or so I'm told) and, most importantly, a stroke of gamblers' luck that gave me the confidence to take risks where others shrunk away.

When Oriole, the most stunning woman I had ever laid eyes on, agreed to be seen on my arm, it stroked my young man's inflating ego. But what set out to be a mutually beneficial professional arrangement, had swiftly turned into an addiction, on my part a compulsory and persistent need. I wanted her as my partner in every aspect of my life.

Prior to meeting her, my grand scheme had never included a wife and family. Falling in love with Oriole may not have changed me, but it radically transformed my ambitions. Loving her wasn't easy, forcing me to confront my self-worth and my one overriding and inescapable deficiency.

Every jewel, every luxury, every kiss was followed by a reminder of what I couldn't give her – my inability to satisfy her needs and, ultimately, to father a family. Later she had turned away from me and sought the comfort of another man.

Although medical science couldn't combat my impotency, it came to my aid in a different form. So it was that when Oriole was finally able to conceive Harmony, I knew she was mine. My precious baby girl became my pride and joy and was growing up to be everything I had hoped for and more. Instead of investing my wealth in a life of grandeur, it was now spent on medical research, charitable acts and my daughter's happiness. Becoming a father had set me on a straighter path, and I swore off anything illegitimate until the day Harmony fell severely ill.

Watching her struggle to draw breath led me to abandon my

best intentions and, in turn, had humbled me into choosing a terrible path.

Saving my daughter's life transcended all else. Surely, any loving father would feel the same? Whatever I had to do, I would do. That's how it all started. Hope for Black provided the life-saving kidney together with the surgery that saved Harmony's life. When we returned from South Africa, full of joy and relief, in the blink of an eye I had got sucked in, sending them massive donations, and willingly using my contacts to provide them with more desperate clients prepared to pay anything for their help.

Inevitably, I suppose, what had started out as philanthropy morphed into a business and my concern for the lives of poor African children became obscured.

Even that didn't trouble me unduly. Wasn't I saving lives where otherwise young kids would die? If governments across the world could turn a blind eye to this, surely, I could too? And so it transpired – not once did I feel threatened or exposed. All I had to do was keep the truth away from my family. Or so I'd thought.

A year ago, I was brought shockingly to my senses when my son, Max, a boy of only seven who we had adopted to provide Harmony with company, slipped off a banister and injured his head. Instead of taking him to the hospital, Nina, his nanny, foolishly took him to the *Aphrodite*. Oriole and I had been away and when we got back, I could see my son was badly distressed. I never found out what he witnessed on the ship because neither he nor Nina would talk about it.

From that day on, I decided to divert my energies into building my wife's singing career and to extricate myself from that so-called charity and the Mafia guys who had taken it over – but that was proving harder than I'd imagined.

Now, my wife and daughter were paying the price.

My train of thought was cut short by the sound of my mobile ringing on the table beside me. It was Jake, my bodyguard and chief of security. He sounded excited and alarmed.

"Mr Nader, I have found the man, Irving. He returned to the UK but without Mrs Nader."

"Where is he keeping her? Let me talk to him!"

"He's not with me right now, but I followed him to his house. I know where he lives, so you don't have to worry about that. According to him, Jones has Mrs Nader."

This revelation didn't surprise me. My suspicions had always been directed at the bloody man until I'd seen Oriole with Gerald Irving in the news. "Did he say anything else to you? Did he know whether she'd been harmed?"

"He sounded very worried about her," Jake paused to let the words sink in. "Irving took a bullet for her. I don't think he's our guy."

I had to make some quick decisions. "I understand. Right, take the Citation with Simon and his team to SA, find Jones' family – he's got a wife, a teenage son and two younger girls. Return with all four of them directly to Gatwick. I'll take the Learjet and meet you at the house."

Dealing with heartless individuals has given me enough experience to recognise one when I see one. When I first met Gerald, I noticed him eyeing up my wife, but that was not unusual given her beauty. Now it was beginning to look as though Oriole had returned his feelings. I was only too aware of how distant she had become even before Harmony went missing, so it made sense that she might have fallen back on a stranger. It had happened before. But her safety was another matter and discovering he was acting as her protector in my absence didn't help. I had to get them both back using any means possible.

With my family crumbling apart, I couldn't entrust Max's safety to a stranger. The only nanny Max had known, Nina, had left and we had replaced her with a temporary, an older Spanish woman, who was doing her best but wasn't the same. It was devastating enough that one of my children had become a victim of my crimes, but when I went to check up on Max, he was fast asleep. "Hey, Max, wake up," I said gently.

Max's golden hair and blue eyes stood him apart in our family, but his mannerisms matched mine. He was curled up in the foetal position; his arms wrapped tightly around his pillow. Slowly, he stirred in his sleep and called out to Nina.

"Nina's not here, kid," I whispered in his ear. "So, rise and shine."

He seemed surprised to find me by his side. "Daddy? Has Mummy come back?"

"No, son, we're going to bring her back. Come on now, get dressed. We're leaving soon!"

* * *

We landed at London Heathrow before the clock struck twelve. Surprisingly, I'd learnt more about Max during that two-hour flight than I had in the past year. He had already perfected French and was on his way to learning Arabic. He liked to take his toys apart to study their inner mechanisms, which always got him into trouble with his nanny. Everything he revealed about himself caused me to feel more pangs of guilt.

"When are we going to see Mummy?" he asked.

"In a few days," I promised.

Dropping him off at the Savoy, I swallowed my pride and dialled a number that I didn't need to look up. He picked up on the second ring. "Hey, Dad?" I asked. There was silence on the other end. "I need your help."

"Why, of course! I heard your wife ran off with another man."

"That's old news." He was straight to the point as usual. "Keep up, old man, will you?"

"How are you holding up, Son? Your mother called you."

"I know." My children had really softened me. "I'm sorry. I've been too busy with all … you know."

"Well, if I turned you down in your time of need, your mother would never forgive me. What can I do?"

"I need to get my wife and daughter back. Can you come to England to look after Max, you can stay with him at the Savoy?"

After I'd torn my walls down, he'd readily done the same. "Of course, Son. Is that even a question?"

* * *

Some sixty miles south of London, a cottage in the heart of the Ashdown Forest was acting as a prison for a certain Judith Jones and her three children.

The beautiful house looked like something straight out of a fairy tale. I'd bought it for Harmony on a whim. It was better than any doll's house and we had dreamed about spending the summers there as a family. What a shame it now had to be put to such use.

When I got there, Jake had already taken care of the situation. The family was locked in one of the unfurnished guest rooms. However, these guests were not content to wait quietly.

The toddler was wailing in his mother's arms and a girl about Harmony's age was sitting by her side trying to comfort her baby brother. The loudest of them all was a teenage boy who came at me with a curtain rail the moment I stepped into the room. Of course, Jake easily blocked the attack, but the boy didn't yield.

"Gag them. And tie this one up."

"Who are you? Why did you bring us here?" the boy asked.

Paying no heed to him, I continued my instructions to Jake. "Bring the boy. Get Jones on the phone and then beat him up so that Jones can hear. If Jones still resists, get the girl. Spare no one."

"Why are you doing this to our family? My father is a good man."

"Your father has kidnapped my daughter and wife," I addressed the boy finally. "So be a good boy and save your breath for when you speak to him. When he gets in touch, you'll need it."

"You'll never find your daughter or your wife! You lay a hand on my sister, and I'll kill you before you can find them!"

His words infuriated me so much that my smack to the side of his face almost knocked him out. It wasn't like me to pick a bone with a kid, but with Jones so far away his son made a good substitute.

With no hesitation, Jake did as he was instructed. I wondered if his conscience stirred as he gagged the toddler, and I wondered about the basis of his loyalty, because I knew it wasn't money.

Maybe, he was in love with Oriole. Like the rest of us.

The rascal wasn't picking up the phone. When eventually the call went through, a woman's voice came across the phone. "Hello, who is this?"

"I wish to speak to Jones. Give him the phone, please."

The woman giggled and replied, "He's sort of busy right now."

"Tell him Henri Nader wants to speak to him."

She conveyed my message, and within seconds, Jones was on the line. "Hello, Henri! Long time, no see."

"Cut the crap. I want my daughter and wife back."

"Henri, my man, we're keeping your wife under the best of conditions here, but we don't have your daughter. Don't worry; your wife is enjoying all the facilities of a five-star hotel with us. Listen, when this media circus blows over, why don't we meet in person and discuss your business with us?"

"To hell with the that! Return my wife and daughter unharmed if you want to see your family again."

Jones let out a mocking laugh. "My family? Even your guys couldn't reach them here."

"Oh, but they did. Jake, bring the boy. Make sure he screams loud enough. His father is six thousand miles away."

Jake dragged the boy by his hair and punched him in the gut. He doubled over and curled up on the tiled floor. Jake repeatedly kicked and threw punches, but the boy was resilient and refused to make a sound. "Hurry, Jake. Jones is waiting."

As instructed, Jake pulled out a pocket-knife and headed towards the girl, crouched silently in a corner.

The boy gave up at once. "No, please don't hurt her."

"Come here, boy. Talk to your father."

His surrender did nothing to affect his insolence, and he was dragged his feet with hate in his eyes.

"Hello, Dad? Yes, I'm okay ... no. They shot them all ... yes, Mom and Timmy are safe ... Yes, Sarah, too ... I know."

When the boy passed the phone back to me, Jones had lost all of his initial smugness. "Henri, don't hurt them. I promise Mrs

Nader will be on her way back to you on the very next flight. Just don't hurt my family." He hesitated, then continued. "We'll talk about the contract later."

"No, we won't. I don't want anything to do with you or your organisation, and don't even think about double-crossing me."

"Henri, listen, you can't just—"

"Are you seriously in a position to tell me what I can or can't do?" My patience was at its limit.

"Fine, fine. Can you do me a favour, then? You owe me that much."

"Depends. Make it quick."

"Remember Black had a boy? His nephew, Isaac? He's staying with that guy, Gerald."

"Go on."

"Can you send him back along with my family?"

"Just return Oriole and Harmony unharmed, and I'll see what I can do."

"Man, how many times do I have to tell you I don't have your daughter?" His voice came through clenched teeth. "And sending your wife back unharmed? That's quite another matter."

His words consumed me with rage again, and I could no longer keep my voice down. "What did you do to her?"

"I didn't do anything! That man with her, Gerald Irving, he knocked the living daylights out of her!"

"He did what?"

"You heard me. My men couldn't even recognise her at first. She was in critical condition when we found her. Got her treated and everything."

"Are you sure it was him? If I find out you're lying . . ."

"I'm not lying! She was the one who told us. You can ask her yourself."

My mind was spinning. God knows where my precious girl was. After all this time, I thought I'd be holding her in my arms again, and my wife ... How could I have abandoned her? When she left me, I was too angry to go after her. Now, I couldn't believe how the Englishman had tricked us both.

Cutting Jones off, I hung up the phone. "Jake. It's your lucky day. You've got more prey to go after."

* * *

A day had passed with relentless pacing, yet there was no sign of Harmony nor Oriole. I was reluctant to believe Jones, simply because it seemed so unlikely that Gerald Irving would hurt Oriole when he had been willing to sacrifice his life for her. However, when Jake reported finding Harmony's hair clip in his car, I became more suspicious and reported him to the police giving them the hair clip as proof.

I'd been put on to a Detective McGraw who appeared to be in charge of the case. He took my statement and reassured me he had obtained a search warrant but, with no evidence linking the man to the crime, I had to do a little coercing to get him to agree to get an arrest warrant as well.

When Jake returned with an injured eye and his leg shot, I realised I had underestimated Gerald. The man wasn't working alone. Augustus' nephew must be helping him. My blood still boiled, recalling how Black had seduced my wife and turned her against me. Well, he'd paid the price. How could I have known that Irving would do the same and be working with another member of Black's family?

Surprisingly, soon after defeating Jake, Irving had willingly surrendered himself to the police. As I heard an engine revving outside the cottage, I rushed outside to find my wife stepping out of an SUV.

I ran to her and gathered her fragile frame in my arms, but she remained stiff and unyielding. I wondered what disturbed me more, her bruised face and body or her recoil from my touch.

"Darling, I'm sorry. I'm so sorry, I'm sorry, I'm sorry." With each word, I was trying to coax her into accepting my embrace.

Reluctantly, she leaned her weight on my arm, and I carried her inside. As she settled on a couch, I told my men to set the table for her. I'd had a meal made ready for her but she refused to touch a thing.

"Oriole, please, say something. I've been so worried. Why did you leave me?"

I tried another approach. "Please, forgive me. I know we've had our ups and downs, but I promise I'll do better from now on." I was horrified by her appearance. "Did Jones do this to you?" She remained lifeless. "Or was it Irving?" Finally, a response – she shuddered at his name.

"Honey, he'll pay for it. You don't have to worry about anything anymore."

For the first time she looked at me. "Henri, please, return my daughter."

"Yes. We'll get her back. We'll find her together."

"No. Where are you keeping her? I'll do anything . . ." She broke into helpless tears. I tried to embrace her, but she fought me off, yelling at me through her sobs. She was barely making any sense, and the more I tried to reach out, the more she shrank away, until eventually, her strength drained away and she fell asleep in my arms, still sobbing.

She woke an hour later which meant I'd had some time to try to work out what she had meant. She seemed to think I had kidnapped my own daughter and, anyway, why would I and where would I have kept her? It still didn't make any sense.

After her sleep she had calmed down considerably but still refused to talk to me. However, she decided to eat as much as she could stomach. Whenever I tried to approach her, she became rigid as a rock, so I decided to keep my distance. After a while, she came up to me on her own.

"Henri, I know about your 'medical equipment' business." Even though it was inevitable that she'd find out eventually, I still drew a sharp breath. "I know about your ship, those poor children, I know you had Augustus killed . . . and if you kill . . . or even hurt Harmony, I swear, I'll kill you myself. I'll . . ."

"Oriole, what are you saying?" Her body was convulsing again, but with every word she spoke, a coldness was washing over me. "Why would I hurt my own daughter – or you? Have you lost your mind?"

Instead of replying, she shut her eyes and started sobbing again. Shaking her head frantically, she repeated the same nonsense. "Give me my daughter back! Give her back!"

"Have they brainwashed you?" Somehow, I managed to keep my tone tender despite the indignation I felt.

Oriole laughed bitterly, "Brainwashed me? Is that all your brilliant mind can comprehend? I am not a child! I'm very much capable of thinking for myself! I know you've been getting cold feet about your criminal activities because of my growing success. Am I just another project to you?"

"I don't understand, Oriole. Yes, I've been trying to get back on the right path again. Isn't that a good thing?"

Instead of making sense, she continued attacking me with her ruthless interrogation. "Is that all your daughter is to you – incriminating evidence you can just erase at your convenience? How could you be so heartless?"

Finally, I was allowing my anger to show. "Enough, Oriole, not another word! How could you trust the word of others over mine?" With that came unbidden tears. "How could you think I'd hurt Harmony for such a . . . how could you think I could hurt her at all?"

She stared at me like a deer caught in headlights. In eleven years of marriage, she had never seen me shed a tear, not even when Harmony was on the brink of dying.

"You can hardly expect me to trust you," she said uncertainly.

"I never gave you a reason to doubt my love for you or Harmony. You, on the other hand . . ."

"You mean your suffocating hold over my life and my daughter's? Is that your definition of love?"

The words spilling out of her mouth were cutting and unbelievable. "I did it for your protection. All of it, it was all for you."

"Protection against what, Henri?"

She was staring at me. I looked away. "Against my crimes and some of those I associate with."

"Why, Henri? It's not like we were short of money. So why?"

I had pondered this question myself a million times. "When I couldn't give you a child, I felt powerless against fate. Eventually, with the emerging technology and my resources, you were able to get pregnant and when I held my little baby girl in my arms, I felt complete. She was ours, Oriole! Wealth has given me power. With my influence and the money to make things happen, I could have anything I set my eyes on."

"Like the *Aphrodite*?" she cut off my response bitterly.

"Yes, that amongst many other things. When Harmony was dying, I felt powerless again and found my answer beyond the boundaries of the law. We dealt with our guilt differently. You were crushed under it, but I embraced it! Not being bound by the conventions of right and wrong gave us a different kind of power, the kind of power that saved our daughter's life."

"What happened, then? Did you get bored with your power?

"No. I was concerned about my children and their upbringing."

"Right."

"Really, Oriole. Should I have decided to set things straight earlier, no one could have stopped me." I realised I had chosen my words badly when her expression returned to infuriation. I was getting angry, too. "The more I learn about Gerald Irving, the more I grow certain that Harmony's disappearance has nothing to do with me or my crimes."

She froze up at his name, giving me silent confirmation of my suspicions. "Oriole, did you learn anything from him? Can you think of something?"

"That guy is twisted. Something is very wrong with him." She wrapped her arms around herself protectively and started shuddering again.

This time when I took her in my arms, she didn't shrink away from my comfort. "Henri, you can't just wipe the slate clean by washing the blood off your hands."

"I know, I know. But let's find Harmony first. She needs us both right now."

"How? Everything leads to a dead end."

"Because we've been following the wrong trail. First thing in the morning, we'll go to the police, and you can give them your statement. Can you handle that, do you feel strong enough?"

"Yes."

* * *

On our way back to the cottage from the police station, Oriole had reverted to her initial state. It had been another ordeal for her and her eyes were glassy as she looked out the car window, rejecting my attempts at an embrace.

"Do you remember how we got this cottage?" I asked, hoping this might be a distraction. She remained silent, so I continued. "Well, according to Harmony, Winnie-the-Pooh had a house in the forest and she wanted to visit it. We started looking to see if there was such a house for sale in the Ashdown Forest, and this one came up. Once we'd furnished it, we were planning to spend that first summer here."

Still lost in her thoughts, Oriole murmured, "I remember . . . I remember, Gerald told us he lived here."

"Here, in Sussex?" I was beginning to recall that conversation. "Yes, you're right, not far from here, he said. You're right."

"Perhaps we should visit his family." Her remark surprised me.

"Now? Do you feel up to it? Are you sure?"

"Yes, I'm sure."

"Very well, then, here."

Balancing the steering wheel with one hand, I fumbled in my pocket to reach for my phone. I handed it to her and asked her to go through my contacts to get the Irvings' number. It only took her a few minutes and I pulled into a lay-by to dial it. It was soon answered by a voice I remembered very well.

"Hello, Mrs Irving, it's Henri Nader here, do you remember, you and your family visited us not long ago in Spain?"

She sounded very hesitant and nervous. "Yes, of course I remember. Why are you calling me?"

"Oriole and I are in England, not far from you. We were

wondering if we might pay you a visit? There is something we would like to talk to you about."

There was a lengthy pause at the other end and I could hear one of her girls ask, "Who is it, Mummy, you look . . ."

"Yes, Mr Nader," Blanche Irving seemed to have made up her mind, "that might be a good idea. When would suit you?"

"Well, we are on the road now, so we could be with you quite shortly, if it is convenient, of course. Could you let me have your address?"

"We're the first house in Rotherfield Lane in Mayfield, you'll see my green Volvo parked outside, you can't miss us."

"Perfect, we are at Wych Cross," I replied, "we should be there within half an hour or so."

"Good," she said, "it will be interesting to see you again, although in rather different circumstances it would seem." I heard the click as she replaced the handset.

'Well, it appears she knows something, although how much is another matter," I said to Oriole. "No doubt we shall soon find out."

The rest of the short journey continued in silence. I had no idea what Oriole was thinking, let alone what she had in mind to say to Blanche Irving.

We found the house easily enough, a smallish, three-bedroomed detached property at the end of a row of identical homes. There was no room to park behind the green Volvo, so I did my best to leave the car in the narrow road without causing an obstruction.

The instant I rang the bell, the door flew open, revealing Gerald's elder daughter, pale and shivering.

"Mummy, Harmony's mummy and daddy are here!"

Before she appeared at the door, Blanche's voice came from a distance. "Nikki, I told you to stay upstairs!"

She rushed to the door, her hands in mittens. For a moment the sight of Oriole left her speechless. Composing herself, she welcomed us into her living room with no hint of malice or hesitation.

"I am so embarrassed, I have nothing to offer you. Nikki is sick, so she's home from school. She's kept me busy all morning."

"Oh no!" I sympathised, "We apologise for intruding. This

must be completely unexpected. We just want to talk about your husband, if you're okay with that. I'm presuming he is not here, of course?"

"Of course," she said, but the expression that crossed her face contradicted her response. "Please, sit down."

Nikki had quietly snuck into the living room with us and sat in a corner, but that hadn't escaped Blanche. "Nikki, please, I asked you to go to your room."

"No. This is about Daddy, isn't it? I'm not going anywhere."

"Nikki, I won't repeat myself," Blanche warned sternly. "Now, go to your room." The girl angrily banged the door behind her as she stormed out.

"I'm sorry about that. She's very disturbed by everything that's going on. Gerald went to see her at school, and she has been crying ever since."

Oriole finally spoke up. "You have nothing to be sorry for. None of this is your fault." Coming from Oriole who hadn't said a word up to then, this appeared to take Blanche off guard.

When they had visited us at the villa, I'd thought she was an attractive woman. Almost the opposite of Oriole, in fact, with her hour-glass figure and closely cropped, boyish blonde hair. Now, her face lined with worry and her tense demeanour, somehow her vulnerability made her even more appealing. I felt sorry for her.

"I can't help but blame myself," she went on. "If only I hadn't ignored the signs earlier . . ." Her jaw tightened as she struggled to hold back her tears. Gesturing towards Oriole's bruised face and arms, she asked in a smaller voice, "Did he do this to you?"

Oriole gave her the smallest of nods. "Has he ever hit you?" she asked Blanche, "and what signs are you talking about?"

"No, he has never hurt me physically, but he has frightened me at times. But he has always had some . . . issues, increasingly as a matter of fact. But they've always been there."

I wanted Blanche to continue but Oriole was looking pale and drawn and I wanted to bring this meeting to a conclusion as quickly as possible. "Forgive me," I said, "it might be too much to ask, but can you be a little more specific? What kind of issues are you referring to?"

"I think he gets triggered in some situations. Under normal circumstances, when he got angry – which was quite often – given a little time he could deal with it himself. But when he was attacked on a personal level, or if I ever did something he didn't expect me to, then he could go crazy."

"I noticed that too," Oriole remarked.

"When we had just moved here, one night, he heard me joking around with my friends. I can't recall what we were talking about, but he assumed I was making fun of him behind his back. Quite often, he would make self-deprecating remarks about himself but that night something must have got to him. He got so mad he went round wrecking our newly furnished home."

"Did this happen often?" I asked.

"No, as I said earlier, sometimes he gets triggered. He also tends to resort to alcohol under stress. That often aggravates his mood swings."

"Has he ever shown any violence towards the children?"

"No, never. As a husband he left much to be desired, but he was an adoring father." Her voice softened for the first time since our arrival. "In fact, he could be overly protective of them." She turned to Oriole. "If it weren't for you sitting before me, looking as you do, I would have refused to believe he could harm anyone so badly, let alone a child. Do you mind if I ask what led him to do this to you?"

Oriole shifted nervously in her seat, and I interjected, "I apologise. My wife isn't well enough to relive the experience. She just gave her statement to the police in vivid—"

Oriole cut me off and answered in a steady voice, "Sure. I'm fine."

Blanche reached out and held my wife's hand in both of her own. "There's no pressure. If you're not comfortable talking about it, I understand, of course."

"We've both been victims of this man. I owe you that much," Oriole replied. She squeezed Blanche's hand reassuringly and continued, "I don't know him well enough to recognise what triggered him." But I knew Oriole well enough to know she was lying. "Before he lashed out at me, he had been having nightmares for days. He used to talk in his sleep."

Oriole looked away as she spoke. She hadn't revealed this piece of information in front of the officer, and my gaze drifted towards Blanche, who was nodding. I could tell she shared my unease.

"One night, he came to the hotel room drunk and started trashing the room. I had never seen him so aggressive, so I tried to escape." With every word, I could feel my anger bubbling up again, and so could Oriole as she rushed through the rest of her story. "The moment he spotted me in the room, he started hitting me. Started blaming me for being the reason he had lost you and his children."

"I'm so sorry! No one is to blame for his actions but himself! How could he be so monstrous! My God!"

Oriole sighed and said in an exhausted voice, "He'll pay for it. I just hope I never have to set eyes on him again."

There was a short silence before Blanche got up. "Well, I wish you luck in finding your daughter. If you need anything else, don't hesitate to call me."

Thanking her for her kindness, we stood to leave. As we reached for the door, I addressed Blanche again. "One more thing, Blanche. If it's not too much to ask, would you be prepared to go public with what you've told us? All the aggression and violence you suffered during your marriage? Why not let them know that he's truly a dangerous man?"

Blanche hesitated, probably thinking about her girls. "Well, I wouldn't exactly describe Gerald as dangerous." I looked at her incredulously. "I mean, I could, but what he really needs is professional help and I'm not sure going public would do any good."

"I see," I replied curtly. This time I wasn't going to get what I wanted.

"Please, try to understand, Henri. When he gets there, it's like . . . he didn't intend to. He can't recall any of his actions later. It's like . . ."

"He has been possessed," Oriole concluded her explanation. Blanche nodded silently.

CHAPTER THIRTEEN

Nina Behrooz

To call them nightmares would be to underrate the terror I was experiencing as my mind roamed randomly through tumultuous episodes from my past, forewarning me of worse to come. So, waking to find I was in a hospital bed rather than a burning pit in hell was a relief. The only thought stuck in my mind as I stumbled into consciousness was, *I'm going to die.*

By piecing together scraps of conversations around me, I had learned that I had survived a bullet through my chest. How did I get here? I tried to find that out from the woman in green looming over me, but my speech was impeded by the tube in my throat. I tried to gesture to her to remove it. To my surprise, she did.

"How are you, Miss Behrooz? Can you nod your head to indicate if you feel anything?" I could barely sense the gentle pinch in my arm, but my muffled response was enough to satisfy her.

Call me Nina. I tried to voice that thought, but the muscles in my throat refused to oblige.

The woman smiled at me kindly. Beneath her cap I could make out a few strands of greying hair. I scanned the room as best as I could from my reclined position. There was a lot of medical equipment clustered around me with several machines connected to my body. Apart from the grey-haired woman, I made out three other people in the room.

"Don't be afraid, you're quite safe with us," she said. "You can call me Dr Maria. All this time, you've been under my care. Do you remember how you got here?"

With some effort, I shook my head and discovered my muscles were beginning to work. "You suffered a critical gunshot wound to your chest," she went on. I remembered that well enough thanks to my recurring nightmares featuring the incident itself. "The loss of blood led to your comatose state. Luckily, your boyfriend got you here in time."

I looked up expectantly. I needed to see Abdul. My fear and anxiety were growing with all these strangers staring at me. Abdul had been my only anchor through my recent turmoils. The doctor noticed my discomfort and asked the rest of her team to leave.

"I'm sorry to disappoint you, but he's not here right now, but don't worry. I'm sure he'll return as soon as he hears you've woken up." My eyes filled with tears. I hated being helpless.

The woman was clearly a veteran in her field. She read desperation and set about answering the question I couldn't voice.

"You have been in this condition for quite a while, but don't worry about it. We're looking forward to your steady recovery!"

Her voice was soothing and gentle and I could feel myself relaxing despite my anxiety. I had never seen or met her, but I was beginning to feel some gratitude.

I needed to find out precisely how much time I had lost and, as she continued filling up her notebook with the occasional clinical look in my direction, I felt a sense of urgency return. I needed proper answers to things I could neither recollect nor comprehend.

Seeing my disappointment, she hesitated before answering. "You've been here for three months. When your friend brought you in, he stayed with you day and night, but then something urgent came up and he had to leave. We haven't seen him lately and he left no details of how we might contact him." Putting away her notebook, the doctor gently took my hand.

"It's going to be okay! Believe me, you are an unusually strong and resilient young woman. Your recovery is nothing short of a miracle, so don't lose hope now. You've come too far to give up. Keep fighting!"

And so I did.

Losing track of time, I focused every ounce of effort on getting back on my feet. I had no idea how many days I must have spent in physical and speech therapy before I could walk, talk and eat again. Whenever I felt like giving up, Dr Maria reminded me that she had never seen a case like mine and remarked again on my unusual strength and physique. But I didn't feel strong, not at all.

Time may have been the best healer for my medical ailments, but the hurt caused by my boyfriend's desertion grew worse with each passing day. His mobile number was unobtainable, and I had given up enquiring with the staff. He was the only one who could fill in the blanks and his lack of concern for my welfare was like a dagger in the heart.

So, with little else to ponder, I resorted to reminiscing about the events in my past and how they had led to me fighting for my life.

After escaping the clutches of my abusive father, I had learnt to survive on my own until I fell into the claws of monsters. The Iranian revolution hadn't brought out the best in my father; he had always been a psychopathic lunatic who got off on seeing others suffer.

I'll never forget how he once mercilessly beat my poor mother so that she ended up in intensive care. When the authorities finally got involved, he suffered no punishment but, luckily, I was taken away to a safer home.

Growing up in my father's household, I had learned to survive. I had learned to always be on the defensive. As I entered my teens, men were often deceived by my sex and invariably let their defences down. Many barely lived to regret their mistake.

The day my mother finally gave up and died, I started using my anger as a weapon – but, with the confidence of youth, never imagined that same weapon would one day leave my life hanging by a thread.

Despite the strict sex segregation in Iran introduced after the Iranian Revolution, a number of Iranian women served in the military and in paramilitaries during the Iran-Iraq War in the eighties. Most were doctors and nurses, but hundreds of others fought on the front line. I was one of them. I had finally found my place.

After the war, life under the Mullahs left my country oppressed and in turmoil and I knew I had to get out. That was easier said than done, but with a small group of ex-army friends I managed to hitch-hike to Beirut. It took us nearly three months and only three of us completed the journey. Tired and exhausted we split up to look for accommodation and jobs.

By now I was in my twenties and I suppose of above average intelligence and looks. It didn't take me long to find a job in a bar lodging with a couple who worked there. At that point in my life, the last thing I anticipated was one day working for a high-profile billionaire.

I clearly remember the night I got caught up in the wretched ordeal that sealed my fate. The exhaustion of working double shifts at the bar, the pungent smell of vomit, the blasting new rock music – it is all imprinted in my mind as if it were yesterday.

That was when I first saw the bulky figure of Jake, although I didn't know his name until later. He had two other guys with him and they had been watching me all night, tracing my every movement.

I left to walk home in the early hours of the morning fully expecting to be followed. There were two of them but no sign of the big man himself. I wasn't even frightened, because I knew I could take them out in a heartbeat – and I did.

The following night, Jake was there on his own. This time he made no pretence of not wanting to see me. He told me that he'd heard of my reputation as an ex-soldier and sent his two colleagues deliberately to test my fighting skills. He'd seen how I'd dealt with them and been impressed, enough apparently to be convinced there was no one more suitable to protect the two children of his wealthy employer. He was offering me a job as their bodyguard, although I would always be masqueraded as their nanny. It soon became clear that money would be no object and that his employer's family and staff would soon be moving to Spain where they had purchased a magnificent villa. It was to become my home, where I would live with the family, all expenses paid.

While the arrangement was not entirely my own choice (to this day I don't know what would have happened had I refused), I was satisfied with it. I was living life in the lap of luxury, and I was being paid a small fortune. Plus, I no longer had to work double shifts to make ends meet. The children were exceptionally well-behaved and affectionate. What was there not to like?

In fact, by far the best thing about my new life was the love I found within that family. It was something I had never experienced before. I got the impression that Mr and Mrs Nader cared for each other deeply, and although Harmony and Max had been deprived of normal parental attention, both parents doted on them. Anyway, it was to my benefit as both children showered me with affection.

Abdul had been with the Naders for two years and had been detailed to show me around and generally help settle me in. He was kind and gentle and it wasn't long before we were spending as much of our free time together as we could. Harmony and Max soon caught on and teased us about it, but I don't think Mr and Mrs Nader were aware of our budding relationship.

One day at Abdul's suggestion I'd arranged for them to meet with his young cousins, Luis and Ahmed. Little Ahmed was the younger of the two, so he was naturally friendlier with Max than Harmony, and I still tremble recalling how the poor boy suffered for it. But Harmony got on equally well with Luis. They were all on cloud nine!

The sound of hushed conversations in the ward interrupted my musings. The room was dimly lit, and it took me almost a minute to focus my cloudy vision on the hands of the wall clock, which showed half past midnight. As the sound of approaching footsteps grew closer, compelled by my instinct for self-preservation my eyes alighted on a disposable syringe lying on my side table.

My restricted movement prevented me from reaching it in time, and the intruder was already walking through the door. Every passing second of my helplessness was accompanied by pangs of loathing. But while I couldn't defend myself, he made no movement to attack me. He just stood observing me, shrouded in the shadows. My voice trembled as I broke the silence: "Who sent you? Are you here to put an end to me?"

Stepping out of the darkness, the man shook his head. "I'm

sorry! I didn't mean to startle you. Allow me to introduce myself."

But before he could, I felt a hint of recognition. It wasn't his features, still obscured by the semi-darkness, but his voice that jogged my memory. Or it could have been the silhouette of a turban.

He stepped forward and extended his hand. "My name is Chandrit Singh. Please, excuse my lack of regard for visiting hours. Dr Maria has been extremely protective of you and wouldn't let me see you. I'm afraid I had to pull some strings to get here today. You should know I work for the same employer as you."

His name had stirred a faint memory and, yes, it was a voice I clearly recognised, overheard in conversations at Villa Harmony, often intervening in verbal battles between Mr and Mrs Nader. Reluctantly, I accepted his handshake. His eyes lit up. "How are you, Miss Behrooz?"

"You can call me Nina. Much better, the doctors tell me. I think I know you? You seem familiar."

For a moment, he remained silent, and then the same concerned expression returned. "No, no, I'm sure we've never met. Are you having trouble recalling things?"

He picked up my medical notes from the foot of the bed and appeared fascinated. "Your GCS score is thirteen – unlike any comatose case I've seen before. Remarkable actually."

My initial distrust returned. He was so polite it sent a shudder down my spine. Instead of replying, I shut my eyes and turned my face away.

Noticing this, he brought his hands together and eyed me attentively with that same look of concern. He had quite the bedside manner. "Nina, I think you may be getting your memories back – and, yes, there is a possibility you've seen me before."

It felt like he was trying to coax me, like a child, back into my comfort zone.

"I'm not exactly a public figure, but my work as a doctor and surgeon has attracted some public interest. It is possible you may have seen me on the news." There was a hint of pride in his voice. "I run a hospital on the ship *Aphrodite,* perhaps, you recall it?"

He went on with false modesty, "Though I am only a cosmetic surgeon, the ship is quite a wonder . . ."

His voice trailed off as he registered the look of horror on my face. The truth had dawned on me – I *had* seen this man before. However, he had been far too busy that day to remember me.

"Dr Singh, I think it's more likely you don't recall we met a year ago when I brought Max Nader to your ship," I said. I felt the exertion making me weaker by the second. "But I know very well why it has slipped your mind."

It had been Max's idea that I should take him to the *Aphrodite* when he'd fallen down a banister and injured his head. He'd heard about the floating hospital from his father, and in his mind, he thought it would be fun. But what happened on that innocent visit had cost him his childhood and probably his friend's life. I knew Abdul had never stopped blaming me for it, but there was nothing he or I could do about it. Ahmed was from a poor family and, frankly, no one cared.

One of the nurses had fixed up Max's head wound and we were making our way off the ship when we saw a motorboat pull up alongside the *Aphrodite*. I thought nothing of it. But when I witnessed a group of frightened young children – six or seven of them – being marshalled on deck, herded together like animals, and then taken below I realised something was terribly wrong. Why were they there at all? What did they have to do with the business of conducting eye surgery and cosmetic procedures?

It was then that I noticed little Ahmed had become separated from us. I called his name over and over but there was no sign of him. That was when I knew that he had somehow become swept up with the other children or, God forbid, gone overboard. Max was inconsolable as my attempts to enlist the help of the crew came to nothing. All I was able to get was an assurance from the captain that, should little Ahmed be found, they would notify me immediately. That was the last we ever heard. Presumed lost at sea. Don't ask me how such a thing could happen. I have no answer to that.

As my story spilled out, Singh's face grew paler. "My God!"

he blurted. "I had no idea, that's terrible – none of that was meant for your or the boy's eyes. I understand your revulsion, but I wasn't involved in any of that. Nor am I now. I simply conduct my side of the business. Everything else is managed and carried out by Henri himself!"

It was an effort to raise my voice, but my outrage was real enough. "You're not involved? You're covering it up! Do you not realise what effect witnessing those poor children being herded around like cattle had on Max? Do you not realise the trauma he has suffered as a result?"

The promising new life I had built with Abdul had crumbled that day. How had I not seen it coming? Abdul had warned me often enough. Everything about the way I had been recruited by the Naders had been bizarre. Since childhood, I had lived in a state of survival, and I'd failed to see the danger signs when they were staring me in the face.

Singh hung his head in shame, yet he still did not leave.

"Nina, calm down, please," he urged. "You must not get stressed while you are in this condition."

"Then leave me alone!" I said as forcefully as I could, "There is nothing more for us to talk about. Whatever you have to say, I don't want to hear it!"

But he was undeterred. "Nina, you must listen to me. You have no choice. We need to work together if you want to get out of this. You must know your life is in danger?"

The urgency in his voice got my attention. "So what – and why? Anyway, why does it concern you?"

"It's everyone's concern," he insisted. "You must see the seriousness of your position, especially in your current state." Lowering his voice, he moved closer to me.

"Listen, please, I haven't told you everything. The day you got shot, Harmony Nader went missing." He took a deep breath. "And she still hasn't been found."

My breath caught in my throat. That's not how it was supposed to happen. First, Max, and now, my poor baby girl was suffering for my recklessness. Harmony had suffered enough already. I was the one who had nursed her through her illness, and she had come to depend on me. Others had warned me against arranging secret meetings for her to play with Abdul's cousins, but watching her beautiful, bright smile fade away in the endless hours of her isolation had persuaded me to go ahead.

Singh seemed to sense that he was getting through to me at last. "Do you remember how you got shot?"

"Protecting her." The answer came mechanically.

"Do you remember who shot you?"

This was what he'd come for, I realised. This is what he needed to know. Dr Maria had never attempted to make me recall that day, and I had carefully avoided doing so. Of all the painful memories I had been enduring, this was the worst. Resigned, I replied, "I can't."

Dr Singh buried his face in his hands. "Take your time. Start slowly with how the day began." He eased away from my bed and settled in a chair. in the corner of the room. I closed my eyes and fumbled through the memories of that day. The events leading up to the shot returned vividly.

When I told Harmony we were going to meet Luis she had been exhilarated. "Nina, I want to wear that pretty, blue floral dress," she had whispered conspiratorially, even though her parents were miles away. The fact that these little trips were our secret made it all the more exciting for her.

I laughed at the giddy expression on her face. "Don't be silly, Harmony. We don't want to draw attention to ourselves."

She pouted before her face lit up as she decided to wear her fancy hair clip instead. In truth, I was just as excited to be seeing Abdul. Despite both working at the villa, we had been finding it hard to spend time alone. We had similar duties. While I was employed to guard the children, his role was to protect and keep an eye on Mrs Nader. When she wasn't there, he busied himself with household chores, menial tasks really but jobs that needed to be done, changing lightbulbs, cleaning cutlery, tidying ornaments – and especially getting things ready for when the Naders returned. He knew how they liked things better than anyone.

But he wanted to see me, too, and our sorties to the abandoned hacienda up the road had provided that opportunity.

Harmony had sat by the villa's big front gates all afternoon, waiting for Abdul's truck to pass by, and the moment it appeared she'd come running to drag me out. As we drove up to the house, I had a premonition of impending danger, but Harmony's excitement wiped it away.

Leaving her to enjoy the company of her friend, I headed for the deserted bungalow, where I found Abdul waiting for me. Secure in his arms, my apprehension faded away. When he started to undress me, I surrendered in a fit of passion. Recalling how my moans had drowned out the crunching of the leaves, how I had not been alert to the safety of the children caused me inexpressible guilt and grief.

I remember the urgent movements of my hands as I fixed myself. Before even stepping out of the building, I already dreaded what might have happened. I remember charging at the man looming over Harmony. But now, when I tried to recall his face, my memory refused to cooperate. If only I could remember who he was!

Frustrated, I opened my eyes to find Dr Singh staring at me intently. He had returned to the side of my bed. "I can't remember!" I cried out hopelessly.

"Was it someone you know?" There was a hint of concern in his voice.

"I just said I can't remember!" Embarrassed and tearful, I turned away but instead of urging me on as I expected, he offered me a handkerchief and a glass of water. Reluctantly, I accepted.

I changed my approach. "Why are you getting involved in all this anyway? I thought you'd be running in the opposite direction."

He let out an exhausted sigh. "What I'm about to tell you, you must not repeat to anyone."

"I can't promise that if it might help to find Harmony."

He nodded. So far so good.

"As I said, we're both in the same place. You can trust me." He took another deep breath. "As it happens, you're right, I am already up to my neck in all this. In fact, I fear that I may have played a pivotal role in Harmony's disappearance."

At this confession, I abandoned any pretence of cordiality. "What do you mean?"

"Nina, you're not the only one who decided to bring one of the Nader children to the ship for treatment."

My voice was barely a whisper. "What happened to her?"

"She was shot. Her clavicle was shattered, and I had to perform surgery to remove the bullet. The girl stayed with me until she recovered. Then, after a few days, she disappeared from right under my nose," he went on hurriedly, "but I have alibis which confirm I had nothing to do with her abduction. She was brought to me by an acquaintance, a man I had met shortly before, who said he'd found her unconscious by the roadside." Before I could ask who that acquaintance was, Singh held up his hand to finish his story. "You need to understand that this man was an acquaintance. Despite not knowing him for long, rightly or wrongly I took him at his word. Frankly, I was more concerned with Harmony's injury and how to treat it, than how she came to be there.

"However, since then some odd things have come to light which have made me reconsider. When he brought the girl to me, he told me that he had never met her before, but we now know he had already met the Naders earlier at the villa.

"Then after the girl went missing, so did Mrs Nader. She has since been found and has reported to the police that this same man had beaten her up. It's all over the news. His name is Gerald Irving. Does the name ring a bell?"

His name was enough to bring all the missing pieces of the puzzle together – wrestling the man to the ground, Harmony's frantic cries, the sound of the gunshot, the blood draining from my body.

As the memories came flooding back, the beeping of my heart monitor grew rapid. The worst thing about recovering this lost memory was knowing I was the one responsible for her getting shot. Instead of protecting her, my selfishness had endangered her young life.

"Now I remember everything. Gerald Irving kidnapped her and he's the one who shot us." Despite my erratic heartbeat, the words came out steadily.

"Are – are you sure?" Dr Singh eyed me doubtfully. "Try to recall everything slowly. Chaotic events of this nature often lead to confusion. I see you're not feeling well. I can visit you later if you'd prefer."

"There's no need for that," I said firmly. "Gerald Irving had come to the villa with his family and they'd taken Harmony out for dinner. I wanted to go with them, but they wouldn't let me. This man has the strangest obsession with both mother and daughter. I am quite positive he shot her and must have returned to kidnap her later."

"So you say, but it seems unlikely that would have happened. After all, he returned to London the very next day, just as he'd said he would. He was the one who brought her in for treatment in the first place. And he couldn't have shot her, because Harmony actually expressed gratitude towards him when she regained consciousness. She expressed her concern about you as well."

"Did she say who did shoot her?"

"No. She either didn't know or didn't say."

"Do you not find it likely that whoever shot her would have needed to keep her quiet? Cowardly men are quick to take it out on those less powerful. He shot her, panicked, and brought her to you instead of taking her to a hospital. Unfortunately, you were foolish enough to believe him. Later, he could easily have arranged for someone else to kidnap her from the ship. That is my explanation, take it or leave it." The alternative was too appalling to contemplate.

Singh stayed silent, pondering my theory before venturing into a new line of questioning. "How was he able to attack the girl when she was under your protection? Isn't the villa heavily guarded?"

The doctor had been honest with me about his failures, so I thought it fair to do the same. "It is. We went for a walk and I got distracted."

"Then it appears we both played our part in her abduction," he said sadly.

I didn't need to be reminded. I knew I had lied but what

else could I do? Meanwhile, Singh was lost in his own thoughts. Finally, he said: "There's something else. I never told the Naders that Harmony had been on the ship."

For once he'd said something that shocked me. "Why? They must have been desperate to know where she was."

"The girl wouldn't let me," he answered. "When she recovered from the anaesthetic, I told her I was going to call them and explained what had happened. She became very agitated and begged me not to. It wasn't good for her to get upset so I agreed to leave it for a while. By the time the Naders got back she'd gone. God knows where. After that, I simply couldn't summon up the courage to say anything. It was cowardly I know, but I reasoned that it didn't matter. If she'd been kidnapped it made no difference where from. So, I never told them. It's too late now."

"That was stupid of you," I said. But he was right. What difference did it make? None. It was as it was.

He seemed to pull himself together and went on. "Then, about a month ago, I got the strangest call from this man Irving. He wanted to know if I had any friends in Johannesburg. I gave him a name. I have no idea why he wanted it."

I stayed silent as he continued his rambling. "God, I could have prevented all of this. Mr Nader will never trust me again. Do you realise what this means for me, for us if he finds out? He will hunt us down like chickens in a coop." His words were alarming but rang true.

He went on, more business-like than before.

"Dr Maria is adamant about keeping your presence a secret until you are fully recovered, quite reasonably so, given your condition. However, if anyone comes sniffing, you must keep your silence."

"Of course, I understand," I replied, "I can barely defend myself now, and no one would shed a tear if I stopped breathing."

Jake hadn't approached me just for my fighting skills. I was the perfect candidate because, just as importantly, I was disposable. Quite literally, if anything happened to me, no one would know or care.

"Nina!" Singh said, "You are the only witness to what happened. So, you see, we are in this together, you and I – we are the only ones who know the truth."

But he was wrong. He hadn't been there with me when the shot was fired.

I lay back against the pillow, completely drained of any strength as the curtains of sleep closed in on me. But I resisted. *Please*, I thought, *no more darkness*.

As my consciousness ebbed away, Singh's voice reached me through a cloud of nothingness. "You're not alone, Nina, remember Harmony still needs you."

CHAPTER FOURTEEN

Blanche Irving

Your best friend's wedding is supposed to be a memorable occasion, but I'd usually found the events leading up to it were more exciting than the day itself. That is until Veronica's big day turned into the best day of my life. Or so it seemed at the time.

To begin with, her day was no exception. Mind you, weddings for me were always tough given my single status, and here I was again, sitting alone at the bar, fighting the urge to yawn . . . or get drunk.

When I'd found out that I would be the only single guest at the wedding, I'd begged Veronica to forego the cursed tradition of the bouquet toss. "Blanche, honey, has no one ever told you how absolutely gorgeous you are? Guys would line up for you! Just keep that smile on your face!" But her attempts at flattery were so obvious that I'd just thrown in the towel and given up on the night.

Joanne, my sister, always remarked that I would attract a lot more men if I could only bring myself to look more approachable. She said I went about with a red traffic light on my head. I wonder what she'd say now if she could see me idly sitting at the open bar nursing a bottle of Chardonnay on my own.

"Did your platonic plus-one ditch you, too?" I was startled by the voice at my shoulder, but the remark couldn't have been meant for anyone else.

"I look that desperate, do I?" I replied, not even bothering to look up.

"No, not at all. Just looking for some common ground." Now I looked up. His ocean-blue eyes were lingering over me. "Guess I chose the wrong girl."

I couldn't help laughing. He sounded slightly tipsy. His

complexion was almost too pale but it was offset by his sandy hair and angular features

"Smooth," I said, "I've never had an encounter with a man who flirts whilst admitting they've been blown out."

"Is that what I'm doing?" His face scrunched up in genuine confusion. "The former or latter?"

Adorable, I thought. "The latter, of course," I replied. He had the perfect balance of humility and confidence, neither too overwhelming.

"By the way, I'm Gerald Irving, the groom's best man. Met him in college."

"I'm Blanche Dougray, chief bridesmaid. Met the bride in kindergarten."

"Well, what a cliché we are," he drawled while topping up my glass. "So, tell me about yourself."

"There's not much to tell. I have a degree in sociology. My mother grew up in France, but my dad is from London. Eldest among my four younger sisters. They were a handful growing up." I went on reciting my boring story without taking a breath. Later, I discovered to my pleasant surprise that he'd remembered every word.

Joanne always got caught up with men twice her age. Our parents had not been entirely neglectful until their separation, but after my mother moved back to her village, things went off the rails pretty quickly. I knew I had a tendency to be overbearing with my sisters, but someone had to play the part of the missing parent. I had no choice but to suppress my own romantic nature and become the fearless heroine they needed me to be.

"What do you like to do for entertainment?" he asked.

There must have been something about his eyes that made me search frantically for anything remotely interesting to say. Letting out a nervous laugh, I replied, "Decorate stuff." He raised his brows quizzically. I went on, gesturing around me. "Organising events. This wedding décor is all mine."

He turned to take in the arched entrance lined with blossoming trees, flickering fairy lights, and the silver candelabra overhead with its suspended floral centrepiece. His expression seemed perfectly in tune with the whimsy of our encounter. "It's breathtaking, you have a gift."

His eyes were reeling me in. I felt my cheeks flush as I caught a whiff of the woody fragrance he wore, with its musky undertones. I pulled myself together. "Thank you. Well, enough about me. Tell me about you."

"I grew up in London. Work at a publishing house. Mainly involved with copywriting services." His answer was more rehearsed and precise than mine. Something held me back from probing further and, anyway, I didn't want to upset the magic of the moment.

So, I simply nodded and he quickly diverted attention away from himself. "William will break down during his toast. Just wait for it. Right when he gets to the part where Veronica knocked down that display in his supermarket."

"No way. The man's hard as steel."

"Not when it comes to Veronica knocking down his precious displays, he's not. Want to bet?"

"Sure." The bet was so silly I couldn't help giggling.

The night went on full of intoxicating laughter, flirtatious remarks, and the most romantic kiss under the twinkling lights. And he was right about William.

For me, that was it. We shacked up in Paris like newlyweds on honeymoon until the day I got pregnant with Nikki. When Gerald asked me to marry him, I didn't need to be asked twice.

His love for me was enthralling to say the least. It had an all-consuming quality that took me to the top of the world. He made me feel wanted, seen. All those years of setting an example to my younger siblings had suppressed my own wants and needs. Now, for the first time, I was able to revel in being adored.

But back then, it didn't occur to me how little I knew about this man.

It first dawned on me when he showed me the meagre list of his invitations to our wedding. It led to our first real argument. That's when he told me about the tragic demise of his parents in a car crash, how he had few living relatives, and that he didn't get on with most of them. The quarrel had left me feeling guilty, but at least I understood why I needed to tread carefully when matters concerning his family came up.

It didn't take long before any conversation with him was like treading on eggshells. Everything he told me about himself contradicted what others had told me about him. Jim wasn't his college friend. When I invited them over for a barbecue, Veronica said they were work friends. When I queried that with Gerald, he reprimanded me for arguing in front of his friends over such an insignificant detail and I was forced to apologise. I could never understand how someone could forget where they first met a friend.

His true demons first showed up when I invited his cousin Michelle over for a family dinner. I have never forgotten the expression on his face when he got home to find her sitting at our dining table. He looked like he'd seen a ghost. Astonishingly, this was only on his part, for Michelle threw her arms around him, clearly delighted. She later told me how close they had been as children, often sharing the same room when he had stayed with her family.

"No, we weren't," he had argued later after she'd left.

"How come you lived under the same roof and never grew close?" Casually pouring tea, I had no idea how this would lead to an incident that I would find hard to forget.

"We barely lived under the same roof. They only moved back to London after my parents died. I spent a short time with them, but as soon as I was able, I moved out." I could sense his barely concealed rage but couldn't understand why. "Anyway, I don't want us getting friendly with that family."

I simply didn't understand. "What's so bad about inviting her over for dinner if she's in town? Is there something wrong with her? Honestly, Gerry, I know so little about you that sometimes it feels like I'm living with a stranger!"

"There's nothing wrong with her! Aren't I enough for you?"

I was beginning to feel this was all my fault. "Gerry, please, surely you can be honest with me. I know you're hiding something. I'm just asking you to trust me – to communicate with me, that's all I want. You can't expect me to settle for 'just because' all the time. This is important to me. I value family relationships, our relationship." But the clench of his jaw said it all.

"Wouldn't it be nice if Nikki had an aunt to look after her sometimes?" I persisted. "My family is miles away."

His answer came back, cold and determined. "I don't want to talk about this any further." I knew he was hiding some truth he didn't want me to share.

"Please, Gerry," I took his trembling hand in both of mine, "Just throw me a crumb?"

He turned on me, his features contorted. "Why can't you fucking take me at my word?" His fist came down on his mug, smashing it to pieces.

I stood before him, shuddering with fear and when I tried to remove the shards of my favourite mug from his bleeding hand, he snatched it away, shoved me aside roughly and escaped slamming the door behind him. I was terrified. Terrified of whatever it was I didn't know. Terrified of him.

Hours later, he would appear as if nothing had happened. After years of this, I had come to realise he must be in some kind of denial – but, then again, he treated me to my favourite meals, praised my successes, sympathised when things went wrong and complimented me on my appearance. It was as if he was the only person I'd ever known, male or female, who truly understood me.

Mostly he managed to conceal his anger from Nikki and Paula. It was as if the beast in him didn't exist when he was in their presence – which was more than I could say for my own parents.

Eventually, I learnt to recognise his trigger points and avoid them. Though I knew little about the human mind, I came to believe his behaviour must have been linked to some deeply damaging event in his past. There were days when he was so emotionally distant that he was like a total stranger.

Sometimes he would even talk in the third person. "Can you promise me that Gerald won't hear about this?" he would say.

This got worse as his dependence on alcohol increased, although ironically, it was on these occasions I often learnt more about his past.

"Yes, of course, you have my word." I had to struggle not to smile at how ingenuous that sounded.

"Well, I'm only telling you because you understand. You've been there and know what it's like. Jack and Hazel always argued over money. Their poor kid had to go without all the time."

Mostly, I let him ramble, but when he paused to listen, I obliged. "That's terrible. Why have children in the first place if you can't provide for them, right?"

"Right. it deeply scars them," he gestured animatedly, his speech composed rather than slurred, "it can totally destroy their self-esteem."

"Parents often don't realise the consequences of their thoughtlessness and lack of control," I added.

Nodding thoughtfully at my every word, he raised his eyes to meet mine with a warm smile. "But you're a good mother."

For a moment, his words bridged the distance between us. "And you're a good father," I said. But my words sent him back into his shell.

"No. I'm not."

Our temporary truce was broken when he started struggling financially. By then he had borrowed some money to set up his own business. It was going well and, on the strength of it, we moved into our house in Mayfield. But the stress got to him. His income was barely enough to pay off his debts, let alone cover the mortgage and raise our two daughters. Night after night he would come home drunk and, when I tried to calm him, he would lose his temper and either hide away or lash out at me. Or both.

When my attempts at reconciliation failed, I started to withdraw into myself. As a girl who grew up with zero praise for my efforts, I was used to making myself inconspicuous – it was as if the clock had been put back. Even when things began to ease at work and his outbursts became less frequent, the wedge between us was widening. I was being destroyed but, instead of crying,

I toughened up for my girls, just like I had learned to do for my sisters.

By the time he finally acknowledged what was happening to us, it was already too late. However, for the sake of our daughters I accepted his attempts to make amends. With a practised smile, I planned our short vacation in Spain naively thinking it might help bring us all together. How could I have known it would cause our lives to take an even more disastrous turn for the worse?

The holiday had been going relatively cheerily, there was even some excitement when we were told we were visiting a wealthy couple in the hills. I felt no apprehension, let alone concern. Not until that TV screen came to life and Oriole Nader's image consumed me.

I felt ill at ease as I caught myself unconsciously biting my lip. Something odd was happening to me and, out of curiosity, my eyes turned to Gerald. I had never seen him so transfixed, except once – only once – when he'd looked at me under that sparkling chandelier the first time we'd met.

My jealousy was as fleeting as the expression on his face. Despite his unpredictable behaviour, I could never have foreseen his infidelity. There was no justification for it. No matter how I tried, I couldn't forgive him for humiliating me so cruelly.

After years of isolation, I had once asked him whether we might experiment with an open marriage. "Should we try seeing other people?" I had asked.

His expression gave away the sense of betrayal he'd felt. "How could you? I trusted you!" The hurt in his voice was so unbearable that I immediately regretted my remark.

"It was just a thought, Gerald. Our marriage is already in tatters. It's not as if I mean anything by it."

"My family means everything to me. You mean the world to me. Do you not love me anymore?" His voice was shaking, and he looked like a vulnerable child.

"No, no. Look, if you're willing to work on things, then so am I. But something has to change, doesn't it?"

"Don't you love me?" he insisted, shaking me violently,

urging me to say 'yes'. But I couldn't.

In tears, he walked away only to return hours later with hatred brimming in his eyes. "I trusted you. You disgust me."

After feeding me all those lies he had walked out on me.

* * *

When she'd heard the loud banging on our front door, it was Paula who had let the policeman in. He'd looked at me with sympathy when I told him the truth – that I had no idea where Gerald was. He stood there, seemingly undecided about what he might do or say next. Not knowing what he expected of me, I asked him in.

That was when I first heard the story of Gerald's affair. My feeling of betrayal was quickly followed by fury that he would do such a thing without a thought for the effect it might have on our girls.

My anger grew with every sordid detail. I knew my husband's mood swings only too well but now it felt as if I had been living with a monster for all those years. Why had I endured all that suffering? To what end? I felt used and discarded.

Well, if he could hurt Oriole, then it stood to reason he could do the same to us. There was a time when I would have been the first to vouch for his innocence. Indeed, that was my initial intention when Nikki dragged me into the living room with tears streaming down her face.

She'd grabbed the TV remote to turn up the volume as I watched, horrified.

"Gerald Irving, the man responsible for the abduction of Harmony Nader and her mother, Oriole, has surrendered to the police."

Taking Nikki into my arms, my hurt turned to hatred. Hatred mixed with relief as it finally dawned on me that a new life, whatever it might bring, lay ahead.

CHAPTER FIFTEEN

Oriole Nader

I could barely make out the muffled schemes and secrets being discussed behind closed doors in the next room – apparently too 'sensitive' for my ears.

After eleven years of living with him, I'd hoped that Henri might have come to trust and confide in me, but to him outward appearances were everything and he wasn't going to change for my sake.

I had learnt too little, too late. My worries and occasional challenges concerning his business activities had always fallen on deaf ears, finally, and I suppose, inevitably, to the detriment of our marriage. After Johannesburg, I had enough evidence to give him an ultimatum but my weakness prevented me from asserting myself.

It was this same weakness that had enabled Henri to always get what he wanted, but now I had lost even the right to protest. Our goals were tragically aligned and I knew I had no choice but to cooperate, even if we were gambling with innocent lives. Not only had I turned a blind eye in the past, now I was his accomplice.

Last night, soon after I had put Max to bed, he told me he was going to hunt down Isaac and if necessary torture out of him Harmony's whereabouts. I had protested: "There is no way that kid is involved, Henri. Leave him alone, please!"

"How do you know that, honey?" he responded in his most supercilious tone of voice. "Firstly, he's Black's nephew and owes me no favours, secondly, he came back to London with that piece of shit."

"You are saying he's guilty by association – then where do you think I stand in all this, Henri?"

The argument had started with him questioning Gerald's reasons for concealing Harmony's whereabouts and quickly spiralled out of control. I think that knowing a relation of Augustus was involved had frightened him. Augustus was possibly the only man who Henri had ever feared – and envied. Even knowing he was dead, Henri was still obsessed with the man.

"Anyway, what makes you think Isaac could help us?" I challenged, "I doubt whether Isaac has any idea of Gerald Irving's true nature. It just doesn't figure."

Henri showed no signs of remorse. "The kid's motives don't concern us, Oriole. Perhaps he wants to avenge his uncle's death, who knows?"

"Can you ever, just for once, trust my judgment?"

"Why would I?" he replied angrily, "you were the one who trusted Gerald Irving, for God's sake! You don't know these people like I do."

"Yes, it takes one to know one." Henri had hit a nerve, and my words stung him exactly as I had intended. But he was good at repressing his anger.

"Look, Oriole, just think about this for a moment. What were the chances of that man finding you at the Hope for Black headquarters? It was just too much of a coincidence. He was putting his life at risk – for what, just because he fancied you? Look, Gerald surrenders, my men return badly hurt and the young Black kid goes missing. For God's sake – and on top of all that, Harmony disappears! Can't you see, it's a calculated plot against me and my family?"

"Our family, Henri!" I was shouting now. "Gerald's case is completely different. I know better than anyone that there is something seriously wrong with him. God knows I suffered the consequences." I rolled up my sleeve to display the red and purple bruises. "So, just remember that before you call me out on that again!"

He was silent for a moment and then made a clumsy attempt to cup my face. I pushed his hands away, exasperated. "Henri, let the police take care of it. Promise me, you won't torture Isaac. He may have got caught up in all this, but he's not part of the problem, I promise."

Before he could respond his mobile rang and, as was his habit, he walked away from me to take the call. I knew in his mind he had already dismissed what I'd said and there was no way I was going to change his mind. As he reached the door, he cupped his hand over the phone.

"For Christ's sake, Oriole, the kid left his life behind in Joburg and moved six thousand miles to be with your former lover! Connect the dots, will you?" With that he went out into the hallway, shutting the door behind him.

Another row had finished with him having the last word. Every lover I had ever taken had let me down, even Augustus although that wasn't his fault. But my experience with Gerald had been the worst. Yet, despite it all, I couldn't forget that sweet smile. But then, don't men always let us down?

* * *

"Mummy, have you taken your painkiller?" Max was awake, standing at the bedroom door. His voice brought me back to reality. Max was insightful and sensitive, in fact, both my children were too mature for their age and had mastered skills that much older children could only dream of. I knew Max felt devastated by his sister's disappearance and my heart ached to see him suffer.

"Yes, baby, come back to bed." I took him by the hand and let him back into his room where I made a blanket fortress. He joined me under it.

"Mummy missed you so much," I said, holding his tiny frame in my arms. It was the only source of comfort I had.

"I missed you too, Mummy and I miss Harmony. I was very lonely without you. Daddy told me that Nina wasn't feeling well either. I miss her, too."

"She's getting better now, darling. When Daddy brings Harmony back, we'll visit her at the hospital. Okay?" In fact, I had no idea where Nina was, or Abdul for that matter, who seemed to have disappeared as well.

Max tightened his arms around me. "Mummy, Harmony will come back to us. She's safe, I just know it." The responsibility of comforting his mother was hard on the little boy, but he did a better job of it than his father ever could.

Hugging Max could only do so much to alleviate the pain of losing my daughter. Call it maternal instinct, but I couldn't shake off the feeling that Harmony's abduction was linked to Henri's precarious business dealings.

Although Gerald had refused to say where he was keeping her, there was no doubt in my mind he had her. Whether or not he and Henri were working together, I had no idea, but Gerald had as good as confessed in those last awful moments of our relationship.

My naïveté may have left me battered and bruised but it also afforded me some precious time. Foolishly, I had taken Gerald at his word, believing all his lies – even shedding tears for him. I now see that after the frustration of all those years with Henri, desperation had led me to make an appalling mistake that had endangered me and, unforgivably, my daughter, too.

Meanwhile, she was in God knows what condition.

* * *

My suspicions were first aroused when Gerald started muttering my daughter's name in his sleep, yet I never thought for a moment he meant me any harm. How could I have been so stupid? Like a silly teenager, I had seen him as my knight in shining armour. Now he had become my enemy.

I had my own demons, too. Whenever I saw a flicker of hope of getting my daughter safely back in my arms, my past caught up with me. Prior to my escape, my remorse had haunted me all night. When my cries had awakened him and he tenderly took me in his arms, it was my conscience that was tormenting me. He deserved the truth, I'd thought. The man had been willing to lay down his life for me, surely, he would understand.

Gerald had freely given me the reins, respected my decisions, and acknowledged my abilities. For the first time in my life, I wasn't pampered or held back. In him, I had finally found a partner who looked out for me whilst, at the same time, treating me with respect.

When I admitted my sins to him, I had expected his anger, not disdain. "Let me go!" he'd said and as he spat out those words my veneer of calm self-sufficiency evaporated. How selfish, I thought, that I had spent our crusade together looking out for myself with no regard for him – the loss of his family, his health, or his happiness. But it was too late. The hatred in his eyes told me that.

Surely, I could make him change his mind? I clung tightly to his arm. "No, Gerald, you must listen to me."

"I told you to let go, didn't I?" To my surprise, his voice no longer held the edge, nor was his body trembling with rage. The anguish from a few moments ago was replaced by calm. Tentatively, I raised my palm to his face.

"Gerald, I . . . I can't do this without you, not anymore." I was shedding my façade of independence layer by layer, making myself vulnerable before him. "Can't you see, I love you?"

The words he had been so desperate to hear for so long were met with a sneer, but his temper had subsided and it gave me the strength to go on. "I was wrong in believing that I was bound to Henri for life. Lately, I've felt more like a hostage than his wife, until you came along, and saved me."

Gerald freed himself from my grip and settled back on the bed. Everything about his attitude seemed bizarre, but then, he had surprised me before. When I hesitated, he urged me on. "Go on," he said, his voice devoid of any emotion.

"Everyone admires me, Gerald, even Henri. He has always treated me like a possession, a trophy on a pedestal. Whatever I may have done, I did it for my daughter, but I was never Henri's accomplice. The way I was raised . . . you see, when my parents were exiled from my native land, I was expected to turn a blind eye to things far more horrible than . . ."

His raised eyebrows made me change my tack mid-sentence.

"You are the first person who saw past a pretty face and loved me for who I am."

He thought for a moment, staring at the end of the bed. Then he looked me straight in the eyes. "You're mistaken there, not about the pretty face, I'll give you that." His rage flared up, but he looked composed. "Why are you so full of yourself? Gerald has a family he dearly loves. He never loved you. The fool was deceived by your beauty." I managed a smile. "This is not funny, Gerald, please, don't joke!" But my plea fell on deaf ears.

"No day goes by when he doesn't yearn to hold his daughters in his arms again. He suffers, just because of you, knowing that his wife will refuse to take him back."

His voice was full of anguish but his callous words still sounded like a hoax. Had he been honest I wouldn't have felt so offended. But he was playing the fool, taking advantage, mocking me. I said: "What the hell is wrong with you?"

"What the hell is wrong with me? What's wrong with you?" He stepped away from the bed, towering over me. I felt defenceless in his overbearing presence. There was no way I could have anticipated what was coming next, but the look in his eyes was enough to tell me I should have let him go when he had given me the chance.

"You, despicable, manipulative woman! You think you can get away with everything? A child has died to save your daughter! How dare you flaunt your virtue in front of me?"

"Gerald, can't you see you've twisted my words in your mind?" I spoke as tentatively as I could.

"How do you think Harmony would feel if she knew? She's a good kid. No wonder she wanted to escape the prison you'd kept her in!"

His words made little sense, but I couldn't disregard his wild accusation and claims. "She said that? When you took her out, she said that?"

There was a prolonged silence of hesitation before he responded. "When she was shot. The poor child was bleeding so profusely, yet she couldn't rely on her own parents to take care of her."

The ground shifted underneath my feet. There was no humour in his voice, only cold, hard bluntness. His eyes revealed the truth, even if his mouth spouted nonsense. Without thinking, I grabbed a knife from the bedside table, the same knife I had used to peel fruit for him an hour ago.

"Where is my daughter?"

"She shouldn't even be with you. Doesn't it concern you that she's terrified of you both?" Surprisingly, his voice sounded sympathetic, but I could only see red.

"What are you? A bloody vigilante?" Holding the knife against him, I angrily demanded, "You say you shot her! Where are you keeping her? Tell me, now!"

"Put that thing away, woman. Gerald didn't shoot her, he'll tell you."

All my fear had dissipated. "Gerald, for God's sake, tell me the truth, where are you keeping my daughter? I'm her mother!"

"Put away that knife. I won't be held responsible if you try to hurt him."

"This is my last warning, Gerald. Where is Harmony?" I spoke the words through clenched teeth.

Instead of replying, he laughed in my face. Due to my small frame, this was not the first time I had met with intimidation, but desperation had never got the better of me. Without thinking twice, I lunged at him with the knife. He knocked it out of my hand easily and grabbed me around the waist.

Wriggling out of his grip, I scrambled for the weapon which had slid under the bed. My fingers had barely wrapped around the hilt when he wrestled me to the ground. My second attack was thwarted when he pinned my hands above my head, snatching the knife out of my hand. He was out of control and his fists came down on me in a fit of rage. With every assault, his voice bellowed through the night, "I told you not to hurt him!"

After battering me into semi-consciousness, he had gone back to sleep without a care in the world. "Leave before Gerald wakes up," he had said nonchalantly. "You look terrible. He'd be upset if he sees you like that."

And so, I did. My bruised, wounded body had kept me from moving very far and he soon found me at the pharmacy around the corner from the motel. The pharmacist had sold me a first-aid kit and was now phoning the police. Gerald approached me in sheep's clothing. "Oriole, where have you been, I was worried sick!"

His relief was replaced by horror as he saw the scars he had left me with. But by now I was terrified of him and recoiled.

"Stay away from me!"

The commotion was now attracting the attention of others in the store. A middle-aged, muscular man came to my rescue. "Is this guy bothering you?"

"Yes," I answered with no hesitation.

"The cops are on their way," the pharmacist said, "they'll be here shortly."

The look of anguish on Gerald's face was excruciating. I could hear the sound of police sirens. His eyes were begging me to intervene on his behalf as he was dragged away and it took all my remaining self-control to keep from running in the other direction.

"They will need to talk to you," said the pharmacist.

"Thank you, I appreciate what you have done but I really have to go now, I'm sorry." I picked up my first aid kit and he followed as I staggered towards the exit.

"Hey, ma'am, wait! Look, I'm not going to hurt you. We're in public, right?" Instead of trying to physically restrain me, he came after me at a slow pace, reasoning with me in a soothing voice. "Calm down, please, let me drop you at a hospital, okay?"

"No, not a hospital." I knew I needed medical attention urgently and considered visiting Diopka. But I knew if he saw me in that condition, he would've given me up to Henri without thinking twice.

"Let me give you a ride or book you a cab, at least," the pharmacist pressed on. "You're not safe. You walk out of here, and that guy will hunt you down again. Wouldn't want you going to the cops, would he?" My mind was spinning, and I could barely make sense of his words. "Look," he said, "I have a six-year-old daughter. Believe me, I wouldn't do anything to hurt a woman. Let me help you, please. If I were you, I wouldn't go anywhere alone. Is there no one you trust, no one who could help get you the help you need?"

There was someone I could trust – someone who was just as caught up as I was in this bloody game. Isaac. He'd told me he was lying low, and I guessed I would find him at his apartment which I knew couldn't be far.

"No, really, thank you," I said, leaving him on the pavement outside his shop. "I have a relative nearby. I'll be okay, I promise, but thank you."

I started to walk and half run as the sound of the police sirens grew louder as they drew up to the kerb. But they couldn't drown out Gerald's last words as he shouted: "Oriole, please, come back! I love you."

How I managed to find Isaac's apartment I shall never know, but I did. I knocked and rang his doorbell.

"Isaac? It's me, Oriole. Please, let me in, I know you're in there." As I knocked again repeatedly, I realised exhaustion and pain were stopping me thinking straight. Then, in a brief flash of awareness, I realised I might be walking into a trap.

That same instant, I felt a rough hand cover my mouth with a piece of rag. I recognised the fruity smell of chloroform and, as I hit the floor, my last shred of consciousness was gone.

Later, I found myself in what looked like a hospital bed set up in a hotel suite. The room was well furnished and a vase of fragrant yellow flowers had been placed on the bedside table.

"Good morning, Mrs Nader. I hope you slept well?"

Every nerve in my body was screaming with pain but I recognised the voice instantly.

Jones let out a cheerful chuckle. "I wouldn't move if I were you. Don't worry, we will look after you."

CHAPTER SIXTEEN

Nina Behrooz

"Be careful," said a voice behind me.

"I can handle myself!" I raised my right hand, forcing my stalker to step back. The narrow aisle between the seats was making me dizzy. Or maybe I was finding the bright lights disorientating – or that I had been shot in the chest and been in a coma for so long I couldn't even count the days.

"Our seats are to the right," the voice came back, this time more insistent. I turned around and found Chandrit Singh carrying the bags, almost barging into me.

"Sorry, I just . . ." He paused and looked down at my chest reminding me of the ugly wound as if it was nothing more than a stain on my shirt. Oh, it was so much more than that and far deeper than the bullet that had caused it. It hadn't been intended for me, yet it had ripped through my skin and flesh, spreading fear and guilt in its wake.

"I think I can read the seat numbers pretty well. I haven't lost my wits, okay?" That should have been enough to put him off, but it wasn't. As I seated myself by the window, Singh stuffed our bags in the overhead locker.

He had been there throughout my recovery and, though he was a doctor with a natural inclination to help the sick and injured, I resented him.

I neither wanted nor needed assistance – it wasn't my style. I was built to look after myself, not accept help from others, even when I most needed it. How I worked was fuelled by my childhood. I saw red every time a man tried to help me, or woman for that matter.

The plane began to move.

"Here we go," Singh said. I couldn't understand why he was sitting right beside me. Why was he accompanying me on this journey at all? I was perfectly capable of conveying my story to Henri on my own.

As I noticed Singh's leg twitching nervously, I realised that I wasn't the only one feeling guilty. He was holding back on something, too, but I couldn't put my finger on what.

Nevertheless, between us I could only see one who bore the blame for this entire predicament. Me. Truthfully, nothing had felt right since I opened my eyes in that hospital. Perhaps the absence of Abdul had taken a greater toll than I'd first thought. I did miss him.

"Are you cold?" Singh asked. "Shall I call the flight attendant? I still don't think you should be travelling."

Singh kept pulling me back to reality every few seconds and I wasn't sure I wanted him to. Barely hearing his words, I turned to the window to look at the airport, desolate and vacant. I knew how it must feel.

It had taken years to find not only a safe space for myself but some people I really loved – Max and Harmony, both of whom were now suffering because of me.

Singh knew what I was thinking and just wouldn't keep quiet. "If you're wondering about Harmony, I must remind you that she disappeared under my watch. She had been safely transferred to my care, I helped her recover and then . . . well, if you want to blame someone, don't blame yourself. This entire trip is going to be a waste of your time because you have absolutely nothing to prove."

But his words were falling on deaf ears. They always did. The sounds of the struggle in the dirt and Harmony's screams as I tried to put an end to Gerald Irving's stupid interference were the last things I recalled and these vivid memories would not, could not, ever be erased.

There was something else. Why hadn't Abdul reached out to me? Didn't he care whether I was alive or dead? Or would he never forgive me for little Ahmed's disappearance? The question made my blood run cold and the worst part was I had no one to confide in. I was certainly not going share my grief with Singh, who I was now fully aware had his own part in the tragedy to cope with.

"I don't need consoling," I finally told him. "The child is gone and this is no time to play hot potato with who is to blame. It's better we talk to Henri and see what he has to say about it all."

"You'll lose your job," he stated.

"Don't you get it? I don't give two shits about my job! I need Harmony to be safe and sound. She's been through a lot. More than you can imagine."

"And what about you?" Singh insisted. "Whoever has the girl might well be looking for you. You're a person of interest, Nina. Telling the truth might get you out of the frying pan but it could put you straight back into the fire." Singh pressed the button located above his seat and a minute later a tall blonde flight attendant approached, wearing the brightest smile.

"May I have a blanket and a glass of water, please?" Singh requested politely. As he reached for a magazine from the seat pouch in front of him, I wondered what I could tell him, anyway? That it was I who encouraged Harmony to meet with Luis? That I had left a young girl playing with him alone because I had something more important to do?

The plane journey was agony. It felt as if the skin was being pulled off my wound, which had just started to heal. As the nails dug deeper, the moments and memories of that day replayed themselves over and over in my mind.

It didn't seem long before the plane began its tedious approach to London Gatwick. Time was running short and I had to decide what I was going to say to Henri. Most importantly, I had to find the best way to explain what had happened to Harmony. I walked out of the arrivals hall and made for the taxi kiosk with Singh close behind. His demeanour had shifted from that of a concerned doctor to an anxious man who couldn't stop nervously looking around him. He produced a slip of paper with Henri's address and passed it across the counter. After a few minutes wait, we were on our way in a black Mercedes.

We hadn't spoken since the plane landed, which I thought was for the best. There was no need to declare our individual plans until we had to. We must have been on the road for nearly twenty minutes before we exchanged a word.

"How far is their place?" Singh enquired, clasping and unclasping his hands. It was getting dark and my eyes were trained on the trees lining the road as we approached the Ashdown Forest. "Not long," I replied disinterestedly, "another fifteen minutes or so."

It was quite a while since I was last at the cottage, under very different circumstances. It had been Harmony's fifth birthday and she was visiting Pooh's Cottage for the first time. Henri had bought the house specially for her and I remember her excitement as we rounded the corner of the drive and she glimpsed it for the first time. It was a stunning English summer and the house looked picture perfect with its thatched roof, carefully manicured grounds and roses around the door. Harmony's joy was second only to Henri's as he witnessed the ecstatic expression on her face.

As I looked away from the road, I noticed the doctor undoing the top buttons of his shirt. Years of accompanying Henri's visitors here had accustomed me to the suffocating effects the forest could have. To them it looked like an endless web of trees with nothing but shades of greens and browns extending up to the sky. As we drove further the trees got denser.

I pressed the button and as the window rolled down, I noticed the doctor was breathing quickly and beginning to perspire. What was bothering him so much? Certainly not the trees.

"Can you stop here?" he asked the driver. "I have to get out of the car. I need some air." He turned to me. "You say the cottage is not far? Tell me the way and I'll walk the rest."

"Suit yourself," I said. "We're nearly there. It's about a quarter of a mile. You'll come to the village in a few hundred yards, take a right down the first lane you come to and the cottage is at the end of the second driveway on the right. It'll take you ten to fifteen minutes. You'll need to use your phone as a torch, there are no street lights. I'll tell them you're on your way."

He got out of the car and we drove on, quickly arriving at the entrance to the long gravel drive which shielded the cottage from the road. As Henri would have wished, the house itself was sufficiently isolated to be virtually secure from unwelcome visitors. The taxi pulled up outside the front door.

The metal outer door that would normally have been open was covered with broken branches, as if to cover up whatever lay beyond. I paid the cab driver and asked him to return within the hour. As he drove off, I walked around the front of the building and through a small gap in the brick wall to the side.

Something was wrong. There were no exterior lights on and the usual sense of welcome I'd felt on previous visits was absent. That's when I knew something was going on. With all my senses alerted, I moved stealthily towards the front door, hid in the shadow of the porch and tossed a handful of gravel on the ground. A few seconds later, the door opened and two men I recognised stepped out with guns pointed straight ahead of them. Once they'd satisfied themselves there was no one there, they tucked their guns away, exchanging a few words. That's when I made my move. With my left arm around one man's neck, I reached into his belt and pulled out his gun, pointing it the other man's head. "Good evening," I said as steadily as I could, "How about letting me in?"

"Nina?" one of them said, "is that you?"

"The very same," I replied. "Sorry to be unsociable, but I don't like guns. Now, perhaps you'd be good enough to tell Mr and Mrs Nader that I've come a very long way to see them. I'm exhausted and would like a drink." I released the guy from my trademark armlock and, rubbing his neck, he gestured me through the front door. His colleague remained outside for a moment to check the periphery of the house and drive.

"Clear," he stepped back in and closed the door behind me as I stood silently between them.

"You are something else," the older man said with a wry smile as they accompanied me through the stone-floored hallway stopping outside the living room door. "They're in there," he said,

"I guess they'll be surprised to see you."

He opened the door and I peered into the richly panelled living room. Henri and Oriole were sitting by the fireplace. Not for the first time, I seemed to have stepped into a heated argument between the two of them. It was one of the things I'd had to get used to when I started working with them but, unlike other times when I would choose not to hang around, today I needed their attention. I hadn't been joking when I said I was exhausted. My latest manoeuvre had taken it out of me and I barely noticed Oriole's cuts and bruises.

I wasted no time with niceties and collapsed into a spare chair. "It was Gerald Irving. He shot Harmony – but he didn't kill her." My words were like a tripwire, in a fraction of a second I had everyone's attention.

"Nina, what did you say? Here let me get you something, you don't look well!" Oriole stood up and embraced me and Henri let out a sigh.

"Nina, how did you get here? Are you okay? I saw you on the news and . . ." Oriole had me at arm's length and scanned me from head to toe. I had never been held with such warmth and attention as at that moment. I would have lost control of my emotions if it weren't for the tragedy at hand. "Please, could I have a glass of water?" I asked. One of the bodyguards went to the cocktail cabinet and poured me a glass from a decanter. I drank it gratefully.

"What do you mean Gerald shot Harmony? How do you know?" Henri enquired, stepping closer. He fetched some cushions and placed them behind my head. I knew that Henri's apparent concern for me was a façade aimed at pleasing his wife. "Were you with them at the time?" he persisted.

Oriole intervened, "Henri, please, leave the girl alone, she obviously needs some rest. We can ask these questions later."

"I'm okay," I said. "I saw him. I saw him abduct Harmony." I knew what was coming next. *How could you have let that happen? You were supposed to take care of her.* I was ready for it.

"Oh no . . ." Oriole fell back on the sofa with a look of defeat that told me she had expected this all along.

"If he was there to take Harmony, why did he feel the need to shoot at her? And you?" Henri was not so easily taken in.

"I . . . tried to stop him." I knew my hesitation wasn't helping but didn't let go of the facts. "I tried my best to stop him, but the bullet went right through me and hit Harmony. The next thing I knew I was waking up in hospital with Dr Singh by my bedside."

I paused and looked to the front door, just visible from the living room. "He came with me, actually. He told me Gerald had brought Harmony to the ship and then left her there. He should be here shortly."

"What? Hold on a second." Henri looked at me, perplexed. "So, he shot my daughter and had the audacity to bring her to the *Aphrodite* to be treated?"

"Are you sure that's what happened? Where is the doctor?" Oriole stood up, placing both hands on her hips.

"He decided to walk the last—"

"He ran away, that's what happened, isn't it? Too scared to face us. That's just great!" Henri shook his head with dismay and turned to his guards.

"Spread out, look for him." He turned toward me once again. There it was. The look I had been dreading. It was the 'How could you let it happen?' question. I had been asking myself the same thing day and night, but the truth was it *had* happened. It had happened, and there was no going back.

I opened my mouth halfway, trying to formulate a sentence that might convince Henri how much I hated myself for failing in my duty but, before I could say anything, the guards barged in with a dishevelled Singh. They let him go and he fell to his knees.

"I wasn't running away. I came with her to see you. I want to tell you everything. Tell them, Nina. Tell them, please!" He was like a child who had been caught fibbing. I wasn't ready to speak on his behalf, so I stayed silent.

"We found him outside, Sir, cowering in the bushes. Too scared to come in, as you said," one of the guards said as he helped Singh up and dumped him onto the sofa. He slithered around and adjusted his position awkwardly.

"Did you treat Harmony?" Henri inquired, leaning over him. His glare was enough to make the man blurt out everything he knew.

"I did. I did. But once I treated her, I didn't see her again. It was like she disappeared into thin air," Singh said, shaking his head in bewilderment.

"Thin air, eh?" Henri repeated his words and gestured at his men to come around. One of them pointed his gun at the doctor's temple while the other one stood above him.

"Tell them," I spoke up. I needed him to tell them he had seen Gerald on the ship. "Tell them it was Gerald who brought Harmony to you."

Singh looked at Henri for a brief second and then nodded unwillingly.

"Oh, God, no!" Oriole exclaimed as though her worst nightmare had come true, making it sound somehow worse than her daughter getting kidnapped. She started to sob feebly. She turned to Henri imploringly. "It's him. He's capable of hurting people in ways you can only imagine, Henri. He's dangerous. He's a thousand times more dangerous than the people you deal with, and I want my daughter back!" She was screaming at him now. "I want her back right now!"

I realised that Oriole knew something none of us did. What was it? I tried to work out where her emotions were coming from, but I couldn't. Not yet. Clearly panicking, she stood up shakily.

As Henri tried to grab her, I also leaped forward. I couldn't bear to see Oriole in such a state. That's when I saw the crimson and purple bruises all over her arms and neck. She had been at the receiving end of a fury that was both sharp and painful.

At the time, I hadn't seen the news of her involvement with Gerald, but the effect on her when she heard his name was obvious. I pitied her vulnerability and sensed the depth of her grief. It was bigger than mine or anyone else's.

She sank to the floor next to me and placed her head on my knee. I bent down and held her for as long as I could, trying to bring some peace and calmness to the distressed mother of the child we both loved. But my action had the opposite effect on Henri. When he saw me holding his wife, he moved away to round up his men.

I looked into his eyes, and that's when I knew for certain he had a plan.

CHAPTER SEVENTEEN

Blanche Irving

Reminders of Gerald loitered round every corner and it dismayed me to see Nikki and Paula suffering. It simply wasn't fair.

At dinner, their unasked questions hung heavily in the air – questions they were stifling for my sake, knowing the distress they had already caused me. I'd always believed I was the glue that held us together, but I was watching my family fall apart in Gerald's absence.

My latest attempt to plaster over the cracks had ended in disaster. Trying to cheer them up, I'd arranged a picnic in the park. But it all went badly wrong when Paula and I left Nikki alone on a bench for a few minutes to go and buy some ice creams, only to find her gone when we returned. Sick with worry I rang the police and reported her missing. Thankfully, before they could respond, I got a call from my neighbour Wendy.

"We found Nikki by the side of the road, trying to hail a taxi," she'd told me almost gleefully. Basically, a well-meaning woman, Wendy Harrald was prone to poking her nose into other people's business.

"What?" I was dumbstruck, "where is she now?"

"Don't worry. I brought her home with me because she wouldn't tell me where you were." She lowered her voice dramatically. "I think she was trying to get to the police station. Might have been trying to reach her father?"

Poor Nikki was frightened when I picked her up and I couldn't find it within me to tell her off. When we got home she went straight to the living room and curled up on the couch. All I could do was wrap my arms around her and let her sob until she exhausted herself.

"Mummy, I want to know if it's all true," she said eventually. "Do you really believe Daddy did all those terrible things?" For a moment, her eyes lit up with hope as I wondered how to answer her. If only she knew that telling the truth would make things far worse.

Finally, I said: "Darling, let's talk about something else."

She leapt off the couch. "I'm really sorry I worried you," she said spitefully. Her eyes were hardened with disillusionment. "I'm tired. Can I go to bed now?"

"Yes, of course you can, darling," I said, relieved that a further litany of lies had been averted.

Left alone, I wondered how many thousands, millions of other parents in broken marriages found themselves in this same quandary – what to say about the absent partner. Whose fault was it, and which parent was to blame? Or was it just fate?

I knew we had to get out of this place. I knew if we all moved back to France, I would have Joanne's support but my daughters were keeping me from escaping Gerald's clutches.

I was startled by the doorbell ringing. The wall clock told me it was getting late. Who could it be at this time of night? A louder rap from the knocker set my heart racing.

"Wait! I'm coming!" I shouted, hurrying to the door. The figure who stood immediately in front of me held a police identity card. There was someone else in the shadow behind him.

"Good evening, Mrs Irving. I'm sorry to barge in on you so late. You'll remember me, Inspector McGraw, we've met before, and this is my partner, Constable Gonzalez from the Anti Kidnap and Extortion Unit, part of the National Crime Agency." The card confirmed it.

I recognised the inspector, but Constable Gonzalez was a new face, offering me a reassuring smile.

"Good evening, Inspector. How may I help you?" I knew that whether I liked it or not, feigning ignorance would only get me so far.

McGraw went on pedantically. "We're here in connection with your husband's involvement in the abduction of Harmony

Nader. I presume you're aware that this investigation is ongoing?"

I nodded. "More or less, yes. Would you like to come in?"

It was chilly outside and they brought a few stray autumn leaves with them. I realised that I still had a scrunched-up copy of the Sunday Times in my hand. Despite my unease, the hostess in me couldn't help it. "Would you like something? Tea? Ginger biscuits?"

"No, no. Please, just take a seat," Constable Gonzalez spoke up in an exceptionally chirpy voice. She was a brunette who appeared to be in her mid-twenties and acted like it. Her eyes were full of wonder as she took in her unremarkable surroundings. "How are you managing, Mrs Irving?"

"Fine." The question required no more explanation.

She looked around her. "I like what you've done with the space, especially this rug. Really makes the interior pop." Judging from the inspector's uneasy expression, I guessed he didn't particularly like her manner. Not his style, not at all.

"Thank you, that's kind of you to say." I meant it. I would rather be coaxed than be pushed. "So, how can I help you?"

McGraw took over as Constable Gonzalez got her notebook out. "If you can just answer a few questions to the best of your recollection, that would be very much appreciated."

Though recent events had made me wary of my instincts, I couldn't help but distrust the inspector. "Sure. Please go ahead."

"We'll also need to search your property." His steely eyes scrutinised me. Honestly, wouldn't anyone be nervous if the police turned up at 9:30pm, announcing they were going to turn your house upside down?

"Okay, though I doubt you'll find anything of interest here. My husband moved out four months ago."

"It's just police procedure in cases like this," he explained. "Has he tried to contact you?"

"Not me. No." Recalling his brief encounter with my daughters outside their school, a shudder went down my spine.

"Are you feeling threatened, Mrs Irving?"

"Yeah, I guess I am."

"Was your husband abusive? Did he ever assault you or mistreat you? Are you fearful that he might return?"

"No, it's not like that. He wasn't abusive, but he was emotionally turbulent. Just . . . slamming and breaking stuff." I sighed in exasperation. These questions were getting repetitive. "It's just, I don't know what to believe anymore."

"Mrs Irving, I need you to relax. We can assure you that Gerald Irving is currently being held in police custody. You and your daughters are quite safe. There is nothing to worry about."

"I know, I know. Anyway, yes, he did contact my girls at school soon after he returned to London. I went to pick them up from school and found him chasing after my elder daughter, Nikki."

"Chasing after? Can you be more specific?"

I tried to piece my thoughts together. "No, let me rephrase that. As far as I know, he went there to see them in the hope of a reconciliation. Nikki wasn't all that pleased after three months' absence, so she stomped off in anger."

"So, your husband went after her? Pursued her? Did you detect any coercion?"

"No, it wasn't like that. Even if he had caught up with her, I doubt he would've done anything to harm her." Out of habit, I was defending him. "At least not in public. In fact, before I could really understand what was happening, he was dragged off by another man."

The inspector's ears perked up at this. "Can you describe the other man's appearance?"

"All I can say is, he was quite a burly fellow, like a military man. I didn't get a proper look. I was more concerned with my daughters' safety."

The constable scrunched up her eyebrows. "Why was that? Being abandoned by your husband might be emotionally damaging, but it hardly raises questions of your children's safety."

"I wasn't scared of . . ." I had to gather up the courage to say his name "Gerald." After days of denying his existence, this all felt unfamiliar. "That one's on the other guy. Gerald looked downright terrified when he appeared, quite understandably. The man looked seriously intimidating. It seemed to me as if Gerald was actually trying to steer him away from the girls."

The inspector produced a photograph of a bespectacled young man from his briefcase. "Does this man look familiar to you?"

"No, no. As I said, the man I am talking about was big, bulky. Quite unmistakable."

Our conversation was interrupted by a crash. I didn't need to look far to know that it was the girls who had most likely had their ears pressed to the living room door.

"I apologise. I'll be right back."

I found them engaged in a noisy argument in the hallway. "Girls, go back to your room."

"Mummy, they're police officers, right? Is Daddy coming back home?"

"Paula, didn't you hear what I—"

But the Inspector had other ideas. "Mrs Irving, actually it would be really helpful if we could have a word with your daughters. too. I hope that's okay with you?" Though he phrased the statement as a question, the insistence in his voice didn't get past me.

"Is that really necessary? It's well past their bedtime."

"Look, we don't have the authority to interrogate minors, but so far this chase has led us nowhere. Talking to your daughters might give us some further insight into your husband's motives. If there's anything you disapprove of, you can intervene. We won't take long."

Still undecided, I forced a nod. "Well, go ahead, then."

Paula sat to my left, while Nikki seated herself on the pouf near Gonzalez who appeared to be taking over from her male colleague. She had the courtesy to introduce herself to my daughters before picking at their wounds.

"Nikki, has your father ever hit you or your mother? Ever hurt you in any way?" Immediately I took exception to this line of questioning. But Nikki got in before me. Stubbornly ignoring the question, Nikki proceeded with her own enquiry. "How is he doing?"

"Nikki, your Daddy can look after himself," I tried to reassure her, but she paid me no heed.

"If you see him, can you tell him that I really miss him?" she asked Constable Gonzalez.

"Sure. I'll let him know. Now, Nikki, back to my question. Has he ever hurt—"

"Obviously not! He would never!" I couldn't blame Nikki for losing her temper.

Paula added in a small voice. "Sometimes, he fought with Mummy a lot. When he got really angry, he went for a walk or punched walls."

Nikki shot her an angry glare. "But Daddy would never kidnap Harmony! He's kind! We went out for a meal with Harmony, then dropped her home, and we never saw her again. Tell them, Mummy!"

"Inspector McGraw, I have already given my statement. I don't see what you hope to achieve by further interrogating my daughters." I struggled to keep the edge out of my voice. "Why don't you go ahead and search the house instead?"

"It's on the schedule, ma'am. I just have one more question before we proceed with the search." When I remained silent, he continued, reaching for another package from his briefcase. "Do you recognise this?"

The exquisite, bejewelled hair clip was unlike any I had ever seen, but to my bafflement, and possibly to my girls' as well, the lie slipped out of my mouth without hesitation. "Harmony left this in our rental car. I meant to have it returned but quite honestly it slipped my mind."

I knew I was removing the only piece of evidence linking my husband to Harmony's abduction. God forbid, I didn't mean to hinder their search for a missing child cruelly torn away from her mother, but my own maternal instincts compelled me to protect my own. I did want them to find something, anything, that might lead them to Harmony, but not under my roof.

The two of them were soon ransacking the house, turning over mattresses and rummaging through draws and cupboards.

Paula sniffled as they muddied the floor with her potted plants. Nikki looked on disparagingly.

They left the house in a mess of half open drawers, unclosed wardrobes and upturned ornaments, but as Nikki and Paula joined me for a cuddle on the couch, I was pleased that I'd been able to distance us all from their enquiries with a single lie about a piece of jewellery.

CHAPTER EIGHTEEN

Chandrit Singh

After my miserable confessions, the last thing I expected was to be released from my confinement – although my six-foot-two-inch companion still lurked behind me at all times. I admit that I had been intimidated by the nanny, but she didn't hold a candle to this guy as he accompanied me back to the ship.

The next time I saw Henri was in the lobby of The Savoy, in the Strand. Being with him in such a public space had done little to alleviate my anxiety.

"I have a job for you, Singh," he'd said, "and I'm expecting you to deliver on our deal this time." Another time, another threat. I was getting used to it.

"Of course, Henri, you know you can count on me. I've always . . ." I bit my tongue as he glared angrily at me. I knew better than to poke a bear, but nerves were getting the better of me.

He went on: "The police here are onto something, I know they are, but it's all based on that bastard's useless testimony! They've done nothing to make him talk. God, if I could get my hands on him."

I'd watched his famous urbane charm disappear before in the course of the last few months. This Henri was a different animal to the man I'd first met and if I hadn't known better I would've taken his outbursts for the ramblings of a madman.

I knew in my bones that Gerald Irving was not our guy, but Henri insisted. "Now, they're sniffing around, and there's a possibility they could raid the ship at any time. They must not get wind of our business." His business, I thought. "Singh, I need you back on *Aphrodite* to get rid of any evidence, anything that could be incriminating, before the police set up a Joint Investigation

Team with the Spaniards."

"Of course," I tried to sound reassuring. "Consider it done. As a matter of fact, I've come up with a rock-solid cover story if they do find anything suspicious."

"What do you mean? They're not going to find anything suspicious, that's your bloody job!" He spat out the words with disdain. "Anyway, you'll be the one held responsible not me!" He calmed down a little. "Now, listen, I'll have the jet ready in a few hours – and don't even think about making a run for it. Jake will go with you, of course."

Despite his demands, I heaved a sigh of relief as he briskly walked off. To be honest, I was grateful for this latest turn of events. Now perhaps I would be able to get back to my medical work without the men from Hope for Black arriving unannounced with a new bunch of kids every couple of months. It felt like going home – in fact, *Aphrodite* had been the closest to a home I'd ever known. All my life, I've followed one destination with another, escaping my roots, forever seeking my next medical accomplishment.

As one passionate man to another, I had always held Henri Nader in esteem. When my breakthrough research into translational stem cell therapy had been widely acknowledged, I had been approached by some of the world's most prestigious research centres. Yet I chose to stay and work for Henri. Yes, of course I was seduced by his promises of state-of-the-art technologies, not to mention an attractive stipend, but not for a moment did I consider I might be exposing myself to any danger.

"What happened to your eye?" I asked my guard. I really preferred the other one. "Look, big guy, you can pretend I don't exist, but you'll be in trouble if the police interrogate us and our stories don't match."

I had his attention. He retorted: "Gerald Irving attacked me with a fork in the eye while I had him pinned by his throat against his living room door. So, how do you think my truth compares with yours?"

"Your truth?" I couldn't help provoking the man with a

chuckle. "Look, I'm familiar with your games, but I've met the man. You can pin it on him all you like, but he's not capable—"

The response was angry. "You don't know what he's capable of, so shut your mouth – doctor!" So much for rational discussion, then.

I turned my mind back to the accused. Based on what I'd heard about his uncontrolled rages, I was starting to form a theory about Irving. Was he conscious of his actions at all? He was certainly demonstrating intriguing symptoms. Anyway, I could see that my hypothesis would be of no interest whatsoever to my companion who was now staring blankly out of the window. The entire flight was painfully boring, to say the least.

Arriving back on the *Aphrodite*, apart from the giant on my tail, everything seemed normal. The sight of the ship never failed to take my breath away. Though I had spent the latter part of my career working on this luxury cruiser, I still couldn't help marvel at it.

John hurried down the gangplank to greet me cheerfully. Although the captain had always turned a blind eye to some of our activities, I knew I could count on him to help disguise them. In reality, there wasn't much to do – the crew was already sufficiently meticulous to keep the illicit side of our business under wraps. All I really had to do was destroy a few incriminating documents and tinker a little with the surveillance security camera footage.

As Henri instructed, I returned to my normal work pattern whilst keeping my eyes open to any possible threat from the law. It was nerve-racking. Three days went by when, with every knock on my office door, I jumped out of my skin. The ever-persistent Mrs Thorpe wasn't helping. With the awards season approaching, she was getting desperate for another rhinoplasty. Although I was somewhat flattered at her keen efforts to see me and no one else, my mind was occupied elsewhere.

There was one significant change that didn't sit right with me: the absence of my loyal PA, Julia Swartz. In all our years together, she had never taken a single day off, so it was highly uncharacteristic of her to take extended leave. Despite her unwavering loyalty to me personally, on occasion her conscience had got the better of common sense. More than once she had been adamant about going to the police and exposing the nature of our business and, had I not talked her out of it, she might have succeeded in getting herself killed. Her absence now was some cause for concern.

The fragility of my own situation didn't dawn upon me until the day the police finally raided the ship. The moment I had been dreading had arrived. Along with an officer from The Policía Nacional.

"Mr Singh, Officer Manuel Artunez is here to see you."

"Bring him in," I instructed Julia's replacement, whilst noting she lacked her predecessor's talent for hospitality. "Have you offered him something?" As expected, she only blinked in response. "Very well, then, carry on with your duties – oh, and leave the door open."

Artunez was a tall, lean man, in his early thirties. As he greeted me, I detected what I thought to be a distinctly Catalan dialect in his speech.

"I am sorry to disturb you, Dr Singh. I know how busy you must be."

"No worries, Officer. I am sure whatever brings you here must be important. Can I offer you something to drink?"

"No, no, but thanks for offering. I just need to ask you a few questions."

"You should sample my Scotch whisky, Officer. Believe me, it's truly top-shelf. Fifteen years old, aged in the Highlands with notes of chocolate, cherry, pecans, honey, and cedar. I insist you have a sip. It would be a waste if you didn't." I hoped I was doing a good job of masking my fears but knew I was rambling.

"Please excuse me, Dr Singh, but I'm on duty." The officer looked rather irked by my persistence. "We need to discuss your involvement in Harmony Nader's abduction case."

"Yes, yes, very tragic, indeed. God knows the girl might be lying dead in a ditch somewhere. Well, I'm sure you're aware of the statement I have already submitted to the police in the UK?"

I was well-acquainted with the procedure of questioning by now.

"Dr Singh, nothing significant has yet been pinned on Mr Irving. The missing girl herself was last spotted on the *Aphrodite*, so there might be some evidence around here that could lead us to her. I have a warrant to search this ship, but before we can proceed with that, as I said, I need a few questions answered." Despite being prepared for what was coming, I still couldn't help but flinch at this.

"Of course, do tell me how I can be of assistance."

"To start with, you can fill in the details of when the girl was brought here?"

"Yes, the circumstances were unusual. Gerald Irving said he found the girl bleeding by the side of the road. I could see she was severely wounded. Her clavicle was shattered. He said it was only out of concern for her safety that he brought her here. Of course, since then we have found much of that to be untrue but, at the time, I had no reason to disbelieve him."

I went on gabbling. "He's a family man, you see, introduced to me by a trusted friend and I had no knowledge of his connection with the Naders. Officer, allow me to say this – there is one significant request he made which I did find strange; he asked me not to disclose his involvement to the police. I didn't think much of it back then, but now it seems an odd thing for him to have said."

"Did he remark upon why he brought her to you rather than to the hospital? After all, the HR International isn't far away, he would have virtually passed it on his way to the port." The officer looked almost uninterested in my reply.

"He didn't explain that. In fact, he didn't say anything of note. Mind you, he was at his wit's end and obviously distraught by the entire ordeal. He asked me to keep the whole matter confidential because he had told his wife he was at work and didn't want to upset her."

"Ah, I see." He referred to his notes. "Now, you said in your statement that you treated the child's wounds and then she disappeared from the ship soon afterwards. I see you've installed far more surveillance cameras than one would expect in an average luxury cruiser. It would seem unlikely that nothing was caught in the footage?"

I ignored his rather offensive description of my ship. "Believe me, officer, I have given much thought to that question over these last few months. I have personally checked that footage countless times myself but whoever kidnapped the girl, knew how to avoid the eye of the camera."

"You're right. Could even have been someone from your crew, might it not?" I realised my error but kept my composure.

"In any case," he went on, "I'll need to see the footage from the last three months." He glanced at his watch, before abruptly rising from his chair.

"Of course. Is that all, officer?"

"Just one more question. What is your relationship with the Nader family?" It had been delivered almost as an afterthought.

"It's strictly professional, Officer. Henri Nader owns this ship. I merely run the medical facilities."

"I see. In that case Dr Singh, I will need to see the ship's documents to verify that ownership."

Though the request was delivered flatly, it felt like a thinly disguised threat. I faced it off with what I hoped was a bullish tone.

"Allow me to ask, but how does that relate to a search for a missing child?"

The answer was unequivocal. "I need to verify that the documents are genuine and not forged. Believe it or not, these cases are mostly personal. Especially as some of these billionaires tend to have made enemies."

"I see. Well, I believe both of us are on a schedule here, so shall we proceed? Allow me to show you around."

My fears eased a little as I conducted him on a tour of my floating hospital. John had made sure he wouldn't find anything amiss. We started at the top and worked our way down. I was pleased to see how he appeared impressed at the futuristic facilities. Like most visitors, he began to loosen up as he explored the luxuries of *Aphrodite*.

The captain took it all in his stride and dealt with the interrogations courteously as did the rest of the crew who remained alert and polite. Our only obstacle arose when the officer demanded to see the security footage. This was going to be tricky.

"There's are gaps in this footage," he explained. "The recordings have been tampered with."

"Not at all!" My explanation was already prepared. "You see, celebrities from all over the world have their cosmetic surgery done here on the *Aphrodite*. It's a matter of exclusivity and confidentiality. Most of them prefer to keep their procedures under wraps, especially from prying media. Security footage can be misappropriated, usually for money. I'm sure you know of such cases."

"Of course, but this is a criminal investigation. We will respect the confidentiality of your clients I can assure you. This information will not be released to the media, but in order to identify the culprit we need to go through all of this footage. If you refuse, you will be obstructing the course of justice."

"I see. Then we had best continue this conversation in the presence of my lawyer."

Artunez shot me a sharp look but decided to change tack. "Is your entire staff present on the ship?" he asked. I guessed they had already been through the list of crew members so didn't bother to answer. I was right. "Your personal assistant, Julia Swartz, is not here is she? Any idea where she might be?"

"She's taken some sick leave. However, you don't need to worry about her. She's a very talented, reliable asset to my team."

"How long exactly has she been away?"

"Not long. She has only been absent since I got back from London." In truth, her attendance had been rather sporadic for a while. Julia is a recovering alcoholic and I'd long since agreed to cut her some slack. The policeman seemed content.

"Thank you for your cooperation, Dr Singh, this tour has been enlightening." He smiled, but I regretted that I had inadvertently signposted one of the few people in this world I truly cared about.

After he'd gone, the worst seemed behind me, but I was restless. Julia had a good heart but, combined with the alcohol, it had sometimes led her into trouble. So, when the Macallan failed to calm me, I decided to check up on her.

It was surprising that in all the time we had worked together, I had never once visited her apartment. Our relationship went a little beyond the strictly professional and I valued her as a friend as much as an employee. She had stood by me through thick and thin and was always invited to my house parties – yet all I knew was her address. She lived in a not quite so fashionable part of town, but in a pleasant enough apartment, a block back from the sea.

As I stood knocking at the mahogany door, I noticed how everything was precisely as I had imagined it would be. The hallway was decorated with ceramic potted plants, mirrors and cute paintings of bowls of fruit. The minimalist yet chic décor was suitably tailored to her taste. However, when she came to the door what I hadn't anticipated was to be met with a chic-looking, albeit frightened, Julia. She was dressed in straight-legged denim, paired with a vintage T-shirt and with her chunky yellow earrings she looked far from the sick woman I expected to see.

The cause of her concern became evident as she opened the door wider, letting me in without a greeting, Officer Artunez, accompanied by another middle-aged man in uniform had beaten me to it and were sitting on the couch in her living room. While the policeman's eyes were following her movements, the older man had his pinned in the direction of her bedroom.

"Julia! How have you been, my friend?" I asked her summoning as much good cheer as I could. "Truth be told, work has been tough without you." Tight-lipped, Julia only managed a nod.

"Dr Singh, what brings you here?" Artunez interrupted. "We're in the middle of an investigation, so, if it's not a matter of urgency, could you drop by at a more convenient time?"

I know he was beginning to suspect me, but instead of excusing myself, I shook his hand enthusiastically instead. "Twice in one day, Officer! What a small world!"

Before he could react, I settled myself next to Julia. "Julia is rather shy," I said, "and I'm sure my presence will help rather than hinder your interrogation." The two officers shared an exchange of dubious expressions while I continued with enthusiasm. "So, shall we continue?"

"Very well," Artunez said in a resigned voice. "Miss Swartz, you appear to be healthy enough. So why haven't you been at work? Dr Singh told us you were on sick leave?" I could tell Julia was struggling to keep her composure.

"Well, can't a girl look hot when she's sick?" Julia responded, flicking her hair over her shoulder, "Is that a crime?" I was proud to see her giving as good as she got.

"Please, answer the question, Miss Swartz."

"Well, yes, I have been off colour. Not at all well, in fact. But, I've felt much better over the last day or so. I was hoping to go back to work next week."

The other officer spoke in a solemn voice. "Do you live here alone?"

"Yeah, only with my dog. Well, not anymore." Julia looked away, tears welling in her eyes. "Tannie passed away a fortnight ago. That hasn't helped. It's been very difficult."

"Well, that explains the mess," the officer stood up abruptly, "but not the toys." I noticed Julia freeze.

Artunez pulled out a Barbie doll which had been lodged between the cushions of the couch. Before either of us could react, the older man had crossed the living room and opened Julia's bedroom door. Nothing could have prepared me for what the others had already guessed they would see. But there was the child, rushing under the bed to hide, only just a second too late.

As the policeman struggled to pull her out from underneath the bed, she was clawing at his arms. Harmony Nader, the missing girl, was dressed casually, looking healthier than I had ever seen before. The little girl who had been forced to grow up too young was desperately clutching her doll as if it represented the end of her childhood.

"Julia Swartz, you're under arrest for the abduction of Harmony Nader. You don't have to say anything, but anything you may say could be used in evidence against you in a court of law."

"Wait," it was Harmony addressing the policeman. "You can't arrest her, she saved my life." She turned back to the bedroom. "You can come out, now." And with that, another child, a little boy, emerged from under the bed. Harmony went to him and held his hand tightly, smiling reassuringly. "And this is my friend, Ahmed. Julia saved his life, too."

And with that, Artunez arrested and handcuffed Julia Swartz for the abduction of Harmony Nader.

PART THREE

CHAPTER NINETEEN

Gerald Irving

The cell reeked of sweat and vomit. Every bit of fight had gone out of me, leaving me defeated and resentful.

Each time I closed my eyes, I saw images of a member of my family lying wounded, while others stood by staring at me with contempt.

My court hearing had led nowhere. Without the money to afford professional legal defence, my arguments had only prolonged my detention. I hadn't anticipated this fate in my wildest of dreams and now I had no idea how to fight my way through it.

So far, my only visitor had been none other than Vinny. He had managed to locate Isaac but, soon after, the young man had gone into hiding again. A wise move, I might say.

Although my imprisonment was a direct result of his foolish advice, Vinny's obnoxious attitude didn't change in the slightest. "Gerry boy, I'm not daft enough to try to bring down a billionaire without evidence."

"How do you even have the nerve?" I knew he enjoyed riling me, but I had lost the appetite to play games. "Anyway, what are you up to now?"

"Just trying to dig up some real nasty dirt on our philanthropic friend, Henri," he'd said with a smirk and left it at that.

In the past our dealings had always been on the basis of a quid pro quo. This time round, however, he claimed he'd showed up just to check up on me. I was touched, that is, until I saw him being chummy with Officer McGraw outside. I knew he was up to something.

"Hey, Gerald, wake up!" It was my guard, Jacob, shouting out with his boisterous voice. He was far too amiable for the job

303

he had to do and I truly appreciated him for it. His friendly small talk had kept me from losing what little remained of my sanity but today, despite his friendliness, I preferred to be left alone.

Still, he went ahead, turning the key in the rusty lock and entering the cell. My heartbeat quickened. Something must be happening.

After Muriel's well-meaning but fruitless attempts to help me, they'd left me in this rotting cell whilst they went off to find answers elsewhere. Anyway, my apprehension appeared to be justified as Jacob led me towards the interrogation room for what felt like the hundredth time.

Officer McGraw and Dr Muriel were already waiting. As usual, the inspector offered a curt nod while Muriel gave me warm smile. "Gerald, how are you feeling today?" she asked.

"I'm okay," I answered with a defeated shrug.

"Well quite a few revealing things have come to light, Gerald – not so much about the investigation as you might expect, but about you."

"Well, that depends on what exactly has come to light." Although my voice was nonchalant, my head was spinning. I tried to reassure myself with my mantra: *I have nothing to hide, I am not guilty of any crime.*

"Let's start with this DVD we found at your apartment." Officer McGraw held up Oriole's DVD, no longer in its fancy case.

Why the sight of it sent a shudder down my spine, I don't know. I had seen it enough times before. There was nothing suspicious about it, and I told my persecutor so. "This is just concert footage, a little gift from Henri Nader as a token of gratitude, nothing more."

Muriel turned the disk around a few times before putting it carefully down beside him. "You're mistaken, Gerald." She peered into my eyes as if she was letting me in on a deep secret. "The films of those performances, along with the footage played on the large screens at the arenas, have been deliberately interfered with to stimulate the subconscious desires of the public by subliminal messaging. Such manipulation of the unconscious mind for commercial, or for that matter, any purpose has been banned in most parts of the world for years."

Honestly, I was surprised, but I chuckled in response. "Believe me, if you investigate Henri Nader, you'll find far worse than subliminal messaging. While you're at it, you might also find his missing daughter."

"Drop the charade, Gerald," McGraw interrupted.

The psychiatrist silenced him with a cautionary glance. "This might seem like a minor offence, but it has been banned for good reason. Subliminal messages are meant to slip past the viewer's conscious perception. So, if a person has an unconscious ego, it could be stimulated in this way."

"Speak in layman's terms, please, doctor." I couldn't work out why I was going on the defensive.

"I think, you know exactly what I mean."

"I'm afraid I don't."

"Gerald, you have to start communicating. Have you experienced any lapses in time? Periods of unconsciousness? If you ever want to get out of here, you have to trust us. Trust me. I'll ask Officer McGraw to leave us alone if it might help?"

"I have been communicating, I've told you everything I know!" Had my hands not been cuffed to the chair, I would have slammed my fist on the table.

Officer McGraw was having none of it. Just like me, he was on the brink of unleashing his barely contained rage. "Gerald, two witnesses have come forward to say they saw you at the crime scene."

I couldn't disguise my shock. It gave room for Dr Muriel to reach out to me again. "Reports from both your wife and Oriole Nader suggest a sudden drastic change in your personality. Can you entertain the possibility that despite your better judgment, you may have been a party to this crime?"

Ignoring the doctor, I addressed Officer McGraw. "So what? It's my word against theirs. I know you don't have any evidence."

"Yeah, there's no evidence," McGraw replied. "That's funny,

eh? Had a little ride down to your house yesterday. Strange how your wife's story precisely matches yours. Tell me, is she part of your scheme to kidnap the girl, or just scared of you?"

"Have you lost your mind?" I was getting angry with him now.

"By the way, your daughter . . . what's her name, Nikki? She said she misses you. Do you really want to disappoint her by staying holed up in here forever?"

With his every word, my pent-up frustration got worse. "Is this another way of coercing a confession out of me? Using my daughter to do your dirty work? How dare you!" But despite my words, I knew I must have sounded helpless.

The doctor finally decided to put an end to my torment, but I couldn't make out what she was saying and felt myself slipping into oblivion.

When I regained my senses, I was surprised to find I hadn't been moved. I was in the same chair in the same room. But now there was a syringe in the doctor's hand and my interrogators were engaged in their own conversation, unaware that I could hear what they were saying. It was Muriel who was talking.

"He's made a breakthrough, officer. As his doctor, I believe he should be made aware of his condition."

"No way," the policeman sounded adamant. "Look, once he finds out, he'll use it as his defence. He is the only lead we've got."

"Finds out what?" I asked. Part of me wanted to know what they were talking about, the other most definitely did not.

While the inspector looked startled, Dr Muriel simply shrugged in response. The air was thick with the stilted conflict between the two.

"Find out what, doctor?" I repeated.

"Gerald, it might be difficult for you to take this in right now, so prepare yourself." Dr Muriel ignored the glare from the inspector. "Based on our observations over the last week and the interview we've just had, I have to tell you that you are seriously ill."

"Er, what interview? I've been unconscious, haven't I?"

"No, Gerald, I'm afraid you have not."

CHAPTER TWENTY

Vincent Lythgoe

"By the grace of God, my daughter has been returned home safely. Police are still investigating this case, so there's not a lot more I can tell you. However, what matters now is the protection of my children and their happiness."

The nightmare she had endured had done little to diminish the allure of that sublime, mysterious smile. Beneath the sunglasses, I knew Oriole Nader's eyes reflected her pain. Surrounded by twenty or thirty hard-nosed reporters, and being beamed all over the world, the woman deserved applause for standing her ground.

Oriole was dressed in a bright red suit, an interesting choice of attire for a press conference. Maybe she was making a statement. Maybe she felt free at last and wanted the world to know.

"Words are not enough to express the gratitude I feel towards my fans, friends, and the public who stood by me throughout this difficult and stressful ordeal."

I recognised the young reporter who was going out on a limb with his next question. "Mrs Nader, is it true you've filed for divorce?" She gripped the armrest of her chair tighter. Though the tiny movement didn't escape my notice, the young reporter remained oblivious.

"No comment." Oriole sighed heavily before continuing, "My children have been put through a lifetime's worth of suffering. If it's possible, I must try to give them some semblance of normality, to experience the childhood they have lost. Harmony Nader does not deserve to be punished for someone else's crimes," she raised her voice passionately.

Looking beyond the obvious, I could see how little she was relishing all of this. But she knew how to manipulate an audience.

"My daughter needs time to recover. The last thing that will help is for the media to hound her every step of the way. Please, for her sake, I request you all to show some compassion and respect for her. Thank you." She rose to leave, but they hadn't finished with her yet.

"Mrs Nader, who's the real culprit in all this? Who kidnapped your daughter?" another reporter asked.

Oriole Nader gathered her bag, hesitant, blind to the flashlights in her face. It was all a crying shame. Blessed with talent, beauty and wealth, she was born for the spotlight.

"Is it true the police are investigating your husband?" No response.

"Is he responsible for your daughter's abduction?" No answer.

"Did Gerald Irving kidnap you, too? How did you manage to escape?" She visibly flinched as she was ushered out of the room by her bodyguard, a man who towered over her.

I paused the footage. There was nothing more for me to gain from this recording, yet I couldn't help myself and hit the replay button.

The girl had been found, but only a few pieces of the puzzle had fallen into place. The mystery remained, and the public thrived on it. As far as they were concerned, Gerald Irving was to blame for everything, the crimes he had committed as well as the ones he hadn't.

If there was anyone who could understand the torture of not having total control over one's actions, it was me. In the eyes of the world, Gerald Irving, the mystery man, had become a violent, misogynistic pervert. Honestly, despite the man's glaring flaws, I knew he wasn't, and that the current narrative was doing him a grave injustice.

There was a familiar knock on my door.

"How many times have you watched that?" Pete came in and sat down opposite me. Pete had started as a court reporter, but once I'd spotted his budding skills of observation, I took him under my wing. True dedication is rare in my field and in his own way, Pete was dedicated. He would never rely on selling lies to make a living.

"Oriole Nader won't crack," I said, "Gerry boy told us everything, but we can't do anything about it. There's no story."

Pete smiled gleefully at my frustration. "I've never seen you so bothered with the truth. This whole fiasco with Gerald has upset you, hasn't it?"

"What are you talking about?" Although sweet Pete and I had little in common, he did sometimes see through me. "I tell lies to get to the truth all the time."

"Exactly, and that's what you're going to do now," Pete had a self-satisfied look on his face. With some excitement, I realised what he might be getting at.

"No way! She agreed?" My voice jumped a few decibels in excitement.

"Yeah, Julia Swartz has agreed to do the interview. 7th January, Monday morning, nine o'clock, live." Pete was grinning ear-to-ear. "You owe me an overdue vacation, mate."

"All in good time. Right now, you've got your work cut out."

Julia Swartz was an aloof girl, and with good reason, I thought. She was gorgeous and sassy. I'd tried to convince her to meet us before, but she'd refused point blank. Honestly, it would've been in her best interest as well as mine. With every passing day, the excitement was growing, and our news channel had seldom had such a big story. I simply couldn't comprehend why she wouldn't want to tell her side of it, especially as I had offered her sight of my questions in advance. Still, she must have had her reasons. Anyway, it appeared that Pete had worked the oracle. Good for him. And he'd get his vacation. Eventually.

When we got to the news studio, it turned out Julia Swartz was not scared at all. In fact, she couldn't wait to let the world know the truth – as she put it, the unfiltered, absolute truth. Dressed in a burgundy blazer, pencil skirt, and stilettos, she not only looked spectacular but exuded confidence. As Pete accompanied her into the Green Room, she offered me her hand with a tight-lipped smile.

"Hi, Ms Swartz, please make yourself comfortable." I admired her more by the second. She was amongst the very few who didn't dwell on my wheelchair.

"So, what do you think of London?" I asked.

"I love the fish and chips. The weather? Not so much." Before I could continue with more mandatory small talk, she broached the business of the day. "Mr Lythgoe, I've done my research, and I'm impressed with your credentials. But I need to make one thing clear before we start; I will speak the truth, but if it comes out differently, I'll sue you, your employers and anyone else connected with your news channel and this interview."

"Of course." I couldn't help chuckling at her forthright manner. I was up against a redoubtable force of nature. "Ms Swartz, I'm incredibly glad you agreed to do this interview. I hope we don't disappoint each other."

Throughout my career, I had never felt nervous before conducting an interview, yet my palms were sweating as the floor manager counted me in and the camera zoomed in on me. Julia Swartz, however, sat unbothered, taking in the unfamiliar surroundings calmly. Her eyes were fixed on the blue and red logo displayed on the huge flatscreen.

"Good morning, UK and welcome to Fresh News! My name is Vincent Lythgoe. Today, I'm hoping to shed some light on the mystery of Harmony Nader's abduction, a story that has taken the world by storm. Harmony Nader, the golden child of business tycoon, Henri Nader, and the mesmerising prima donna, Oriole Nader, was reported missing six months ago. After an extensive search, the missing girl was found by Spanish police. Who would have thought she would be found right under the nose of her distressed parents? Let's meet our guest, Julia Swartz, to find out more." Julia adjusted her skirt as camera two moved in. "Ms Swartz, it's a pleasure to have you with us."

"Thank you, Vincent, I am also grateful to you for giving me a platform from which to speak the truth." It was refreshing to see how gracefully the young woman conducted herself.

"Okay, thank you. So, let's start with your relationship with the girl. How did you meet Harmony Nader?"

"I met Harmony aboard the luxury hospital ship, the Aphrodite. I worked there as personal assistant to the Medical Director, Dr Chandrit Singh. Had it not been for meeting that sweet little angel, I would've cursed the day I joined the staff on that ship."

Julia paused as she went off topic before continuing, "She was brought onboard by Gerald Irving, injured severely with a gunshot wound to the shoulder. At the time, he said he didn't know her. But there was no doubt he genuinely, I might even say desperately, wanted to help the girl."

So far, her story aligned with Irving's. "How did he know to bring her to the ship?" I'd decided to test the water.

"Gerald Irving had taken a tour of *Aphrodite* just a day earlier, so we took him at his word when he said he found her by the side of the road, bleeding." Apparently, my guest had prepared her answers thoroughly.

"So, at the time, you believed him. What do you think now? Was he telling the truth?" I knew my approach was direct, but I wanted the facts laid out on the table.

"Oh, I know he was lying about where he found her, but I also know for a fact, he didn't hurt Harmony. He would never." The moment the words left her mouth, I let out a breath I didn't know I had been holding.

"How come?" I inquired, hoping for the answer I wanted.

"Because Harmony only ever had good things to say about him. And let me tell you, that girl is smart, so you can be sure she meant every word." She sounded like a proud mother who'd had her child taken away. Dignified, yet regretful.

"I take it you've developed a, er, close relationship with her?"

"Definitely. You see, Gerald left her at the ship in Dr Chandrit's care. When Harmony came round, she was terrified out of her wits – not for herself, but for her nanny's safety. No, I'd say she was scared for everyone's life." I saw sorrow reflected in Julia's eyes, and I could only hope, so would the world.

"We know that her nanny, Nina Behrooz, was shot, but what do you mean by 'everyone's life?'" With each delicate question, I found myself holding my breath. How far would this woman go?

The moment she's decided to broadcast the truth, she had already put her life on the line.

"I can't answer that. These rich men have their ways of settling scores. That's all I'm going to say." Honestly, she'd said more than enough. "Anyway, she didn't want to go back home. I was nursing her back to health, so naturally, I wasn't blind to her feelings. The poor girl would cry at night, praying for her friends' lives.

"I was so concerned I tried to communicate with her, but every time I demanded a name, *'Who shot you, Harmony?'* I was met with the same response, 'No one. It was all an accident, just a big misunderstanding.'"

I had to suppress the laughter bubbling up inside me. "So, you're saying the girl and the nanny were injured accidentally? Two bullets were shot and neither one missed." I knew my inquisition wasn't just going off the script, but also worked against the narrative I stood for.

"I'm just telling you my side of the story. No one knows the real target of those shots, but I think I can determine a lot about the truth solely from the fact that this wounded girl, stranded alone on a ship amongst strangers, was far more scared of returning to her father than some phantom kidnapper. About Gerald, she only had one thing to say: 'He saved my life.'"

"Phantom kidnapper, huh? You're saying there was no abduction, yet there had been a ransom demand and Harmony Nader disappeared off the face of the earth for more than three months!"

"Of course not. She lived with me at my apartment." I'd always fancied I was pretty good at concealing my emotions, but this latest revelation took me aback. However, my guest continued speaking without a hitch, "I looked after her, made sure she was properly nourished, nurtured, and loved. God knows the poor child needed that. Her face lit up like a Christmas tree at the tiniest of gestures – going out shopping in disguise, baking cookies together, heck, she was even desperate for a walk in the park." To my astonishment, I almost missed the tears trickling down her cheeks.

"Ms Swartz, you took in the child, fully aware of the consequences?" I inquired gently, offering her a box of tissues.

"These past few months, I've been sleeping with one eye open at night. I've been following the news, so I thought about it many times. Especially when Oriole Nader made the headlines. It was heartbreaking for me." Ms Swartz wiped her mascara-streaked eyes. "Every single day, I returned home, convinced that I'd talk to Harmony about giving ourselves up and every time she greeted me at the door with an enormous hug. I failed. How could I bring myself to wipe that beautiful smile off her face?"

"Harmony wanted to stay with you? She was living with you of her own free will?"

"Absolutely. I'd be behind bars if it wasn't so." I found myself appreciating every well-prepared answer Julia Swartz came out with.

"So, if I understand you rightly, Harmony was at odds with her father, but what about her mother? The woman mourning the loss of her beloved child?"

"Her mother had been neglectful at best. It is not my place to criticise her parenting, but those children were not being raised in a healthy environment. Having grown up with an abusive and alcoholic father myself, I think perhaps I would have turned out to be a better, more functional adult if I had found someone to look after me when I was younger. Someone who would've taken me away from a world of deceit and lies. I couldn't watch it happening to another child, a child I had grown to love deeply." The word hung heavy in the air. My guest had decided to go all the way.

"I just have one more question, Ms Swartz. A ransom call was made to Henri Nader. If you did everything out of the goodness of your heart, why demand money?"

"I never made a ransom call, and I don't need to rely on extortion. My father left me a small fortune; it was the only good thing he ever did for me."

"So, you don't know who made that call?" I enquired cautiously.

"Perhaps it was someone who recognised her on the ship or a member of Henri's staff trying to grab a small fortune for themselves out of it – who knows or cares? Anyway, why wouldn't a billionaire pay up to get his daughter back. What does that tell you about Henri Nader?" Julia had retaliated with a question of her own, putting the final nail in the coffin.

"Oh, and one last question. We understand there was another child involved, a little boy called Ahmed. Is that right?"

For the first time, I detected a note of uncertainty in her reply. "Yes, that's right. I didn't think it fair that Harmony was on her own with no one to play with – especially when I was away at work. Little Ahmed lived nearby and sometimes came by to keep her company."

"Thank you, Ms Swartz, you've been very brave." I turned to face the camera. "I've asked that same question a billion times, and I'm sure, so have you. Why didn't Henri Nader pay the ransom? Why did his daughter run away? Why is his wife divorcing him? Julia Swartz has given us a rare insight today. The rest, I hope, will be answered by more official sources in due course."

Despite Julia's revelations, not much had been revealed about Gerald's involvement, but it was enough to absolve him of his tainted reputation. Folks will always find a way to demonise the unknown, stigmatise the sick, and condemn others for crimes they didn't commit. That's what the news business thrives on. But the cat was out of the bag and Henri Nader, the billionaire who had hidden behind his wealth and celebrity for years, was beginning to look like a crook. Big time.

Oh, and one more thing: despite her promise to tell the absolute truth, I didn't believe a word Julia Swartz had said about the second child, Ahmed. She was protecting someone. The question was, who?

CHAPTER TWENTY-ONE

Gerald Irving

It was late afternoon, and the dwindling rays of sunlight did little to brighten up my dull surroundings. Nor did the white linen-padded bed and pale blue walls help my mood. Shouldn't mental health facilities be livened up with a splash of colour? It would certainly be more conducive to one's recovery than 'group art therapy'.

The view from my window of unkempt grass and daisies was peaceful enough, yet any kind of peace was furthest from my mind as I contemplated what, if any, future might be in store for me.

There was gentle knock on the door.

"Gerald, we're watching 'The Wizard of Oz', would you like to join us?" It was Katie, a smart, young woman in her early twenties who occupied a room just down the corridor. Though I had been careful not to ask how long she had been in the facility, her infrequent bouts of psychotic behaviour explained how such an apparently sweet-natured girl had ended up here.

"No, thank you, Katie," I replied, already reaching for my journal. She came in anyway and stood coyly by the door.

"You know, you shouldn't worry too much about tomorrow. You'll survive in the wilderness – one way or another." She offered me a crooked-toothed grin.

She had her own problems and it was good of her to offer kind words. After all, it would only be a few hours before I escaped these drab surroundings. She might never.

"I know, and thank you, but I just have a lot on my mind." Katie and I had little in common but, in fairness, she had been my only friend during my stay. "Hey, Katie, don't worry about me. Enjoy the movie," I reassured her.

She looked sad and I felt guilty but, with a disappointed nod, she left me alone. I reverted to my journal, my index finger tracing through my notes, searching for the person I used to be.

Dissociation is a mental process that produces a lack of connection in a person's thoughts, memories, feelings, actions, or sense of identity. I know this now, although it has taken nearly two years for me to understand that it is a disease. Despite how ridiculously unbelievable it may seem, I have only just started to accept that I have been suffering from it to a greater or lesser extent for most of my life. Coming to terms with this condition has been the most agonising journey I've ever tackled – and that's saying something.

Fate enslaves us all more or less equally and as time goes by, it becomes easier to accept what it throws at us. Eventually, we begin to harness whatever cards we have been dealt to exercise some semblance of control in our lives. Though two years have passed, I still struggle to wrap my head around the revelations that accompanied my diagnosis. How could I learn to accept the horrors committed by a fragment of my damaged mind? How could I shut my eyes anymore to the beast that lay within in me?

However, as hard as it's been to accept the lack of control I had over my actions, every step of this journey has enlightened my path to self-acceptance.

After all the anguish, rage, and desperation, such optimistic notions sound bizarre, even foreign to me. Nonetheless, as I learn more about my disorder, I unlock gut-wrenching memories which, despite adding to my torment, paradoxically comfort me too. Every time I fear the unknown, I find myself turning to Dr Muriel's notes and my own to remind myself of all that I now know.

February 6, 2015

I believe every diagnosis, especially a mental health condition, is followed by a string of epiphanies. Once you've set foot in this labyrinth, there's no going back to the bliss of ignorance. You start to recognise patterns and all those unexplainable events of your life start to make sense. You start to see your entire life unfolding in a diagnostic manual and reflected in a list of symptoms.

After uncovering the truth, I can neither forget nor ignore my demons, not even if I wanted to, but Muriel insists I write everything down. So here goes . . .

Repeated dissociation may result in a series of separate entities, or mental states, which may eventually take on identities of their own. These entities may become the internal "personality states" of a Dissociative Identity Disorder (DID). Transitioning between these states of consciousness is often described as switching.

What are the symptoms of dissociative identity disorder? People with dissociative disorders may experience any of the following: depression, mood swings, suicidal tendencies, sleep disorders (insomnia, night terrors, and/or sleepwalking), panic attacks and phobias (flashbacks, reactions to stimuli, or triggers), alcohol and drug abuse, compulsions and rituals, psychotic-like symptoms (including auditory and visual hallucinations) and eating disorders.

Additionally, individuals with dissociative disorders can experience headaches, amnesia, time loss, trances, and out-of-body experiences. Some people with dissociative disorders have a tendency toward self-persecution, self-sabotage, and even violence (both self-inflicted and outwardly directed).

Who gets dissociative disorders? The vast majority (as many as 98-99%) of individuals who develop dissociative disorders have documented histories of repetitive, overwhelming, and often life-threatening trauma at a sensitive developmental stage of childhood, usually before the age of nine, and they may possess an inherited biological predisposition for dissociation. In our culture, the most frequent precursor to dissociative disorders is severe physical, emotional, and sexual abuse in childhood, but survivors of other kinds of trauma in childhood (such as natural disasters, invasive medical procedures, war, kidnapping, and torture) have also reacted by developing dissociative disorders.

Why are dissociative disorders often misdiagnosed? Dissociative disorder survivors often spend years living with misdiagnoses, consequently floundering within the mental health system. They move from therapist to therapist and medication to medication, getting treatment for symptoms, but making little to no actual progress.

Do people actually have multiple personalities? Yes, and no. One of the reasons for the decision by the psychiatric community to change the name of the disorder from multiple personality disorder to dissociative identity disorder is because "multiple personalities" is a somewhat misleading term. A person diagnosed with DID feels as if they have within them two or more entities, or personality states, each with its own independent way of relating, perceiving, thinking, and remembering about themselves and their life.

If two or more of these entities take control of the person's behaviour at a given time, a diagnosis of DID can be made. These entities were previously often called personalities, even though the term did not accurately reflect the common definition of the word as the total aspect of our psychological makeup. It is important to keep in mind that although these alternate states may appear to be very different, they are all manifestations of a single person.

When a person is dissociating, certain information in the brain is not linked with other information as it normally would be. For example, during a traumatic experience, a person may separate the memory of the place and circumstances of the trauma from their ongoing memory, resulting in a temporary mental escape from the fear and pain of the trauma and, in some cases, a memory gap surrounding the experience. Because this process can produce changes in memory, people who frequently dissociate often find their senses of personal history and identity are affected.

Of course, these things may not be severe enough to rank as an illness. Daydreaming, getting lost in a book or movie, and even being hypnotised by telegraph poles on a highway, all involve losing touch with one's immediate surroundings.

However, at the other extreme is complex, chronic dissociation, which may result in serious impairment or inability to function. Doctors refer to these as dissociative disorders, although sufferers can hold highly responsible jobs, appearing to function perfectly normally to those around them. In fact, it can take years for the problem to manifest itself in such a way that the sufferer or those around them need to seek help from a specialist.

Muriel told me that, faced with overwhelmingly traumatic situations from which there is no physical escape, a child may resort to "going away" in their head. Children typically use this ability as an extremely effective defence against acute physical and emotional pain, or even just anticipation of that pain. They become anxious that something painful they experienced in the past might happen again. That's when they dissociate. Thoughts, feelings, memories, and perceptions of past pain and its causes are separated off psychologically, allowing the child to function as if it had never occurred.

I suppose that on the positive side, you might see this as a highly effective survival technique, allowing someone to endure hopeless situations whilst preserving some areas of healthy functioning. Over time, though, in the case of a child who has been repeatedly physically or sexually assaulted, for example, defensive dissociation becomes reinforced and conditioned.

Because this method of escape is so effective, children who are very practiced at it may automatically use it whenever they feel threatened or anxious, even if the threat is not extreme. In other words, long after the original source of pain has gone, the leftover pattern of dissociation remains, leading to serious dysfunction in work, social, and daily activities.

Can the condition be cured? Yes. At least, I hope so.

I'm sorry if this sounds like a lecture. I wouldn't blame you if you decided to dissociate yourself right now! It has taken me so long to understand what has been wrong with me that it is cathartic to write it down. I have to.

I still can't forgive myself for what I did. Muriel tells me I have to let go of the blame, to move on. I'm not ready to do that yet, and finishing this book is part of the journey I must tread.

There's only so much comfort the pages of a spiral-bound notebook can bring. Every time I struggled to accept myself, I turned to these entries almost religiously. Honestly, I've been clinging to my diagnosis for the validation I've sought all my life, but now this journey has come to an end, and I need more than self-love to process this transition. I need a friend.

It has been painful, terrifying even, and I would not wish to go through it all again. I was fortunate to find Muriel. She became a friend and companion as well as my therapist, and it is thanks to her that I have been able – far too late, of course – to piece together what actually happened in those terrible weeks.

Muriel is an expert in individual psychotherapy, or talk therapy, as she calls it. This is not to say that they didn't try everything else first, mainly at the insistence of the police, including hypnosis and powerful drugs with vicious side effects.

My talk therapy has been going on for eighteen months, and it's not over yet. Mostly, it has involved remembering and reclaiming the lost experiences, going back to when I first "contracted" the illness. I'd love to know how the recollections of others might differ from my own. Still, I doubt I ever shall – unless, of course, someone like Vinny gets on the case, which I wouldn't put past him!

My contemplation was interrupted by the sudden presence of

a larger-than-life nurse called Marsha in the doorway. As usual, she barged into my room without apologising.

"Gerald, you have visitors. It's your lucky day." She had rapped so loudly on the door it had made me jump. "What are you up to anyway? You didn't show up for dinner. I thought you'd be busy packing."

"Gosh, Marsha, you scared me!"

Truth be told, I didn't mind her nagging one bit. Her fussing reminded me of Pru. Putting away my notebook, I accompanied her to the visitors' lounge. It was a cramped space filled with the lingering smell of cigarette smoke and disinfectant.

Though I tried not to show it, I was not only surprised but also secretly delighted. Throughout my confinement, I'd had only had two visitors and I hadn't expected them both to show up the day before my release.

"Gerry boy!" I couldn't help grinning at hearing the two words that had never failed to make me scowl. Success suited Vinny well.

"Hey, Gerald!" Every time Isaac visited me, he greeted me with the same excited curiosity. His interest in my illness had eventually overtaken his distrust and anger. However, his curiosity remained largely unfulfilled and I had little inclination to share with him what I had learnt.

"Hey, Isaac! Long time, no see," I greeted him, returning his hug. Ironically, I had grown more distant from my young friend only to develop a stronger bond with my old adversary. Of the two of them, it was Vinny who had visited me more frequently. Still, I could hardly fault Isaac for that – he'd had his work cut out running my publishing firm for the last eighteen months and, as far as I could tell, making a pretty good job of it.

"How's work?" I asked him.

"Tough." It showed in the dark circles under his eyes.

As I caught up with Isaac, Vinny occupied himself with a magazine, criticising it more than reading.

"I've heard you've been busy, Vinny. Is it true they put the *Aphrodite* up for auction?" I asked.

Vinny looked up sharply at the mention of the ship.

"Yes, that's right as far as I know," he replied. "Henri has been arrested along with the mob in South Africa. I don't know what they'll charge him with, we're still waiting to find out, but the game's up and I imagine he'll be going inside for a few years at best. If he avoids a murder charge, he'll be lucky, but I wouldn't be surprised if he wriggles out of it. Of course, a lot of other big'uns would go down with him – that's his best bet. Plus the fact the law moves at a snail's pace and he'll slow it down even more if he can. In the meantime they've frozen most of his assets, including the ship. No one is quite sure where Singh is. Probably done a runner, maybe back to India. But they'll get him eventually, he's too recognisable for his own good."

No one had supported me through this ordeal more than Vinny. Though I had told him little about my childhood, he seemed to understand. Knowing that I had lost my family in an accident not unlike the one that had stripped him of his mobility was enough to sow the seeds of a highly unlikely, unspoken bond between us.

"And what about Oriole?" I asked.

"Oh, she's alright," Vinny chuckled. "As a result of all the media coverage, she's more famous than ever! She's a consummate performer and in great demand. Every chat show host on the planet is after her and, if she chooses to carry on performing she's guaranteed a fortune." He paused before continuing. "But, you know, I wouldn't be surprised if she'll end up doing something completely different. Wouldn't put it past her to start a charity or foundation, or something like that – there'll still be a lot of Henri's money secreted away and she might want to use it to make amends for his misdeeds. Or maybe she sees them as hers. Anyway, who knows what she's thinking." He paused to look me in the eye. "Still, no concern of yours now, eh, Gerry boy?"

Following suit, Isaac shared the same thought. "Yes. More trouble than she's worth," he confirmed.

A heavy silence followed. I wasn't so scared about the past anymore. The future was my challenge now.

Reading my mind, Vinny broached the subject I had

been studiously avoiding. "Gerald, you're getting discharged tomorrow. Why do I get the impression you're not facing up to things – again?" I was reluctant to comment. "Have you thought about your plans? What are you going to do about Blanche and the kids?"

My family. The three people I most wanted to see and yet were most terrified of confronting. Frankly, I had no idea how to answer him.

"The truth," I muttered. I'd thought long and hard about this; how to venture into the future without dragging with me the mistakes of my past.

I'd told so many lies to them. I could see from my notes that I'd said I was seventeen when my parents died in a car crash. That isn't true. I was eleven. I said I was an only child. Another lie. I had a sister who was older than me, Lizzie. She was twelve. I have blocked out the truth about that night for thirty-four years.

Now I must find the strength to set this part of the record straight.

CHAPTER TWENTY-TWO

1963

My parents had dropped us off at the party two hours earlier. There could not have been more than ten of us assembled in that sterile front room. The girls had separated into one group, the boys into another.

If only girls knew how hurtful they can be, how fragile is the ego of a young boy, and how easily scratched the thin veneer of fledgling male bravado. I felt abandoned by my beautiful, self-possessed older sister. As I write I can see her in my mind's eye, her blonde hair gathered loosely with a blue ribbon, her pale green eyes aglow, the skin of her bare arms and legs gleaming in the half-light. She was the most beautiful girl there, I thought proudly, pleased to bask in her reflected glory as we entered that grey room together. She set the room alight, I was her brother and I was safe.

Then she abandoned me. I didn't expect her to. I did nothing to cause her to. She just did.

Looking back, she must have thought I was perfectly capable of looking after myself; that I would quite naturally want to be with my friends. With the benefit of hindsight, I can see that she was probably nervous too, anxious to create a good impression, to appear 'cool' in front of her peer group.

I shambled towards the other boys who were already in an animated, over-excited conversation. I knew them all. Most were at my school; two or three were friends of the girl whose party it was, Deirdre, I think her name was, but I can't really remember.

I still don't know how it started. One of the girls – it must have been Deirdre – came across and said we were no fun, how could we stand there in a group talking to each other? Weren't the girls pretty enough, didn't we want to talk to them?

We were just kids. The oldest boy was twelve, no match for a twelve-year-old girl. I was eleven. Girls mature earlier than boys. Boys might catch up later, even overtake, but a girl of twelve is a young woman to a boy of the same age. I didn't understand that Deirdre was just practising on us, testing her budding feminine wiles, teasing, flirting, in training for the power game that was to come. Why should I? To me, she was the most sophisticated, sensual creature I had ever set eyes on.

None of the boys knew how to respond. Typically, we froze, hapless, ill-equipped to deal with her advances. Seeing that she was not achieving the desired effect, Deirdre turned on her heel and, with a toss of her auburn head, returned to her friends. She whispered something and they all giggled, pointedly, in our direction, hands to their mouths scarcely bothering to conceal their disdain.

I looked at Lizzie. She was giggling, too, her beautiful face creased into a mischievous and, to me, incomprehensible grin. I noticed she was wearing lipstick. I was sure she hadn't been when we left home. Like a hammer blow, it struck me that we were on opposing sides. Lizzie was laughing at me. This couldn't be the Lizzie I knew and loved, my Lizzie, this was some caricature, an impostor bearing only physical resemblance to my sister.

One of the older boys attempted a riposte. It was probably pitifully inept, for the girls were now squaring up, hands on hips, taunting us openly, ridiculing us for our shyness.

I think it was Deirdre who had put a record on. It could have been the Elvis or the Everly Brothers, I can't remember. But I watched as they danced with each other, twisting and curving their bodies to the beat, their young faces assuming that heavy-lidded, trance-like expression, induced by songs with words of love, sex and desire.

My child's mind was bewildered by conflicting sensations. I wanted to go home, of that I was sure, and I wanted Lizzie to revert back to being the sister I knew and loved, and felt safe with. Yet these child's thoughts were clouded by stirrings of another kind, unprecedented and inexplicable.

"Gerry!" It was Deirdre again, sidling up to me, brushing close to my ear, and taking my hand. "Come and dance with me, show us what you can do."

I tried to resist and struggled, but she was pulling me into the centre of the room, into the throng of twisting and turning female bodies. I was out of my depth and scared.

Clumsily, I tried to match Deirdre's moves, watching her, copying her as best I could, desperate not to make a fool of myself. Suddenly, the music changed and she had her arms around my neck, her body pressed against mine. I must have recoiled from this intimacy for she said: "I'm not going to eat you, Gerry, there's no need to be frightened."

I now remember the next moment vividly. All I could think about was getting away, escaping from her uninvited embrace, not knowing what I was supposed to do, how I was meant to react. Before I knew what had happened (I assume I must have pushed her) Deirdre was lying on her back, hand to her head, crying. The other girls were on to me, pulling my hair, tearing at my clothes and there, looking on was Lizzie. I shouted her name, but she turned away.

I couldn't make out what they were mouthing. I didn't need to, the expressions on their faces were enough. They hated me, that much I knew. Hated me for hurting their friend, for not being a good dancer, for being a young boy, too young, much too young, frightened and shy. But, mostly, it seemed, for just being me.

What I had done to deserve this frenzied attack I had no idea. In hindsight, I suppose it could have happened to any of us. But I was 'it' and now something worse was happening. Egged on by the others, Deirdre had returned to the fray, blood trickling from her ear, a gash on her cheek from her fall. She seemed crazed, her pupils dilated, her nostrils flared, her face flushed and ugly. She started to undo the buttons of my shirt, ripping it apart and then set about removing my trousers. I was struggling with all my puny strength, fighting (it seemed) for my life. I had never known terror, combined with such intense embarrassment. It was my first taste of humiliation, my first taste of helplessness, of being subjugated totally to someone else's will.

I can hear their voices now, their jeering, all these years later, and those twisted, cruel faces still feed my nightmares although not always as children, but as devils, gargoyles, and monsters.

They overpowered me easily, and soon I was lying there pale and naked, exposed and shamed with little to hide and nothing to hide it with. Tears streamed down my cheeks although I was hardly aware of their taunting and derision. All I could do was throw myself onto my stomach and lie sobbing in the middle of the room.

The moment had gone, the music had stopped, and the jeering abated replaced by a sense of foreboding. I heard new voices, adult I thought, but only fragments of what they were saying drifted in and out of my consciousness.

"Ring his parents, I'll get his clothes back on." It must have been Deirdre's mother and I became aware of grown-up hands muscling my arms and legs back into shirt and trousers.

"I've spoken to his parents, they're on their way. Now, what on earth's been going on?" This time a male voice, the father, perhaps. The question hung in the air.

"He hurt Deirdre," a girl piped up eventually.

"Deirdre, darling!" It was the mother again. She must have noticed the blood on her daughter's head. "Oh, my God!" Then, to me, harshly: "Did you do this, did you?"

By now I was sitting up, shivering uncontrollably. My mouth opened but there were no words. She turned to Lizzie, still on the outside, looking in. "Did he? Did he hurt her?"

Surely Lizzie would explain, set the record straight, explain exactly what had happened.

"He pushed me," Deirdre broke in, "I fell and hit my head. He pushed me, on purpose!" Her voice was shrill, redolent with disgust.

"Lizzie," said the mother, "is that what happened?"

"I'm sorry," I heard Lizzie say, "I couldn't really see, but, if that's what Deirdre says, I'm sure it's true."

Deirdre's mother surveyed the scene before her. "Well, then," she said, "the less said the better."

Although an eleven-year-old boy would have trouble comprehending many adult emotions, betrayal was not one of them. In that instant, the unquestioning love, admiration, respect and trust I had always felt for my sister turned to loathing. And in my confusion, one thing emerged crystal clear; the terrifying torment I had suffered had been her fault.

When my parents arrived there was a brief inconclusive adult conversation and then we left. As we drove home, my mother and father were in the front of the car, Lizzie and I in the back, I looked up at Lizzie's face. The lipstick had gone.

"You're very quiet, Gerald," my mother said, kindly enough. "So, what was all that about, then?"

"He attacked Dede, Mummy, he pushed her over and she cut herself." Lizzie couldn't wait to get the first word in.

"On purpose," my mother went on, "or accidentally?"

"Gerald, was it an accident or did you push her on purpose?" Lizzie remained silent.

I was containing a fury such as I had never known, consumed by the cruel treatment that I had been subjected to and about which nobody seemed to care. I had been cast as a perpetrator, not a victim. It was excruciatingly unfair.

"Gerald, darling, is there anything you want to tell me?" There were a thousand things I could have said but, more than anything, I wanted to hurt my sister.

"Lizzie was wearing lipstick," I croaked. My throat was dry and it came out louder and more aggressively than intended, perhaps because these were the first words I had uttered for nearly an hour.

"You liar," Lizzie cried, "you little liar! Mummy, it isn't true, he's making it up! He wants to get me into trouble to cover up what he did!"

I threw myself at her, pulling her hair, and pummelling her with my fists. She had to share my suffering and I have no doubt that, in the frenzy and frustration of that moment, I would have killed her if I could. Instead, I started to rip at her clothes, the way her friends had ripped at mine.

"Gerald, for God's sake, what are you doing?" My mother was reaching back trying to separate me from my sister. But her position, craning over the back of her front seat, made it impossible.

Lizzie was screaming now, beginning as a low whine, becoming shriller and more terrified as I started to rain blows on her. I don't think she had ever been frightened of me before. Now I had my hands around her neck, squeezing her throat. She grabbed at my wrists, trying to wrestle herself free of my grip.

"Jack, for God's sake, stop the car!" cried my mother clambering over the back of her seat to reach us. What happened next was a haze although I was conscious of the car swerving from side to side as if out of control.

"Christ!" was the last word I heard my father say.

What followed was like a video on fast-forward with no sound. A thousand images flashed before me. Then there was a shattering impact and everything went black.

When I regained consciousness all was white.

* * *

In the following weeks and months, through terrible mind-numbing pain, I can now recall being angry that my parents didn't come to see me.

Later I was taken to live with my mother's sister, Aunt Alice, and her husband Des. I never set eyes on my home again, nor my parents, nor my sister.

When they judged the time was right, they explained to me gently that my parents and sister had been killed in a car crash and that I had been lucky to come out alive. There was no one to embellish or contradict this simplified account of what really happened and, so I've been told, I never raised the matter again, never questioned, never grieved.

There must have been a funeral. I may have been in no fit state to attend or, more likely, others decided it would be less harrowing if I didn't.

In any event, by the time I returned to school nearly a year later, life had moved on. My aunt and uncle assumed that it was kinder not to dredge up memories of the tragedy and, not surprisingly, those involved in Deirdre's party had their own reasons for not wanting the details of what had happened to be resurrected.

Quite simply, nobody knew that I had killed my family.

* * *

It is only in the last few months that Muriel has explained to me how I had obliterated the memory of what happened that night and dissociated myself from the circumstances that had caused the crash. It took many hours of her 'talk therapy' to regress me to the point where I was forced to re-live the agony and horror of that night so that, together, we could reconstruct the origins of my disease. As an eleven-year-old boy, I couldn't bear the responsibility for the deaths of my parents and sister, so, in my mind, it had all been erased. I resumed life from a later point. There it is – sounds easy, doesn't it?

As time went by, other aspects of that traumatic night emerged to haunt my sub-conscious. Muriel has pointed out that as I moved into adulthood, I would have experienced difficulty in forming successful, enduring relationships with the opposite sex. Regrettably, this turned out to be true, as you will have realised by now.

My adulation of a beautiful older sister, so suddenly demolished and replaced by loathing, has had consequences too many and complex to list. In addition, the sexual humiliation of a pre-pubescent child, male or female, is certain to have had long-lasting consequences. Perceiving woman to be angels on a pedestal one moment, then aliens bent on destroying you the next, is hardly a recipe for successful long-term relationships. I am afraid that my poor Blanche and, to no lesser extent, Oriole, have been gravely hurt as a result.

CHAPTER TWENTY-THREE

I realise now that I omitted to record certain events that occurred during that fateful week when I had first met Oriole and Henri.

It was the day after we had taken Harmony into Estepona – a Wednesday, I think. Blanche and the girls had persuaded me to join them on the beach but, after an hour of lying around doing nothing, I had become bored. I'd told them I needed to go into the office for an hour or so but, when I got there, Lawrence was out. I didn't relish the prospect of more sunbathing and, besides, they weren't expecting me to return so soon.

That's when I discovered Harmony's precious carrier bag in the back of the car, tucked under one of the front seats. Quite what went through my mind I can't recall; whether it was simply a childish desire to see the pleasure on Harmony's face when I gave it back to her or was I hoping her parents would be impressed by my kindness, or, more likely, was it that the seeds of my obsession with Oriole had already been sown and I wanted to see her again.

In any event, I reckoned I could be at Villa Harmony in twenty minutes, stay perhaps for five, and be back on the beach within the hour. For my apparently 'casual' call to be effective, I could not stay long. Thus it was that I again set off along the Ronda road. The weather had clouded over and there was a heaviness in the air which threatened rain overnight.

As I approached the entrance to the villa, my attention was diverted by the sight of two figures ahead of me in the road. They were walking away from me, a hundred meters or so ahead, up the slight hill beyond the house, both female, one taller than the other. A woman and child. From her gait I was sure the child was Harmony, the woman, I thought, could be Nina, the nanny/bodyguard.

I stopped the car just before the gates and switched off the engine. All was still and quiet, the two figures clearly having no idea I was there. I thought for a moment: there was no point in going into the villa if Harmony wasn't there, but what was she doing outside at all? Surely Henri and Oriole would disapprove. On the other hand, maybe she was allowed to set foot outside providing she was accompanied by Nina.

Disappointed that I wouldn't see Oriole but realising that my purpose for being there was to deliver the bag, I started the car again and set off up the hill. I had temporarily lost sight of them but, as I rounded a corner, spotted them again turning into the entrance of what appeared to be an old, unoccupied single-story dwelling surrounded by open land. In front of the modest building was a yard across which Harmony and Nina, for now I could recognise her clearly, were walking. Still, they seemed unaware of my presence. A small open-topped truck was parked just inside the yard.

Aware now that I was spying on them, I stopped the car twenty or thirty metres short of the dwelling and walked the rest of the way. The sound of children's voices was coming from the yard. A few steps further and I was able to take in the picture ahead of me.

Harmony, dressed simply in jeans and T-shirt, was happily embracing a stocky, dark-complexioned boy of roughly her own age. As I watched, she grabbed him by the hand and dragged him down to sit next to her under the overhanging bough of an ancient olive tree. Old pieces of wood, branches and some rusty corrugated sheets had been nailed to the tree. It looked like a half-completed playhouse – I remembered as a child erecting something similar myself at the bottom of my garden. When it was finished, the area where the two of them were sitting would be totally enclosed. The two children were conversing vigorously in Spanish. Of the nanny there was no sign.

Ashamed to pry, and yet curiously puzzled by the set-up, I circled the crumbling outside walls of the building and made towards one of the small unglazed windows at the rear. Taking care to move slowly, I peered through the small opening into the shadowy interior. There, on a makeshift bed, in what must once have been a bedroom, was Nina the nanny lying back, her skirt around her chest, her powerful thighs parted, passionately responding to the attentions of a swarthy man whose head was buried in the darkness between her legs. As I watched, the girl grasped his hair, pulling him roughly towards her, shuddering and moaning loudly. Leaning against the wall beside them was unmistakably a rifle with a white jacket draped across it.

I watched as she climaxed, noisily and clumsily, arching her back in one final convulsive spasm. Giving her no time to recover, the man got to his feet and manhandled her violently into the prone position, her face buried in the course blanket, her buttocks in the air. Entering her from behind he began thrusting quickly and powerfully, grasping her waist and pulling her to him as he pushed against her. The act was bestial, yet I was riveted by it.

When he finished, bellowing at his own pleasure, I saw his face for the first time, contorted as if in rage. It was the servant, Abdul, from Villa Harmony.

I moved quickly from the window, knowing that such a man would always have half an eye watching his back and that once his physical preoccupation was satisfied, it would not take long for him to discover my presence.

Returning to the front of the house, heart beating, I decided to do what I had come to do and then make a hasty retreat. Taking the carrier bag from my pocket, I boldly walked into the yard to where Harmony and the boy were playing. Despite the eerie stillness under the blackening sky, so engaged were they in their fantasy world that I was on top of them before they heard or saw me. It was the boy who reacted first. Springing to his feet and backing up against the tree, his eyes wide with terror, his knuckles came up in a childish caricature of a street fighter. Harmony was equally startled although she clearly recognised me.

"Gerald, why are you here?" Her voice was anxious and as she spoke her eyes darted around her, then to the house.

I held out the bag.

"You forgot this," I said as cheerfully as I could in the tense situation, "your aeroplane?" What had started out as a harmless if infantile gesture now felt pathetic.

"Thank you," she said graciously, taking the bag from me and looking again in the direction of the house. I held my ground, smiling at her, not quite knowing what to say next. The boy was still regarding me as though I was his mortal enemy. The plan had misfired; it was obvious she was not pleased to see me, and I should have left then and there but, like a fool, I thought I could make things better.

"Harmony, your friend need not be frightened. Tell him you know me, that I am your friend."

"His name is Luis. Gerald, please, do not tell my parents you have seen me here, please, promise you won't say anything?" She was looking me straight in the eye, pleading.

"Alright, but I don't quite see . . ."

"I am a prisoner, you know that. Nina brings me here sometimes, maybe once a week, when my parents go to Madrid or to the studio. Abdul likes Nina, he comes too."

So, this was a regular arrangement, I thought. The nanny and the guard get to have sex in the house whilst Harmony meets her little boyfriend to play in the yard. Presumably the rest of the staff turned a blind eye.

"Who is Luis?" I asked.

"He is my friend," she replied, "and Abdul's cousin."

"Your parents would be very angry if they knew, Harmony. You are doing wrong, you know that don't you?"

"Please, you must not say anything. I'll just get told off and they won't let me see Luis again, but Nina and Abdul, my father will never forgive them."

This was a very special little girl, a child deprived of the company of others her own age, as the events of our earlier visit had shown. Now, threatened with her parents' anger, she was still able to bear a thought for her two adult co-conspirators.

"Don't worry," I said, "we're going back to England tomorrow. I won't even see your parents. But look, shouldn't you get back to the villa, anyway?"

Harmony smiled her wonderful, radiant nine-year-old smile,

"Thank you. But now you must—" She never completed the sentence. The look of fear had returned and I followed her gaze past my shoulder to the house where Nina had appeared in the doorway. She came rushing towards me, arms flailing like a windmill.

"No, Nina, no!" Harmony cried. But it was too late and she was on me fighting like a Dervish. It was all I could do to protect myself such was her strength as her fingernails raked my arms and face. I was backed up against the wall, trying to hold her by the shoulders.

"For God's sake," I cried, "I'm not going to harm the child, look, you must remember me, I was at the villa yesterday! I am a friend of her parents!" I wasn't fighting back, thinking I would get further by relying on persuasion.

"Why are you here, how did you know where to find us?" she hissed. Her pupils were dilated, the vein in her neck pulsing visibly. I didn't know what she was on but there was more than post-coital adrenalin coursing through her system. For a moment she relaxed her grip, and I managed to regain my balance. "Look," I was going to tell her how I had seen them walking along the road, how I had brought a harmless gift for Harmony, how this was all a terrible mistake. Instead, three things happened at once. As I stood up, Nina stepped back, caught her foot on a loose plank and stumbled, falling heavily to the ground. Harmony and I rushed forward to help her. There was a short burst of gunfire from the doorway. Abdul had emerged from the house, the gun at his hip.

"No, no, don't shoot," I cried at him, "wait, for God's sake." But it was too late. The shots aimed at me had missed their target and it was Nina who was lying at my feet, blood staining her white blouse and (God, how my heart sank) Harmony, too, clutching her shoulder, blood seeping from between her fingers.

"You bloody fool," I screamed. "You bloody idiot, look what you've done! Christ, look what you've done!"

He was stationary at the door, thin acrid smoke spiralling from the barrel of the gun, still aimed at me, his stare fixed on the carnage it had taken him only a split second to wreak. The boy, Luis, broke the tableaux and rushed to Harmony's side. Tears of pain streaked her child's face as she rocked from side to side, holding her shattered shoulder. The boy looked up at me, speechless, his face telling me all I needed to know. Suddenly, Abdul made his move. With an anguished scream, he ran to kneel at Nina's side, cradling her head in his arms. Throwing down the gun he turned to face me with unmitigated hatred in his eyes

"You should not have come," he rasped and lowered his head onto Nina's bloody chest.

We stayed like that as it began to rain. At first in small irregular droplets and then harder and more persistently, stinging the skin like sleet.

"She bad, need doctor, quick!" It was Luis' pigeon English that broke the silence. He was talking to me, expecting me to take the lead, to get us out of this chaos of our own creation. I felt nauseous, tempted to run for it, to escape, to leave this nightmare behind, get back to England, forget, forget . . .

The horror of what had happened was causing my body to convulse uncontrollably, incontinent with panic and fear. I vomited on the spot. Abdul watched with undisguised contempt in his eyes, but I knew that he, too, was waiting for me to act, to think of what to do next. I took a few faltering steps towards him. He was still holding the swarthy woman tenderly in his arms. Lying there, weak and vulnerable, she suddenly looked very young, I thought, not at all the wild creature who had so ferociously attacked me only a minute before.

"Is she dead?" I asked.

Instead of replying he carefully removed his arm and gently laid her head back on the ground. Then he stood and stepped back as if inviting me to inspect her for myself.

"I'm not a doctor," I said apologetically, but I knelt just the same and took her limp wrist between my fingers and thumb. I thought I felt a fluttering and recalled that powerful vein pulsing in her neck as we had grappled only moments earlier. The rain was turning her blouse transparent and diluting the stream of blood oozing from the wound above her left breast. I instinctively looked to the spot on her neck to see if there was any sign of a pulse. A slight movement convinced me that there was.

Harmony was now sitting up, eyes open, bewildered but attempting to come to terms with reality. God, she has courage, I thought. I turned back to Abdul.

"We must get them to the villa," I said, "they both need medical attention and fast."

"No!" It was Harmony, her voice shaking with fear and pain, but speaking firmly and with the authority I had come to expect from her. "We cannot go back. There is no one who can help us, and my parents will be back tomorrow evening. They must not see me like this. They must not know what has happened. We must think of an explanation. My father will not . . . he will not understand."

"But, Harmony, what can we do?" I asked. "Do you know a doctor nearby, somewhere I could take your—" But Nina's eyes had closed again, she was drifting into unconsciousness.

"I don't care where you take me, but not home, please, not home." I looked at Abdul, he was waiting for his instructions, too. I made up my mind.

"I'll take the girl to a doctor in my car. You look after Nina. Is that your truck?" He nodded. "If you can come up with an explanation you think Mr and Mrs Nader might believe, I suggest you go back to the villa and try to bluff it out. Otherwise, take Nina and make a run for it. Find help in the mountains somewhere, its up to you. If all goes well I'll get Harmony patched up and back to the villa before they return from Madrid tomorrow. Do you understand?"

He nodded again. "You should not have come," was all he said as he gathered the lifeless-looking Nina in his arms and carried her towards the truck. The boy Luis went to follow but Abdul hissed at him to go away. Obediently, the child turned on his heel and ran off into the fields.

As an afterthought I said: "Oh, and when you've got the girl sorted out, come back up and tidy up. If anyone comes snooping it won't take much for them to work out what's happened here."

I lifted Harmony easily enough and carried her to the Opel. We were both drenched by now and she started to shiver in my arms. Her eyelids fluttered.

"I'm sorry, Gerald," she muttered, "it was kind of you to bring me my aeroplane."

* * *

My mind was racing as I drove back along the road, past Villa Harmony, towards town. The rain was easing and I looked at my watch. I'd been gone for less than an hour. Harmony was slumped beside me, my handkerchief clutched to her shoulder to staunch the blood. I had no idea where to take her although I thought there was a hospital some way beyond the town centre on the road to Calahonda.

"What are we going to do, Harmony?" I said through clenched teeth, "we've got ourselves in a pretty mess this time." But she had fallen fast asleep as only children who are hurt or sick know how.

I racked my brain for an alternative. Once she was admitted to a hospital they would quite rightly ask a lot of questions which neither of us wanted to answer.

Of course, our positions were rather different. Despite Harmony's obvious anxiety about being found to have ventured outside the villa against the express wishes of her parents, not to mention her loyalty to Nina and Abdul, nonetheless, of course, whatever anger her parents felt would be outweighed by their relief to see her safe. They would forgive her immediately, fire the nanny and the guard and tighten up the rules to prevent a recurrence. Of course, if the nanny were to die, and she had looked close to it to me, then the position would be more serious, but Harmony would hardly be held responsible.

I was in a more difficult fix. Unwittingly perhaps, and with no ill intent, I had been a party to, even the reason for a shooting. Moreover, I had agreed to conspire with the perpetrator when I should have gone straight to the police and reported the whole ghastly mess. I had listened to Harmony, a child, when I should have followed my own adult reasoning. Not to mention that Blanche thought I was at the office. Still, it was not too late. If I could get Harmony safely to a doctor – hopefully one who would disinfect and dress her wound while I waited and not ask too many questions – then, perhaps, I could return home with a relatively clear conscience. After all, I was leaving Spain the following day. Maybe I could leave this nightmare behind me.

The answer came to me in a flash. Singh. Although I had only met him once I felt I could trust him, firstly to do a first-class medical job on the girl and, secondly, to be discreet. It was, after all, the nature of his business. Relieved by this idea, I turned left into the town, and headed for the port.

I took the car along the quayside and stopped outside Mamma's. It was midday and a few customers were eating lunch under the sunshades, others propping up the bar inside. I was glad to see *The Aphrodite* gleaming white at anchor in the bay. Leaving Harmony in the passenger seat – my jacket around her shoulders so that to a passer-by she would appear to be sleeping – I locked the car from the outside and went into the restaurant. I imagined I might see Julia Swartz amongst Mamma's regular clients, but I was not to be so lucky. Mamma greeted me warmly, her smile fading as she registered my appearance. I had wiped the blood from the scratches on my face, but I knew I looked unkempt and bedraggled. I gestured to her to move to the end of the bar where it was quieter.

"Mamma, I need a favour," I said with as much cheer as I could muster; there was nothing to be gained by alarming her. "I have to get in touch with Dr Singh or Julia on *The Aphrodite.* Can I use your telephone?"

"Si, of course," she replied, "do you have the number?"

"No, I don't, I was hoping you might?"

"Wait." She reached behind her and produced a business card. It was Julia Swartz's. "There," she said, "on the back I wrote her home number, you see, but she will be on the ship at this time, I think."

"Thank you, Mamma," I replied gratefully as she pushed

the telephone in my direction. "You are very kind." I dialled the number from the front of the card.

"Is everything okay, Mr Irving?" Mamma enquired.

"Yes, of course Mamma. I got caught out in the rain, that's all." It was a poor explanation, but she had no choice but to accept it before tottering back to her regulars. There was a ringing tone at the other end.

"Hello, this is *The Aphrodite,*" said a polite English voice, "may I help you?"

"May I speak to Dr Singh or Julia Swartz?" I asked.

"One moment, please, just connecting you."

"Hello, this is Julia." The warm American tones were instantly reassuring.

"Hi, Julia," I said, "this is Gerald, Gerald Irving. Can I come aboard?"

"Hi, Gerald, yeah, of course. Sit tight, I'll be over to get you. Give me two minutes."

I put the phone down and thanked Mamma. Outside the sun was burning down again with a vengeance. I unlocked the car and got in. Harmony was as I had left her, sleeping peacefully, breathing steadily. I looked across the short expanse of water between us and the ship and saw the little launch set off. Julia with her lion's mane of blonde hair blowing in the breeze was easy to distinguish at the helm. I sat tight until she neared the quayside, then got out and went around to open the passenger door. I stroked Harmony's brow to wake her and spoke her name urgently in her ear. After a moment her eyes flickered open.

"Where are we?" she asked glancing round.

"Can you walk a little?" I asked her. "I could carry you, but I don't want to arouse suspicion."

"I'll try," she said, and turned in her seat ready to get out.

I half-walked, half carried her the short distance to the jetty where Julia was waiting.

"Hello," she said, "what have we here?" I didn't reply.

"Well, we'll soon find out, I guess, come on let's get you as comfortable as we can." She helped Harmony to an upholstered seat where she promptly lay down, almost out of sight. We were soon heading back towards *The Aphrodite.*

Julia didn't say another word until we tied up and then confined herself to telling us to stay in the launch while she summoned some assistance. It took no time for two nurses, one male the other female, to appear. Harmony was looking very ill now, the loss of blood showing in the pallor of her complexion. It was all she could do to stay conscious but, as always, she didn't want to miss anything. The two nurses carried her easily and gently aboard where, for the first time, Julia removed my jacket from around her shoulders and saw the extent of her bleeding. With a sharp look in my direction, she spoke briefly to the nurses in Spanish. A wheelchair appeared and Harmony was whisked away to a nearby cabin.

"That's nasty," Julia said. "I'm no expert, but it looks to me as if she's lost a lot of blood."

"I'm afraid so," I replied, "its a bullet wound. A few inches to the left and she'd be dead."

"Let's hope its mainly the flesh and that the shoulder itself isn't too badly damaged." She thought briefly and then looked me full in the face. "Who would want to shoot a little girl?" It was not so much a question as an expression of dismay.

"They didn't," I replied.

She led me to the panelled lounge with its antique furniture which I had so recently, and yet, it seemed, so long ago, admired. There was no one else about.

"Would you like a drink, you look as though you could do with one?"

"Thanks," I replied gratefully, "a brandy would be fine. She'll be alright, won't she?"

Julia went to the bar and poured an arbitrary measure of VSOP into a large cut-glass brandy balloon.

She handed it to me.

"Wait here," she said, "I'll see if Chandrit is available."

I fell back into the sofa and gulped at the warm liquid. My watch told me that I had been away from the beach for nearly two hours, and I still had to get Harmony back to the villa. I hoped that whatever they had to do would not take long.

A woman came in, her face heavily bandaged so that only her eyes were visible. She wore a long, floral top coat. It was impossible to tell how old she was. She nodded a cursory greeting in my direction and began to browse amongst the books and magazines neatly stacked by the mock fireplace. Julia had only been gone for a minute when she reappeared with Singh in the doorway. Seeing that we were not alone, Singh was formal to the point of curtness.

"Would you like to come this way, please, we can speak in my office." He turned on his heel and disappeared again. Julia waited politely by the door. Leaving the glass on the polished table, I got up and followed her to Singh's room.

He was standing with his back to us, gazing through the large porthole at the sprinkling of small craft going about their business on the thin stretch of azure water between us and the serried ranks of yachts and cruisers moored in the port. Beyond I could see the Opel parked as I had left it. Julia closed the door behind us. Singh turned to face me.

"What the hell is the meaning of this? We are not a casualty unit." His voice was hardly above a whisper but redolent with suppressed anger. This was a different Singh to the man I had met the day before. I felt uneasy and it showed.

"Have you examined the wound?" I asked, hoping not to have to explain what had happened and my part in it.

"Yes, of course. You must know the child is seriously injured. There is extensive damage to the shoulder. There is a bullet still lodged in there and she has lost a great deal of blood. I am having the wound cleansed at the moment so that we can see what we are doing. Mr Irving . . ." he paused and then went on, "do you know who this girl is?"

The question took me by surprise – it had never occurred to me that he might know her.

"No, I found her like that and brought her straight here. I could see that she was in urgent need of attention and you were the only doctor I knew."

How easily the untruth tumbled out – thoughtlessly, irresponsibly, without consideration as to the consequences. Why? Fear, perhaps; blind optimism that I might escape from the outcome of my foolishness without being found out. Like a schoolboy, I was trying to lie my way out of something from which there was no chance of escape, stupidly believing that if I acted the innocent convincingly enough others would have to believe me. For the moment, however, Singh was appeased.

"I see. Where did you find her?" he asked, more reasonably.

"On the Ronda highway, a mile or so from the country club, by the roadside." How easily came the re-enactment, the fabrication. "I don't know how long she had been there she was barely conscious when I found her."

Of course, if he had recognised Harmony then he would know where she lived. My story would have indicated to him that I had found her not far from her home. That, at least, would add up.

"Have you informed the police?" he asked.

"No," I replied, "as I said, I came straight here."

He seemed to relax, inclined to believe my story.

"Don't worry, her parents are away at the moment. I'll let them know as soon as possible but she'll be quite safe here for a day or two." He crossed thoughtfully to his desk and sat down in the large swivel chair.

"You are certain you don't know her?" he asked, looking at me sharply.

"Of course not, why should I? I'm only a visitor here, after all." My answer seemed to satisfy him.

"I shall have to operate on the shoulder as quickly as possible to remove the bullet and repair as much of the damage as I can. With luck, at her age, she should recover full use of the shoulder. Naturally, her arm will be in a sling for some weeks. She owes you a debt of gratitude, Mr Irving, it was fortunate you were in the vicinity and saw her. That road is quite busy, I'm surprised no one else stopped. Where shall I tell the police to contact you?"

Panic, more lies.

"I don't quite know how to ask you this, but I would be grateful if my name could be kept out of this. You see, I have my family down here with me and we're due to return home tomorrow. I really don't want to get delayed."

"I see. That might be difficult. You may be the only lead the police have in tracing the perpetrators of this appalling business."

"But, as I have told you, I will not be able to help them." My brain was working overtime. "Not only that, there is something else." I glanced in Julia's direction. "I wonder if I might have a word with you in private?"

"Of course. Julia . . ." He gestured and, unhesitatingly, she left the room closing the door silently behind her.

"Now, Mr Irving?" He sat, fingertips together forming a pyramid, questioning.

"Thank you. It's just that, I'm sorry, its rather embarrassing, I'm afraid. You see, my wife doesn't know where I have been this morning and, well, I'd rather she didn't find out. She thought I was working in my office in town. You appreciate the delicacy of my position, I'm sure?"

Singh looked at me intently over his fingertips, sizing me up, calculating the odds as to whether he should trust me.

"You realise, don't you, that what you are asking would be out of the question in England?" It was a pointed remark with only the slightest tinge of irony. I did not answer, holding my breath. "But we are not in England." The semblance of a smile played around the corners of his mouth at last. "Very well, Mr Irving, your subterfuge is safe with me. After all, in your circumstances, I am not sure how many of us would have stopped and helped the child in the first place. You did the honourable thing and should not be made to suffer for it. Now, with your permission, I will attend to our young patient." He stood to usher me out. "You know, it is a coincidence. I have . . ." He appeared to change his mind. "Well, be that as it may, you need not worry about her. I know her parents. Had they not been away I cannot believe they would have let her outside the walls of their villa. So, I shall contact them as soon as they are back and arrange for them to collect the child, when she is strong enough. By then you will be safely back in England."

I felt a huge surge of relief. It seemed too good to be true. But for one thing. I stood up and took a pace towards the door.

"May I say goodbye to her?" I asked as casually as I could. Singh was all smiles now, the old Singh of Thursday and our PR visit.

"I'm sorry, Mr Irving. By now she will be in pre-med. She wouldn't even recognise you. After the operation, when she is aware of where she is, I will pass on your good wishes. What shall I tell her? That her anonymous knight in shining armour wishes her well?"

"Thank you," I replied, "yes, that would be perfect. Oh, and maybe you would instruct Julia . . ."

"Of course, Julia understands the nature of discretion. It is her job, after all." He held out his hand. "Mr Irving, goodbye again, you need have no shame about your conduct today. I hope we meet again under less alarming circumstances." He opened the door. "Julia, Mr Irving is leaving, would you be kind enough to escort him back to the quayside?"

Julia appeared on cue and smiled at me reassuringly picking up the tone of Singh's voice. I shook his hand.

"I am most grateful to you," I said, "for everything."

Julia walked me back to the lounge.

"Would you like to wash and clean up before I take you back?" she asked. "You can use one of the empty staterooms."

"No, no, thanks," I said, keen to get away, "I'll shower back at the apartment."

Outside the sun was blindingly bright. My sunglasses were in the car. Squinting, I followed Julia as we clambered into the launch. She didn't speak until we were tied up at the quayside.

"Goodbye, then, Mr Irving. I think you may have saved a life today. She'll be fine, don't worry. Lucky for her you were around, I guess." For a split second her brow furrowed and it seemed as if she was going to ask me something else but then she smiled, leant forward and brushed my cheek with her lips. It was a gesture, innocent and affectionate. I rested my hands on her shoulders briefly and smiled back.

"Thanks," was all I could find in my heart to say.

She removed the rope from the capstan, throttled up the engine and was gone in a creamy wake. Hurrying, I walked back to the car.

CHAPTER TWENTY-FOUR

As I lie here, back in the same flat that Pru had arranged for Isaac and me nearly two years ago, with the autumn sun low on the horizon and the green grass beyond my window strewn with burnt sienna, I have to look forward, try to imagine a new life built on the ruins of the old. There seems little hope that I might regain even a semblance of what I had before, wasted and frittered away for lack of understanding of my own fragility.

There is still the business, I suppose, although what shape it is in, I have no idea. To begin with, Pru and Isaac would telephone me in a well-meaning attempt to keep me abreast of developments and keep me involved. Isaac visited me several times but, as the enormity of my problems dawned on him, he stopped coming, and stopped telephoning.

I have not seen Blanche or the children for nearly a year. They have made no effort to contact me, nor vice versa.

* * *

Yesterday, the telephone rang. It was a child's voice. For a moment I didn't recognise it and then, hardly believing it possible, I knew it was Nikki.

"Dad," she said, "is that you?"

I didn't know what to say. That Nikki had rung me at all was open to so many interpretations: did Blanche know, had she put her up to it? Was Nikki trying to build bridges? Or was she just curious? All these thoughts rushed through my head in the split second I had to decide what to say.

"Does your mother know you're ringing, darling?" was the best I could do. There was a pause.

"Dad, I'd like to see you, but I don't know how I can get to you. Can you give me directions?" She sounded grown up, matter of fact, but what she was asking unsettled me. Besides which she had ignored my question.

"Nikki, I need to know about your mother, whether she—" but Nikki, the new Nikki, older and wiser it seemed, wouldn't allow me to finish the sentence.

"Dad, I can't speak for long. How can I get to you? I need to know."

"Nikki, darling, I can't tell you how much this call means to me, it's wonderful to speak to you, but I'm not sure that it's a good idea for you to come here, not on your own, it's a long journey and—" Again, she cut in.

"I've got to go now, I'll try to call again. 'Bye, Dad . . ." she hesitated and then: "You are alright, aren't you?"

"Yes, darling, I'm fine – well, I will be, soon." I was suddenly conscious of the tears running down my cheeks. "Darling, I'd love to see you, you know that but . . ."

"I'll say goodbye then, for now. We'll speak later, okay?" This was in a different voice as if she was talking to someone else. The line went dead.

I was enthralled and puzzled by our conversation, firstly because it was the last thing I had expected and, secondly, because it raised more questions than answers. I picked up the phone and dialled 1471. The answer came back as 'number unknown'. Where was she ringing from? From home or had Blanche got her a mobile? I had no idea. I would just have to wait for her to call again.

The thrilling news was that my daughter wanted to see me. That was more than I could ever have hoped for. The bad news was that, typically, I had failed to grasp the opportunity and couldn't be sure I would hear from her again.

* * *

But I did hear from Nikki again.

Since her last call, I had thought about little else. She'd kept me waiting for two days. This time I was better prepared and had talked to Muriel first.

As usual, Muriel had turned the question back on me.

"The fact that your daughter wants to see you is not so surprising," she'd said. "The question is are you ready to see her?"

The old me would have answered 'yes' immediately – typically, ploughed in with both feet, worried about the outcome later. But I must have learnt something under Muriel's care because now I took her question at face value. Was I ready? I didn't know. It could be Nikki was offering me a lifeline, bless her, a way back, an opportunity, a chance. Somehow, I knew that I wouldn't get another. Mess this up, Irving, and that's it.

Over the next twenty-four hours (I don't know, it could have been longer) I thought of little else; how I should react, what to say, how much I should tell her – capped by the biggest conundrum of all, how much did Nikki know? What had Blanche told her, how much had she pieced together herself?

I had just finished lunch when the phone rang.

"Dad?" the voice was nervous, more childlike than last time.

"Hello, darling, how wonderful you've called again."

"Dad, Mum and Paula are here. Mum would like to talk to you."

EPILOGUE

Sib Khumalo

Yeah, I remember. It was a Sunday night.

I'd been working late. Picked him up at the airport. He had a suitcase. It didn't take me long to see he was drunk – well, not bad, but, you know, bad enough. Didn't know where he wanted to go. He asked me whether I knew a nice hotel not too far. Could I take him there – said he'd pay me when we got there, he had some money in the suitcase. Hell, everyone pays when you get there.

I said I knew a nice place, The Cottage in Grove Road, not too pricey. He said fine, so that's where we went.

He was chattering away in the back, I could hardly make out what he was saying. Something about he didn't like sitting in the back of a car, could I stop so he could change and sit in the front beside me?

I told him no, we hadn't got far to go and, anyway, he was drunk. I was watching him on and off in my mirror. He was in a bad state, but I could see that underneath it all, he was a nice-looking man, down on his luck maybe, and under the influence, but decent enough, I would say. I've seen worse.

We were nearly there when he threw up the contents of his stomach over the back of the car and down the back of my front seat, too. It was a really bad smell. Disgusting.

I stopped and told him that was it, he'd have to get out. He pleaded with me to take me to the hotel. When I said no, he stuck his fingers in my back as if it was a gun. I'm too old and been doing this job too long to fall for that old trick. Then he passed out.

The guy was in a terrible state and it wasn't just the drink. There was something else but I couldn't make out what. One thing

350

was sure, he was down on his luck.

I'm seventy years old. I've lived my life and done okay without reading or writing. Always been poor but lucky. Started out in a tin-roofed shack in Soweto. But my parents stuck together. We had nothing but we were happy. I've taken a lot of visitors there. They get all shocked, thinking it's a slum and the people who live there are poor, dirty and helpless. They're wrong. People like my dad travelled a hundred miles on foot to live in Soweto, some never made it – there are electricity points, water taps, churches, and schools. Kids do well, buy suits and go off to work in the banks. With luck, you can get on in Soweto. And then you can get out. My old man did, got himself a clapped-out car and started ferrying kids to school for a few rands. Later he took the young bucks who worked in the banks into the CBD of Jo'burg. Then when I was old enough he bought a second old car for me.

We went to church on Sundays, the four of us, my parents, younger bro and me. We were brought up as Christians. Lots of us were churchgoers and those ten commandments stuck. "Remember the Sabbath and keep it holy."

Maybe that's why I didn't abandon that young man. He'd passed out by then and I could have left him on the pavement. But I didn't, I carried on driving until we got to the Cottage.

My friend, Tommy we called him, was on the night desk. Together we carried the guy upstairs and left him on the bed to sober up. I opened his case and, sure enough, there was some money wrapped in polythene. I took enough to cover the fare and some for Tommy.

And that's the last I saw of him. I went home to hose down the back of the cab. Never did get rid of the smell. Had to use one of those hanging air fresheners until I could buy a new old car.

I don't think he was a bad guy, just someone down on his luck who'd taken the cares of the world on his shoulders. He might have been ill for all I know.

Often wondered what would have happened if I'd left him in the gutter. I'd be surprised if he'd made it through the night.

ACKNOWLEDGEMENTS

I would like to thank the following for their enthusiasm and patience during the many months of editing and re-drafting of this book. Without their help its completion would have been infinitely less rewarding:

James Willis, Chris Hancock, Libby Ashmore-Short, Stefan Proudfoot and Abbie Starling.

The Author

Printed in Great Britain
by Amazon

29262447R00200